# Deranged Marriage

*Also by Faith Bleasdale*

Rubber Gloves or Jimmy Choos?

Pinstripes

Peep Show

FAITH BLEASDALE

# Deranged Marriage

Quality Paperbacks Direct

This edition published 2003
by QPD
by arrangement with Hodder and Stoughton
a division of Hodder Headline

CN 115067

Typeset in Plantin Light by Phoenix Typesetting, Burley-in-Wharfedale, West Yorkshire

Printed and bound in Great Britain by
Mackays of Chatham Ltd, Chatham, Kent

For Mum and Dad. The best parents in the world.

# Acknowledgements

This book was not based on experience so there are quite a few people to thank for their help. Thanks to everyone who gave me pregnancy and birth advice (too much information to be honest). Thanks to the lawyers who gave me advice about suing people (just waiting for the chance to put it into practice). Thanks to the man (if there is such a creature) with whom I might have made a marriage pact for not trying to enforce it.

Thanks also to:
Mum, Dad, Thom, Mary, Andrew, Claire, Gareth, John and Paul – my wonderful, brilliant family.
Jo, John and baby Lucy, Emma, Matt and baby Archie for making me an honorary Auntie Faith.
Holly for making a wise choice in naming the sexy Joe McClaren.
Kat and Guy, thanks for a great line.
Sara Hulse, who will always have claim on the heart of my books.
Diane Banks and Sara Kinsella for the drinks (next time we must eat, really we must).
To everyone at Hodder.
Simon Trewin and Sarah Ballard at PFD who are my favourite agents.

A special thanks goes to the people who read my books, especially those who e-mail me via my website, www.faithbleasdale.com

Finally to Jonathan, there will never be enough thanks for your love and support. Your encouragement is priceless, as is your ability to make me laugh. You're still a top fellow.

# Prologue

At some stage in life, most people make a marriage pact. This arrangement is an undertaking to marry someone as long as you are both unattached by the time you reach a certain age.

There are certain guidelines to follow when you are entering such a pact:

- You should be much younger than the deadline you set as the marriage-pact age. This gives both parties ample time to find their destined life partners before the agreement expiry date.

- It has to be a verbal commitment. No lawyers need be involved in this type of contract.

- Both parties should feel vulnerable and unloved before entering the agreement.

- Both parties must be intoxicated.

If you adhere to these simple guidelines, then you have made a successful marriage pact. However, the rules do not end there. They carry on into the aftermath of the 'deal':

- Once made, it must be forgotten. A distant memory, only recalled when you are both happily married to other people.

- The main condition is that once made, you do not ever intend to carry out the pact. Because destiny will wash your true love up on to your shore. It's a bit like panic-buying: when you hear there's going to be a shortage of something, you buy because you have to, not because you want to.

Take a word from the wise, as my mother would say, because I am now wise. I was twenty when I made my marriage pact. Without knowing the rules, I failed to adhere to some of them. Yes, I was drunk, as was he. I was vulnerable, as was he. I wasn't in love with him; he wasn't in love with me. We had set a ten-year deadline – adequate time to find the true loves of our lives. However, we failed, by ignoring the simplest of the rules: we didn't make a verbal agreement, we produced a written one.

We didn't stop there, we rolled drunkenly to the local off-licence with it and asked the man behind the counter to witness the 'document'. Looking back, I think we took the intoxication rule a tad too far. Afterwards, we left our wayward path, returned to the rules, and forgot about it.

Then, one fateful day, it all came back to haunt me in the most unimaginable way.

# Chapter One

―――――◆⊠◆―――――

## *Two Men*

'What do you wear to court?' I screamed in frustration at my wardrobe. I was staring at rows and rows of clothes as if they would tell me. Of course they wouldn't, clothes had a habit of refusing to answer important questions. I had been awake for hours, I felt sick and tired, and more than a tiny bit hysterical. Joe came up behind me.

'Try to stay calm,' he said. Like a red rag to a bull.

'I'd like to see you try to stay calm, if you were me.'

'Sorry.' Joe looked suitably contrite, although none of this was his fault.

'What do you think I should wear?' I asked, nicely, throwing in a smile for good measure.

'A suit,' Joe replied.

My resolution dissolved immediately. 'Yeah thanks, mastermind. What colour?' I felt awful for the way I was treating him but I had no control over my bitchiness.

'Well, I'm wearing a grey suit so wouldn't it make sense for us to match?'

'Yes, maybe, but I don't own a grey suit. It's a pity you didn't think of that earlier.'

'Holly Miller, I'm not your enemy. I'm on your side. Let me have a look.' He proceeded to flick through my clothes. He was trying so hard and didn't deserve my wrath.

I sat on the bed in a sulk while Joe worked his way through my wardrobe. I could tell by the way his back was hunched that he was worried about making the right choice. I couldn't see his face but I could picture the look on it. His brows would be furrowed the way they did when he was concentrating, and his lips would be pursed together tightly. He was so beautiful when he was engrossed. Just as I was about to kiss him and apologise for my earlier outburst, the buzzer interrupted. I answered the intercom to my boss Francesca, and my friend and work colleague, Freddie. I waited at the door for them to climb the stairs. Within seconds and like a slightly out-of-breath fanfare, they arrived.

'You poor lamb,' Francesca cried, hugging me. I experienced another blast of nausea as I inhaled her generous perfume. She was such a maternal boss; it was all I could do to stop myself from crying. I chastised myself, I'm not a big cry-baby and I hate tears.

'We've come to help with the outfit,' Freddie said, giving me a kiss on the cheek and one of his famous ladykiller smiles. I stood, frozen in my dressing gown, as they pushed passed me and made their way to my bedroom.

I watched Francesca, Freddie and Joe discuss what I should wear. I stood back, nervously chewing my bottom lip. I felt invisible. Finally they decided on a navy-blue shift dress and jacket; the most conservative items in my wardrobe. For some irrational reason, the outfit made me feel even more sick. I went to the bathroom and threw up, praying no one would notice. That would have involved fuss I wasn't equipped to deal with. Now all I had to do was dress, leave my flat, and go to court. Then it would be over. I tried to be confident, after all it wasn't even a proper court, but I was still worried. I was in the right, I knew that, but it didn't help that there could be another outcome, however unlikely, and that outcome could ruin my life.

It came down to two men. Joe, the man I loved, and George,

my oldest friend. Not a love triangle; actually, it was anything but a love triangle. Two men and two things happened to kick off everything. I realised I was in love with Joe, then George, my oldest friend who had been out of touch and in New York for the last five years, returned home. How did those two events manage to get me in court? Well . . . it's a bit of a long story.

At the time, I was twenty-nine and on the fast track to being thirty. I felt that my life was settled; not boring, but tranquil. Every morning I woke, despite the frequent hangovers or lack of sleep, I woke smiling. Always. I had a job I loved, great friends and a new man in my life. I was even looking forward to being thirty. What I discovered was that I had 'sorted out the lumps in the cushions', as my mother would say.

The lumps in question were my twenties. I had some bad relationships, a few drunken encounters with equally drunken and unsuitable men, I lost my best friend, George, to New York, and I had had some disastrous jobs. But that was behind me. I was a woman of the new millennium and I was enjoying what that meant. Obviously there were day-to-day problems in my existence, but that was par for the course. The fact remained that I was deliriously happy most of the time.

Perhaps that's why it went wrong. I had enjoyed selfish happiness for long enough, and now someone wanted to take that away. If fate was always in control of people's lives, then fate decided to slam on the brakes, and take my life in a more downhill direction.

I was no longer as happy as I was. Two men in my life, one good, one bad. That was how it all started and that is why I am about to go to court.

# Chapter Two

I realised that I was in love with Joe McClaren the moment we had our first row. That row will be stored in the chronicles of our relationship along with our first meeting, our first kiss, and our first time. The row was important because it consolidated my feelings; it opened my slightly closed eyes.

All the signs were there, only I probably hadn't recognised them as such. Knowing what I know now, I am sure they were. Big neon, flashing lights telling me that I was in love. Once I had identified my feelings, or accepted them perhaps, I knew I had never felt like that before. I was tipsy the whole time but also a little bit vulnerable. There wasn't a more specific way for me to describe it, which is why people say you just *know* when you've met the right person. You do know, but you don't always know why. I was different, I had more energy. I smiled more, I laughed, I was nice. More than nice, I was wonderful.

I was also terrified, scared of losing that happiness. Even though it's good, it's bad, but you have to take the bad with the good and the bad didn't even feel bad because I certainly wasn't miserable, just a bit vulnerable and I could cope with that. I could, because although it was confusing, it was amazing.

Over three months ago, in August, I met Joe at a party thrown by a mutual client. They were celebrating a successful publicity campaign; Joe's company were the designers, my company provided the PR. I had never met Joe before.

I don't like parties, I never have. Parties are too full of

anonymous people and I liked my social life to be familiar. If I am standing in a room I like to know the room, I don't like to look out on a sea of strangers and hope that one of those strangers might be interesting. I'm a bit of a bitch when it comes to new people; with men – unless I am going to fall in love with them or at least have sex with them – I can't be bothered. Usually I judge women really quickly. However, that is part of my job, and normally I manage to put on a façade and be civil when duty calls. I can boast, unhappily, that I have gone to every type of party; from the corporate, dull ones, to film premières where, naturally, I was ignored by celebrities. Parties are part of my professional life, but not a part of my personal lifestyle.

Certainly I wasn't enjoying myself on this particular evening. The party was in a cavernous bar, somewhere which was trendy once, but was definitely passé. The invitation – a white card embossed in gold – declared an evening to 'celebrate success!' Although the sentiment was nice, the reality was quite different.

Approximately one hundred people were crammed into the dark cave, that wasn't big enough for half that number. The decor was minimal, but that was fine because there wasn't room for much. Most of the people there were company staff; it was a personal finance organisation. They were all wearing suits. I felt distinctly odd as I was not wearing a suit, but a pair of black Joseph trousers, high-heeled boots and a black cashmere polo neck. More like an undertaker than a PR director.

The evening started with sparkling wine. The waiters were trying their best to distribute the drinks, but were unable to penetrate the human wall that had formed, so they stood around the perimeter of the room, shoulder to shoulder; all that was missing were the riot shields.

'Champagne madam,' a bespectacled youth offered. It was an indication of the complete unfashionable nature of the whole proceedings that the waiters weren't rude. I took a glass of 'champagne', sipped and wrinkled my nose. I know I am a dreadful snob, but when your taste buds are prompted by your brain, which has been informed by a horribly polite waiter, to expect champagne, they are bound to be disappointed when they discover it is in fact slightly warm, slightly sweet, sparkling wine.

There was no way I could talk to people even if I wanted to, everyone was practically touching each other, and I have a problem with strangers invading my space. The music was blaring and my head throbbed. I couldn't see my client anywhere, and the attempts I made to ask anyone about her extracted blank looks. Just as I was about to consider my options the microphone screeched. The sound grated through my body, as the taste of the wine had earlier. A rather plump woman wearing a navy-blue suit stood smiling behind it. I groaned and picked off another glass of sparkling wine. I had positioned myself as close to the drinks as possible deciding it preferable to the 'mob'. The speeches were about to start.

I have a problem with a certain type of employer. The kind that makes a load of money off the back of its hard working employees, then decides to reward them with a party like that one. I found it demeaning to their dedication and hard work. I think I might be a bit of a socialist in that way. Although I have to say, as I studied the sweaty, smiling faces sipping wine, they didn't look exactly demeaned. I think I was the only person there who wasn't enjoying myself.

I should explain why I am being so horrible about the evening. Yes, it was too crowded that night, yes the wine was sweet and warm, and yes the speeches were bound to be boring. But there was more to it. I was the senior account director at Francesca Williams PR. I had worked there for a few years and apart from my boss and owner, Francesca, I was the most senior member of staff. Therefore, I was totally annoyed when I was told that I had to attend the party in person instead of sending one of my team. I head a group of eight: Freddie my account director and deputy, two account managers, two senior account executives, two account executives, and a personal assistant. But, I was the chosen one and had come to this party because the client demanded it. I would much rather have been at home painting my toenails, or unblocking drains.

The speeches started. I had three glasses of wine to alleviate the monotony, and by the third my tastebuds seemed to have adequately recovered. First, a man in a grey suit, pulled out a giant pie-chart and began talking about company performance. Apparently he wasn't really a boring suit; he was a comedian because the throng of people were bellowing with laughter. Quite a feat as they didn't appear to have much room to breathe. I shuddered to think how on earth they had managed to expand their lungs to that degree. I moved closer to the drinks waiters; I knew whose side I was on.

After the grey man finished to rapturous applause, the plump navy woman returned. Her speech was reminiscent of the worst Oscar acceptance speech: long, dull, fatuous. At one point I am sure I saw her sob.

Thankfully the formalities ceased and the music blared again. I took another drink, well, I had nothing else to do, smiled at a few of the pressing mob who were brave enough to smile at me. I vowed to speak to Francesca the following day about getting a better class of client.

I spotted a gap near a bar. It wasn't a drinks bar, more of a ledge really, but I homed in on my prize: peanuts. Oh how the mob were missing out. If they knew there were four bowls of peanuts nestling behind the wall of waiters, they would have been where I was.

I put down my glass of wine on the ledge and picked up a handful of peanuts. My tastebuds were delighted with me.

Just as I had put a third fistful into my mouth, I turned slightly to my right and noticed a guy observing me. My first impression was that he was sexy. He had light-brown hair, cropped short, and was wearing a black V-neck top, with a small tuft of chest hair protruding, as if it belonged to the jumper. I couldn't see the colour of his eyes, but he had two, and his smile was lopsided but definitely interesting. I stared at him; he stared back. I tried to swallow my peanuts so I could say something witty, but they seemed glued to my tongue. The man was tall, much taller than me; it was then I noticed he was also wearing black. We matched. He wasn't the best-looking man in the world, but there was definitely something incredibly attractive about him.

'I have never in my life seen someone eat so many peanuts at once,' he said. Embarrassment flashed briefly across my eyes. Then I choked.

I really choked; my whole body shook. My face turned puce, although I couldn't see that, but I could feel it. My eyes began to water. The man, the man who had caused this distress, stepped towards me and slapped my back, rather too hard. Unable to protest, I just coughed and coughed, until at last I regained control.

As I felt what I hoped was my face resuming its normal colour, I wiped my eyes. Still, I had no energy to speak.

'Are you OK?' he asked, looking slightly mortified. I nodded. All my witty repertoire gone, I couldn't think of a single thing to say.

'Do you smoke?' he asked.

I don't smoke. I gave up smoking when I turned twenty-nine because I was worried about getting a cat-bum mouth, and other unsightly wrinkles. I only relapsed when I was inebriated.

'Only when I'm drunk,' I replied.

'Are you drunk?' he asked, his mouth curling at the corners, ever so slightly. His voice washed through me. It was melodic. Which made no sense, because I had already identified his accent – slightly Essex. My eardrums were as happy as my taste-buds.

I pulled myself back to his question. Was I drunk? No, not really. After all I drink for a living. But, even if I wasn't, I could be. I drained my glass in one, large, quite unladylike gulp.

'I am now,' I replied, flirtily, as my man handed me a cigarette.

We started talking and it was so easy. I discovered all about his job in design; I told him all about mine. His name was Joe McClaren, an incredibly sexy name. He was from Essex, but lived in north London. I told him a brief history of myself and proceeded to drink another four glasses of wine. I think he matched me glass for glass, although I noticed that he shuddered every time he took a sip. He smoked four cigarettes – one per glass – I smoked only the one. We stood away from the mob; we laughed. He called me 'posh', and was clearly mocking me. That proved to be a huge turn on.

Finally it was announced that the party was over, they switched off the lights, which made me giggle and say to Joe, 'my father will be waiting outside to take me home'. He didn't quite get my school disco meaning and asked me why my father was picking me up. I explained it to him and he laughed. Actually he was embarrassed, but that was because he told me that it took him longer to get my 'posh jokes'.

Despite the fact that we did not get off to a particularly auspicious start, he asked for my phone number and I gave him my card. As he put me in a cab and told me he'd call me, I was radiator warm from the inside out.

Freddie, who works for me is also one of my best friends. He says that I only go out with 'suits'. He would say that I will only go for men who look as if they can pay not only their own rent or mortgage but also take care of mine. He says that I am 'classest' as well as 'walletist'. I only go out with middle-class men and that's only because I am too common for upper-class men. It can sometimes be hard to understand why I love Freddie so much. When I ask him what personalities he presumes I go for, he replies that I am far too mercenary to care about personality. As long as they had the semblance of one, that would do.

So, Freddie would say that Joe isn't my type. After all he has an Essex accent, he wasn't wearing a suit, and he's creative. I had no idea at that time if he was rich, or even solvent, but I didn't care. I didn't analyse my feelings; I was too busy enjoying them.

The day after the party I stormed into work and launched an attack on Freddie because I had a hangover. Hangovers were also part of my life. I was used to them, but I didn't like them. I also didn't like the fact that they seemed to get worse as I negotiated the ageing ladder. If they were that bad at twenty-nine I would be unable to get out of bed at forty. In fact, as I held my pounding head that morning, I wondered if I would make it that far.

'Next time there's a client party you are bloody well going,' I shouted. I am not at my discreet best when I'm hungover.

'Oh dear,' he replied. 'Was it pants?'

'Utterly,' I stormed.

'No one interesting there?' he asked.

'No.'

'Not even the designer chap. What was his name, John or Joe or something?'

'The designer?' How the hell did he know?

'Yeah, I met him once, just thought he might be there.'

'What and he's interesting?' My attack was ruined.

'Very, but not your type.'

'Why?'

'Because he's a bit common, darling. Successful, yes, probably got an OK salary, but not posh enough.'

'Freddie, stop. Anyway I didn't meet him last night.'

'Really? I wonder how he got your e-mail address then.' Freddie laughed.

'You've been checking my e-mails?' Now I was really angry. My attack had been completely foiled.

'No, of course not, Dixie told me.'

I scowled at Freddie, and went off to shout at my assistant. Dixie is brilliant. She's the most efficient person I've ever met and she keeps the whole team in check. She also has access to my e-mails because I have been known to forget to check them. She has access to my entire life, and if it weren't for the fact that she liked gossip then that would be fine. It didn't matter though, because he had e-mailed me.

He told me he had enjoyed meeting me. He asked if I was quite recovered from my peanut attack and he suggested going out on Friday. I e-mailed him back and said that Friday would be great.

The other thing Freddie would tell you, about me and men, is that I don't play hard to get, or even a little bit unavailable.

I never have believed in love at first sight. My relationship history would lead any sane person to think that I barely believe in love at all. But of course I do. I'm a Piscean, our whole being is founded on love. It's just that my past relationships weren't right, I wasn't right. But when I met Joe I was.

My twentieth year saw my first major heartbreak. Some said that I was lucky to have waited that long. At the time, I didn't see it because Harry was the man for me. Being twenty, any man is the man for you as long as he is around. I had been living in London for a year, and I'd met Harry almost straight away. I was sharing a flat with Lisa, the daughter of a friend of my mother's. My mother thought that nineteen was very young to be fleeing to London in search of my fortune, so she entrusted me into Lisa's care. Lisa was ill-equipped to look after a goldfish, let alone a person, so unbeknown to my mother I ran wild. Perhaps not wild, but I met Harry, who was a model and a colleague of Lisa's, and he was a bit wayward.

Going out with a model at such a young age was a triumph. He was gorgeous and I only wanted a gorgeous man. I didn't mind that he was vain and self-obsessed. That he rarely knew how to use a telephone, or how to tell the time. It didn't matter. I handed my heart to him on a platter and he in turn dropped the platter, making a clang that would end all clangs.

It was another woman of course, boring and predictable I know, but for a first heartbreak, it had all the ingredients I needed to be thrown into uncontrollable grief. At least for a little while.

I didn't stay heartbroken for long. I had always held the belief that misery was too draining on one's energy, so I went straight for the rebound relationship. The general rules in rebound relationships are that they are not built to last. Mine lasted for one and a half years.

Ewan was at university. I met him in a bar when I was trying to meet my Mr Rebound. He was posh, he was arrogant and he was a bore. But, and it is an enormous but, he had a car. By the time I reached twenty-one, I had decided that a man with a car was far more necessary than a man with looks, despite spending most of our relationship in London traffic jams.

That characterised our time together. Ewan plodded, his car sat in traffic. But the thing I loved about the traffic was sitting in the car next to him. I felt safe, I felt secure, because unlike Harry he seemed to really care about me. And I liked his wheels.

We broke up when Ewan failed his end-of-year exams and decided to go home with his tail between his legs. I was even more heartbroken than I was with Harry. I really loved that car.

I took a break from relationships at that time to concentrate on my career. I worked hard, got as much experience as I could, and I got myself a job as an account executive at a PR firm pre-Francesca Williams. It was there that I met Marcus. Marcus was sort of my boss. He was the account manager there, so he was absolutely my senior. It was about a year after Ewan's car had deserted me that we started dating. You know the scene; boring story of drinking too much at the pub after work, flirting wildly over a bottle of white wine. Almost the entire office witnessed our getting together, so it was no surprise to anyone when we became a couple.

Marcus liked to boss me around at work and at home. I liked his flat. My main priority was dating someone with his own flat. I was going up in the world. Marcus's flat was a small one-bedroomed basement abode in Fulham. At that time, Marcus and his flat were my ambitions. I felt like the woman of the house as I provided all sorts of food and even did his housework. I loved that flat.

We broke up when I changed jobs to become an account manager. On reflection, I think that him telling me what to do at work turned him on and when he could no longer do that there was no passion. I had never thought of him as kinky while we were together, but deep down I think he was. We didn't break up straight away, but that was because I was too blind to see that he had lost interest in me. Eventually he spelled it out. So I said goodbye to Marcus and I cried buckets over that flat.

From then on my relationships and dates don't even warrant cataloguing. As my friends watched on, they exclaimed my love life a disaster. Which it was, but I wasn't unhappy about it. I had flings, little meaningless fun flings. I had one-night stands. As long as you're safe I don't think that admitting a need for sex is a problem. The trouble is that one-night stands are like buying sweets. You so want them until you've got them and then once you've devoured the last one they leave you feeling a bit sick. Or like when you're in the sweetshop and there's this big selection to choose from and then you get them home and find that you've picked out gobstoppers instead of aniseed balls.

But Joe changed all that. He changed my relationship history, for ever, simply because I knew I didn't want him to become part of it. I wanted a future with him, and I realised it on the day when we had our first row.

The day of the row dawned ordinarily enough. I was at work, arguing with Freddie.

'"Stand By Your Man",' Freddie said.

'What?' I asked.

'"Stand By Your Man", Tammy Wynette?'

'I hardly think that gives across a strong feminist message.'

'Yes, but we are talking about *new* feminism aren't we. No longer the dungarees and lesbian brigade, the new feminist isn't afraid to wear nail varnish.' Freddie smiled as if he had discovered the meaning of life. I sighed. Our brief was to come up with a promotion for *Zoom*, the new deodorant for women who wanted to be in control of their lives. The advertising agency was producing ads for a new girl band who would be sponsored by *Zoom*, and we were publicising the competition. We were trying desperately to come up with the perfect song to front the campaign. I was trying but Freddie was, as usual, taking the mickey.

'Although you might have a valid point about *new* feminism being different, I still think that standing by your man is pushing it a bit too far.'

'I thought you might appreciate the sentiment,' Freddie teased.

'Freddie, this is about *Zoom*, not about me and if you want to use this whole exercise as another excuse to take the piss, then go ahead, but I am warning you that if you do, I will pitch for a foot odour campaign and make you run it.'

'Point taken.' We smiled at each other and went back to our brainstorming.

Freddie had already won. The more I tried to think, the worse it got. All I could find in my head was a wobbly rendition of 'Stand By Your Man'. And as I only knew the first few lines, it was a repetitive rendition. By association, it led me to think of Joe.

Joe and I had, at that point, been together for three months. The beginning of December heralded not only incredibly cold weather but also the fact that Joe and I had come through the precarious early days. I hadn't spent too much time analysing my feelings, but when I thought about him (which was a considerable amount), I would warm up, fluff up and my insides would do a funny little dance.

'So,' Freddie interrupted. 'What are we wearing tonight?' He clapped his hands together.

'OK, we have fifteen minutes to go get a coffee and discuss my wardrobe, after which we will come back and you will finish that proposal before I let you out of here.' I was such a commanding figure as a boss.

'Whatever,' Freddie replied in deference to my authority. I rolled my eyes, grabbed my purse and set off for Coffee Republic.

We sipped lattés and talked through my wardrobe.

'What are you doing tonight?' I asked, finally remembering that I wasn't as selfish as I made out.

'I'm seeing Hannah.'

'Hannah?' Yet another girl I hadn't heard of.

'She's just some girl, nothing for you to worry about.'

I laughed. Freddie liked to think that I was jealous of all the other women in his life. Of course nothing could be further from the truth. I liked having him as a friend, and I enjoyed working with him, but I certainly didn't fancy him. Freddie's views of women were just a touch cynical. 'So, how come you never ask for wardrobe advice?'

'From you?'

'What's wrong with my dress sense?'

'Your dress sense is great for you, but you always try to make me look gay.'

'That's because you act gay.'

'Oh, here we go. Ten reasons why Freddie is really a closet case . . .'

'You have impeccable taste, you love gossip, you always wave your arms around, you are incredibly pretty, you work in PR, you are afraid of spiders. I can't think of any more at the moment.' I used to be able to come up with a longer list, just to annoy him but the novelty had faded. The whole Freddie 'gay thing' had become a bit tedious.

'You just want to be a fag-hag, and because, despite all your attempts of stereotypical accusations, I am straight. *I love women*. Generally I want to sleep with all women – you excepted. But, Holly darling, if you want to continue this crusade of yours to try to convert me, go ahead. I am far too secure in my hetero-sexuality to be even remotely upset.'

'Fine, let's go back to work then.' I laughed, despite his protestations, it still riled him.

Freddie was indisputably straight, he wasn't even camp. But when Francesca interviewed me for my job she told me that Freddie was gay. She told me that he would be my deputy, and then she leaned across her desk and whispered, 'You do realise he's gay', into my ear. I didn't; I hadn't met him but I didn't tell her that. When we became friends, I soon discovered that if Freddie was gay, he was doing a wonderful impression of a womanising cad.

Freddie explained to me that Francesca believed that only women and gay men should be allowed to work in PR. He hadn't told her he was gay, she had just assumed, and he left it at that. The first office party we had the Christmas after I joined, Freddie engaged in some very public saliva-swapping with Francesca's PA and the boss discovered, much to her disdain, that she couldn't sack someone for being straight. They had since developed a healthy working relationship, and I had since developed a need to tease him about it. Although we behaved like schoolchildren most of the time, we were very good at our jobs.

Francesca Williams PR is a growing company, so the roles that Freddie and I had were advancing with it. Being a big believer in delegation, Francesca left the day-to-day running of accounts with me, while she concentrated on new business and marketing. I, in turn, ran the accounts with dictatorial control and Freddie as my right-hand man. We both worked hard, and although Freddie was supposed to defer to me, I regarded and treated him as more of an equal.

At six-thirty, I approved all the work that needed my authorisation and left the office.

I paced the flat and waited for the doorbell to ring. It was almost painful. I had arrived home from work at quarter past seven, which left me forty-five minutes until Joe was due. But I was ready early, which annoyed me because being early was uncool. I had bathed, changed and applied my make-up. I even painted my fingernails and I still had ten minutes to spare. I sat on the sofa and inspected my nails, fighting a strange urge to bite them. I felt unsettled but had no idea why. I was sure that it couldn't be the fact I was ready early.

When Joe and I first started dating we met in bars or restaurants, but soon we had progressed to the stage where he could meet me at my flat, we could go for dinner around the corner, we could get home without hassle. No pretence. We had cleared the pretence hurdle. The pretence hurdle is when you don't want to assume you are going to end up sleeping together although you know you will. So you arrange to meet somewhere equidistant between both flats – Joe in Camden, me in Clapham – and then at the end of the evening, you wait until he utters the classic line, 'My place or yours?' Sometimes we met in Clapham, sometimes Camden. And if we did go out to the West End, for example, we always discussed whose flat we'd be staying in that night. It was a relationship landmark. *It was a relationship*.

It was quarter past eight and he was late. The buzzer hadn't buzzed. The phone hadn't rung. I would have called his mobile, but I figured that fifteen minutes was probably too soon and if I did call I would come across as being neurotic and I definitely wasn't. Maybe I was, but there was no way I was going to admit it.

I had just emptied my second glass of wine when finally he arrived. The first thing I noticed after I let him in and he kissed me, was that he had been drinking. The smell of beer and the fact he was late annoyed me.

'You've been drinking.' I sounded like a fishwife.

'Only a couple. Sorry I'm late but I had to see a mate about something.' Ugh, that is such a male thing to say.

'About what?'

'Shall we go to dinner? I'm starving, I'll tell you on the way.'

I should have known then, or even before then, that the evening would go wrong.

'I forgot about this stag do I have to go on this weekend,' Joe said as we walked to the restaurant.

'This weekend?' I repeated.

'Yeah, this weekend. It's a mate I knew from college, haven't seen him in ages but when he told me he was getting married, I promised to go on his stag weekend.'

'Where is it?' I could feel my indignation rising.

'Amsterdam.' Joe was smiling.

'Amsterdam?'

'That's why I was late. I had to meet him to make the travel arrangements.'

'But Amsterdam is full of whores.' It was all I could think of.

At this point we arrived at the restaurant.

'Are we going in?' Joe asked. 'Holly, come on, I'm sorry I forgot to tell you, but I promise I won't sleep with any whores.' He had a smile on his beautiful lips. His eyes glistened the way they always did when he'd had a drink. He looked so sexy.

'Does that mean you'll sleep with women who aren't whores?' I was so angry. Irrational, I know, but I was past the point of no return.

'Of course not.' His smile disappeared; he looked hurt.

'Joe, we were going to dinner on Saturday.'

'I'm sorry, I forgot. But Tony is only getting married once.'

'You hope.'

'Holly, don't be like this. Look, you can go for dinner with one of your friends.'

'I could, Joe, yes, but I wanted to go with you.' My voice was ice-cold. A total overreaction.

'Holly I'm sorry, if it means that much to you then I'll cancel.'

'Good.'

'You mean you really want me to let down an old friend who's getting married?' He looked incredulous.

'Yes.'

'Well I won't.'

'Why did you say you would then?'

'I didn't think you'd be so unreasonable.'

'Well, now you know, don't you. I'm going home and if you follow me I'll scream.'

I walked off without looking back. Then I went home and cried.

A while later, when the anger had subsided, I felt blanketed by warmth. Here I was trying to be mad at him, but instead I couldn't help but smile. My feelings had been there from the beginning, but in true twenty-first-century form they were buried beneath the rubble of 'dating'.

Dating is a game. It's a battle of wills: who calls who, who chases who, who concedes defeat. You're so busy sitting by a phone that has taken a vow of silence that you forget the reason you're sitting there. That was what it was like in the early days of the Holly and Joe saga. We played games, we cancelled dates, and we kept our cool. Not any more.

If it hadn't been for the convention demanded by modern relationships, I would have known I was in love with him from the word go. I would have let my emotions flow through me enjoying the sensuality of every single drop. But instead I hid behind the dating game.

I understand why we behave this way. Because although I felt elated, I also felt naked. I stood there without my skin, my defence. I was stripped bare and every single emotion I possessed was on show in my personal exhibition. Love is incredibly welcome, but it is also unwelcome, because it brings with it vulnerability. Happiness and vulnerability go hand in hand in love.

I had sorted out my feelings for Joe, I could only hope that he hadn't decided that I was a mad banshee, and that he felt the same way I did. After all, my reaction had been out of character. But I couldn't find out, because it was too late, and I didn't have the words. Instead, I wrapped myself in my duvet, and smiled myself to sleep.

# Chapter Three

———◆◆◆———

Early the following day I took my smile with me to the office. The first thing I did was to send Joe an e-mail. I told him that I was sorry. I asked him to forgive me and call. How could he resist?

E-mail might be thoroughly modern but it's just as annoying as every other method of communication. I still had to wait for his response, which hadn't arrived by lunchtime. I was terrified in case I'd blown it.

'Holly, *Zoom* are on the line.' I looked at Dixie and my smile became a grimace. I picked up the phone to Phil Can, my biggest client, and managed to behave professionally through the conversation. As soon as I put down the phone I told Dixie I was going out and left the office.

My office is near Leicester Square, so I walked around, clutching my mobile phone and willing him to ring. He didn't. I didn't feel like eating so I just walked. I debated giving him a call but couldn't. I'd held out my olive branch, it was up to him to take it. Bastard. Lovely, sexy, delicious bastard.

Reluctantly I returned to the office. I turned to my computer screen to check my e-mails. There was nothing from Joe, but there was a message which almost managed to distract me.

It was an e-mail from George. George, my best friend, whom I hadn't seen for five years. The only contact we'd had in those five years were Christmas cards, where we'd swopped work details, but not personal ones. That was how he'd had my e-mail address but he had never used it. Until now. I could barely believe my eyes. As I read it, I began to feel better. George was coming home that weekend and he wanted to see me.

My mood of depression evaporated. George was coming home! So the love of my life was ignoring me, but at least my best friend was coming to see me. I knew that everything would be all right. George was an omen. You see, I had realised I was in love with Joe; my oldest, best friend, was coming home; and I was wrapping up my twenty-ninth year. Everything was falling neatly into place.

I didn't have an abundance of friends. I was the type of person who put all her eggs in one basket. I always thought that as long as I had one best friend, I wouldn't need any more. I could be aloof with people who aren't that important to me. When George left me, he left me a bit short on the friends front, but I barely replenished my supplies. I had Lisa and her boyfriend Max; Freddie, and even my boss Francesca, but that was about it. As for acquaintances, they can't always be avoided, but they aren't the same. As far as friends went, no one was the same as George.

When we had first met, George was my arch enemy. The reason for his status was that at the age of eleven he was going out with my best friend Samantha. Of course going out was probably the wrong way to describe it because they didn't really go anywhere. They walked to school together (they lived in the same street), they held hands at lunchtime and they walked home together. It was a typical eleven-year-old's relationship, and I was the typical jealous best friend. I would look at them covetously as they held hands, standing in the playground. I would trail behind them, scuffing my sensible school shoes, much to my mother's annoyance. My relationship with George was one of mutual scowl throwing, and not much else. My friendship with Samantha changed beyond all recognition. I was no longer the most important person in her life; I had to share that honour, and in reality, I knew I'd been usurped.

They lasted for a year, until Samantha informed me tearfully that her family were moving to Australia. I was distraught, George was distraught, Samantha was distraught. I believed that my life was over, I wouldn't have the requisite best friend any more. George was heartbroken, he declared undying love and even asked his parents if Samantha could live with him. I asked my parents the same. But off she went to the other side of the world leaving two very upset twelve-year-olds who both believed that their lives were over.

Before she left she had a farewell party. It was a disco in the village hall and nearly everyone from school was invited. Halfway through, I went outside to weep dramatically and found that George had already beaten me to it. Instead of scowling I sort of smiled at him, and through his tears he sort of smiled at me.

That was it really. When Samantha left we united in our grief and became friends. We were inseparable. At first we talked about how much we missed Samantha, but after a while our conversation diverged a little, then a bit more, until Samantha was no longer the main focus. Our friendship flourished, and it lasted long after our contact with Samantha had tapered off. George became my new best friend and he also became the most important person in my life.

We lasted in our roles of best friends until we were both twenty-four. It was an incredible friendship.

The only disappointment was that we didn't fall in love. Everyone expected it; people would have put money on it. They guessed that at some point after our hormones kicked in we would end up together. But we never so much as shared a kiss. I never wanted to kiss him and he never wanted to kiss me. In fact nothing could have been further from our minds.

When we finished our A levels, we both decided to travel. We worked to make some money then we went away together for seven months. Even today I remember that time as one of the best of my life; it was magical. I was sharing the most wonderful experiences with the most wonderful person. One day, when we were in a Thai market, I remember looking at him. He was trying to barter for a fake Rolex, and he was so bad at bartering. The price was going up instead of down and I was trying not to laugh at him. I remember looking at him and thinking that this sensible boy, the serious boy that I had known for what felt like all my life was truly the best friend anyone could ask for. I couldn't imagine life without him; I didn't expect I'd have to. And I certainly had no inkling at that time that he would ever, ever hurt me.

We returned from travelling and George got ready to start his law degree in London, while I looked for a job. I soon found one as a lowly office junior in a respectable PR firm. I had chosen PR as my career path at the same time George chose law.

'Why public relations?' he asked.

'Because I think it'll be quite glamorous.' I had read about all sorts of media careers, and thought that PR sounded the most exciting. I had done my homework, and decided that I would rather work than study. I wasn't sure why I shunned university, despite my parents and George's views, but I wanted to start making a career for myself. I was too ambitious for education, or at least too impatient. I had never been in love with school and therefore I knew I didn't want to go to university. Despite the efforts of everyone around me, I stood my ground.

So as George moved into student halls, I moved in with Lisa, bought my first suit, started work and got on with my life. I saw George about once a week. It was an enduring special friendship.

I felt as if no one would ever understand me as he did. I knew no one would care for him the way I did. The only thing missing in our platonic love affair was physical attraction. It's hard for me to understand this. George was nice looking even when he and Samantha were together. He was tall, had very blond hair, he wore glasses which made him look cute rather than geeky. At twelve, he was considered a good catch. As we grew up, he improved. He got taller, broader, he changed his glasses so he always looked trendy and he didn't suffer from spots. He grew into his face which was quite a serious one, but also warm. All the girls liked him, but I didn't, couldn't fancy him, although I used to wish I could. I believed that falling in love with my best friend would be the most sensible thing I could do. However, I have never been particularly sensible and neither of us showed the remotest signs of doing that.

Post-Harry I spent a lot of time with George, crying and lamenting. Uncannily he had just split up with his first university girlfriend, so we were a mutual depression zone. It was around that time that we made our marriage pact.

'No one will ever love me,' I cried with a lip that could win the world record for trembling.

'No one will love me either,' he replied, although he didn't cry.

'I love you,' I said, shakily.

'I love you too, but I don't want to shag you.' Never one to mince his words was our George. So, we decided, after drinking in the student bar, that we would design a contingency plan for ourselves. If our twenty-year-old prediction came true and no one would ever love us, then we would love each other and despite the fact that we didn't want to have sex, we would get married. We both found the idea hysterically funny, and like any discussion you have when under the influence, we thought we were geniuses. It didn't matter if no one wanted to marry me because George would. Even though I didn't want to marry him.

In a drunken state we found our way back to George's room, where he typed out our arrangement on his computer and printed a copy. At this stage I would like to add an additional marriage-pact proviso: don't ever make one with a law student.

I remember the look on the man's face when we rushed into the off-licence to buy six cans of Stella and ask him if he would witness our marriage-pact agreement. Although stunned, he agreed and signed it, probably because we were buying something and, after all, the customer is always right. Even when they are clearly bonkers.

In our drunken state, we found our way to the photocopier at the all-night library and made a copy for each of us. We were so drunk that I was sure that the wording made no sense, although George thought the word 'decree' was appropriate and I had no idea what it meant. It read:

I, Holly Miller, hereby decree that if I am unmarried by the time I reach my thirtieth birthday I will marry George David Conway.

Signed: *Holly Miller*                              Date: 23 October 1993

I, George David Conway, hereby decree that if I am unmarried by the time I reach my thirtieth year and if Holly Miller is also unmarried, (her reaching thirty six months after me), then I will marry Holly Miller.

Signed: *George Conway*                         Date: 23 October 1993

Witness: *Michael Harris*                         Date: 23 October 1993

The following day we woke up with monster hangovers and didn't mention the pact we'd made. When I went home, emptied my bag and found it, I put it in my special shoebox with my other keepsakes. We never mentioned it again.

George graduated with top honours, and got a job with a leading law firm. We were twenty-two with our best years ahead. He was spending the summer away, and it was the longest time we'd been apart from each other since we'd first met. I missed him, but knew it wasn't for ever. I spent time at home, hung out with

Lisa, who was very good at showing me how to have a good time, at this point I was with Marcus.

Our flat had become a party zone. People filled the place every night, mostly models. It was a good job that my main focus in life was no longer looks because otherwise I'd have fallen in love every day. I divided my time between my flat, and Marcus's. I didn't want Marcus in my flat, because it was full of beautiful women. His was only full of us.

When George started working, he stayed at our flat. It wasn't ideal because he was camped in my room, he had to work every day, and the party atmosphere almost threatened to destroy his career before it started. Lisa understood when George and I decided that it would be a good time for us to find a place to share. We moved into a two-bedroomed flat in Victoria, and we became flatmates as well as soulmates.

I don't remember much about the events preceding George's big announcement. My career was going well, as was his. Our flat was a hive of social activity; we often had visitors. We had established a life in London, which we both enjoyed.

Then he dropped his bombshell. He was so excited, I remember that. It was the greatest honour bestowed on a young lawyer. He lost his usual cool when he told me, his words cascading from his mouth. I giggled as I told him to calm down and tell me again. On the third attempt I finally understood what he was saying. A major American law firm that had connections with his company had chosen George to go and work in the New York office where he would be on the fast track to lawyer greatness.

He had bought a bottle of champagne and excitedly poured the drinks hugging me again and again. I had never seen George so enthusiastic. Eventually he calmed down enough to phone his family and tell them. Then he called some friends from university. He wanted to tell the whole world. And while he was on the phone, I put my glass of champagne down on the coffee table, and went to the bathroom where finally I let the tears fall.

I was happy for him, of course I was. I loved George and love is all about wanting happiness for that person. If George had what he wanted, then I had what I wanted. But there is always a selfish side to love, and although I was determined to quash it, it still needed an outlet. Of course I was happy for him, but I was sad for me, because I was losing my best friend.

We were twenty-four when he left. I knew our friendship was effectively over. It was the second time I had lost a best friend to another country and although I was older when George left, I didn't believe our friendship would endure any more than mine and Samantha's had. It's hard to explain, but I knew.

Although the world these days is a global village, a move to New York need not precipitate the end of friendship, but it did. There were cheap flights every day, but for some reason I never got on a plane and he never asked me to. Our physical proximity had kept us together – but space between us became space in our friendship.

He visited his parents at Christmas for the first two years, and I saw him. But something had changed. Our childhood friendship had endured the rocky road of puberty onwards, because we saw each other all the time. When either of us changed, our friendship was able to adapt but when he left and I couldn't see him, he changed without me and I changed without him. Our friendship couldn't keep up.

We became Christmas-card friends and eventually I forgot to miss him.

Then the e-mail arrived and George was back. We arranged to meet on Saturday night, the Saturday night that had become Joe-free since my abandonment. At the thought of seeing George, I felt my old feelings return. He might not have been in my life, but he was still in my heart.

# Chapter Four

I didn't give my outfit too much thought when I was getting ready to meet George. Even though I hadn't seen him for ages and I wanted to look my best, I still couldn't bring myself to fret about clothes. In total contrast, every date I've had with Joe, my wardrobe has been ransacked, in order for me to try on every outfit I possess more than once. It was natural for me to want to look sexy for Joe; for George, I didn't care about that. I chose an outfit which was warm (it was the beginning of December), but smart because we were meeting at his swanky hotel. I looked nice, but not sexy. It was difficult because I was naturally sexy, but not overtly so.

As I left, I thought of Joe. My emotions were a little bit jumpy. They danced across my mind, then went to wait in the wings before returning to the stage. I was upset about the non-communication. Did Joe love me or was he just playing with me? I had just decided how I felt about him, but I was so confused. Why hadn't he contacted me? After the row I apologised but he had ignored me. Had I blown it? I was terrified that I might have ruined everything. But as I couldn't get hold of him, I had no way of knowing.

Although I couldn't wait to see George, I was worried about Joe. What if he was so angry with me, he ended our relationship? Just as I had admitted to myself that I loved him.

Panic and excitement are things that shouldn't be mixed, like drinks I guess. I suppose if I had to tell you how I felt that night, it would be the lethal combination of red wine and tequila.

There is little certainty in life unless you know someone inside out. How can you do that? George is how. He had always been a constant in my life, or at least he had until he left London. It was ironic really. I was uncertain about the man I loved, but I was seeing my best friend. Even if Joe never wanted to see me again, I knew that George would always be George and he'd always be my friend. I loved that certainty; it's so rare.

I needed George that night, I needed to see him and to remember how he made me smile for most of our childhood. I needed to see him and know he still cared about me regardless of Joe's feelings for me. I wasn't sure if I was suffering from uncertainty or rejection, but because you've just admitted to your cynical self that you are in love with a man who you rowed with because you were behaving irrationally, then all you want is someone you are one hundred per cent sure of. Someone who won't reject you or hurt you. Your best friend.

George had been there for every one of my heartbreaks. My first boyfriend was Andrew, aged fourteen. He took me to the local park where he shoved his tongue into my mouth and wiggled it about a bit – my first real kiss. I had never had a boyfriend before so I was just grateful, if not a little shocked at that kiss and a little scared of it happening again; so I still let him. Then when he dumped me for some girl from another school, who was a little more willing than me, George hit him. He hit him really hard in front of everyone. He was my hero.

All the men before Joe had been compared to George. He was my benchmark. That was why it took me so long to get over him when he moved to New York. George was my perfect man, and sex didn't come into it.

Joe was the first man I didn't compare with George. He was the first man who bowled me over; all that mattered was Joe. And now he wasn't even talking to me.

\*

When I saw George standing at the bar in his hotel, I studied him for a few moments before approaching. He was tall (of course he had been tall when he left, but he looked taller somehow), his dark hair was sprinkled with grey flecks, and he wore a shirt and trousers; he looked preppy. American, I suppose. Although I could see he was George, he wasn't quite the same George that I remembered. He wasn't a stranger exactly, but he wasn't as familiar as I had expected. I took a deep breath, tried to banish my thoughts of Joe and told myself to enjoy the one night I had with my old friend. It could be another five years till the next time.

'Hi,' I said, grinning broadly.

'My God, Hol, you look incredible.' His smile was the same. An obvious grin, and an honest one. But he sounded different.

'So do you, and you sound so American.'

'Do not.'

'Do too.' Some things change, but others don't, although cosmetically we were different, our friendship had been set in cement. Instantly teenagers again.

He ordered champagne, said we were celebrating. We drank a bottle before going to dinner in the hotel restaurant. It was obvious that George was doing very well. He was staying in one of London's trendiest hotels, eating in one of the most expensive restaurants, wearing quality clothes, even his nails looked manicured. But I didn't ask him about that. We didn't talk about our lives as they stood, we talked only about the past.

The past. It's amazing how strong your grip on it can be. George and I didn't have a present in common. We both knew we were unlikely to have a future, so we looked to the past, which is where we would always be. We were nostalgic and sentimental as we recalled stories, experiences, our entire childhood from when we were twelve. If anyone could have heard us they would have been bored rigid.

I didn't mention Joe, he didn't tell me if there was anyone in his life. I didn't find out about his job, he didn't ask about mine. It wasn't so much a conversation, we were reminiscing. The thing about that is that you talk and talk and talk and don't realise how much you've drunk.

George paid the bill, he insisted. I watched him take his platinum American Express card out of his expensive-looking wallet and I felt proud of him. He had always been ambitious, always certain about where he was going; he appeared to have achieved his goals. He was still the serious, sensible boy I remembered and it had certainly paid off.

'Do you want to come up to my room and drink the minibar?' he asked. It sounded like a line; or it would have done coming from anyone else.

'Of course I bloody do. I haven't seen you for five years and probably won't for another five. Let's go.' I took his hand and we walked to the lift. I was so comfortable with him that I didn't even think about taking hold of his hand before I did it.

His suite was huge. I explored it with an enthusiasm I reserved for all hotel rooms. There is something about them that makes me feel decadent and special. I opened all the cupboards and drawers. I flicked all the channels on the television. I ransacked the bathroom, putting a number of the small bottles in my handbag, leaving George with just essentials. He was lining up the bottles from the minibar, getting out the ice tray and requesting a packet of cigarettes from room service all at the same time, and with an efficiency and confidence that I knew so well.

'You never smoked,' I said. It was true, he didn't. I smoked. I smoked from the age of eighteen until I gave up.

'I don't really, but you know . . . sometimes, I just . . . Well when I'm drunk anyway. It's just this thing, no big deal.'

'I thought Americans hated smokers,' I said.

'Yeah well in the privacy of your own home it's nobody else's business. I'm hardly a full-time smoker, it relieves the stress.' He shrugged.

It was the first thing he had told me that I didn't already know. Although I was having a wonderful evening, I had to admit it was slightly bizarre.

George handed me a vodka, I gulped it down.

'Don't you think it's weird that we have revisited the past but not talked about the here and now,' he said, sipping his drink.

'I was just thinking that.' I smiled, amazed at how in tune we still were. I remembered that we always seemed to think the same things, and always thought we had some kind of weird psychic link. We didn't, as the distance between us proved, or if we did it was a connection that only worked when we were in close proximity. Actually I think it was just a result of the amount of time we spent together. Nothing more.

'Maybe we should start by being completely honest,' he continued. I looked at him, bemused. I must have been more drunk than I thought. Before I had time to reply, there was a knock on the door. George came back with his cigarettes. As he filled our glasses with ice and alcohol (I think it was gin this time), I took and lit one of the cigarettes. I felt unsettled, I was drunk; I needed nicotine. The atmosphere now was slightly charged. I had no idea at that point what had happened, but I was sure I was going to find out.

'I am honest with you,' I said after an age. We were both smoking and drinking.

'Kids stuff, Hol, that's what it is. Remember when we were young and everyone said we would end up together?' I nodded.

'Well haven't you ever thought about it?'

Now there was a question. Had I thought about it? Of course I had, I would be a liar if I said I hadn't. But when I had thought about it, and that was an age ago, the answer had been no, categorically no. I loved George more than I've ever loved any other man but it was purely platonic. That was the one thing I had always been certain about.

'George, I'm not sure where this is heading.' I felt uneasy. He was knocking me off balance, pushing me over, trying to take our friendship into uncharted territory; no man's land.

'It's leading to a kiss,' he replied.

As soon as the words were out, he leaned in and kissed me. I wanted to run away, because within a few seconds I had gone from having one of my best nights in ages to having one of the worst.

But I didn't stop him.

I looked at him totally bewildered. I was trying to figure out my feelings, trying to discover why I didn't put a stop to it. I felt sick, I was angry with myself, I was disappointed with both of us. *Why did I let it happen?*

It wasn't a passionate kiss. It was just a kiss. The way he had looked at me told me that he felt the same. The mechanics were there; it worked as per kiss guidelines, but the magical ingredients which differentiate a kiss from a *kiss* were missing. Lips were functioning, tongues even made a brief appearance, teeth didn't clash and saliva didn't get out of hand. But there was no passion, no enjoyment, and certainly no pleasure.

I lit a cigarette. It was amazing how easily I was able to slip back into being a smoker. As the room began to spin slightly I realised just how drunk I was. I felt as if I had lost control of my faculties. Desperately I needed to regain them.

'Why?' I asked. I felt nauseous, but I had no intention of being sick.

'Holly, don't sound so angry, it was inevitable. Remember when we first met, we were sworn enemies, but we became so close. We grew up together, we travelled together, we even lived together. Hol, there was bound to be some point where we had a physical encounter.'

'A physical encounter? Shit George what has happened to you? How can you refer to what just happened as a physical encounter?' I had never been able to get angry with George, ever. Our friendship, which I cherished, had always been tranquil. I had never refused him anything, been angry with him or had his anger vented on me. But now, now I was looking at a stranger, and one whom I had experienced 'a physical encounter' with.

'I'm sorry, Hol, but that was what it was. I know it was hardly romantic.' I snorted my agreement, no it certainly wasn't. He continued. 'What I mean is that I haven't been entirely honest with you. I think perhaps I should explain.'

I stared at him while he told me his story.

He was in love. He'd been dating a woman called Julia for three years. She was a fellow lawyer: American, tall, slim, gorgeous, athletic, oh, and she had a lot going for her. The thing was that their relationship was at a junction. (Believe me, along with physical encounters, George also talked about junctions). They both had their own apartments, but they split their time between the two. They were known among their 'circle', as a power couple. Successful, rich, good-looking, made for each other. George agreed with them. Nevertheless, and of course in the life of someone who talks 'a corporate match made in heaven,' there would be a but, I was an unresolved issue.

I became more incredulous by the second.

He had always expected us to cross the boundaries of friendship at some point in our lives. He knew, from the age of twelve that our hormones would get the better of us, but they never had. That didn't matter to him until he thought about marrying Julia. He was ninety-nine per cent sure that she was the right woman for him, and he was planning on proposing, but there was a worrying one per cent chance that she wasn't. I was the one per cent. It wasn't terribly flattering.

I was the tiny little doubt in the back of his mind; a speck of uncertainty. What if he and I *were* made for each other after all? He couldn't take the chance of not knowing. He sat there and told me this as if it made perfect sense. I blinked a few times in the hope that I would find myself dreaming.

George had said he was here on business but he wasn't. He was here for the sole purpose of checking that I wasn't the girl for him. So, he took me out to dinner, then he pounced on me, and having done what he came here to do, he was delighted because he realised that our 'physical encounter' wasn't right. It didn't – or rather I didn't – do for him what Julia did for him. His exact words were: 'Holly, there is no use pretending that that worked. No point in thinking that it was right. I don't mean to be blunt and I'd never hurt you intentionally but you didn't rock my world.' He smiled as if it was all some sort of joke. I wasn't laughing.

I was filled with fury. I was also incredibly drunk having managed to consume most of the minibar while George was relaying his tale.

'George, I have a boyfriend. I love him, I really do. Then you swan back into my life, you get me drunk, you do this when I'm not prepared and then you tell me that you only did it because you wanted to propose to your superwoman girlfriend and you had to check that I was crap.' I think I managed to sum it up succinctly. Even if I was doubting my status as a girlfriend at the time.

'Hol, don't be like that, you make it sound so crass. You must have thought about us in that way too, women and men can't be platonic without it crossing their minds. Now, the good news is that you can carry on with your guy and I can marry Julia and we will know, for sure, that we weren't meant to be together.' He smiled. He actually smiled, as if he was pleased with the situation.

'You're a fucking nutter, George, I can't believe you'd do this. For your information I wasn't curious about us. I have never wanted to kiss you, and I don't know why I did, but I suspect it has something to do with the gallons of alcohol you poured down my neck this evening.' I could feel my head expanding as if it would pop off. I had another cigarette to try to calm myself. I knew it wasn't all his fault, much as I wished it was, but he had lured me into his web with the sole intention of seducing me. I felt cheated, and I felt betrayed. I felt betrayed by the one person I never thought would do that to me, which was a zillion times worse.

'Christ, Hol, you have certainly managed to develop your temper in later life. I remember when you were quiet as a lamb.' He seemed to be mocking me. Where had my friend gone? Why was he doing that? I understood less than nothing.

'I have never needed to raise my voice the way I need to now.' I looked at him and realised that it was fruitless to carry on. He looked so smug, sitting there in his plush hotel room, like the cat who got the cream. Or the cat who had the cream waiting for him back in New York, and who had just sampled the skimmed milk. 'I'm going now and I want you to know that I am incredibly pissed off with you.' When it came down to it, the anger didn't in any way manage to manifest itself. I couldn't even do my feelings justice.

'When you calm down you'll realise that we did the right thing.' With George's words ringing in my ears I walked out of his hotel room and out of his life without even a backward glance.

My lifelong friendship was over.

# Chapter Five

I woke on Sunday feeling suitably horrible. I know I deserved it. As soon as I was sober again, the anger and guilt set in. Joe didn't deserve to have a loose woman for a girlfriend, especially since I was in love with him. Why on earth did I kiss George? I couldn't figure it out, I had no answers. If it was lust, or something like that then I could almost understand. Even if it was just curiosity I would have known why I did it. But I didn't have any of those reasons. I did it because he wanted me to and that was unforgivable.

I really loved Joe. So why would I jeopardise that with anyone? What sort of woman am I? A raging harlot, a slut, a whore? How could I have let anything happen when my true feelings for Joe had only just been recognised? I couldn't forgive myself. I hated George, but I hated myself more. I couldn't bear to think about what I'd done. I couldn't bear to admit to what I'd done.

I crawled out of bed and into the shower. As soon as I dried myself and dressed I went out to buy the papers. I also bought food to make myself a fry-up. I cooked, ate, then dragged my duvet to the sofa where I lay, feeling miserable, reading the papers.

The phone didn't ring all day. I thought Joe would have called and just let me know that he was still talking to me, but he didn't. I wanted to send him a text message, but knew that wouldn't be a cool thing to do so I hid my mobile phone in the laundry basket. I then tried to figure out what I was going to do.

Normally, at times like this, I would turn to friends for advice. But I couldn't face talking to anyone, couldn't bring myself to try to explain the situation. I decided there and then that I would never tell anyone what had happened with George. By not telling anyone, then I could pretend it never happened. Like magic, I obliterated the previous night from my mind and concentrated on how I was going to make my relationship with Joe work. After all, George was now firmly relegated to my past, and I had a future to look forward to. I just had to ensure that Joe still wanted to be part of it.

Finally I pulled myself together that evening and called Lisa. Lisa is the best person to speak to when you feel a little bit down because she doesn't believe in dwelling on problems. She is better at ignoring her own moods than anyone I have ever come across; she is also better at ignoring other people's moods. Ever since I first moved in with her she was the one person who could always cheer me up. She was brilliant after George left for America all those years ago, she moved me straight back into her flat and nurtured me in an alcoholic sort of way until I was ready to move on and get my own place. Then she helped me find the little two-bedroomed flat in Clapham which is still my home.

We arranged to go for supper at our favourite Italian, conveniently located down the road from my flat. Because I was meeting Lisa, who was stunning, I put on a bit of make-up, and because she was tall, I put on my high heels. I looked at myself in the mirror, and I could still see the hangover. I smiled and tried my best to look human, then I left.

'So, you and Joe aren't talking,' Lisa said when we were settled with a bottle of red. She was wearing jeans and a black long-sleeved T-shirt, but she still looked amazing.

'I don't know. We haven't spoken since it happened, and I guess he's pissed off with me, but I don't know because all there's been is silence.'

'Call him?' Lisa didn't believe in game-playing.

'I thought that it would be better if I didn't.'

'Holly, you're a bloody idiot. Anyway did you say you saw George last night?' This was my line: I met George, he told me that he was going to ask his girlfriend to marry him, we had dinner to celebrate and catch up.

'Yeah, he looked older.'

'No offence, but you look older.'

'Today I do.'

'Every day darling. Listen, you're going to be thirty soon, I was wondering what sort of a party you had planned.'

'I don't like parties, you know that.'

'I wanted to have a roller disco for my thirtieth but the insurance premium was too high.' Lisa lit a cigarette.

'As I remember it your thirtieth was a drugs and disco party.'

'That's back in the days when I was on the drugs and disco diet.'

'The what?'

'Well, in order to stay thin I took a little coke and danced a lot.'

'And now?'

'Now I smoke a lot, but generally I don't do much else.'

Not sure how we had got to this point, I decided to change the subject. 'What are you doing for Christmas?'

'Oh, Max has invited his family to come to us for Christmas Day. He tried to persuade me to invite mine too, but no way. What about you?' Max was Lisa's boyfriend, they'd been together for years and she adored him.

'Well, I'm probably going to Devon, but I'd quite like to spend Christmas Day with Joe.'

'If he's still talking to you.' We had come full circle.

Later, as I lay wrapped in my duvet, I realised that recently I had begun to hate sleeping alone. It had never bothered me before. Sure, I liked to spread out in bed, but I wanted Joe there.

I chastised myself for sounding so sad. Instead, I looked forward to a new day, a new week, and I would concentrate on Joe, I wasn't ready to let him get away.

'Freddie, why didn't you buy me coffee?' I asked as I sat at my desk glancing enviously at Freddie's overpriced cappuccino.

'Because it's bad for you and now you have a boyfriend you have to be careful.'

'But I don't even know if I have a boyfriend at the moment.'

'Oh God, I wondered how long it would take you. Holly it's ten o'clock on Monday morning and already you're whingeing.'

'I am not.' What I didn't tell Freddie was that I had already taken action on the Joe front. I decided not to be too proud and so sent him a text message on the way to work asking him to call me. I hated the idea I was coming across as desperate but felt that I didn't have any choice.

'Good weekend?' I asked, changing the subject.

'Yeah, yours?'

'Yeah, it was lovely seeing George again,' I lied.

'So why do you look so ghastly?' It was a good question. One which reaffirmed that I looked the way I felt.

'Joe.'

'Oh the whores,' Freddie teased. I shot him a look. This was Freddie's idea of lending a sympathetic ear.

'No, I don't think that's it. I'm not a total moron. How do you get a man to fall in love with you?'

'Red dress, no knickers,' Freddie responded without appearing to think.

'I didn't ask how to get a man to shag me, I asked how to get a man to fall in love with me.'

'Trust me that works. It's not about sex, you don't have to make any effort to make a man want to sleep with you. In fact you only need a hole in the right place.' I knew before I had started that he wasn't the right man to ask, but he was all I had.

'Freddie, I'm serious.'

'So am I. Red dress, no knickers; nice meal, nice wine. All any man wants. Trust me.'

I wondered if I had a red dress. I knew I could do no knickers.

Later, I was just drafting an e-mail to *Jet*, my household cleaning product client, about their New Year campaign – 'Clean Away Those January Blues' – when Dixie appeared at my desk carrying an enormous bunch of flowers. Everyone crowded around to exclaim how lucky I was, but still my hands shook as I opened the card. It just said, *Sorry, Joe*. My heart soared. He wasn't going to finish with me and he cared enough to send flowers. My love life was on course again.

I called him straight away and arranged for him to come over to my flat that evening. He apologised for not calling but said he wanted to send flowers before we spoke. He said that he didn't get my e-mail before he had left, and he'd spent the weekend worrying that I wasn't speaking to him! So, I was going to cook dinner, and look nice (Freddie style), before addressing the subject of our relationship (My style). It wasn't much of a plan, but it was the best plan I had.

I spent the rest of the day in a little bit of a flurry. I know that I am trying desperately hard to convey the fact I was an intelligent, sensible grown-up, but underneath there were some conflicting emotions that were hard to control. It wasn't my fault, it certainly wasn't my style. I actually felt a bit cross with myself about it.

Weighed down with the flowers, I had to get a cab home, giving me the feeling that my evening was starting off well. Joe was due round at eight, which gave me just over an hour to go to the shop, make myself look stunning and tidy up the flat. Joe didn't stand a chance.

I cheated on the food and bought fresh pasta and sauce from the organic shop. I also bought a lipsmacking cheesecake. The wine was chilling and I was wearing a knee-length, tight black skirt (no red dress in my wardrobe), no knickers, high heels and a small strappy top. It wasn't the most sensible outfit seeing as it was minus six degrees outside and my central heating was escaping through the cracks in the window, but the stiff nipples it produced were a genius addition. Freddie would have been proud.

Joe, or he who is normally late, was on time. I threw my arms around him and kissed him to within an inch of his life.

'So I'm forgiven?' he said.

'I was being neurotic,' I replied, leading him to the dining table. I decided beforehand that we would eat without talking about ourselves, have a nice normal dinner, then we would talk about us.

'You look fucking sexy,' he said. I giggled and kissed him again. The only problem was that if I wasn't careful the plan would be abandoned and I would be in bed without sorting things out. I couldn't let that happen.

'I made your favourite,' I said, disappearing into the kitchen. I was like a teenager on a first date. My adrenaline was pumping, a feeling that I liked because not only did it make me feel young, but it made me feel alive.

I returned with a dish of steaming pasta.

'This looks fabulous,' Joe said, although he was looking at me, not the food.

'I know how much you love pasta,' I replied. Actually, I had no idea if he loved pasta, but I wanted to be in control.

'I like it a lot,' Joe replied, slightly puzzled.

'Good.' Then I asked him about his stag weekend.

'It was all right,' he said cautiously.

'Look, I don't mind if you had a great time, in fact I hope you *had* a great time.' After that we managed to have the natural conversation I had planned. We chatted about work, I even told him about seeing George (but not about going to his hotel suite). Everything was on track. Finally it was time for brandy.

'What I love about dating a posh bird like you is that not only do you know about knives and forks, but you also give me proper drinks after dinner.' I raised my eyebrows. Joe always played up his humble beginnings. He might have been from Essex but so what. He wasn't poor, he hadn't been brought up poor, he'd had an average childhood as far as I could gather: two parents who were still together, and a younger sister. Just because his father was a plasterer and mine was a suit didn't mean anything, but I think he liked to play on the class differences between us.

He went to state school, I went to private school; his parents lived in a semi, mine live in a detached house with an acre of land. Anyway, I hadn't met his parents and he hadn't met mine. He called himself my 'bit of rough', but he worked for a top design consultancy, he spent most of his days in designer clothes, and he drove a beautiful 1960s Porsche.

'How much do you like dating me?' I asked.

'Why do you ask?'

'Because of that silly row we had. I felt all vulnerable at the weekend and I hate to put pressure on you but I just need to know that what we have, what we're doing is more than a bit of fun.' I was quite proud of the succinct way I had voiced my feelings.

'Has that been bothering you?' I watched as a huge grin spread across his face.

'Yes,' I said, not smiling back.

'Holly, I adore you, and yes what we have is much more than a bit of fun. I was worried too, thought about you all weekend, which wasn't easy with all the whores there. Joke. The thing is that I'm not really good at the boyfriend thing.'

'That's a typical man-thing to say.' My hackles were raised, despite my resolve to stay calm.

'Let me finish. I'm just not used to it. I haven't had a girlfriend for ages and I'm just a bit selfish. I don't want to be, but I am. I want us to make a proper go of it, and I'm going to do that.' He stood up, took my hands and pulled me up. He nuzzled my ear.

'I'm not wearing any knickers,' I whispered. He took me to bed to check and afterwards he told me that he loved me.

There followed a blissful few weeks. We were in love, head over heels in love and it was everything that I'd dreamed of. Life was wonderful, really wonderful. We spent more and more time together, until I had underwear and cosmetics firmly lodged in his flat and he had deposited his shaving gear and shirts in mine. It was nearly Christmas and Christmas was truly magical. I wasn't going to write a letter to Santa that year, I had everything I wanted.

# Chapter Six

I spent Christmas Day with Joe, and that made me feel grown-up. We woke up, had breakfast and champagne in bed where we exchanged our presents. We'd purchased a Christmas tree and put up a few tasteful decorations. We cooked turkey together, we drank a lot, we made love a lot. By the time we were ready to watch Christmas TV, Joe was drunk and singing Christmas carols and I was blissfully happy.

Then, on Boxing Day I borrowed Lisa's car, and drove to see my parents and sister for a few days, while Joe went to visit his parents. I didn't want us to be apart but it was the first Christmas where I hadn't seen my family and I think it was the same for him so we went our separate ways.

Then the morning after Boxing Day, I got the call that was to change everything.

George's mother rang. George had called in the middle of the night saying he was getting the first available flight back to England. She didn't know why and was worried about him. When she asked me, I panicked, thinking it might have been to do with his recent visit, although I told her I had no idea. It couldn't have been because of me. Could it?

When I put the phone down, I turned to my sister, Imogen, who was at my parents' house with her husband Jack.

I haven't spoken much about Imogen, mainly because I don't really see her that much now. I adore her and she adores me, but in a sisterly, sort of way. She's four years older than me, but she got married when she was twenty-one. At first my parents thought she was making a terrible decision, her intended was a man she had been at university with and he came across as a bit of a hippy. Immi had no intention of a career (she had always maintained that), so my parents fretted about how they would survive. But they were so in love that we all accepted it, and they proved their devotion when Immi took a job in an office to support Jack while he wrote his first children's book. The book was an instant success and he quickly became one of the most successful children's authors in the country. Now he's loaded, so Immi gave up her job. They live in Devon, near my parents and near where I grew up, which is why, in London, I see her rarely unless she comes up with Jack when he visits his publishers, and we have lunch. However, our meetings are always brief.

'Can we go for a walk?' I asked her.

'You, walk?' She raised an astonished eyebrow. 'OK, we'll take Bertie.' Bertie was Jack's highland terrier. We put him on the lead and headed out.

'George's mother called me,' I said. 'Seems he is getting a flight home and she asked me if I knew why.'

'Do you?' My sister is quite astute and I thought it would be pointless not to tell her the truth.

'He kissed me.' I told her what had happened. Then I told her about Julia.

'There's nothing in that story that would link his homecoming to you. I don't mean to be rude, Holly, but he told you that you didn't set him on fire.'

'I know, but there's this nagging thing. I mean if he asked her to marry him, why would he be coming back home so soon. I just hope he didn't change his mind. I'm not being vain, I don't think it's to do with me, I'm just worried in case it might disrupt things.'

'Joe?'

'Yes, everything's going so well, I really love him. I can't think why George would come home, other than he's changed his mind.'

'I can. What if this woman turned him down.'

I looked at Imogen, and as much as I hoped that Julia hadn't, it was almost a relief to think that that could be the case. I hated myself for thinking such an awful, selfish thought, but when George went back to New York, I was banking on the fact he would be staying there. For the first time ever, I didn't want him around.

I stayed in Devon for two more days. The day before I was due to drive back to London he called me. He said he was at his parents' house and asked if we could meet up. Actually he didn't, he demanded we meet up. I arranged to meet him at the park we used to hang out in as children.

The park had changed. The swings were new and brightly painted. The climbing apparatus more complex. The gardens were neat and full of flower beds. It looked nothing like the way it did when we were younger. This was almost a comfort to me. I sat on a bench and, although it was freezing, I was feeling quite flushed. It was less than a month since I had seen George, and here we were again. I saw him pull up in what I presumed was a hire car. It was a small Ford and it seemed too small for him. Until I watched him get out that is. He seemed to have shrunk; diminished. With a heavy heart I watched him approach.

'What's happened?' I asked as he sat down beside me. He had refused to tell me over the phone.

'She said no, Holly. I couldn't believe it. We've been together for three years, practically living together and she turned me down, said she wasn't ready. We're both thirty. Thirty for God's sake. You should be getting married at that age; *I* should be getting married, to Julia.' He broke down sobbing.

I saw a glimpse of the old George. The George that I had

adored. The one who was kind, sensitive and caring. He was crushed.

'So she didn't want to get married, but why did you split up?'

'It was her idea to break up. She said that if we both wanted such different things then maybe we should take a break from each other.'

'A break maybe, but a total split?'

'Obviously she doesn't love me enough.'

'Not necessarily.'

'Holly, it's obvious. Women want to get married, most women do. So the reason she turned me down is because she doesn't love me enough.' Just as I was about to protest he started crying again.

The first time I saw George cry was when Samantha left. I had cried too and he made me promise not to tell anyone. Our friendship was sealed on that promise. I don't think I ever saw him cry after that. Until now.

Not knowing what to do with a blubbing grown man, I folded my arms, well I was frozen. My mobile beeped at me to announce a text message; it was from Joe. I was about to read it when George moved towards me, his arms extended for a comforting hug.

'I missed you,' he said.

'I missed you too.' It was true I had, at one time. I didn't feel that in his current state he needed me to bring up the last time we met.

'I've never had a friendship as good as ours.'

'Me either.' I wanted to ask him why he had been so willing to sacrifice it, but that wasn't the appropriate moment.

'Friends for ever?' he asked, looking at me the way he used to when he was a teenager.

'Of course,' I replied. Well, what else could I say? I looked at him. His manic eyes seemed to have taken on a life of their own. One minute they were full of tears, the next they were staring at me, the next they seemed to be crossed. I experienced a huge jolt of genuine concern, although I couldn't pinpoint if it was for him or for me. Although why I should need concern when George had been dumped, I had no idea. I just felt I should.

'I thought she loved me,' George exclaimed, interrupting my thoughts. This time his eyes were boring into mine and he was incensed. I felt scared. 'I was so sure she loved me. I loved her, she loved me. That's the way it works isn't it Holly?' His eyes continued staring into mine and I wanted to cower, but I didn't. Although this was a George I had never, ever seen before, I stayed put. 'I did nothing to deserve this,' he continued. His voice was rising, getting harsher, meaner. Then into a softer cadence, but not for long. 'Everything . . . I did everything for her. And now the bitch has taken everything away from me. My job, my life; she took it all and she burned it and handed me back the ashes. I was wrong Holly, I must have been wrong.'

'About what?'

'About love of course. The only explanation for all this, the only thing that will ever make any sense is the fact that I got it all wrong. I got love wrong. I did it, not her. Me. Yes that's it, I am the one who got it wrong.' I had no idea what he was talking about, but he was scaring me now. 'There was this fug in my brain. Thick fug and now I think it might be going. Yes, something is clearing the way so I can think again.' He looked at me with those manic, stranger's eyes. His mad rant had tapered off. He appeared to be deep in thought, although the edge of madness that had crept into him was still lingering.

'I'm going back to London today,' I said, for want of changing the subject. I knew it was totally inadequate, but this conversation had to be re-routed.

'I'll probably be moving up later in the week.' He was regaining control.

'Really? You're transferring your job?'

'No, I'm going to take a sabbatical. I've got to clear it formally but I put the request in and signs are it will be approved. Then I'm going to rent a flat in London, and sort out my life.' He laughed, unconvincingly.

'I guess I'll see you when you're in London then.'

'You bet you will.'

As I drove back to my flat and my life in London, I couldn't shed the unsettled feeling that had taken root within me. I tried to concentrate on the fact that I would soon be seeing Joe. I felt sorry for George, I really did, but I was also looking forward to my own future. A future that up until now I never thought would include him.

Friendships changed, that was a fact of life. I can't say how I would define my friendship with George had he not left me for New York. I don't know if we would have been as close as we were, or if we'd have grown apart. But from the age of twelve, he was the single most important person in my life, that much I do know, and there was no way I was turning my back on him. The question of whether I still liked him was one which I couldn't answer. Our first meeting after five years was too weird for me to talk about; our second consisted of him scaring me and crying a lot. I wasn't certain that I knew George any more.

# Chapter Seven

It was the first day of the new year and I was going to meet Joe's parents for the first time. We were a bit hungover, having been out with Lisa and Max the night before but we'd promised that we'd go to lunch, so we dragged ourselves out of bed, and cursing our stupidity, got ready to leave. Joe was far more nervous than I was, apart from feeling ill I was looking forward to meeting his parents. After all I was meeting the people who brought up the man I loved. I already adored them.

George's parents had taught me from an early age that grown-ups are not all scary, alien beings. They're just people. I quite liked talking to people's parents, I found them interesting, I have never understood anyone being intimidated by grown-ups, I think *they* are far more afraid of us.

'They don't live in a big house,' Joe said.

'Sweetheart, for someone who is supposed to love me you don't think much of me if you think that matters.' I tried not to be angry, but Joe's impression of me being posh was a little unfair to say the least and the implication that I was a snob (although of course I was a bit), annoyed me.

'It's not that. I know you're not going to judge them, but I just want you to know what to expect.'

'I don't care if they live in a hovel, I still love them because they gave me you.' We kissed.

I love to kiss, but especially I love kissing Joe. He has the best lips I've ever been near. I sometimes think our relationship is

teenage, in the way we seem to 'kiss each other's faces off'. (I
heard that expression on television once, I have no idea if it was
appropriate but it was said by a teenager.) My mobile rang and
interrupted the delicious kiss. I shrugged and answered it
without recognising the number.

'Holly, it's George.' I hadn't heard from him since the day in
the park. I had thought about calling his parents to check that he
was all right, but something held me back.

'Are you OK?' I asked, as Joe helped me into my coat.

'I'm better,' he said.

'That's wonderful.' Something about the tone in his voice set
me on edge. It didn't sound right.

'I need to see you.'

'Sure, when?'

'Now.'

'Impossible, I'm off to Joe's parents' for lunch.' I mouthed the
word 'George' at Joe. I had told Joe about George's rejection,
and he already knew about our friendship.

'After lunch then,' George said.

'Look, to be honest George I'm going to be back late tonight,
we're spending the afternoon there.' I didn't want him to spoil
my day with Joe.

'It's in your interest,' he said. That took me aback. I know that
things hadn't been quite right between us since the kiss, but he
was sounding like a second-hand car dealer.

'I really can't.'

'OK, well tomorrow after work. I'll pick you up from your
office at six.' Again, I was stunned. He sounded upbeat and
assertive. The last time I'd seen him he was convinced his life
was over, now he seemed ready to re-start. I just wasn't sure
where I came in. Joe stood by the door, looking gorgeous and
impatient.

'OK, I'll see you there.' I gave him my office address, hung
up and forgot about him.

*

The village that Joe grew up in was incredibly pretty. It didn't tally with him. Joe who drove a black Porsche and always wore black or grey grew up in a flowery haven. It seemed incongruous.

His parents greeted me as if they'd known me for years. I got the impression that his mum was quite relieved that Joe seemed to be 'settling down'. He was only thirty-one but she made a few references to his age as if he was older and a confirmed bachelor. Luckily, she didn't mention grandchildren. I didn't get to meet his sister, whom I had heard lots about, but had apparently disappeared to her boyfriend's for New Year's Eve and hadn't come back. She was only twenty and her brother and his new girlfriend weren't of much interest to her. Or not as much interest as the new man in her life. His mother told me all about Hannah, so I felt as if I'd met her. She didn't have Joe's ambition or talent, her mum said, which seemed a bit harsh, and she hadn't shown any interest in leaving home as Joe had done. I think Joe was her shining star, and every time she raved about an achievement of his (from his first swimming badge to his degree), she sparkled, and Joe got more and more embarrassed. I think he was more upset about his 'cool' image being thrown out by his doting mother than anything, which was highly amusing.

After a huge, perfect hangover lunch, Joe and his father cleared up while his mum showed me his baby photos. She was hilarious, really mumsy, whereas his father was fairly quiet, but liked to tell old jokes which made Joe cringe. We all went for a short walk after lunch, where his mother pointed out all the local places of interest: Joe's school, Joe's cub hut (really he was a cub), and Joe's first girlfriend's house. Then we headed back to London.

As we drove back I felt as if Joe was more than ever a part of my life. We went back to his flat, where we opened some wine and debated whether we should be gluttonous and have a take-away.

'I'm not sure I should, I might get fat,' I pointed out.

'Then I'd have to dump you.'

'How shallow,' I pouted.

'Well I have an image to uphold and you being a fat bird could seriously damage that.'

'I am not a bird.'

'No, you're lovely.'

'Are we getting really sad?'

'I think so. I can't stop looking at you.'

'I can't stop feeling warm.'

'Holly, I love you, I really love you.' It was time for another kiss. Which again was the cue for my mobile to ring. I not only ignored it, but switched it off.

# Chapter Eight

'Why do you hum when you're happy?' Freddie asked.

'Because I'm happy.'

'It's extremely irritating.'

'Thanks. Freddie can you update me on the latest *Zoom* proposal? Then I want a meeting with everyone to go over the state of all our accounts. New Year and all that, let's start it efficiently. I think we're on top of everything but I need to make sure.'

'My God, happy but still bossy.'

'Freddie, I hate to remind you that I am your boss. Can you rally the troops for after lunch, I'll get Dixie to sort out a room.'

I went to check my e-mail. I had a number of e-mails from clients, to which I responded, and about twenty from George. It was confounding. I'd spoken to him the previous day. I had agreed to see him that evening. I was flummoxed by the nature of his communications:

From: georgec@hotmail.com

To: Holly Miller

Subject: Your phone

*Why didn't you answer your phone last night?*

From: georgec@hotmail.com

To: Holly Miller

Subject: Response

*I would like a response.*

From: georgec@hotmail.com

To: Holly Miller

Subject: Response

*HOLLY WHY ARE YOU AVOIDING ME?*

There were ten more messages. He asked if I was ill, he asked if I was being a bitch, then said he'd called me at home and I wasn't there so he was presuming I wasn't ill. It was all incredibly tiresome and I didn't understand. All I could think was that rejection by Julia had left him feeling very insecure, and I was his only friend in this city, so I was the only person he had for reassurance. I felt guilty. I responded immediately saying that my mobile battery was flat last night and that I had been in a meeting all morning (it was only lunchtime). I was unsure why I was lying to placate him but it was the easiest thing to do. However, George wasn't going to be so easily fobbed off. He replied with a huffy e-mail asking me why I was being so uncaring. I replied saying I did care. How he had tied me in knots was beyond me, but he had. He went quiet for a while, I guessed he was sulking but eventually another e-mail arrived saying that he would give me the benefit of the doubt and that he'd pick me up from my office as arranged. As much as I would have liked to try to make sense of his erratic behaviour, and discuss it with Freddie, I had work to do. I put George to the back of my mind.

He was sitting in reception when finally I walked out at quarter past six. I knew he was there, but couldn't quite get out on time. I ignored the funny look that the receptionist gave me as I took a deep breath and went to greet him.

'You're late,' he said, thrusting a bunch of roses at me. Which did I address first, the accusation or the flowers?

'Sorry, I had a last minute crisis. The flowers are lovely.' I had no idea why he had given me roses, it set me on edge. George had never given me flowers in my life. And the anger, why the anger? I was beginning to tire of the situation, although I didn't know what the situation was.

'I've booked dinner at San Lorenzo,' he announced.

'Really?' I was surprised, San Lorenzo was one of my favourite restaurants in the whole of London, but I rarely got taken there.

'Come on, I don't want to be late.' He sounded terse. He took my arm, a little roughly, and started to lead me out. Then I heard my name being called. I turned around to find Freddie standing behind us.

'Hi, I'm Freddie,' he stuck a hand towards George.

'He works with me,' I explained. George took the outstretched hand and shook it.

'I'd love to stop and chat,' he said, sounding like he really wouldn't, 'but we're late.' I smiled weakly at Freddie as I followed George out.

George had always been in charge of our friendship. I firmly believe that in childhood friendships, someone is always in charge. George was the leader. He always decided what we were doing; I always agreed. I had become stronger and more independent after he left, more out of necessity than anything. Still, I found it hard in adult life to break the pattern, and even though we had been apart for five years and I was an intelligent independent woman, as soon as he came back I was thirteen again and following him around. Or that was what it felt like. Only this time I wasn't so happy to be doing so.

We sat in silence in the cab. I had no idea what to say and he just stared out of the window. Although he looked much better than he had the last time I saw him, he looked too unemotional; trancelike even. I tried to see the streets we were passing through his eyes, but all I could see were the streets through my eyes and my eyes were filled with Joe. I gave myself a mental jolt: stop thinking of yourself and try to think of George and his broken heart. No matter how hard I tried it all came back to San Lorenzo (not a restaurant for the broken-hearted), his rudeness to Freddie, and the fact that I was sitting in a taxi, clutching a bunch of roses, next to a stranger. A stranger I had known for ever.

It wasn't until we were seated that George looked at me, properly. Then it was only to ask me what I wanted to drink. Before I had responded he ordered a bottle of champagne. That was it, I'd had enough!

'What is this?' I demanded.

'What?' he snapped.

Winter had entered the building.

'You know, dinner here, champagne? George, last time I was with you, you were in pieces, and now I feel like we're celebrating, although I have no idea what we're celebrating.'

'We *are* celebrating.'

'What though?'

'Us.'

'Us? You mean our friendship?'

'No. Holly, you're a bright girl, so I am surprised that you haven't got it yet. I'm almost disappointed that you haven't got it yet.'

'Got what?' I was totally confused.

'We are meant to be together, that's what. Holly, you and I are meant *to be* and no one can keep us apart.'

I was stunned; mortified and stunned; rendered speechless. While my brain tried to process the information sufficiently for me to respond, George continued.

'It makes perfect sense. You are the only person who has *never* let me down; I am the same for you. This whole mess with Julia has made me realise the truth. I guess you'll realise soon enough that Joe isn't the man for you . . . I am.'

'George, this is absurd. The time we met, when you wanted to make sure that Julia was the "one", you said that you were sure that I wasn't. I presume you remember all that "physical encounter" stuff? You said that you were one hundred per cent sure that Julia was the one for you, and I wasn't. And to be honest, although I was angry with you, I agreed. So how come, now when you arrive back here, minus the fiancée, I am the woman for you all of a sudden?' My voice was raised ever so slightly.

'Holly, calm down. To be honest, I expected you to react like this, but that doesn't change things. I guess I am just more enlightened than you at this moment, but don't worry, you'll come round.'

'I will not.' I stopped as I realised that my last comment was a little too loud and had drawn attention from other diners. I tried to compose myself. 'George, you're mad. I have Joe now and I love him. Just because your relationship didn't work out, doesn't mean that I am here to be your second-best.' I had managed to keep the volume down.

'You're not second-best Holly, you're the *best*. You're the one, I know that now. I was just blinded by Julia's physical qualities, but looks aren't everything. You might not have her looks, or her success, but you are a much better person, a much better person for me.'

I cannot describe my feelings at that moment; they were disparate. But I do know that I had never been so angry in my entire life.

'I am not,' I hissed. 'I am not anything for you. George we were friends, try to remember that, we were friends for years and years; best friends. You do not do this to your best friend.'

'I don't see why you're upset, I am telling you that I love you.'

'You don't. For God's sake George get a grip.'

'Holly, no offence but as I said, I am further down the road to enlightenment, and I know you'll come round. I do love you and I know that soon you'll realise that you love me too. It *will* happen.'

'You'll have a long wait,' I replied as I stood up and, discarding the opportunity of lovely food and drink headed for the exit.

'Wait,' George shouted after me. 'You've forgotten your flowers.'

Walking out of the restaurant hungry and minus the flowers I hailed a taxi and headed home. My head spinning I tried to make sense of what George had said, but I couldn't. In a short time so much had happened, too much had changed and I felt unbalanced.

I had an overwhelming desire to laugh. He had propositioned me with the warmth of an ice cube and there was definitely a distinct lack of romance in his declaration. Obviously he had lost his marbles. We were meant to be together? I wasn't yet enlightened? It was unimaginable. I knew that I didn't want George, not in that way, not in any way now. I was more certain of that than of anything else. I just had to convince him.

Over the next few days I sought advice. Despite my resolve not to take it seriously, I wanted to know the best way to deal with the situation. I could have left George alone with his delusions, but knowing him, that wouldn't work. Then there was Joe. Should I tell him about his love rival or not? Freddie told me that I should explain the situation to Joe straight away, Lisa told me not to tell Joe because George was obviously mad and hopefully would soon go away. Imogen told me that I should write a letter to George asking him nicely to stay away from me, and only if he failed to do so should I tell Joe. My mother said that it would be lovely if we did get together.

I was busy at work. We had some new business pitches coming up and the team were pushed to the limit. I needed to stay focused. I wasn't going to let George ruin things.

At this point I took a wrong turning because I decided to ignore him. The day after dinner, he bombarded me with e-mails. I deleted them, barely glancing at them. Actually, Dixie, who declared herself bored, read them all and gave me the edited highlights.

'Well, Holly, he's clearly quite disturbed, he says that you are definitely the only woman for him and he loves you more than life itself.' Dixie had been spending too much time with Freddie.

'Thanks, why does that make him disturbed.'

'Because you don't feel the same.'

'Oh, yeah.'

'Anyway, he wants to see you again, he's sorry if he shocked you with his declaration, but it had to be said. He's visiting his parents this weekend and he wants you to join him. Says you could talk about old times.'

'Well I won't.'

'Shall I tell him that?'

'No, leave it, he'll get the message.'

'But I thought you said that he was your oldest friend.'

'He was.'

'Is that wise then?'

'Yes. Stop questioning me. Is there anything else I should know?'

'Yes, you've got an away day with *Zoom* on Friday; you need to do a presentation. You've got lunch with Francesca tomorrow, to review your accounts, and you're due at *Candy Confectionery* in one hour. Oh, and George says you have the sweetest lips.'

'Thanks, Dixie.' I gave her a peck on the cheek.

I vowed to carry on with my life. The life that it had taken me most of my twenty-nine years to get right. The life I loved.

George had become a little irritating niggle that was underlying my happiness. But that was all he was, a niggle.

George got the message that I wouldn't be responding to his e-mails, because the following day I received a single red rose. Actually from ten o'clock in the morning I received a red rose every hour on the hour . . . from George. Francesca noticed and called me into her office to ask if Joe had popped the question. Francesca might be my boss, she was also a friend.

'It isn't Joe.' I sighed in answer to her question.

'Who is it then?' She looked excited.

'George.' I barely had the energy to explain.

'Who's George, an ex?'

'No Francesca, he's a friend from way back. He's been in New York for the past five years, and he's come back because his girl-friend turned down his marriage proposal and now he says that he's the man for me.'

'Gosh, that sounds bizarre. What does Joe think?' Francesca looked delighted with the developments.

'Joe doesn't know. Well he knows he came back but he doesn't know anything bar the fact that George is my old friend.'

'Oh dear, I think you should tell him.'

'Funny. Lots of people think that.'

'You have to. There is no way that you can have a relation-ship where there are secrets, no way. And I don't wish to be pessimistic but I don't think you can bury your head in the sand with this. We need to do something.'

'But what?'

'Leave it to me. I'll have a think and let you know.'

The day after the roses, I heard nothing from George. That night I was going home and Lisa was coming over because Max was away and she hated being alone. I had changed out of my work clothes, opened a bottle of wine and was about to prepare some food when the buzzer went; it was Lisa.

'Hi honey,' she said brandishing a bottle of champagne and some chocolate ice cream.

'Are you OK?' I asked.

'Yes, although I hate Max being away. He had to go to France, he's photographing some horribly glamorous French model, and I miss him.'

'You sound more of a sap than me.'

'Impossible. Talking of that, how is "Mr Perfect"?'

'Perfect.' I giggled. 'But wait until you hear the next instalment in the George saga.' I told her about the roses.

'What did you do with them?' She looked at my roseless flat.

'Gave them to Dixie, I didn't want them.'

We opened the champagne and drank it quickly. Lisa smoked constantly (which I think is how she kept so thin), and I refrained. Lisa was such an elegant person. She has grace from her old catwalk days when she used to swan up and down wiggling her hips. When I lived with her I was amazed at how ugly some of the models were, well not ugly but not beautiful in the traditional sense of the word, but Lisa, well she *was* beautiful, still is. Anyway, she even smoked beautifully. If you saw her smoking you'd want to take it up because she made it look like an art form. Her long fingers seemed to make the cigarette dance and when she exhaled the smoke, well it was enough to make a grown man weep. When I used to smoke, I didn't manage to make it look as good as that. I know this because I practised in front of the mirror. Then, because of Lisa's smoking grace, I wanted to smoke again. Which I did. My will-power leaves a little to be desired.

'I can't believe what a creep he's become,' Lisa said.

'It doesn't make sense. George is this big-shot corporate lawyer and all of a sudden he's taken a year off work and thinks he's going to get me to fall in love with him.' At that point, it all seemed too bizarre to take seriously. I had no idea how far he would go.

'It's a bit out of character.'

'The thing that worries me, Lisa, is that he seems to be an entirely different person from the guy I met when he came back for that weekend. He seemed in control then, but now he seems to be . . . well I don't know exactly but he seems to be all over the place. It just doesn't make any sense at all.'

'Shall we eat?' Lisa suggested. She was renowned for changing conversations in mid-flow; I was pretty sure she had a low attention threshold.

'Are you hungry?' I asked, surprised. Lisa did eat, but she never admitted to being hungry.

'Not really.' She lit another cigarette.

'I was going to do some tuna steaks.'

'Sounds fantastic. I'll just finish this and then I'll come and help.'

I was a bit tipsy as I walked into the kitchen and switched on the light. I put my half full champagne glass down on the kitchen counter and went to the fridge. Then I stopped feeling slightly on edge. I turned around and looked out of the window. He was standing opposite my flat, leaning against some railings, just looking up at me. I didn't even know that he knew where I lived, although of course he had my address from when I'd first moved in. I'm not sure if he saw me, but I rushed back into the sitting room.

'Lisa, he's staring at my windows.' In my flat, the kitchen was a large room at the front, my living room was adjacent and also had windows facing the front. My two bedrooms and the bathroom were on an upper floor. I shuddered as I realised that my bedroom was also at the front of the building.

'Who?'

'George, that's who.' For some reason I was whispering. I

have no idea why because he couldn't hear me. Lisa ran up to the sitting-room window, the blinds were closed, which explained why we hadn't noticed him. She pulled up the blind. I was right behind her, he was looking straight at us. I couldn't believe that he was there. Lisa opened the window.

'George,' she shouted. 'George, what are you doing?' I was so grateful that Lisa took control because I couldn't. I was too stunned by the fact that he was even there. Had he turned into some kind of pervert?

'I'm waiting for Holly to tell me she loves me,' he shouted back.

'Then you're going to have a fucking long wait,' I was angry, but luckily had Lisa to voice that anger.

'Did you like the roses?'

'George, I didn't want roses from you. What if Joe were here?' I found my voice.

'Well he has to find out sometime.'

'Find out what?' Lisa asked.

'Find out about us.'

'But there is no us,' I replied.

'Oh, but there will be. Don't worry about that. You can't fight destiny Holly.'

'Look, George, be an angel and piss off,' Lisa shouted. I groaned as I saw other lights going on in the street.

'No.'

'George I'll call the police,' I threatened.

'I don't think you will, I really don't think you will.' He was right.

I grabbed Lisa's hand and dragged her into the kitchen, where I pulled down the blind.

'What should I do?'

'Ignore him,' Lisa suggested.

'He's in the street, outside my flat, he can see into my bedroom. My God he's stalking me!'

'Draw the curtains. I'm staying here tonight anyway and we can always sleep with weapons if we're worried.' Was she serious?

'But he wouldn't do anything would he?'

'Darling, a month ago I wouldn't have believed you if you said he was standing outside your flat stalking you. I have no idea what is going on in his mind.'

He was still there while we cooked dinner, I could see his silhouette through the closed blind. By the time we had finished eating and washed up he was still there. Lisa and I spent hours planning what to do. Her suggestion was to throw things at him; mine was to wait and see what he would do next. I was tempted to call Joe, but I wasn't ready to explain the whole sorry saga to him. In the end we did nothing but drink and hatch elaborate plans.

I took one last look out of my bedroom window before I went to bed. It was 1.30 a.m. and he was still there. Because I was so incredibly paranoid I got changed in the bathroom, at the rear of the flat, and climbed into bed ignoring the fact that a madman – formerly my best friend – was standing in the freezing sub-zero temperature outside my home.

By the next morning he had gone. I had half expected him to be lying on the ground in the advanced stages of hypothermia, or even dead. Although, on reflection, if he had been, that might have solved a lot of things. I didn't mean that, or if I did, I only meant it fleetingly.

I went to work. I was exhausted having slept fitfully. I was far too worried about George to unwind, and by the time I believe I drifted into sleep he had taken on those half-dream proportions of being an axe murderer. But the problem was, and my lack of positive action can be explained by that problem, he was still George. Despite everything he was the boy I grew up with, my closest friend, and I couldn't decide what to do about him because I didn't have a clue what had happened to him. Had he been affected by a full moon the way men can be? (Or did that just apply to werewolves?) Was he in the grip of temporary madness having lost the love of his life? I couldn't help but think that there was some rational explanation for his strange behaviour (probably nothing to do with the full moon, however). I wasn't only angry at his intrusion into my life, but I was worried about him. I was quite maternal in my own way. Sometimes I think I don't have a maternal bone in my body, but for some reason when it came to George, *all* my feelings were maternal. I guess that can go some way to explaining why I freaked out over the kiss. When I first met him – his tears, his shoulders hunched, defeated – all I could do was take him in my arms and try to comfort him. Ever since that first meeting, I always needed to make sure he was all right. The way he fell apart, in a twelve-year-old way, was quite extreme. And from that moment, I had vowed to take care of him.

How could I take care of someone who wanted me to fall in love with them? Did he even want me to fall in love with him or was he just mad? I don't mean mad in the way that he wouldn't fall in love with me, after all I am not bad if I do say so myself, but mad because he should know that that is the one thing he could ask of me that I wouldn't be able to do. Despite everything, I still didn't think it was the right time to tell Joe.

'What are you going to do?' Freddie asked, as I finished recounting the night's events to him and Francesca. We were in the boardroom for a 'brainstorming session', which is such a crappy phrase, but businesses everywhere love to use it. It makes me feel like a complete moron every time I hear myself say it.

The boardroom is my favourite in the whole office. It's large and it's got the most beautiful paintings on the wall. They were commissioned by Francesca from some poor art student whom I expect will go on to win the Turner Prize or something and they'll be worth a fortune. The table is square which I like; I dislike oval and round tables for some reason, and the chairs are comfortable, I hate going back to my desk after being in there. The best thing about it though, is that Francesca's PA brings us coffee, tea and chocolate biscuits. For some obscure reason it reminded me of being at my mother's kitchen table at home, a strange association that I'm sure a psychologist would love to get their hands on.

'I have no idea,' I replied, as I yawned for the hundredth time.

'You're going to tell Joe,' Francesca said.

'But . . .'

'No buts, you are going to tell Joe and you are going to do it tonight.' I felt as if telling Joe had come as an order from my boss, and I decided not to defy her.

Telling Joe was quite painless really. He was upset for me, chastised me for not telling him sooner and he said that he would stay with me to ensure that there were no repeat performances. Actually Joe became all macho and said he was going to 'deck' George, which I found quite sexy in a base sort of way. I thanked him kindly for the offer but said that violence was way down my list as a solution. This intrusion into our relationship brought us closer together. I began to feel that we were impenetrable and there was no way that George could hurt me. I was in love, Joe was my protector. The situation was almost sexy. I was the damsel in distress, Joe my knight in shining armour and, ironically, George was the dragon.

I reported back the following day and, encouraged by my initial success, Francesca decided to take control of the situation. Both her and Freddie stood over me while I phoned George and arranged to meet him. Of course he was free that very evening, and so we arranged to have a drink. I named the venue, I set the standard, I was managing the whole thing and I quite liked the feeling. After that, the rest of the day was spent working on my clients. I had a couple of meetings, a problem to solve, the usual. I didn't have too much time to dwell on George, but that was fine, because I planned to put an end to this nonsense once and for all.

# Chapter Nine

The bar I had chosen was quite an ordinary one. It was busy and just round the corner from my office. When I say ordinary, that doesn't mean it wasn't nice, it was one of those big chains, so it wasn't too fancy. It certainly wasn't romantic. Because I was going straight from work I was wearing a black trouser suit and a cream jumper. I looked smart but not dressed-up. I didn't even reapply my make-up before meeting him, and I didn't brush my hair.

As I opened the door I saw him. He was sitting at a table nursing a beer, shoulders hunched. I tried to keep myself in check as I felt my heart plummet into my shoes; he looked so sad. I couldn't help but feel for him. I strode, as confidently as I could, over to the table.

'Hello,' I said, pulling out a chair.

'Hi,' he replied. He smiled at me; a sad, lonely smile which tugged at my heart once again. His hair was brushed neatly, he was wearing a striped shirt and some chinos, a jumper across his shoulders. I remembered telling him that he would become preppy. He used to be so determined not to appear a typical lawyer that he wore old battered jeans and T-shirts when he wasn't working, but now he was that typical lawyer.

So much history between us and that counts for a lot. It means loyalty, caring, it means so much. Our history could still be precious to me couldn't it? Even if the present was not.

'George, we must talk.' Assertive; check.

'You know how I feel.' Again, he appeared to slump into his seat.

'Yes, but I don't think that *is* how you feel.' Even more assertive.

'Holly, don't take offence but how can you know how I feel?'

'I always knew how you felt.'

'Yes but that was then. This is now. We're not kids any more.'

'I know that. You're thirty, I'm almost thirty. We're adults, grown-ups.' Quite a speech, although I wasn't sure how relevant it was.

'So, you can see that you know how I feel about you, and you have absolutely no right to dispute it on the basis of our child-hood.'

Eh? Why did I feel as if he had tied all my logic, assertiveness and determination into one big knot. Not only was I having trouble following him, but I was also having problems recol-lecting my line of argument. 'It's not that. George, you saw me before Christmas and you told me that you loved Julia.'

'I was wrong.'

'How can you be?'

'Fate, Holly. Remember fate? Remember how when we were growing up we'd look at the sky and say that the sky held our fate, and sometime it would send it down to us, the light that meant we knew where our fate lay. Then, when we accom-plished one thing, like our careers, we said that it would send down another bit to us and at some point we'd get the whole picture. But fate plays games, doesn't it? It plays with us, and doesn't always send answers . . . it sends clues. Fate does that, fate *has* done that and now we have to be together for ever.' No wonder he was a good lawyer, my whole line of reasoning had walked out of the door in disgust. I knew he was wrong. I just didn't know how to tell him by dissecting his words.

'You're wrong.' Great.

'Holly, there is no point in us meeting unless you are going to tell me what you *have* to tell me. You'll realise at some point that we are supposed to be together, I'm only trying to prevent you wasting Joe's time,' he paused to smile. 'I know so much about you. When I leave you now I'll picture you trying to work it out, and I know that you'll have those creases in your brow and your mind will whirl. But you'll see sense in the end. I'll call you tomorrow. I need your decision by then.' And, leaving me feeling totally flummoxed, he got up and walked out. I hadn't even had a drink.

As I left the bar, I tried to make some sense of our encounter. Why he'd given me a day to make a decision when I had already given him my answer was beyond me.

It was only the second week of January, and already I felt that this year was spiralling out of control. I had called Joe and told him I was meeting George. He wanted to come and do his macho act, but I assured him I could handle it. But I didn't because I had no idea what I was handling. I called him from the taxi and asked to come over. For some reason I felt uncontrollably tearful. I chastised myself for a bad job done, and for being such a wimp about it.

Joe found me crumpled in tears.

'Holly, it's not so bad. It's almost flattering. This guy is in love with you and I totally understand that because I'm in love with you myself.' I wasn't comforted by his words.

'The thing is it's not flattering because it doesn't feel right. He's not in love with me. He's not. I don't know much about this situation but I do know that. He said that I'd got until tomorrow to think about it, and he sounded almost threatening.' A fresh batch of tears coursed down my cheeks.

'What can he do?' Joe said as he took me in his arms. 'He can't do anything.'

# Chapter Ten

How wrong Joe was. The following day George called me as promised. I told him, as calmly as I could, that I was in love with Joe and not him. I told him we had no future in *that* way. I told him there was nothing more to say. And that was when he told me, yet again, that I was wrong.

'It's your birthday in just over a month,' he said.

'Yes. So . . . ?'

'You're going to be thirty.'

'I am.'

'And you're not married to Joe are you?'

'No, I'm not.'

'You're not married to anyone, nor are you likely to be by the time you're thirty. Do you remember our marriage pact?'

I did. The memory flooded back. 'Yes.'

'Well you signed an agreement saying that if you were single by the age of thirty you'd marry me. So, Holly, you have to marry me.' As simple as that.

I put down the phone.

I am not sure where 'my George' ended and 'stalker George' took over. I knew it was still George, but I couldn't equate the madman with the man who had been my most important friend. People forgive a lot in life, and I would have forgiven my friend George anything, but I didn't know who he was any more, and there was no room to forgive a stranger.

I was squashed in the biggest conundrum, and not only could I not sort it out but I also couldn't explain it. Joe wanted to hit George, but because the man who was harassing me wasn't George, couldn't be George, I wouldn't let him. Lisa told me that it was time to call the police, but I couldn't have George arrested. Freddie agreed with both Lisa and Joe, and he accused me of being flattered, hence my reluctance to act, but I wasn't flattered; I was confused. I had no idea what to do, but how could I hurt him? Imogen thought that part of my friend was still there, she thought I could reason with him. But how could I reason with the unreasonable?

I was frustrated through my lack of comprehension. Feelings, emotions, they can be trapped inside you, and there isn't always an effective method of communicating them, even to yourself.

Every time he did something to annoy me and I got angry, I recalled something from the past, a fond memory. It seemed that my mind was playing games. He would call me and demand my hand in marriage, and just as I wanted to scream, into my head would pop a vision of us when we were in our teens on holiday in France. We'd be swimming, and joking and laughing, and his wet hair would be stuck to his face. His smile would be always there and I would be trying to look cool but failing and it was just the sort of moment that only happens when you have a wonderful friendship. And we did. Or we used to have.

Joe accused me of rewriting history when I tried to tell him that this was the problem, but I wasn't. George and I had a friendship which could have won awards. Whether my mind was playing tricks with me, or whether my subconscious was refusing to believe that the George I knew and loved would behave like this, I don't know. I could be angry with him, but I couldn't be too angry with him. I couldn't do anything to stop him. All I could do was hope that he would go away and come to his senses.

I knew that the old George was still there, somewhere. He

would come back and he would be sorry. He would apologise for the incident at the beginning of December when he wanted to check out his feelings and used me to do so. He would then apologise for using me as his fall-back partner when Julia turned him down. And I would accept his apology because he was my best friend.

I just wasn't sure how far he would go before he came to his senses and I didn't believe for one minute that he would go so far as to try to legally enforce our marriage pact.

I had a number of phone calls from George about the marriage pact. After the initial shock, I tried to tell him that he was crazy, that we'd made the pact when drunk and heartbroken and that we both knew it would never actually happen.

He disagreed. He believed that we made the pact knowing full well that we would get married. I accused him of rewriting history, he accused me of rewriting history. I knew I was right, but he believed he was right. Finally, I had taken enough and went on the offensive. It had gone too far.

'Holly, we need to get things straight.'

'They are straight.'

'No, they're not. I have a contract here, in which you put in writing that you agreed to marry me if we were both unmarried when we reached the age of thirty.'

'We've been through all this. We didn't know what we were doing.'

'I did.'

'Right, so when you asked Julia to marry you that was just because you forgot about the pact and you had no real intention of marrying her?'

'No.'

'No, George, you asked Julia to marry her because you were in love with her, you probably still are.'

'No, asking Julia to marry me was a mistake. It's you I love.'

'Really? Well you've got a crap way of showing it. If you loved me you'd leave me alone.'

'I can't do that.'

'Evidently. But why not?'

'Because it wouldn't be right. *We*'re right. So, will you agree to marry me and fulfil our pact.'

'How many times do I have to say no?'

'Final answer.'

'Yes, Chris Tarrant, final answer.'

'Who?'

'Forget it George. My last word on the subject is no. I will not marry you, I will never marry you and if you're not careful I'm going to slap a restraining order on you.' In reality I had no idea if I could, but it sounded threatening enough.

'Holly, I wish you'd be reasonable about this.'

'Oh yeah? Reasonable? Like agreeing to marry you would be reasonable would it? Sorry George if I saw my wedding day as being something more than reasonable.'

'I can't talk to you when you're like this. I'll write to you.'

'You'll what?' Of course, he had hung up.

Why I lost control every single time I spoke to him I don't know, but it was beginning to piss me off.

I fumed silently, all happy memories of George notably absent and all I could do was wait.

I don't know if it was misplaced loyalty or what that meant I kept some of George's conversations from other people. Of course, it might have been something else. Buried somewhere inside me may have been a measure of guilt. Guilt for what happened when we met at his hotel that time. Although he precipitated the incident (hereafter it is known as 'the incident'), I complied, and even if I don't think I complied, I didn't stop him. Actually thinking about that night makes me feel physically sick, because that was the night I felt that our friendship died. I have pushed it so far to the back of my mind, that I can almost believe that it didn't happen. If I had had any idea then of the consequences of my actions, then I hope I would have found the strength to stop him. What worried me most was that if I let myself dwell on it, my panic attacks would return.

I had my first panic attack when George first left London for New York. I would wake up, and the first thing I'd feel was dread, and then the palpitations would start and I'd burst into tears. It was the most fearful experience, my heart was hammering so fast, I thought it would break out of my body. I truly believed that there was something seriously wrong with me. After a week, and having drunk four bottles of Rescue Remedy (something I still have a slight addiction to), I went to the doctor, convinced I was dying. He explained I was merely having panic attacks and asked if I was under stress. He offered me anti-depressants, but I decided to stick to my Rescue Remedy. When I had got used to him not being there for me, anxiety revisited only rarely.

After the phone call, I rummaged for my copy of the fateful marriage pact, and found it in a shoebox, along with other 'George stuff'. I called Joe, told him I had a headache and was going to have an early night, and then sat in my white living room with the shoebox and a cup of coffee at my feet. I felt that I should be opening the box (a pale white box with 'memories' written across it in black marker), with a bottle of wine, but for some reason I didn't want any. I was feeling irrationally tearful and I didn't want to add to that.

It was like delving into an old love affair. A scene from a movie where the tearful heroine sits alone and laments her lost love by reading everything he ever wrote to her: looking at pictures, conjuring memories, wiping her tears. But it never was a love affair and that wasn't what I was feeling. I felt a loss, but my feelings for Joe were so vivid that I knew that I wasn't confusing love with friendship. I was just being nostalgic, that was all, and the George of my shoebox was the person I still missed, and the George of my everyday life was someone else altogether.

I sipped my coffee, as I opened the box. The first thing I pulled out was a photograph. It was my favourite photo of us, taken when we were about sixteen. We were sitting in the garden of my parents' house, in sunloungers. I was wearing a pair of tatty denim cut-offs (I almost lived in those shorts the whole summer, they were so short you could almost see my bum cheeks and the treads hung down all over the place but I thought they were so cool). George was wearing some baggy Bemunda shorts and a pair of Ray-Bans, which he lived in. He hated taking them off even when he was inside. He said it was because they were prescription sunglasses but really he just liked them. We spent most of the summer that way, so the picture represented more than a moment. We'd finished our GCSEs and we thought we were so grown-up as we talked about our A levels and the future.

There were other photos, mainly of us on our travels. I was permanently in a sarong and George was always in baggy, brightly coloured trousers. We looked like wannabe hippies, which was exactly what we were at eighteen. One good thing about growing up is that one's taste improves. I looked at the photos and more than anything saw the physical change that George had undergone. He was unrecognisable, from the slick, suited lawyer who probably only wore chino shorts in beige with creases ironed down the front. Mind you, I wouldn't wear tie-dye sarongs either. We'd both changed. We'd both grown up.

The cards I kept weren't all the cards he ever sent me. I kept the birthday cards from my sixteenth, eighteenth and twenty-first birthdays. I kept the joke valentines he sent me, saying that he never wanted me to be his valentine but he thought he'd be kind (he did that every year before he went to New York). And I kept the Christmas cards he sent once he was in New York. There were various other items of memorabilia to remind me of our friendship: tickets to plays, an old school badge, postcards from when we were travelling together – happy times.

As per the scene from the film where the distressed heroine sits on the floor surrounded by her memories, tears slowly began to roll down my cheeks. Then I pulled out the marriage pact (which was tucked right at the bottom of the box), and regained my composure.

It was as if someone had given me an electric shock. I realised how amazingly bizarre it was. I reread the pact and laughed at the recollection that when we'd made it we had no intention of it ever coming true. I remembered the night vividly: the drink, the fact we were both feeling so sorry for ourselves. The hang-over the next day was more serious than the pact had been. I made a decision then that I would not take it seriously and I would try to persuade everyone else to do the same.

Which wasn't easy. Lisa insisted on taking me out, or at least being with me if Joe wasn't, and Max was also a tower of strength. They both seemed to enjoy the fact that in their minds George was a psychopath and my life was in danger. I didn't mind too much that they were living their lives vicariously through the one they had concocted for me; at least it also kept me amused. My mother had decided that she didn't want me to marry George, now she had seen how obsessed he was. She was there for me, but also giving me space. My father had taken action and gone to see George's family, but as they explained, they were as baffled as he was, but there wasn't anything they could do, George being thirty, not thirteen. My sister sent me food parcels. Bizarrely she thought that I might forget to eat. Actually it was the opposite, my appetite was voracious and I was putting on weight. Adversely I thought that maybe if I got fat, George would leave me alone, the only flaw in that plan was that Joe might do the same.

Joe seemed to be more affected by it than anyone. He wanted to 'do something' although I never found out what he meant by that. He felt that I needed his protection, which I did. Actually, I think that I spent more time calming him down than anything. Which, if nothing else, kept me busy.

Finally the promised letter arrived by courier when I was at work. George really was a class act. The letter informed me, that if I did not agree to marry him, he was going to take me to court to enforce our marriage pact.

My hands were shaky as I opened the letter, as if they knew what was in it. I clutched the letter and ran to Francesca's office, Freddie at my heels.

'He's going to take me to court!' I screeched. Eventually they managed to calm me down. Francesca took the letter, read it and reached for the phone, while at the same time she instructed Freddie to get Dixie to make me a strong cup of tea. When my hysterics finally abated, Francesca informed me that her solicitor was going to be at the office later that afternoon, and she didn't believe there would be anything to worry about.

Susan Lord was the solicitor in question. She looked a bit like a female George and I wondered for a minute if she might be like Julia. She was very businesslike as she took the letter and read it, having placed a large briefcase on the table. She was very to the point as she requested a copy of the marriage pact and the story behind it. She then asked me if I wanted to marry him.

'There is no way that you will ever marry this man?'

'No. We've never even had a relationship.'

'So he's a friend?'

'Yes, that's exactly what he is . . . what he was.'

'Fine. Holly, I cannot see how this will be enforceable. Has he given you a ring?'

'A ring?'

'An engagement ring. If you had accepted a ring from him then the matter might be slightly complicated, but still, I cannot imagine a judge enforcing this. I will write a letter on your behalf, telling him that you are not going to marry him, and that in my opinion the pact is unenforceable. You said he was a lawyer?'

'Yes.'

'Then he must know that. Unless he's insane. Is he insane?'

'Quite possibly.'

'Well, I would say that the best course of action is to write the letter. I would guess that he is doing this to antagonise you, almost bully you. I can't imagine that he actually believes this will work, unless he *is* insane. I'd be surprised if he took it any further.' We discussed her fee, which was a bit of a shock, but I have to say that engaging a solicitor made me feel quite competent. My confidence seared.

But then I still had to tell Joe.

Predictably he didn't take it very well.

'He's a stupid fucker if he thinks he can bully you this way.'

'I know.'

'But who in their right mind would force someone to marry them?'

'Exactly.'

'If I got my hands on him he'd be really, really sorry.'

'I'm sure.'

'In fact, that's it. I am going to get hold of him and nothing you can say will stop me.'

'Joe, it's in the hands of my solicitor, you can't get involved, it might make things worse.'

'I don't care. What sort of man stands back while another tries to force his girlfriend to marry him.' Joe was angry, but looked so sexy.

'The sort of man who is clever enough to leave it to the solicitor, and take his girlfriend to bed.'

It worked every time.

★

I received a copy of the letter Susan had sent to George. It was very much to the point, a bit like her actually, and for a few minutes I really believed it would do the trick. But, not for long, because I knew George, and although I keep saying the old George was totally different from the new model, they still share some of the same characteristics and one of those is that they don't give up easily. I used to think it was a good quality with the old George, but now . . .

The George of my childhood was always relentless in pursuing his goals. If he wanted to play the lead in the school play, he would; if he wanted to get straight As he would; if he wanted to date someone, they wouldn't stand a chance. George's constant certainty about 'what next' in his life, was responsible for his single-mindedness. I used to take comfort in it; if I went under his wing then a little of his assuredness would rub off on me, because I didn't have any. Now there was no way I wanted to be under his wing, and I hated the thought that for the first time in his life *I* was one of his goals. It scared me to my core, but then it didn't. The contradiction that George was my friend, and when it came down to it wouldn't be able to hurt me, crept in again. Everything would be fine.

George was experiencing temporary insanity – I was sure of that – and soon he would realise that he didn't want to marry me; realise he'd made a huge mistake and I would live happily ever after with Joe. It was just a matter of time.

# Chapter Eleven

I received my court summons pretty quickly. Even Susan was surprised at the speed in which it came through. She implied that it wasn't normal for things in the British legal system to happen so fast and I wondered if George had some 'mason-like' connection with a judge. I hoped not. She was actually a bit huffy that her letter hadn't worked, which I found a bit amusing. After all I was expecting George to go as far as he had to, at least until he regained his sanity. I might sound calm describing this now, but at the time I was a wreck. I was terrified at the prospect of attending court, terrified because my solicitor had already been proved wrong. I had visions of being in a dock and being asked to plead while a horrid jury watched on. How could anyone find me guilty of not standing by a marriage pact made when drunk and desperate? I dreaded to think.

Susan recovered from her sulk and explained to me that I was not going to appear in court the way I thought. There would be no need to engage Kavanagh QC for me. We were going before a judge, in chambers rather than court, to see if there was a case to answer. George was suing me for breach of promise (which sounded pretty serious to me, but what did I know), and he and I would face a judge who would then decide if there was any grounds to take the proceedings to the next level. Susan assured me that there wasn't a judge in the land who would take George's case seriously in a legal way. But then she had said that her letter would put a stop to it, which it hadn't, so I was a tad reluctant to believe what she said.

I decided to believe her 'there's nothing to worry about', line simply because the alternative was too exhausting. It was tiring enough anyway. Daily I would put on my make-up and try to be normal. I'd laugh about the Legal proceedings to the people I worked with. I was my usual businesslike self with my clients. I reassured Joe by making flippant comments and jokes; I did the same with my family. I was so busy that I didn't even know how I felt about it any more; there simply wasn't time for me to analyse my feelings. I just wanted to sleep and wake up and hope that when I did, George would have given up his crazy crusade.

I felt completely stupid for worrying; after all I couldn't be forced into marriage, I knew I wouldn't be, so I pretended not to worry and I teased others who did.

So I waited for the date to be announced (all George had done was to issue notification of intention to enforce the pact), and then I would put the whole sorry mess behind me.

Nearly thirty years old, in love and being sued to enforce a marriage pact that I really didn't want enforced.

Finally I lost any sympathy I had for George. I called him, told his answerphone that he was a wanker and put down the phone, feeling better. That was as revolutionary as I got. I told Joe, who seemed to have changed his tune and decided that I shouldn't rock the boat.

'You're the one who was talking about hitmen the other day,' I accused.

'Holly, George is definitely unstable, I don't think that telling him he's a wanker is going to help.'

'I didn't tell him, I told his answerphone,' I shouted. Then I smiled. I didn't like being told I was wrong, but I didn't want to argue with Joe. I gave him a kiss.

'What are we going to do?' Joe asked, suddenly looking sad.

'Not sure,' I replied, truthfully.

'We have to do something Holly. I don't like the idea of leaving it to the law, especially as he's a lawyer.'

'Me either, but we don't have a choice. We'll wait to get the date and then we'll go and we'll win and put it all behind us.' For some reason I felt as if I was talking to a child, but I think that was more for my benefit than for his.

'But George is taking you to court to try to enforce your marriage pact.'

'Yes, but there is no way any judge would go in his favour.'

'You're sure about that?'

'Well as sure as my lawyer can be. What do you suggest?'

'I was talking to Dave about it last night and he thought that I should do something. He suggested that you let me deal with George.'

'Oh did he? And when you say "deal" I guess you mean "kick the shit out of"?' Dave was a friend of Joe's and looked a bit thuggish. But Joe said he was a pussy cat.

'No. Just talk to him, maybe I can make him see reason.'

'I don't mean to be rude to you or Dave, but neither of you know George. You can try to talk to him but remember I already did that and he tied me up in knots. He'd do the same to you, in fact he'd probably end up getting your support.'

'That wouldn't happen.' Joe was indignant.

'No, I didn't mean it like that. But George is a lawyer, a good lawyer, and he's also nuts. A crazy lawyer is a lethal combination, we've already discovered that and I think we'd better leave it alone.'

'I feel like I should be doing something.'

'You are, you're supporting me. And you're doing it marvellously.' I smiled. Containing macho male behaviour was becoming something of a regular thing.

'Why did you make that marriage pact?' he asked. It was the first time he'd asked me that.

'Because we decided no one would ever love us. I was

incredibly drunk; it was a joke, something that should never have come back to haunt me in this way. I keep asking myself the same question, but I could never in a million years imagine that it would have had this effect.'

'I bet you wish you hadn't done it though.'

'Of course I do. Joe, can we forget it for now?' I wanted to relax, and although I knew that Joe was feeling threatened by the whole thing I just wanted to pretend that I was Holly Miller in a normal relationship, without the black cloud of George hanging over me. But I wasn't going to get that opportunity. Joe stood up and started pacing.

'I can't forget it. I feel like I should be doing something. There must be a way to stop him.'

'We could kill him,' I joked.

'That's not funny Holly. There is one way to put a stop to him, though.'

'What?' I was listening to Joe but my brain was beginning to tune out. Discussions about George were getting tedious. I looked up at Joe wondering if it was time for me to be a bit more understanding. He was pacing the room. 'Joe, what is it? You know that the only reason I'm able to be flippant about this is because I feel certain in my love for you.' I thought that should help.

'I know, but if we didn't have to worry about George then things would be much better, wouldn't they?'

'I guess.' I was finding the conversation tiresome. I was also finding Joe's pacing irritating.

'Then let's get married.' I nearly fell off my chair. Did I hear right?

'Joe, did you just say what I think you said?'

'Yup. It makes sense. If we get married quickly, and I think we can, then you'll be married by the time you're thirty and George won't have a case.' Joe had stopped pacing, and although he hadn't gone down on one knee he looked so earnest. I did something that I really shouldn't have done; I burst out laughing. Joe adopted a very sulky expression.

'I'm glad you find my proposal amusing.' This made me laugh more. It was probably closer to hysteria than normal laughter and once I started I couldn't stop. Joe tried really hard to look upset but, he couldn't quite stop his lips from twitching.

'Sweetheart, I'm sorry for laughing,' I said, when I had resumed control. 'But you have to admit that it's not the most romantic of proposals and it's the second non-romantic proposal I've received lately. You know, every girl dreams of the day when the man she loves asks her to marry him, but you just asked me to stop George, not because you want to. I couldn't marry you for the wrong reasons, it's not the proper basis for a marriage.' Now I was serious. I didn't want Joe to ask me to marry him just to get George off our backs.

'But I do love you,' he protested.

'And I love you, but this isn't right. And when I do get married I want the works. You know: big dress, hen night, church wedding, great big reception. Not a day organised in a hurry and conducted in a Registry Office.'

'I understand. Yeah, you're right. Shit, do you think I'm turning as mad as he is?'

'No, darling, you're not, but I think you're possibly letting this affect you a bit too much.'

'Then I'll try not to.'

'Good, come on, I'll buy you a pint.'

We left the flat for the pub and not only was a row averted, but also all talk of George ceased.

# Chapter Twelve

Two days before my thirtieth birthday I received a call from Susan, who told me in her monotone voice (for which I had developed an aversion), that we would be going before the judge in the first week in March. Again, she droned on about how soon it was and she seemed wrong-footed by this. I put down the phone, went straight to Francesca who assured me that Susan *did* have a law degree.

'Holly, you don't have to like her, you just have to let her sort this out for you.'

'What if she bores the judge so much that he decides to make me marry George?'

'I hardly think that's likely.'

'Well, she doesn't sound very sure of herself. She said she was surprised that the date came through so quickly. I would rather have a solicitor who wasn't surprised.'

'What's really bothering you?' Francesca could be very perceptive.

'Don't know really. Look, let's plan my birthday celebration. Do you want to know what to buy me?'

The long-awaited day arrived; I was thirty. I had shelved all plans of parties, because I realised that I would rather spend time with the people I really cared about, my close friends. I know it sounds a bit boring, but at least it meant that I wouldn't have to put up with a load of drunken strangers. In order to placate people I arranged to have a meal with my work colleagues after my birthday.

I had visited my family the weekend before (Joe was at a work conference), and I was spending the day with Joe and the evening with Freddie, Lisa, Max, Francesca and Joe. It was exactly what I wanted. Not very rock and roll, but then I was a grown-up now and I wanted to do grown-up things. My first dinner party of my thirtieth year, it seemed a good and civilised way to start.

When I woke up and saw Joe lying next to me, I finally realised that for once I was right, and this was my life and I would no longer let George run or ruin it. I shook Joe awake.

'Happy Birthday!'

'I can't believe I'm thirty. I don't know whether to be happy or in mourning for my youth, but I believe it should start with my first fuck of my new decade.'

'Holly, you can be really dirty.'

'Shut up and get your pants off.'

After we made love, Joe went to make breakfast. I opened the cards and presents that I'd been sent. A cheque from my parents and a necklace; a box of Jo Malone goodies from my sister and her husband; cards from various relatives; and Joe gave me a painting of a beach, which reminded me of home.

I spoke to my family, and Joe took me ice-skating, which was hilarious because neither of us could skate. Then we went back to my place.

I opened the front door and found a small package with a card attached sitting on the doormat. It had no stamp, and was wrapped elaborately with ribbons flowing everywhere. I recognised the handwriting on the card immediately. George!

'Why couldn't he leave me alone for one day,' I said to Joe as I picked up the package with shaking hands. Instinctively I knew what it was, and I thrust it at Joe as I ran up the stairs, let myself into my flat and flew to the bathroom. I felt sick. When I came out, Joe was waiting for me with a look of concern on his face and the package in his hand.

'Open it please,' I asked him. He kissed my forehead and read the card. Looking concerned he handed it to me.

*Dear Holly*, it read, *Happy thirtieth birthday to my future wife. All my love and more, George xxxx*

I looked at Joe. 'He's lost it, completely.'

'Holly, don't let him ruin today, please.'

'Joe, open the present.' He looked at the wrapped box in his hand, then looked at me. I think he knew what it was. 'Open it,' I whispered. His hands shook as he removed the paper, he did it so delicately as my mother used to do when she was saving wrapping paper, a habit we never managed to get her to break. Finally he pulled out a small leather box. He stopped and looked at me again, but already I had tears streaming down my face. 'Open it,' I begged him.

The ring was platinum with a large solitaire. It wasn't the sort of ring I would choose, a thought I banished as soon as it entered my head. The ring wasn't relevant. What was relevant was that my boyfriend was standing in my sitting room holding an engagement ring bought for me by someone else. Although I was crying, the absurdity of the situation hit me. Joe looked upset, I thought he would soon be crying too.

'I am going to take this ring and shove it up his arse,' he said. I laughed. 'Holly it's not funny. Not even a bit funny.' His face was full of rage and I didn't doubt he would take the ring to George.

'Sorry, but I am not letting him ruin today. We've had more fun than in ages because of him, so I reckon that we should just order a courier and get them to return it to him, without an explanation.'

'I'd rather shove it up his arse.'

'I know, but darling he's already suing me, I'm not sure that it would be wise to have him suing you as well.' I started laughing, as Joe stood there shaking his fist indignantly at the ring box.

'Promise me something,' I said as the tears of laughter streamed down my face. 'Promise me if you ever want to marry me you'll get me a nicer, more subtle ring.' Finally, Joe cracked a smile and the situation that could have been a disaster was aborted.

I put the ring in an envelope and called a courier to bike it round to George's flat in the city. I instructed them that if he wasn't there to sign for it, they could just drop it through his letter box, after all that was what he did, although he probably delivered it himself. Then I persuaded Joe to content himself with tearing up the card. Suddenly I realised that I had been very selfish. I had been crying, confused and upset over George's behaviour, but it was hard for Joe. He wasn't allowed to exercise his macho instincts and beat up George, or even warn him off. I was the person dealing with it, but he had to deal with me and with the fact that his relationship was being threatened.

'You know, one day we'll laugh about this,' I told him, trying to believe it would be true.

'Maybe, but at the moment he's gone too far.'

'Let's forget it just for today.'

'OK, but if I ever get my hands on him.'

'I know. If you do he'll be pulp.'

Joe isn't a big man. He's tall, about six foot, and he's slim. He doesn't have a hard look about him, his features are almost pretty. His dark hair is shortish, his eyes are friendly, his mouth is nearly always smiling. George is bigger than Joe and I wouldn't like to say who would win in a fight, but I have a feeling that George would. George is a maniac, he's proved that and Joe isn't. Maniacs are always stronger than sane people, like in films. When psychos are dying, it always takes them for ever to draw their last breath.

Freddie turned up to help Joe with my birthday dinner. He

gave me a beautiful white orchid, and brought a couple of bottles of champagne.

'Thought you might need a drink,' he said.

'Why?' I asked.

'Now that you're old of course. I was going to see if everyone in the office would chip in for a facelift but I think it's a bit late for that.'

'Freddie, I love you.'

Freddie and Joe insisted I take a long bath and get ready while they cooked. I was banished from the kitchen and made the most of the time I had to pamper myself. As it was my birthday, I put on a dress and some stockings and high heels. I put up my hair and applied my make-up as if I was going out. I was pleased with the result; I scrubbed up quite well even if I say so myself.

Everyone was sat round my dining table. I had received more gifts, drank more champagne, and we had just been given our starters: prawn cocktail. I realised that although Freddie and Joe had spent a long time in the kitchen, they hadn't actually cooked much.

'What's for main?' I asked as I scooped up a spoonful of prawns.

'Beef Wellington.'

'That's ambitious,' Francesca said, looking mildly relieved that he didn't say fish fingers and chips.

'Actually the butcher made it, I just ordered it,' Joe admitted. Francesca looked even more relieved.

'But we did bake the cake,' Freddie said.

'You did?' I asked, feeling touched.

'Yes, and I think you'll be impressed,' Joe said.

'I'm sure we will,' Francesca agreed, but didn't look very certain.

'We could have gone out,' Lisa said, playing with her starter.

'It's not that bad is it?' Joe asked.

'No, it's fine,' Max replied, then he laughed. 'No offence to you guys, but well you bought a beef dish from the butcher, you shoved some prawns in the mayonnaise, it's not exactly Delia Smith is it?'

'But I appreciate the effort,' I said quickly, in case they took offence. Just as the last prawn was being polished off, the phone rang. Immediately everyone went quiet. 'I'll get it,' I said as Joe started to get up. As I walked to the phone, all eyes were on me.

'Hello,' I said, knowing full well who was on the other end.

'Happy Birthday Holly.' He sounded sad. Again I almost felt sorry for him but sternly and silently told my heartstrings to stop tugging.

'Thank you.' At least I could be civil.

'Didn't you like the ring?' he asked.

I laughed. 'George, it has nothing to do with whether I liked the ring, the fact is that I don't want an engagement ring from you and I don't want to marry you.' I saw that Joe had got out of his seat, then I saw Freddie pull him back down.

'Well that's blunt. I'm still taking you to court, Holly.'

'Fine George, that's absolutely fine. Brilliant. Thanks a fucking bunch for calling me on my birthday to remind me of that.' Actually I was quite calm but George had got away with enough.

'Nice language. You didn't have to be so horrible about the ring.'

'I did. And now I have to go. See you in court.' I hung up before he could respond.

My guests had gone all quiet.

'Come on, don't look like that. Let's all get absolutely pissed, and forget about George.'

'Right. Who needs more champagne?' Freddie entered into the spirit.

Everyone stuck out their glasses. The beef was delicious, a credit to the butcher. But the triumph of the evening was a lopsided cake, decorated with jellytots and Smarties with the words, *Happy Birthday Hol* iced in very uneven letters. They put one candle on it and insisted on singing to me as they brought it out.

'That is *so* sweet,' Lisa said, giggling.

'I'm not sure about sweet but you have made a wonderful effort,' Max agreed.

'It looks like a monstrosity,' Francesca pointed out.

'Yes, but at least we made it ourselves,' Freddie said.

We cut the cake which tasted better than it looked. Then we kept on drinking and talking into the early hours when we were all too drunk to carry on.

I awoke on the second day of my thirtieth year with a monster hangover. I was so bad that I was actually sick. I knelt with my head over the bowl of the loo wondering why I hadn't quite got the hang of being a grown-up. Then I smiled, because I was definitely happy. Being thirty was going to be all right after all, George or no George.

February turned into March, and it was time to go to court. Now I knew I would see him, whatever happened I would have to face him. I stood up, and brushed imaginary dust from my sensible navy outfit and went to the front door.

'I have to go back to work, but call me the minute it's over,' Francesca said. I kissed her cheek and thanked her.

'Let's go Hol,' Joe said, taking my hand.

'Freddie?' I asked.

'I'm with you.' He winked and took my other hand. With my two new men, I was as ready as I would ever be.

# Chapter Thirteen

## *Love and Litigation*

I felt like my old self for a while as I stepped into my suit. I was George Conway, the lawyer. I looked the part. In the legal profession, looking the part is so important. My suit was made to measure; charcoal grey, with three buttons on the jacket. A plain tie; I've always been a firm believer in plain ties. White shirt, crisp and straight from the dry cleaner's. Plain black socks sitting snuggly in polished black brogues. I was ready and for the first time since I left New York, the adrenaline rush that my job gave me was revisiting.

I wasn't proud of what I was doing, but I was proud of how I looked.

I know that if there has to be a villain, then that's how I'll be viewed. I'm sure that Holly sees me that way, and that upsets me. When there is someone special, someone you expect to spend the rest of your life with then you have to fight, with everything you've got, to get them. Love is such a rare commodity, that you have to do everything in your power to get it and keep it. That is simple common sense.

Of course, a few months ago I didn't expect to be standing here, in my tailored-suit about to take the girl I love, to court. But she left me no option, she had hurt me. She discarded my feelings. I believe that deep down I always knew that she was the one for me, I just forgot for a while but it all made sense now. Unfortunately, Holly was not yet as enlightened.

When I first met Holly, I hated her. She was always surly and she resented me because I was her friend's boyfriend. I still remember Samantha, my first girlfriend, the first girl I snogged. I was besotted with her in an adolescent sort of way, but then she left to live in Australia and Holly and I became friends and we spent all our formative years together.

She was always with me. My family holidays (I was an only child), included her. School included her. Weekends included her. We spent so much time together; we were barely apart. But even though I was young, and had lost my first girlfriend there was never any question of Holly being girlfriend number two. I liked her as a friend, I liked her company. As we grew up, she became so important to me I wasn't willing to jeopardise her friendship by becoming romantically involved. So we didn't. We grew up, to be best friends.

Not that Holly was completely unattractive. At twelve, her eyes were too big for her face, she looked a bit like an alien. Her knees, sticking out of her white school socks were knobbly, her teeth, encased in a brace, were crooked. But still she was pretty, and I was no film star.

Then she certainly blossomed. She grew to about five foot six, she was slim, her teeth straightened, her face filled out and her dark hair was long and glossy. I did, at certain times in our life, think about her in 'that' way, but I suppressed my feelings. I was a man though, and I wouldn't have been normal if it had never crossed my mind.

I remember a time when we were in France on holiday with my parents. We were fifteen and Holly was wearing a bikini and sunbathing by the pool of our villa. I noticed for the first time that she had boobs, small and pert. I was fifteen and being fifteen isn't easy. Your penis seems to have a mind of its own and I remember having to stay in the swimming pool until I turned into a prune waiting for the boy to go down. I thought about kissing her then. I really did, and part of me wanted to, but then by the time we were alone she was in her jeans and top and we were messing around. No kiss but very close friends.

Then, when we were travelling in Thailand, we had to share a room and that was difficult. I exercised such restraint when I saw her half naked coming out of the shower, or getting dressed in the morning and undressed at night. I wasn't sure if she was taunting me with her body or if she was just so comfortable with me that she didn't think about it. I didn't make a move, just in case it was the latter.

The last time I thought about it was when we were both broken-hearted, or she was broken-hearted and I was suffering from a bruised ego. She looked so vulnerable, her big brown eyes glistening with tears, that I just wanted to reach over and kiss those tears away. We made our marriage pact that night, and I half expected it to come true.

The thing that held me back, was the fact that I knew if I was to do anything with Holly, I had to be one hundred per cent sure that it would last, because there was no way I would ruin our friendship.

When I was offered my job in New York, the only thing that would have stopped me going was Holly. I knew I would miss her as much as I would ever miss anyone, but I also knew, as I think she did, that our friendship wouldn't survive. Not in the same way. Not being able to see her every day, not being able to talk over all my problems with her. The only reason I didn't invite her to visit was because I thought I might never let her go home, and I wasn't sure if that was what she would have wanted, or if it was *really* what I wanted. She never asked to visit; I assumed she felt the way I did. We were so in tune, and I had never met anyone like her.

I had never been as close to anyone as I was with Holly. Friendships like ours aren't normal among guys. At school I was teased by all the other boys, they couldn't understand why I would want to hang out with a girl like Holly unless I was putting my tongue down her throat or my hand down her knickers. Close friendship with a member of the opposite sex that isn't physical isn't near the top of most teenage boys' lists. But I ignored the teasing because being with Holly made me feel good.

I put all my energy into my career which flourished, and the only times I saw her after I left were a couple of Christmas visits. Even then I felt the gulf between us. Then I stopped going home, and only saw my parents when they visited me. I can't explain why I let our friendship go the way I did; but I knew that friendships changed. Yes, Holly was the most important person of my youth; I would rather have lost her altogether than watched that friendship go wrong. It may not make sense, but that was the truth at the time.

I made my life in New York, and tasted success. I loved it: friends, girlfriends, gym membership, tennis lessons; I had it all. Skiing in Colorado, surfing in Hawaii. I lived a pretty good life out there.

Then I met Julia.

Julia was a truly amazing woman. Looks-wise, she was straight off the pages of *Cosmopolitan*. Intelligent, with a good job and a certainty about her that I'd never experienced with a woman – I fell in love.

We first met at a work-related cocktail party. A friend of hers, who was a colleague of mine, introduced us. My first impression was that she was pretty sexy. She wore a trouser suit, I don't remember the colour, but I do remember thinking she had a great body. She had long, thick, black, glossy hair and gorgeous lips, curled into a smile that captivated me totally. There was a definite physical attraction. We talked all night, first about work, then about us. We clicked intellectually. I was direct and asked her if she was seeing anyone. Thankfully she wasn't. She asked me the same, I told her I was single. Technically that wasn't true, but the girl I was seeing was only a casual fling. In my mind I was single. So at the end of the night I asked her for a date.

The following day I instructed my efficient secretary to book a table for me at one of New York's hot spots. I wanted the full works: champagne cocktails, dinner, dancing. It was perfect.

We became a regular couple pretty quickly, with a hectic social life: dinners, parties, weekends away; we did everything together, apart from going to work. I fell head over heels in love with her very quickly. I believed she felt the same about me.

Before I met Julia, I had measured my girlfriends against Holly, and they couldn't compete. It was confusing, often I wondered if I was in love with her. I often thought about whether we were going to end up together. There was always a doubt in the back of my mind where she was concerned. I thought she felt the same. The relationships she had when we were in London were never as important to her as our friendship. I felt sure that the reason for this was that she measured each man against me, and they didn't compare favourably.

But then there was New York and then there was Julia. Julia and I had a fantastic relationship. The physical side was amazing; our conversation was always interesting. We had so much in common. Everyone around us thought we were the real thing. *I* thought we were the real thing, and *she* thought we were the real thing.

Everyone says that turning thirty is a real milestone in your life. That often it changed the way you looked at your life. Prior to my birthday last October, I thought about what I wanted in life. My career was going great guns, and the partnership I coveted was in sight. My life was firmly in New York, so the only thing left to do was to consolidate my relationship. I was done with bachelor life, although for the three years I'd been with Julia I could hardly call myself a bachelor, but we hadn't made a commitment. We didn't live together, we weren't married. I realised then that that was what I wanted. I wanted to get married, but I had to be sure I was marrying the right girl.

I was pretty sure that Julia was the one for me, we were this dynamic couple, both successful, both had money, we entertained high-profile people, we went for weekends away with high-profile people. She was beautiful, sexy and intelligent. I liked to think I was a pretty good catch. All the ingredients were there but I had to be one hundred per cent sure.

Holly was my only doubt. So I decided to do the only thing I could to sort it out. I went to London for the weekend, not giving it much thought and taking a last-minute flight. I told Julia that I had to visit our London office; I told the office that I had to visit my parents. I didn't contact Holly until I was in London, so she would have no choice but to see me, but she didn't even protest. Typical Holly.

She had always been there for me. She'd never refused me anything. She was quite a girl, and I guessed now she was a woman she'd be quite a woman. I was terrified in my own way of what I might find. The complications of Holly being the one for me were vast. Would she move to New York? Would I have to move back to London? These were details that I didn't want to contemplate. Being a lawyer I am attentive to detail; unfortunately there is no way you can be romantic about the whole thing. It all comes down to detail. Something I learned a long time ago.

If you're in love you have to think like that. I was sure I was in love with Julia, but I wasn't sure if I was more in love with Holly. When I was younger I used to be quite the fatalist. I used to tell Holly to look up at the sky because that held our fate. I thought that fate would give you clues and guide you in the right direction. I still believe that, but as you get older you realise you can't leave too much to fate. I could have ignored Holly and just asked Julia, but because of that niggling doubt, I thought that maybe fate was giving me one of the clues I used to look out for. I determined that I would act on it, I had to get things right. Getting things wrong is something I would never contemplate.

So I arrived in London and booked myself into the St Martin's Lane Hotel. I thought that as the rest of my life was being decided that very weekend, I would let it be decided in style.

I checked into the hotel, checked in with work, called Julia, then I e-mailed Holly. It was Friday, but because I told her that I was over on business I asked if we could meet on Saturday night. It meant one night alone in a hotel room, but that was necessary. Everything hinged on this one night, so I was prepared to spend an evening sitting in a bathrobe, enjoying room service, watching television. It wasn't too much of a sacrifice, considering.

The following day, I walked around London, and noticed how little it had changed. There were some new bars and shops, but the atmosphere was the same. I tried to decide if I'd missed it, but I didn't. There was no question, as I walked along the grey streets, that I loved New York. I went to get coffee and smiled to myself at the American-style coffee houses that had sprung up. There seemed to be more in London that in New York. There weren't any when I had left, but now there were three to every street. It reminded me of the 'Big Apple'. It was time to meet Holly.

I had to make sure that I looked the part. I wore beige slacks, and a light-coloured shirt. Brown brogues, fawn socks. It was the look I had cultivated in New York. It worked for me. I always looked smart, I was always expensively dressed. Always immaculate. That was something my job had taught me.

I sat at the bar sipping a beer waiting for her and my stomach was full of butterflies. I hadn't seen Holly for what . . . five years? That's a long time and I wondered what might have happened to her. I smiled to myself at the thought that maybe she was really fat now and her hair was totally grey, but I knew that five years didn't do that to a person. No, I knew that I would recognise her the moment I saw her.

I felt, rather than saw, someone looking at me from behind, and instinctively I knew it was her. I decided to wait until she approached me, I didn't turn round. When she reached my table and I stood up to kiss her, I realised that she was the same Holly I'd kissed goodbye all those years ago. She looked a bit older, but not really, she looked more confident, more sophisticated, but she was still the knobbly kneed twelve year old I knew and loved.

I ordered champagne and we talked about the past. I hadn't thought about what conversation would be like, but it was weird that as soon as I saw her I felt a reluctance to talk about the present. As we relived our childhood everything was about what life had been like. And for some reason I didn't want it to be any other way. I had an agenda, that I knew, but seeing Holly made me yearn for the old days, I guess when we were young and care-free. I know I sound like an old man, but it wasn't like that, it was just that my childhood seemed so far away.

As we talked, I devised a plan. Thus far, I had no answers, or not the answers I'd come for. I did find Holly attractive, but she wasn't as attractive as Julia. I found her amusing, but she was a bit scatty, which I had always teased her about. She wasn't as self-confident as Julia. Holly had a tendency to jump from one topic to the next as if she was in a real rush, whereas Julia would speak in an orderly, methodical fashion. If I was being cold and calculated, I would have chosen Julia on the grounds that she was better for my image and my career, but that wasn't why I was here. I was simply here to do the right thing, to ensure that the woman I married was the right one.

There was one other thing: Holly drank like a fish. Julia was always very controlled when it came to drinking. Holly wasn't.

She seemed to be drinking for England. I noticed she'd given up smoking and I was a little disappointed. Holly had smoked, from the age of eighteen and I had always disapproved. Ironically I had taken up smoking. In my early days in New York I would sit in my tiny apartment, and light a cigarette because that's what I always imagined she would be doing in her time zone, at the same time. It made me feel close to her. I know it's crazy, but that's how I felt. I wanted to ask her why she'd quit, but I didn't in case she told me it was for a man. I took up smoking for her; I didn't want *her* giving it up for anyone else. I only smoked occasionally though, and I hadn't had any since I'd been in London. I probably could have done with one for my nerves, but decided to hold off a while.

After we finished dinner, she turned down coffee, so I suggested we go to my room and I invited her to drink the minibar. She agreed enthusiastically. She took my hand as we walked to the lift, and there was a distinct lack of electricity in the action. But it felt like the most natural thing in the world at that moment. It was then I realised that I was trying to decide between passion and security, when really I wanted both. I had booked a suite, so she sat on the sofa while I picked out the bottles from the minibar and lined them up. I challenged her to a drinking contest.

'I won't let you go until we've emptied the fridge,' I joked.

'You're on,' she replied, and I knew she meant it. Holly was definitely fun, always ready for a challenge, for doing something that would not exactly be seen as sensible in the morning. Julia, well Julia didn't do anything that wasn't sensible. Not that she was boring, she wasn't, but her idea of fun was different. I knew that if I had suggested to her that we empty the minibar she would have looked at me as if I was completely mad, 'Stop messing, George,' she would have said, with her lips pursed together in case I meant it, and I'd pretend it was a joke and that I hadn't meant it. Not like Holly. I pulled out the ice tray, and while I poured the drinks I called room service for a packet of cigarettes. Holly acted shocked and I felt embarrassed, I couldn't tell her the real reason that I smoked, so I fobbed her off with some lame excuse.

The cigarettes arrived and I lit one. Holly followed suit. She looked as if she was uncomfortable and I guess it was my fault, because the uneasy atmosphere in the room was down to me. It had changed in a split second, we could both feel it. I was tense because I had to know, and I couldn't beat around the bush any more.

Most of the evening after that was a blur. For someone who is meticulous in recounting events, I had a major lapse. I think because it was so important, it threw me off my normally sturdy guard. I started by asking her if she'd ever thought about us in *that* way. I think I mentioned kissing her. I remember her face turned red, she looked flushed, she couldn't quite look at me and as she said she didn't, I couldn't help but feel that she was lying. A major skill you acquire as a lawyer is knowing when a person is lying and I believed in my heart that Holly was telling me one.

Then I kissed her. She responded, not at once, but after a while she did, and it was a satisfying kiss. It was a gentle kiss, a soft kiss; it was a kiss that needed to be taken further. I remember when we pulled apart she looked at me and I wondered, for a split second, if I was doing the wrong thing. She looked at me as if she had a million questions in her eyes; as if I had turned her to stone. I probably should have left it there but I needed to know. I put my hand to her cheek.

'Are you OK?' I asked. She nodded and I kissed her again.

As I peeled off her top, I tried to work out if I had my answers yet. As I undid her bra, my hands shaking as if I was a teenager again, as I put my hands to her breasts and caressed her nipples, as I took my shirt off and watched her tentatively put her hands on my chest, as I pulled her shoes off, then her socks, then her trousers, as I pulled her up onto her feet, and left her there for a minute while I undid my trousers, as I led her to the four-poster king-size bed, as I gently pushed her down and finally made love to her. I had my answer at some point in that whole process, but I don't know where it was exactly.

Afterwards, I tried to figure out why I'd done it. I guess I should have realised that it wasn't right from the start, but I needed to be sure. She looked so shocked as she sat up on the bed, before realising she was naked and rushing to put her clothes back on. I put on a bathrobe and followed her into the living room where I poured her a whisky. She looked as if she wanted to kill me and I worried for a moment that I had forced myself on her. I knew I hadn't. She had kissed me, she had let me take her clothes off, she even orgasmed, I know she climaxed.

The sex was good, but rather passionless. It wasn't as good as with Julia, and it didn't leave me feeling warm as she did. So I had my answer: Julia. It was the answer I wanted because it meant that I wouldn't have to turn my life upside down.

Holly regained her composure pretty quickly, and then the recriminations started. Suddenly I got a Holly I had never seen before. She screamed at me; I think she was angry with herself and she needed to blame me. She screamed something about a boyfriend, but how was I to know. I wasn't responsible for her fidelity, she was. Nevertheless, I don't believe that I handled the next bit so well, but she was angry and I was happy. I was happy, because now I was sure that Julia was the woman with whom I was going to spend my future.

I tried to explain everything to Holly. About her being a doubt in my mind, about Julia, about the proposal. I thought she might find it flattering, but I guess it didn't sound too good because she was mad. Holly had never been angry with me before. I tried to explain everything, but she just screamed at me. She said I got her drunk and took advantage of her. You know that's what I hate about women, they always blame the man. I didn't make her drink like a fucking fish, I didn't force her into my room at gunpoint and I didn't hear her complaining at the time. However, I let her have her accusation, because it didn't matter any more and she was feeling guilty, I guess. I wasn't though, I didn't feel guilty one iota because I believed that being unfaithful to Julia, with Holly, meant that I was going to be faithful to her for the rest of my life.

At some point Holly stormed out. I was hoping we could salvage our friendship, but it didn't look likely. I found it hard to comprehend her anger, after all we were bound to have a physical encounter at some stage. But I let her go because my mission was accomplished. Although I was sorry that I hurt Holly, I can't say I regretted it.

# Chapter Fourteen

One minute life was perfect, the next it was ruined.

I flew back to New York, it was the beginning of December and instead of saying anything to Julia straight away, I decided to plan something special. I'm not a romantic man, although I know what flowers to send, and when, but I wanted the proposal to be special. I was only intending on doing it once. I decided to propose on Christmas Day because we were spending it together in her apartment. Therefore, while we discussed buying the tree and ordering the food, I planned to give her the Christmas present of her life. I called her best girlfriend and swearing her to secrecy, we went shopping for a ring. We both decided to go for the traditional Tiffany solitaire. Amanda (Julia's friend) managed to get her ring size somehow. So then we went and picked up an expensive, but beautiful diamond set in platinum. It was perfect and I felt quite emotional about the whole thing. The ring is a symbol of love. I was feeling more romantic than I ever had in my life.

On Christmas morning I presented Julia with her gifts. My plan was to exchange the ordinary presents, and then I would produce my surprise. I gave her a tennis racket, a cashmere jumper, and some books. She gave me a couple of shirts, jumpers, and some CDs. I didn't care about my presents, I was too concerned about the ring. I was going to make breakfast, but she wanted to make love, so I obliged her. It was more intense than usual, or so I thought. Afterwards I told her I was bringing her breakfast in bed. She smiled that post-coital smile she has: sexy and dreamy which makes it hard not to go back for seconds, but I had more important things to do. I left her and went to rustle up some smoked salmon and scrambled eggs. I took the chilled champagne from the fridge along with two glasses from the cupboard. I wasn't sure if I was nervous, I think I was, but I was also excited. I took everything to her on a tray, including the ring box. As she sat up eagerly awaiting her food, she did not see it at first. Then she did and that was the end of Christmas.

She picked up the box tentatively and opened it. She looked at the ring, then looked at me, then back at the ring.

'What . . . ?' she asked, but it wasn't a very reassuring what.

'I want you to be my wife,' I replied. I felt emotional.

'George . . . but why?' Not the response I was expecting.

'Because I love you, you are the most beautiful woman I have ever met and I want us to spend the rest of our lives together.' Julia got out of bed slowly and headed for the kitchen with the breakfast tray in her hands.

'What are you doing?' I asked.

'Putting this down. Look George, you should have discussed this with me.'

'Discussed it? I have just asked you to marry me, why would we have a discussion about that? I wanted to be romantic.' Suddenly, it seemed I was talking to a stranger; it was scaring me.

'That's not the point. The point is I don't want to get married.'

'You're turning me down?' She was fucking turning me down.

'George, marriage is a big step. I don't want to be rushed.'

'We've been together for three years, I'd hardly say that was a rush.'

'No, not necessarily, but well I just don't think we're ready. We're not that old.'

'I'm thirty.'

'That's young.' Julia had pursed her lips, she always did that when she was angry, but I couldn't understand why she was on edge with me. For God's sake I had just asked her to marry me. She'd told me she loved me enough times, OK maybe we hadn't discussed marriage exactly, but we'd been together, happily, for three years. It was the obvious next step.

'I thought we were ready. I know I am ready.'

'But I'm not. If you'd told me you were thinking of doing this then we could have talked.'

'So you're saying no.'

'George, I do love you, but I don't want this, not yet, maybe not ever.'

'I see.' I looked at her face but she was giving nothing away.

'Perhaps we should take a break from each other.'

'What?'

'Well we want different things from life. Let's take some time out.'

'Is this your way of dumping me.'

'No, well . . . yes. I think it might be best if we break up.'

'Break up? Look Julia, we should talk about this. You made it clear you don't want to marry me, but you said you loved me. So where's breaking up come from? Christ, Julia.' I was lost for words.

'I haven't been planning it, but when you asked me to marry you, well . . .'

'OK, then let's forget about marriage and talk about our relationship, I thought it was perfect.'

'Maybe on the surface it was—'

'Julia, what in hell is that supposed to mean?'

'I just haven't been feeling right about us for a while now.'

'And, when you said you loved me?'

'I know it sounds awful but I think maybe it's habit. You have to admit our relationship has gone a bit stale.'

'I don't. I am blissfully happy with you, I thought you were with me. I was happy enough to propose to you and now you want out.'

'Yes, George, I do.'

'Happy Fucking Christmas, Julia,' I yelled before snatching the ring off the tray and storming out of the apartment.

I spent the rest of Christmas on my own, getting drunk in my apartment. All I remember is that the alcohol numbed the searing pain at first and eventually it obliterated it altogether. There was no turkey, no crackers, nothing of a traditional Christmas. The first clear thought I had, once back in my apartment was of the two glasses of champagne, untouched, gradually losing their fizz. The rest of the bottle, not drunk. Did Julia pour it down the sink? Of course she did. Julia was not the type of woman to drink flat champagne. She would have poured it down the plug hole, one glass, then the other, hesitating while deciding what to do with the rest of the bottle before pouring that away as well. She wouldn't drink it because that specific bottle of champagne represented me. She would have poured it down the sink with my proposal.

People talk about an event happening that turns their lives upside down, Julia's response did that to me. Apart from the hurt, which was bad enough, there were other things. I had been so certain of my future, now I had no idea. I thought I was going to marry the woman I loved. It wasn't a fairy-tale ending I was looking for, it was the ending that best befitted my lifestyle. Julia, a big apartment, nice holidays, children one day. Now I had none of that on my horizon.

I felt shipwrecked; how was I going to salvage my life? I had always seen Julia as perfect, but she had just proved the opposite. I was furious. I had gone to so much trouble and for what? I was so sure that Julia was the right one for me, I'd even upset Holly for her. I'd done everything for her, and she threw it all back in my face. Obviously I had been wrong all along. She wasn't the woman I was in love with, which left me with the question: who was I in love with? Was I even in love at all?

On Boxing Day I made a decision. Or maybe the decision was made for me. I was in the basement gym of my apartment block, pounding the treadmill and trying to pound Julia out of my mind. I realised now that fate had been telling me something, and I wasn't going to sit around in New York moping and drinking. That wasn't my style. I had to regain control of my life; I needed to get away, I needed to rethink. I needed to go back to England. The following day I was going home. It was a drastic decision perhaps, but one that needed making. I needed distance and I needed to think. It seemed clear to me that New York wasn't going to hold the answers. And Julia had given me her answer. Not the answer I was expecting, but maybe the one I needed after all.

That afternoon she turned up at my apartment with a box of my things. They included the Christmas presents. I felt cold as I looked at her, she didn't look over the moon but she looked OK. She stood at the door of my apartment, clutching the big brown cardboard box, I could tell she felt awkward and I did nothing to make her feel any easier. She told me she was sorry, and I told her I was too. When I let her in, part of me wanted to take her in my arms, but I didn't, I just didn't want to give her any comfort. She reiterated her thoughts of the previous day, but I didn't need to hear it. I told her I accepted her decision. That was all – I accepted it. I didn't offer her a drink, I didn't ask her to sit down. I thanked her formally for returning my things and I held the door open for her to leave. As soon as she left, I closed the door so that I couldn't see her walk away.

Two days later I was at home in Devon, where I'd grown up. Things were a bit of a blur but I had managed to get on to my flight. I'd hired a car at Heathrow and I'd driven home. I was feeling numb, I still hurt. I admit that I had also shed some tears.

I had not cried over Julia until I was back in my old childhood bedroom. I remembered the last time I'd cried. The last time was just after I'd said goodbye to Holly before moving to New York. The time before that was when Samantha had moved to Australia. All connected to Holly. Even this time was connected with her because it was right after I saw her that I had proposed to Julia. And that sure worked out. I felt that maybe Holly was more intrinsically linked into my life than I'd thought. Part of me felt that my life had ground to a halt, the optimistic part felt that perhaps it was just beginning.

In my childhood bedroom – now an anonymous space, all traces of me hidden away in a cupboard – I wiped my tears away with an angry gesture. It was time for me to regain control of my life.

I called my boss and requested time off. I cited a family crisis. Later we arranged a proper, unpaid sabbatical on this basis. I think he understood more than I expected him to and he promised that this wouldn't in any way harm my career prospects. With that reassurance I could turn my attention to how I was going to rebuild my personal life. How I was going to re-create myself.

I met Holly in Devon (she was visiting her parents) and told her what had happened. She was no longer the angry woman who had stormed out of my hotel room, she was the sweet, loving girl that I had always known. She held me while I cried and she told me she'd be there for me. She looked so genuine, that I realised that I'd made the wrong decision. In a moment I realised that Holly was the girl for me. I should have known. There were two women, Holly and Julia, and it looked like I had picked the wrong one. Simple.

I'd walked away from Julia, from New York, from my job, but I wasn't going to walk away from her – not Holly.

I rented a flat in London and tried to sort myself out. For a few days I stayed in bed, didn't eat, didn't shave, didn't wash. I had my head to sort out, my feelings for Holly. I had to do it before I explained them to her. I stayed in bed and I thought and I thought, then the truth manifested.

When you realise the truth everything feels better. Since Julia had rejected me my whole body had suffered. My hands shook so I just tried not to use them. I wasn't hungry. It was as if she had taken all my energy and left me with nothing. But in those days when I was lying horizontal, unable to lift my head, the truth seeped into my consciousness. Holly was the most important woman in my life apart from my mother. My friend Holly. We'd grown up together and our lives had always been linked. But then I had messed it all up by going to New York. I shouldn't have gone. I should have turned down the job. I should have stayed in London where Holly and I would have fallen in love and lived happily ever after. There would never have been a Julia, she was a hurdle too far in the true course my love life should have run. But her rejection was necessary because now I had been returned to Holly.

Holly. The girl that represented the best times in my life. The girl who made me laugh more than any other. The woman who was my destiny. The uncomplicated, unconditional love she had always given me should have made me realise sooner. But I hadn't. Until now.

I felt better so I got out of bed, shaved, showered, dressed. Then I contacted Holly and started trying to explain my feelings. She said she wasn't interested. She accused me of stalking her. She had turned into a bitch. She told me that I had become a stranger but *she* was the stranger. Not me. I was angry with her, although I put her feelings down to fear. She was under the impression that she was in love with someone else, and all I could do was try to get her to come to her senses. I tried to explain this to her, but to no avail. I was in London, I had no friends, only a handful of acquaintances, and it was a lonely time, but Holly was the goal and I stayed focused on it. Flowers, dinner, phone calls, visits. I tried everything to get her attention, and I did get her attention but she stayed resolutely immune to my charms.

It really hurt when she shouted at me, when she called me names, but there was nothing I could do. I had to make Holly see that I loved her and that she loved me, there was no way that I could give up on that.

I visited my parents one weekend and found our marriage pact. I was looking through some of my old things and there it was, the answer to everything. Holly had shunned every attempt I'd made to develop our relationship, she had become cold and hostile. But the pact, our marriage pact represented something special. It would make her see sense. Everything fitted into place.

Unfortunately, Holly didn't agree. She said I was crazy. I wasn't. Believe me I wasn't. All I wanted was a happy future and I knew that that would mean Holly. It wasn't Julia after all it was Holly. The only reason we didn't know it was because that night, that night in the hotel, we were drunk, so it didn't register, but it would work because we were so obviously destined to be together. Crazy? I wasn't crazy, I was saner than I'd ever been.

But she told me to get out of her life. *Get out of her life.* The one person I'd always loved, told me to get lost. She couldn't do that and get away with it. We had a pact; she'd signed it. It was there in black and white. It was a contract. It was our bond. It represented our future. When I tried to point this out she laughed at me. I had to make her see sense the only way I could. The only way I could was to sue her for breach of promise.

The British law system is quite different to American procedure, but I had contacts. I called a guy I had worked with when I had started out in London, he was still with the firm with whom we'd both trained. Clive Parsons met me for a drink and I told him everything. He told me I had no chance of getting it to court, and he tried his darndest to talk me out of it. I told him there was no way I would give up, so he said that as I was serious we could issue proceedings for a preliminary hearing. He helped through the process, and although we weren't exactly friends, it was good to have someone to talk to. I issued a summons for a preliminary hearing in a civil court. If the judge agreed I had a case then I would go ahead and sue; I'd sue until she saw sense. Although Clive said this was doubtful, I was still determined to give it my best shot. I asked Clive to represent me but he refused. He was very nice about it, but told me that he couldn't take on a case like that, he mumbled something about it not being his 'area'. I was going to represent myself. I knew what I had to do, and I knew why I was doing it. I thanked Clive for his help and I prepared myself to battle.

'Why are you really doing this?' Clive asked me.

'Because I love her,' I replied, simply.

'George, I don't think this is going to work, I'm telling you that as a mate.'

'Fine, but I'm still going to do it.'

'I suppose I should wish you luck, I just don't know if I can. I feel that I should try to stop you, that I shouldn't have let you come this far.'

'Clive, I'll take it from here, there's no need for you to be involved further. There's nothing more to say.'

'George, good luck . . . I think.'

'Thank you Clive.'

Just one more person who refused to understand me.

I wasn't trying to hurt her. There was no way I would ever hurt her, but I couldn't let her throw our future away and I had to use any means within my power to ensure that that didn't happen. All I was trying to do was to keep myself in her life, that way she would soon come to her senses.

Love is a funny thing. Everyone who has ever been in love must know that. It is something that makes you feel strong and weak at the same time. I knew in the weeks following my departure from New York, that I wanted to go back there. I knew that I wanted to return to my old job and resume my career but I also knew that the only way I would do that was with Holly as my wife. Surely she was going to realise how right we were for each other? It was just a question of when.

So, today, I am once again George Conway, super lawyer, and I am going to ensure that Holly Miller is so impressed with what I can do that she will come running into my arms. Where she belongs.

I checked myself in the mirror one last time. Gave myself a pep talk and tried to contain my nerves. I had to; my future depended on it.

# Chapter Fifteen

———◆◄►◆———

## *Post Coital*

I went to court, although it didn't look like a court, but saying that, I was too nervous to pay attention. As we met Susan's words washed over me. All I could imagine was myself and George shackled together in marriage, enforced by an old judge who had never married himself. It certainly wasn't like on television. I kissed Joe and Freddie before we were taken to somewhere called 'chambers', and all I could think was that the British legal system was archaic because what they called chambers, any normal person would call an office.

It was over quickly. If I had paid attention rather than concentrating on the nausea I was feeling, I would have known that it was going to be all right from the start. The judge asked how it had been allowed to get this far. I wondered the same. As this was a preliminary hearing and not a proper case it was just Susan, myself and George in front of the judge. The judge said that the contract would not stand up in any court of law and that was to be an end to the matter. I watched George's face crumple and I felt sorry for him. I then kicked myself for that, because he had tried to force me to marry him. He was ordered to pay any costs and then we were thrown out. As Joe and Freddie hugged and congratulated me I watched George leave dejectedly. I did notice that there was a woman there and I wondered if she was a friend because she led him out. I didn't care because it was all over as far as I was concerned and I could get back to my life.

It was three months since George had first come back into my life and finally I was rid of him. Any sadness I tried to feel about this, was washed away with relief.

'Susan, thanks,' I said, with as much affection as I could muster for my solicitor.

'Just my job,' she replied, said her goodbyes and left. I noticed that she smiled a little more than she had on our previous meetings, and I decided that if I was going to need a solicitor ever again, I would contact her.

'I think that we should celebrate,' Freddie said.

'How about Italian food and red wine,' Joe suggested.

'No champagne?' Freddie asked, in mock-horror.

'OK, so we'll head over to the nearest oyster bar and order champagne and oysters,' I decided.

'Actually, I've got to get back to work, so I better leave you two to it,' Freddie said, winking.

'Maybe I should come in to work, after all I have been a bit preoccupied lately,' I suggested.

'No, Francesca said that I was to call her with the news and then head back, and whatever the outcome you were to have the rest of the day off.' Freddie kissed me and left.

I think you need to pinch me,' I said as Joe took my hand as we left the building.

'Why?'

'Well, now it's over it all feels like it was just a terrible nightmare.'

'It was.'

'I'm relieved, but I'm almost angry with myself for letting it get me into such a state.'

'It's not every day that someone takes you to court to try to get you to marry them,' Joe said, squeezing my hand that bit harder.

'I know, anyway, it is over now.'

'It sure is. Where shall we go for the champagne?'

'Let's go to Blake's, I feel like celebrating.'

In the taxi, I called my parents, then Imogen, Lisa and Francesca to tell them the good news. By the time we got to the restaurant, I was more than ready to celebrate. I hadn't felt this happy in ages, I was as exuberant as the bubbles in the champagne. I ate heartily, but then I had been eating quite a lot. After lunch, I ordered another bottle of champagne, and Joe reached over and took my hand. We were a bit merry I think, but Joe's face was pink, I believe he was blushing.

'Holly, I know that when I asked you to marry me it was for all the wrong reasons. Well, not all the wrong reasons, because I do love you and that's always a reason for marriage, but I guess my timing was off and the overwhelming reason was to get George off your back, but now he is. Anyway, what I mean is that when I asked you, well I hadn't given it a huge amount of thought, but I haven't stopped thinking about it. And well, this isn't how I planned it, but . . . I don't think I'm very good at this, so I should just do it. Holly Miller will you marry me?'

The warmth that flooded my entire body was like a lifetime of summers. Shit, how corny is that, but it was. Here in front of me was the man I loved and he was asking me the question that was perhaps the most important question anyone would ever ask me, and although I was a bit off marriage since George came back on the scene, I knew that the way my body, and my head, and my heart were feeling right now, was the right way to feel. I squeezed Joe's hand and felt tears stinging the back of my eyes, I didn't want to cry, not even with happiness because there had been too many tears. Joe was looking at me intently, looking for the answer, and his face was still pink.

'Yes,' I squeaked, unable to hear if my voice was audible.

'You said "yes"?' Joe shouted.

'I did.' He jumped up and to the surprise of the rest of the restaurant, he lifted me high in the air.

'You mean it?' he whispered into my ear, as if he couldn't believe it.

'I do, do you?' I asked, unable to believe it either. Then we kissed, and we laughed, and this time the tears did return.

We finished the second bottle, and then we paid the bill and went home.

'I want to tell the world,' Joe said.

'Well you can't. You have to ask my father's permission don't forget.'

'I haven't met your father.' Suddenly Joe looked scared.

'He's a softie, but really you ought to meet my parents before we tell anyone.'

'When can I meet them?'

'How about the weekend after next? It's a bit of a trek to Devon, so we could try to take Friday afternoon off.'

'Sounds fine by me. But I have to keep quiet until then?'

'Absolutely.'

'I love you Holly Miller.'

'I love you too Joe McClaren.'

The court case was over, I was marrying the man I loved, but immediately following the proposal, life got back to normal. I went to work and threw myself into it. I found it hard keeping quiet about our engagement but if ever I was tempted to talk about it, I called Joe. On Saturday, following the court visit, I had work to catch up with and Freddie was coming over to my flat to help. We'd got behind on a couple of projects, although nothing major, and as it was my fault, I resolved to sort it out. Freddie was being a darling about the whole thing, and I really felt things getting back on track. Joe was spending the weekend catching up with friends he'd neglected before the court case. I kissed him goodbye and I realised that although he would only be gone for one night, I really would miss him. I was totally sad.

When I think back to first meeting Joe, I was cool. Before Joe

I was cool, but gradually I have been sliding off the cool tracks and now I am just a loved-up sap. The awful thing is that I'm quite happy to be uncool. I have no use for cool any longer. But then, the relationship has had an unusual path. Pre-George it was normal, but George did turn it on its head. He tried to split us up but that brought us closer together and I am sure that if it hadn't been for him we wouldn't be making this mammoth marriage decision for a while yet. He made me realise how much I loved Joe, which is ironic because that was the opposite to what he wanted, and I guess he must have made Joe realise how much he loved me. In a funny way, I owed a lot to George. I might even tell him that one day.

The buzzer interrupted my thoughts and as Freddie announced himself over the intercom I let him in.

I could hear him bounding up the stairs, and he stood at the door looking like the cat who got the cream.

'Let me in,' he said, impatiently, as he pushed past me.

'Why the big grin?' I asked.

'Just had a good shag last night, you know.'

'Actually, I do. Who was she?'

'No one you'd know.' Freddie coloured slightly, suggesting the opposite of his words.

'It better not be anyone at work or I'll castrate you.'

'Course not,' Freddie replied, filling the kettle.

'So?' I pulled two cups out of the cupboard and reached for the instant coffee.

'Instant? You are so bourgeois,' Freddie said.

'I'm not sure that you mean that. I thought instant was common.'

'Actually bourgeois is the new common.'

'So, no more details?'

'Nope. What about you? How is life in the land of the romantics?'

'Perfect. It's been so nice since the court appearance. First off

I am relaxed, and second Joe and I are happy and I don't snap at him all the time and, of course, George is nowhere to be seen.'

'Holly, touch wood quickly, I hate it when you say things like that, it's like you're tempting fate.' I humoured him by touching wood.

'Sorry. And the other thing is that I've stopped being sick.'

'I didn't know you were being sick.'

'Oh yes, practically every day, it was the stress. Anyway, it's stopped now.' I smiled, Freddie didn't.

'Holly, you know I teased you the other day about putting on weight?'

'Yeah, but that was stress too, anyway, it's barely noticeable.'

'I know. But . . . well I thought you might take up smoking again, you know when George was stressing you out.'

'I did, but I couldn't bear the taste, just shows how effective giving up was.'

The kettle had boiled and I made the coffee. He was leaning against the cooker looking perplexed. I handed him the coffee.

'Can I ask you something without you shouting at me?' he said.

I nodded, confused by the strange look that had appeared on his face. 'As long as it's not about the fact that I've put on weight. I feel bad enough about that already.' I giggled, Freddie didn't.

'Holly, can you in any way be pregnant?'

'What?' I laughed. 'Don't be ridiculous, I'm on the pill.'

'And you take it regularly?'

'Like clockwork, you know how organised I am. I get out of bed in the morning, take a shower, then I drink a glass of fruit juice and take my pill before getting dressed. Freddie, why did you say that?'

'When was your last period?'

'Don't . . .' I was about to tell him that I didn't know, and then I remembered I *didn't* know. Stress can be insidious, I know, I've seen what it can do. People lose their hair and all sorts, and I was really under stress. I had been trying to come to terms with my best friend turning into a madman, then it was the harassment, then the court threats. Almost three months of torture. Shit, three months.

'Holly, please, tell me. I had this hunch . . . I thought you looked, well you look different, if you've missed your period do a test.' I looked at him, surprised that he would be the one to notice such things. Even if he was totally wrong. 'Hol, don't look at me like that, my sister was pregnant last year remember, she phoned me up daily as soon as she found out with symptoms. I never thought her harassing me would come in handy, but it has.'

'Freddie, I told you, I'm on the pill, and anyway, stress can affect you in many ways you know.'

Freddie had grabbed his coat and abandoned his coffee.

'Where are you going?' I asked, confused, scared, and unsure.

'I'm going to buy you a pregnancy test kit.'

'I don't need one.'

'I think you do.'

'I don't.'

'Tell me when your last period was and I'll stay.' He looked at me with concern and a bit of impatience. I shrugged as I looked back at him, then watched him leave the flat.

I clutched my coffee waiting for him to return, but I didn't drink it. It was all so absurd. How could I be pregnant? I'd know. I'm sure I'd know. There was no way on earth that I wouldn't know something that big. I hadn't even put on much weight, just a few pounds. Freddie was being melodramatic.

The coffee cup slipped from my hand as something entered my mind. I walked to the sink to get a cloth but I held on to it for dear life. No! I screamed to myself. This could not happen. There were too many things, no, too many bad things. I was not pregnant, because I would know if I was.

It seemed like hours before Freddie came back, and I had

mopped up the spilt coffee and regained some of my composure. Freddie had scared me, but that was all, and as soon as
I took his negative pregnancy test I would then go to the doctor
and tell him about the stress and see what he could do for me.
Everything would be sorted, Freddie was definitely wrong.

'Holly, you know I care about you, and I'm not doing this to try
to hurt you?' he said as he handed the package to me. I smiled
and busied myself reading the instructions, but although I knew
that there was no way I was pregnant, holding the test in my
hand scared me.

'Go pee on the stick,' Freddie instructed.

'I'm just reading the instructions and anyway I don't know if
I can pee to order.'

'You've got one of the weakest bladders I've ever met, go on.'
He ushered me to the bathroom and stood there.

'Well I can't do it if you're watching,' I said.

'I don't want to watch, thank you,' Freddie replied, and he
smiled as he shut the door. Suddenly my bathroom seemed
enormous, although it wasn't. The loo was miles away, so I
started walking towards it. I pulled the test out of the box and
did as I was instructed, I peed on it. Then I washed my hands,
wiped the arm of the test with a tissue, thinking how undignified
it all felt. Surely modern science could come up with a more
hygienic way of finding out if I was pregnant or not. I put down
the loo seat and sat on it leaving the test on the side of the sink.
Freddie knocked on the door.

'I'm coming.' I went and opened the door.

'Well?'

'Give it a chance, you have to wait a couple of minutes.'

'Is there a line?'

'I don't know.'

'What do you mean you don't know?'

'I can't look.'

'But if you're so confident that you're not pregnant, you wouldn't mind looking.'

'Fuck off Freddie. You look.' All of a sudden, this huge implausibility was looking a tiny bit plausible. Then increasingly so as the test sat on the sink.

'There's a line,' Freddie whispered.

'Well then, it must be wrong. Faulty tests, you hear about them all the time.'

'Lucky I got you another one then.'

'Well I can't pee again.'

We battled on for a bit, while I paced round the flat. I immediately gravitated back to the kitchen where I stared out of the window. I saw George. I blinked and looked again and realised he wasn't there.

'Holly, please, come on. Have a drink of water and try again.' Freddie was being sweet which worried me because although I adore him, he's not a sweet person.

'Why?' I asked.

'Why what?'

'Why are you so convinced that I'm pregnant.'

'It adds up. Firstly you get sick, then you stop, and you put on weight, and you haven't had a period and you don't like the taste of cigarettes. I recognise those symptoms.'

'But you're not an expert are you?'

'My sister remember. I am not doing this to torture you, but if you are pregnant, and if you have been for a while, then you need to know.'

'Did you think about this before today?'

'No. I thought there was something, but it was only today it fitted into place. Holly, please, I might be wrong, humour me. Do another test.'

I obliged, and although it took longer for me to pee this time, I did eventually. Once I'd finished, I wiped the test again, washed my hands and left the room. Freddie walked into the bathroom as I walked out. There wasn't enough time for me to think about it, there wasn't enough time for me to feel anything. I was too busy trying not to cry.

I sat on the sofa, and Freddie walked in.

'You're pregnant.'

'I'm . . . I'm not.' I burst into tears. Freddie came to sit beside me and hugged me.

'Two tests, and don't say it was a faulty batch because I got two different brands.'

'They could still be wrong,' I looked at him as a child would, trying to get him to take it all back.

'They're pretty accurate Hol.'

'You don't understand, I can't be pregnant.'

'Why not? You've got Joe. George has gone, Joe loves you, and you love him. What's the problem?'

'Did I tell you that when George issued the court summons, Joe asked me to marry him?'

'No, you didn't.'

'Well he did and I said no because he only wanted to marry me to stop George from having a leg to stand on in this court case.'

'You did the right thing.'

'Yes, but then after the case he asked me again. He said he wanted to marry me more than anything, he said that although he'd asked for the wrong reasons the first time, he now knew it was the right thing to do.'

'Well that's brilliant isn't it? He won't mind about the baby as he's already made a commitment to you for the rest of your lives.'

'Freddie, those tests, they don't tell you how pregnant you are do they?'

'No, but it can't be much.'

'It's at least two months since my last period, maybe three.'

'So?'

'So, I don't know . . . I mean I can't be sure who the father is.' The tears had stopped now and the fear started. I had uttered words I never thought I would ever utter. Freddie had his arm round my shoulders; he squeezed my hand, looked at me.

'I think you better explain.'

'Remember at the beginning of December when George first came home?' Freddie was looking at me oddly, but he nodded. 'Well, remember I told you he tried to kiss me?' Again, he nodded. 'I lied.' I stood up and walked over to the window. 'He didn't try to kiss me, I let him. He initiated it, but I let him. Then I let him take me to bed, and I let him . . .' My body rocked with tears.

'You had sex with George?'

'Yes, and I still don't know why. That's why I didn't tell you, or tell anyone. I couldn't remember ever feeling so stupid, so used or so humiliated. I didn't do it because I wanted to, but I don't know why I did. I didn't stop him, I didn't protest. I let him and I even . . . oh shit, I even orgasmed.' I was crying too much to continue.

'Shit! Shit, Holly.' Freddie came to the window and hugged me.

'Afterwards I blocked it out. I almost convinced myself that I didn't do it. I felt wretched for Joe, how could I have done that to him? The week after, he told me he loved me and I told him I loved him and I did and I do. That wasn't a lie. And after I'd slept with George, he told me about Julia and his plan to marry her and how he just wanted to check that I wasn't the one for him. And then he said I wasn't. So I thought that he would marry her and I'd be with Joe and we'd be all right, no one need ever know about it.

'But then George came back and even then I blocked it out, I never admitted it to myself even when he told me I had to marry him. The court case and everything, I really thought he might sue me and I thought that maybe he'd win and it was all so horrible because all I wanted was to be thirty, to be grown up and to be in love and that all happened but then it all went wrong and now I'm pregnant and I don't know who the father is.'

Freddie looked as if he wanted to cry. 'Holly, that was back in the beginning of December. That would make you just over three months' pregnant. Surely you can't be that pregnant, you'd have noticed.'

'You think so? Everything adds up. I am on the pill and I was then, and I have no idea how it failed, but it did. I can't be sure how pregnant I am, and until I am sure I won't know if I can be sure about the father. I feel like such a slut.'

'You're not a slut.'

'How can you say that?'

'Because I know you, and I don't understand this weird bond you have with George, but I can almost understand that you would do what you did without meaning to.'

'No one else will understand though will they? Joe won't.'

'I have no idea.'

'What am I going to do?'

'You're going to have a relaxing bath, I'm going to make lunch, then we'll talk.'

'OK.'

I lay in the bath covered with soothing bubbles. I touched my stomach but it didn't feel different. My boobs had grown a bit I think, but not much. If anyone would have noticed that I guess it would have been Joe and he hadn't said anything. But then most men would know better than to draw their girlfriends' attention to the fact that she'd put on weight. I tried to pull myself together, as I seemed to have been doing for the last couple of months. Life was disrupting but this was way beyond that. I didn't know how I felt about the baby, because I didn't know whose it was. I needed to see a doctor, and I needed that doctor to tell me that I was only two months' pregnant because then the baby would be Joe's. If that were the case then I could put the whole sorry mess behind me and carry on as planned.

We'd have a shotgun wedding. Me resplendent in white with a huge bump and him looking smart in grey or in a morning suit or maybe black tie. A black-tie wedding would be nice. Everyone would look smart and no one would be wearing floral monstrosities. I guess I wouldn't be able to get drunk, but that would be a good thing because then I would remember the whole day perfectly. I would carry lilies, the ones that looked like trumpets because they always reminded me of winter. And I'd have a faux-fur-lined coat, and I'd look like the snow queen, although I am not sure if she was a goody or a baddy but I'd be a good snow queen. That was it, I could focus on the wedding because the baby would be Joe's and we'd be a family. We would be a family before we planned to be, but that didn't mean that we wouldn't be happy. I just knew we'd be really happy.

But, if my worst fears were confirmed and I had no idea who the father was, then would I feel differently. Should I have an abortion, get rid of it before it begins to disrupt my life. I pinched myself hard at thinking such a cruel thought, but then I tried to cut myself some slack. The only innocent party in all this was the baby. And I had no doubt that it was a baby. I even thought of it as so. I have never believed in the anti-abortionist lobby. I would rather a child wasn't brought into the world if it weren't going to be loved, but all of a sudden I knew without a shadow of a doubt that I wanted this baby. I couldn't comprehend not having it, with or without Joe as the father.

The jolt of maternal feelings I had threw me off balance. I wasn't sure if it was my age, or what, but I wanted this baby. It was the one thing I was sure of.

Finally when I emerged from the bathroom, Freddie had not only made lunch, but he'd written the proposal for our work project, the one I was supposed to be writing. I burst into tears again.

'Don't you like tuna?' he joked and I laughed. That was friendship, Freddie was friendship. George wasn't a friend any more and if I was going to keep my sanity I would have to fight him. I read the proposal while I ate the tuna sandwich and although I changed a couple of things, it was fine.

'One down, five to go,' I quipped.

'We don't have to,' Freddie said.

'We do. You've given up your day off to help your ailing boss, when you could have been plotting my downfall and stealing my job.'

'That would be too easy. You know how much I like a challenge, it'll be much harder for me to help you keep your job than get you fired.'

I laughed, properly, and put everything apart from work to the back of my mind. The afternoon was much better than the morning. Focusing on work was pure therapy and Freddie and I resumed our usual banter. It was only when all the work was finished that I remembered my condition. And the possible repercussions.

'I'm going to the doctor first thing Monday. I'll get there when the surgery opens and wait until someone sees me. Until I know for sure how pregnant I am I want to keep this quiet. Just the two of us. Not Joe, not anyone. OK?'

'OK. Remember before when I told you that you should tell Joe about George? How I told you the longer you kept it from him the worse it would be?' I nodded. 'Well, I agree with you this time. Don't tell Joe until you're sure. It's probably his, after all I'm sure you've had sex with him loads of times.'

I smiled. 'What are you doing tonight?'

'I've got a date but I can cancel if you want.'

'No, I need some sleep. It's been a confusing, horrible, scary day. I'm going to sleep now and if I wake later I'll watch TV or something.'

Freddie grabbed his coat and kissed me goodbye. 'If you need anything, please call, I mean it Hol, middle of the night, anytime. You call me.'

I had tears swimming in my eyes again as I kissed his cheek then watched him leave. I fell into my bed, determined to shut off my mind, and it was very obliging as I succumbed to sleep almost straight away.

# Chapter Sixteen

I was woken by the buzzer on Sunday morning, having slept for what seemed like days. I felt a bit disorientated as I pulled on my bathrobe and answered the intercom to Joe. I shuddered as I let him in, then I went to the bathroom to ensure that the pregnancy tests weren't lying around. I think Freddie must have disposed of them because there was no sign. I opened the door and found Joe waiting.

'What took you so long?' he asked, planting a kiss on my cheek.

'You woke me, I had to get my bathrobe,' I lied.

'Why bother, sleepy head, let's go back to bed.'

'No, let's go and get breakfast, I'm really hungry.' I believe I sounded normal, but I didn't feel it, and I didn't want to go to bed with Joe. There was an awful feeling of distaste at the idea of sex. That wasn't Joe's fault, but I felt dirty; angry even. If the baby was Joe's then I could put the other out of my mind, but if it wasn't, or if I wasn't sure . . . I shuddered at the thought.

'Are you all right?' Joe asked, as he followed me into my bedroom and watched me grab some clothes.

'I'm fine, just got a stomach ache,' I lied.

'Women's problems?' he asked.

'Something like that.'

I put on my jogging bottoms and a sweatshirt, an outfit that I wouldn't normally have worn with Joe here, but it was comfortable. I didn't know if it was wise to shoehorn myself into my jeans, I didn't know if it would hurt the baby. I was amazed at such thoughts as they crept into my head, like that, but I let them. I was half behaving like I was pleased to be pregnant, or at least accepting it, and half behaving like the person I was before yesterday happened. Not pregnant.

We walked to the café and I ordered a full breakfast and a cup of tea.

'I don't fancy coffee,' I explained, although I don't know why because Joe didn't bat an eyelid. I was on edge about the way I was behaving, which I don't think was surprising. Here I was harbouring this huge secret and the more I tried to behave normally, the more I thought I was behaving oddly. I felt rotten for lying, but more rotten for what had happened. I almost wanted to tell Joe, so he would punish me and make me feel even worse. It was all I deserved.

'Right,' he smiled at me.

'Did you have fun last night?' I asked.

'Yeah. I had to bite my tongue to stop telling them about us, but I managed. Anyway, they would have laughed at how soft I've become, so I had to put on my laddish front, you know leering at girls and stuff.'

'Never had you down as a leerer,' I smiled.

'We talked about beer and football.'

'Not women then?'

'Nah.' Joe was so cute; my stomach did a somersault as I looked at him. 'I tried to call you but I guess you were asleep. I missed you.'

'Come on Joe, stop being a girl. I was so tired. My body was catching up on the lack of sleep worrying about the court thing.'

'But you're OK?'

'I'm fine, darling.'

I hated it. As soon as I had woken up a bit, I realised that this was the first time I wished Joe wasn't with me. Ever since I had first met him I hadn't felt that, and now, I did. I knew it wasn't

Joe, it was the situation. Me being pregnant, not being able to tell him, not knowing if I would ever be able to tell him that it was his. I was terrified, and I hated lying. I was still hoping that when I went to the doctor I might find out that I wasn't pregnant, or that it was all a huge nightmare, just as I kept hoping that George would go away prior to the court hearing. But he didn't, just as I knew that this wouldn't. I remember thinking my twenties were turbulent, but they had nothing on my thirties, and I'd only been in them for a month.

How I got through the rest of the day, I don't know. Joe wanted to walk on the common after breakfast and I agreed. I thought the cold air and the exercise would do me good. I concentrated harder than ever on him while he talked, so I could answer him, without giving anything away. He wanted to talk about the wedding, he wanted to discuss the ring, he wanted to chat about details and I joined in as much as I could, because I didn't know if there would be a wedding, not now. I didn't know anything any more.

I put Joe off sex by claiming my stomach was hurting. He didn't protest, he was sympathetic which made me feel worse and he held me as we both went to sleep. I didn't have the ease I'd had on Saturday because everything I'd pushed away when I was with him came back at me with a vengeance. My mind was in turmoil and sleep was impossible. I lay there feeling his arms around me as if he was stopping me from falling, and I hoped, prayed, that those arms would always be there for me.

I was up before Joe on Monday morning, telling him I had an early meeting. I left him getting showered as I walked out of the flat and made my way to the doctors' surgery. As I sat in the waiting room, having been chastised for not having an appointment, and only being allowed to stay because I burst into tears, I felt very frightened and very alone. My mind flooded back to that day in the judge's chambers with George. He looked so

confident when he walked in, I wanted to hit him, but then when
he left he looked so dejected. I hadn't allowed myself to think of
him before now, but suddenly I felt sorry for him. He was alone;
he had lost the woman he claimed he loved, and soon I might be
in the same position with Joe. I tried to concentrate on a poster
about pregnancy to take my mind off how I felt, which was
incredibly stupid. Then I looked at a poster for chickenpox that
made me cry even more. I picked up a tattered old copy of *Bella*
and tried to read it through my tears but every story seemed too
sad. Shit, I hope that I don't have months of this ahead of me,
it's painful to be so horribly emotional. I really didn't feel
comfortable with it.

A voice shouted my name twice before I noticed and I
followed the signs to the doctor's room. I was pleased to see that
it was a female doctor, and I sat down determined not to cry.

'What seems to be the problem?' she asked. Her manner was
quite brusque, she reminded me more of a schoolteacher than a
doctor. In fact she looked a bit like one of my old teachers, her
head was covered in tight grey curls and she was wearing glasses.
She was probably in her late forties although I had no idea, she
was stern but at the same time motherly.

'I think I'm pregnant. I did two tests and they were both
positive.'

'I'd say you were then.'

'Don't you want to give me a test?'

'Not unless you really want one. Those pregnancy tests are
very accurate.'

'I was afraid of that.'

'You don't want the baby?'

I told her the whole story, every gory detail. I was waiting for
her to call me names and throw me out, or tell me I deserved
everything I got, but she softened towards me.

'There are ways of finding out. Firstly I will make you an
appointment for a scan. As you could be so far gone, I'll get you

a quick appointment. Then we need to look at options. Have you considered an abortion?'

'Isn't it too late?' I don't know why I didn't just say there was no way I wanted an abortion, but I didn't.

'Until we know how pregnant you are I can't say. I'll book the scan now.' I waited while she made a telephone call. Briefly I thought about an abortion. It would mean that Joe would never need know, if it turned out that it might be George's. It would also mean that George would never know. But was that what I wanted? I had no idea what I wanted.

She managed to get me an appointment for Thursday, and I took the details and thanked her as I left.

'If you need to talk about things, you can always talk to me,' she offered kindly. The second person who'd been nice to me about the pregnancy, and the second person who made me cry.

I went to work straight from the surgery and found Freddie immersed in the proposals we'd done over the weekend. He was holding the fort well and I knew he could do my job. I vowed to thank him by speaking to Francesca about putting us on an even keel. That way we could split into two teams, he could head one, me the other. He didn't give me any knowing looks, or ask any questions, which I was grateful for, until lunchtime when he coaxed me out of the office with the offer of a bowl of pasta.

'How did it go?' he asked as soon as we walked out of the door. I filled him in on everything and found that I couldn't stop talking.

'I don't want an abortion, I'm sure of that. I've got an appointment for a scan on Thursday.'

'That's one decision made, let's wait until Thursday before we make any more.'

'What about Joe? I can barely hold it together when he's there.'

'Say you've got a virus and would be better left alone.'

'Freddie I hate lying to him.'

'You did it before. Sorry, I didn't mean that to sound like a criticism.'

'You're right though, but I didn't think I was lying because I was in denial.' I managed a laugh.

'Somewhere in there is the old Holly.'

'I know, but I'd quite like her back.'

To say it was the worst week of my life would be a huge dramatic statement. One I've used before. The court case was the worst week of my life, the first time I was dumped, losing George to New York, oh you get lots of worst weeks. This one was up there though. If ever I chronicle the worst weeks, I will put that near the top of the list. I managed to get Joe to stay away by pleading illness, but he was so concerned he called me constantly which was almost worse than having him with me. All I wanted to do was burst into tears (hormones rather than stress), and have him hold me. I missed him like crazy. I also felt as if I was lying to everyone. My parents, my sister, Lisa, Francesca, all my team at work. I'm not sure why I felt like that, but I did. Lies seem so easy at first, but then they take on a life of their own; they breed, they take over. Christ, now on top of everything else I had become a drama queen.

Ironically, I got news of George that week. He had been in Devon and my mother had bumped into him. He asked after me and told her he'd be seeing me soon. That news unsettled me, as did everything else. I consoled myself with the thought that if George was safely in Devon he couldn't bother me, and he probably only said he would see me soon because that sounded polite. My mum said that she was civil to him and didn't mention the court case; she knew better than to rock the boat. For once, George wasn't my most immediate concern.

I tried to keep everything as much at arm's length as I could, until Thursday. My appointment was in the late afternoon so I went to work as normal and managed to keep my mind off things by speaking to clients and briefing my team. It was a busy time, with new clients, and existing ones, and I wondered briefly how I would manage with work *and* a baby. I can only concede that I wanted this baby now, that I had grown accustomed to the news, I just wanted it to be Joe's.

I left for the hospital, full of trepidation. This was it, the moment of truth when I'd know, one way or the other, how pregnant I was. I had written down the dates that I could be sure of.

I slept with George on 4 December. Two days later I slept with Joe. I had slept with Joe before the fourth as well. Despite the fact I was on the pill I couldn't remember my periods. Perhaps I bled a bit, I really didn't know. I don't know how I didn't know, but I didn't. On the journey to the hospital I kept thinking how stupid I was. Normally that wasn't the sort of thing you forgot, was it?

The hospital was horrible, I guess all of them are, but as I sat on the customary grey plastic chair in the waiting room the one thing that struck me was that I was surrounded by couples. Freddie had offered to come with me but there was too much going on at work and no one else knew. I could sense everyone looking at me and I thought that they thought I was a single mother, which I was; or maybe a slut, which I was. Perhaps I was being paranoid because they were all smiling. For most it was a happy occasion, for me, well, I still didn't know.

I am sure time takes on a different meaning when you're waiting for something. It seemed like hours rather than twenty minutes when the receptionist cheerfully announced my name. It was time for me to go and see my baby.

# Chapter Seventeen

It was official. I had no idea who the father of my baby was. I was over three months pregnant, and although I kept crying and saying that I didn't know how it could have taken me so long to realise, the doctor told me that my case wasn't unusual. Apparently when people aren't trying to get pregnant they can ignore the signs easily. I told him I didn't know who the father was and he was quite sympathetic. When we'd established that I was keeping the baby, he gave me all sorts of advice about diet and exercise and advised me to go back to my GP. I managed to pull myself together enough to ask about paternity testing. I knew that I didn't want the baby to be George's but the idea of a test terrified me. But I also knew that I would have to face it. Joe would want to know. I owed it to him.

'Ms Miller, we don't do DNA tests on unborn babies here.'

'Why not?' I wasn't sure if I was more relieved about not having the test, so I could keep the illusion that Joe was the father, or upset because it would mean that Joe wouldn't know and wouldn't be able to cope with not knowing. I didn't give a flying fig about George.

'It can harm the baby and there are ethical arguments as well. Some people will do them, usually private hospitals, but unless there is a sound medical reason, such as hereditary diseases, then it can't be done. You should wait until the baby is born.' He went on to talk about reproduction, but I switched off, I had never been any good at biology and had failed my GCSE. The important thing was, that I knew now that a test wasn't an option. So that was the end of that. As I left, clutching what was left of the doctor's tissues, I made my way home, determined that I would sort the whole mess out but having no idea how.

I hailed a taxi, unable to face the bus, and I spent the journey rehearsing the speech I was going to give to Joe. It wasn't good. Not only was I telling him that I was pregnant, I was telling him he might not be the father, which means I cheated on him, and not only that but I cheated on him with George. It wasn't even a question of him coming to terms with being a father the way I was coming to terms with being a mother; I couldn't even give him that. I could lie, and I know that's wrong but it did cross my mind. Although the dates were a bit close it was more likely to be him because I had sex with him more than I had sex with George. And it wasn't as if George was Chinese or anything, they had similar colouring. But I couldn't do that, and also, I knew that if George found out that I was pregnant, highly likely even if he stayed in Devon, he'd know what I knew and I would lie to him, but he isn't the type to let it go. Anyway, there had been too many lies already.

I was in a mess. A rubbish-tip of a mess. The sort where, when you tried to sort through it, something else would crop up. There was too much, it was too serious. I was thirty, pregnant, about to be un-engaged, and there wasn't anything I could do to stop it. I felt as if there was so much rubbish in my personal dump that I would never be able to clear a path, but I had to do something, because I was no longer alone. There was a baby who would be relying on me from now on.

I let myself into the front door and picked up my mail. When I walked into my flat, took off my coat and went to the kitchen to drink some water, I looked at the post. Most were bills but there was a letter, which gave me a start. The handwriting was George's. Before I opened it, I knew it was a bad omen.

I read the letter, and then I read it again. It was a single sheet of typed A4 paper, but it said an awful lot. He was sorry that the judge had been so quick to dismiss his claim, but felt that he probably made a mistake trying to go the legal route. However, and this was the however I had been dreading, he still believed he was right, and he needed to do something, anything, he could to make me see sense. Therefore, he was writing to tell me that he had hired the services of Cordelia Dickens, a PR, to work on his behalf towards getting me to marry him. This was the gist.

Cordelia Dickens is the worst kind of publicist. She takes people who aren't famous and makes them famous. Most of the time their fame is short-lived, but it makes her a living, a good living. She has worked for topless models, people who sleep with famous people, spurned wives, spurned husbands, anyone willing to bare their soul for the tabloids, or daytime TV. Cordelia boasts that she can make anyone famous, and she really can. Now it looked as if she was adding George and his marriage pact to her client list, which meant that I was, by default, going to be famous.

I sat down in the sitting room and tried to think about what she would do. I know PR but her type of PR is different to mine. We work with brands, products, not with people who don't have talent but want publicity at someone else's expense. However, it was pretty clear. She would circulate the story, the marriage-pact story, and George would appear as the heartbroken spurned lover, and I would appear as the bitch who reneged on a deal, leaving him with his broken heart. Oh, and Joe would be involved, and my work. It was almost too much to bear. Immediately I thought of the baby, the baby they didn't yet know about and I dialled George's mobile.

'George Conway,' he answered. Gradually I was growing to dislike everything about him, especially his voice. His voice got on my tits.

'It's Holly.'

'Ah, you got my letter?'

Yes you arrogant wanker. 'Yes I did. George, you can't do this.' My voice was calm, quiet. It was certainly not reflective of how I felt.

'Holly, you leave me no choice. I take it your feelings haven't changed? You're not prepared to honour our agreement?' How could he be serious when he asked that?

'George, we're talking about marriage. Something that is a symbol of love, it's not just an agreement, it's so much more than that.'

'I agree, which is why I have to do this. Holly we're meant to be together, and I can't let you make the biggest mistake of your life.'

'It is *my* life.'

'That's irrelevant.'

I was now seriously wound up. It was pure frustration. How do you reason with the unreasonable? 'I'm going to marry Joe, then you won't be able to do this.' It was an 'I'm going to stamp my foot' kind of statement. George laughed. I was furious.

'Fine, you marry Joe, the press will rip you to shreds. They'll know you're doing it because of the pact and that will cheapen the whole thing. It doesn't matter anyway because you still weren't married by the time you were thirty so the pact still stands. Holly, I have thought long and hard about this and this is the only way I can get you to come to your senses, the only thing left for me to do. I *will* marry you. You'll see.' He was so self-assured; he never got angry or upset any more. He was so calm which was even more frustrating. He was emotionless.

'You won't.' The second stamp of my foot.

'Is there anything else? I don't think there is any point to us having this conversation unless you have something new to say.' He sounded so cold for someone who wanted to marry me. I hung up. Then I went to throw up.

Afterwards I was seething. My eyes were narrowed, my fists clenched, steam belching from my nose, (well almost). I needed to lash out; I needed to hit someone. The anger grew inside me until I thought I would burst. I couldn't find the words to describe how I felt. I needed to kick something, or hit something or scream. I screamed – the easiest option. Out loud. It felt strange to scream being on my own, I thought of the neighbours and hoped they wouldn't call the police, but boy did I need to scream. As the scream rose in pitch I stopped feeling silly, it was at least some sort of release. I felt exhausted, but I felt better. My anger had subsided, only to be replaced with trepidation.

I was thirty, pregnant, about to be dumped, and soon to be exposed in the media as a heartbreaker. Could life get any better?

# Chapter Eighteen

---

*Courtship*

When the judge said that there was no way that the pact was enforceable and that Holly had no case to answer I felt drained. He droned on about the sanctity of marriage and refused to understand that that was all I wanted. He was archaic. A pathetic old goat with no idea or comprehension beyond his own. He said it was unorthodox to get someone to marry you this way. Of course it bloody was, but that was the only way I had. I left chambers and watched as Holly was surrounded by her friends. I recognised Freddie from her office, and I guessed the other man was her boyfriend. They were hugging her, kissing her and congratulating her. I couldn't believe she was so happy; I was her happiness, not them. I had an urge to go over to them, to grab her and shake her and ask her how she could be so stupid. Naturally I didn't, but I did feel a stab of jealousy that I could barely contain.

For the first time since I'd left New York I felt totally alone. Desolate. I had no real friends, no girlfriend, no one. Holly was the only person I had left. Although I had met with some of my old colleagues, and I had seen Clive a few times about the case, there was no one person here I could call a friend. I'd had drinks with some associates, dinner with a couple but it was purely on a professional basis. We discussed our careers, the latest legal developments, boring as hell if you're not a lawyer, pretty boring if you are one. We touched on our personal lives but only in the way that colleagues do.

I thought of my circle in New York. My tennis club friends, my workmates, my drinking buddies. I missed them. It's not very macho to admit to needing anyone, but I did. Isolation wasn't something I enjoyed, nor wanted. But isolated I was. I took one last look at Holly and turned to leave. As I walked out, a woman came up to me.

'George Conway?' she asked.

'Yes.' I looked at her. She was tall, young, not bad looking, I had no idea who she was, and I didn't care.

'My boss asked me to come here, Cordelia Dickens? I'm Sophie.' I looked at her blankly. 'She's a friend of Clive Parsons.'

'OK.'

'Can I take you for coffee?' she asked. I look back at the celebrating crowd, all laughing at my expense.

'Sure,' I agreed. At least it was better than being on my own.

We walked to the nearest coffee shop. She asked questions about the case, I told her. I requested a double espresso, she ordered a latte. She insisted on paying, then we sat down.

'The reason I'm here, rather than Cordelia, is that she didn't want anyone to recognise her.'

'Really? Is she famous then?' I was beginning to come to my senses and realised I had no idea what I was doing in a coffee shop with a stranger who kept going on about someone called Cordelia, who knew Clive. I tried to focus.

'Yes, she is rather well known, she's a publicist.'

'OK.' Still had no idea, but I wasn't sure I was that interested. I knew there was a point somewhere but I wished she'd get to it. I detested women who danced around rather than getting to the point; they really pissed me off.

'Clive told her your marriage agreement story.'

'It's not a story,' I snapped, willing her to get on with it.

'Sorry, I didn't mean it like that. He told her all about you, and your friend, and the court case and she wonders if you'd be interested in talking to her.'

'About what?'

'She could represent you.' Now I'd had enough. Cut the crap, my head screamed. I was finding it hard to be civil.

'No offence, Sophie, but could you possibly tell me exactly why you're here?'

'The law didn't work. She didn't know that of course, and sent me down to speak to you whether you were successful or not. If you were we could have put the story out to the press, but we can do the same anyway.' I still didn't understand; either I was dense or she was.

'Why would I want to do that?'

'Talk to Cordelia.' She handed me a card. 'Believe me, you'll be amazed at what she can do.' Sophie left me sitting there, with an empty cup and a business card.

I put the card in my wallet and forgot about it as I went back to my rented flat. I had signed a lease for a year, but for the first time, I thought I might go back to New York. To my friends, my job, and my life. The flat was still as depressing as the day I had moved in. An obvious bachelor pad with black leather and chrome everywhere; it was dated and characterless. It was much smaller than my New York apartment, which was lying empty, waiting for my return. I could just go straight back. All I had to do was forget Holly and get on with my life.

Just as I was in the middle of my debate the telephone rang.

'George, it's your mother.' I grimaced. She was angry with me and hadn't been holding back on her feelings.

'Hi.' I braced myself for a lecture.

'So, what happened?'

'I'm not going to court. The judge said there was no case to answer.' She would tell me that she told me so.

'I thought he might. George darling, that's why I tried to stop you.'

'Mum, remember when I was younger, you told me that if I wanted something badly enough I should pursue it relentlessly.'

'Did I?'

'Yes, you and Dad. I followed your advice all my life, I wanted to go travelling so I did, I wanted to study law so I did, I wanted a job with one of the top law firms, I got it, I wanted to go to New York. Now I want Holly.'

'But you can't compare a job to a person, George, emotions are involved.'

'Mum, I know all about emotions and I'm not in the mood for a lecture.'

'Fair enough. Just come and stay for a while.'

'You want me to come home?'

'I think it's the best thing.'

All of a sudden, it did feel like the best thing. 'Give me a day or so to sort things out and I'll see you.' I smiled as I put down the telephone.

I don't know why I didn't just jump into my hire car and go straight away. I didn't have anything to sort out. It's just that in talking to mum, and remembering that I always fought for what I wanted, I needed to think a bit. My thoughts returned to Julia. I left her, I didn't fight for her, which means that I didn't want her enough. But, Holly, well I was fighting for Holly, so I must want her. It was so clear, that I knew what I had to do. I would go home, but only after visiting Cordelia Dickens and ensuring that this time, as in all others, I got what I wanted. How I contemplated quitting, I don't know. That wasn't the way I did things.

The next morning I called the number on the card. Although I had stared at it in the coffee shop yesterday, I hadn't read it. Cordelia Dickens PR, it read in black embossed letters, *Cordelia Dickens, Managing Director*, it said underneath. Then it listed the address (Knightsbridge), and the telephone numbers. Interesting; I could beat Holly at her own game.

Sophie answered the telephone and asked me how I was,

which was welcome because no one else seemed to care. Then she put me on hold for a matter of seconds.

'George, how lovely of you to call,' a voice said. It was a strong, confident voice.

'I was interested in what you could offer,' I told her.

'I think I can help you, that's all. Why don't you come in and meet me for a chat?'

'I'm going away tomorrow.'

'Then come today. How does two o'clock suit you?'

'Perfect.' After all I had nothing left to lose.

I made my way to her offices, which were not as grand as the address suggested, but they were in a good location. She was in an old building, on the top floor. As I pressed the intercom I still had no idea what I was doing there. I stood in the tiny elevator and made my way to the top floor. I stepped out and immediately saw her sign on the wall in the tiny corridor. I walked into what I guessed was the reception and saw Sophie who smiled at me warmly. Then before she had to call her, Cordelia walked out. She looked like her voice, if that is possible. She was tall, slim with long highlighted blonde hair and a Pashmina wrapped around her shoulders. She was wearing a short red skirt and incredible high heels. Her legs were lithe and sexy and she looked like the sort of woman you didn't mess with. She also looked as if she would be filthy in bed. I shook my head at that thought and banished it, to concentrate on the meeting. There were only three rooms off reception. One housed four people, and was open-plan, one was Cordelia's office, it had her name on it and the third was a meeting room, which was where Cordelia led me.

'We're a small operation,' she explained. 'There are only six of us, which is how I like it. It's more personal this way.'

I sat down in the meeting room while Cordelia left to instruct Sophie to make us coffee. The room was small, it would only seat about six people comfortably, but the walls were adorned with framed tabloid headlines. Most had pictures of scantily clad women accompanying them. I wondered what I had walked into. Cordelia returned.

'I would have had the room set up but it was a bit last minute.'

'That's OK.' We smiled at each other for a few minutes.

'So, George, tell me your story.'

'I thought you already knew.'

'I want to hear it from you.' I told her everything. About Julia, about my childhood about recent events, about Holly. When I finished she was smiling.

'That's quite a story,' she said.

'It's not a happy one at the moment.' I smiled.

'Which is where I come in. If you want to get Holly, you have to fight for her.'

'That's what I thought, but then I thought maybe it would be better to leave it.'

'Tosh. Never give up, that's my motto.'

'That's mine too,' I smiled at her. I liked this woman.

'You need a friend, George, someone on your side. Therefore, what I propose is this.'

At first, what she outlined horrified me. It would mean putting myself into the public arena to publicise my story, but the more she talked the more it made sense.

'All I want is for Holly to realise we should be together,' I explained.

'And if she sees you in the press and on television saying that, she will.'

'What if it doesn't work? The way you describe it, I would have to gain public sympathy to get story coverage, which surely would alienate Holly further.'

'I'm buying you time George, making sure that she sees you everywhere and as you get the public sympathy, you'll get hers. You need to trust me.'

'The thing is I'm a lawyer, a successful one, I'm not sure my firm will approve.'

'Well, you can clear it with them if you like, or you can just do it. What's more important to you, Holly or your job?'

'Holly.'

'Then you've answered your own question. George you're not like most of my clients. They're all hungry for fame. I give them that and I could get you that. You could be famous for your story, but that's not our aim. Our aim is to publicise your plight so Holly will realise how much you care about her.'

'Yes, that's what I want.'

'Of course it is, and you look as if you could use someone on your side. By the time I've finished not only will Holly be in love with you but so will the entire nation.'

'You're sure about this?' I still harboured doubts.

'Trust me, I know what's best for you, which is why I contacted you.'

'I'm not sure.' I wasn't sure at all. There was a part of what she was saying that made perfect sense, but not all.

'George, I am not going to pressure you, that's what everyone else has been doing. I want to be your friend, I want to help, I think I can.'

'I need a friend.' My resolve was weakening.

'Of course you do, and that is exactly what I am going to be. Look George, I'll be honest with you. You can sign up as a client but you can back out any time you like. I'm not going to harm you, I'm going to help you. Help you get the woman you love to love you. I don't want to push you, so it's totally your decision.'

'You mean I could engage you to help but then if I changed my mind at any time we'd stop.'

'You have my word.'

'I need to be in control.'

'You will be. This is your show, George, and I am only going to do what you want me to do.' I pretty much knew that I needed this woman in my life.

'But why did you send Sophie? Why not come yourself?' As

I looked into Cordelia's eyes I found I did trust her. I just wanted to be sure.'

'I had a meeting I was unable to reschedule. George, think of me as your friend. When Clive told me your story, I knew I had to help. I think that you being still in love with your childhood sweetheart is wonderful.'

'Umm, we weren't exactly childhood sweethearts.'

'Of course you were. Now if we're going to work together to win you the girl then you have to trust my judgement on things. Firstly you were childhood sweethearts, secondly you knew you needed to part but you made a pact that you would one day get married, thirdly you come home from your exclusive life in New York to ask her to marry you before she turned thirty. Then she turns you down and your life is ripped apart. That's the story.'

It didn't sound exactly like what had happened, but it was based on fact. If I had been given my chance in court that would have been how I would have argued my case. I made my decision. Cordelia was on my side and she was my best bet.

'How much?'

'For what?' She acted coy but I knew she knew that I was with her. I think she knew it even before I walked into her office.

'Your services, how much do you charge?' She smiled as she told me that she would only take a percentage of what the media paid me. I was surprised because I hadn't thought about making money out of this, but she told me to relax. I would get paid, she'd take her percentage. She instructed Sophie to draw up a contract, which she did while we chatted about our strategy.

Cordelia was going to get me into one tabloid at first, and let the others pick up the trail. Then we would grant interviews to select press (Sunday supplements were a target as were *Hello!* and *OK!* magazines), then she would arrange a number of television appearances. She was honest with me and said that the story wouldn't last for ever, but would probably have a one month lifespan. That was enough time to get the public behind me and for Holly to realise how stupid she'd been. In one month's time I would have secured my future wife.

I signed the agreement, which was just a one-sided, straightforward, terms-of-business letter. Then I kissed Cordelia on the cheek knowing I was about to turn things around.

# Chapter Nineteen

It was as if someone had removed the millstone from around my neck. And I drove to Devon the following day with a much lighter heart. I had some time before the story broke and I was going to use it to persuade my parents I was doing the right thing. I couldn't believe how positive I felt; yesterday I was ready to give up, but now I felt I'd been given a whole new lease of life. Answers came from the unexpected, now I knew that fate had been at work. My life was going to work out the way I thought it would. I was certain of that.

Once again, I wasn't trying to hurt Holly, that wasn't my aim and Cordelia was the first person who understood that. Everyone was quick to berate me; to judge me. My parents, Holly, her friends, everyone, but they didn't understand my motives. Cordelia saw the truth and I was undeniably grateful for that.

I had never been lonely before. In New York my social life was always full, I barely had time to breathe, and before New York I had Holly. But now I found myself with no one. Loneliness is brutal. It takes away your confidence and leaves you doubting yourself. It's destructive. My heart goes out to anyone who is lonely.

The law had let me down; something I never believed would happen. The media was now my only hope. Either that or quit, and I'm not a quitter. Here I was, holding not only my future in my slightly clammy hands, but also Holly's. I loved Holly and there was no way I wasn't going to fight for her. Whatever it took.

She was behaving like a bitch, but that was all right because I knew as soon as she came to her senses that she would revert back to her old self. Delusion is something we all suffer from at one point or another in our lives. I was delusional about Julia. But now I could see the light, and soon, Holly would also.

As I approached my home town I felt as if I was finally coming home. I had never been homesick in New York, of course I had in the beginning, but not once I had really got my teeth into life there. It was a long time since I'd thought of the small town of Barnstaple as home. Now it was. Fleetingly I thought that maybe Holly and I could live here after we married, but then I tried to be sensible. Holly loved London, I'd lived in a city for years, and Barnstaple didn't offer the fiscal opportunities that a city would. No, we'd have a second home near the coast, in Woolacombe or maybe Croyde, but we would never live here. I think at this point, I still wanted to go back to New York. But if Holly had her heart set on staying in London then I could accept that.

My parents still lived in the same house that I'd lived in my whole life. It was a detached, four-bedroomed house on a hill in Newport, just outside Barnstaple. Very pretty and bigger than strictly necessary for the three of us; because it had always been the three of us. That house gave me my love of space. I remember when I first moved into student accommodation, I didn't think I would ever be able to cope with the lack of space. Then when I moved in with Holly, I found flat hunting just as depressing even with a salary. Most flats in London are not only minuscule but they make you feel hemmed in like living in a rabbit hutch. A very expensive hutch. When I moved to New York, my priority was space, but like London, money doesn't get you much. As soon as I started making decent money, I decided that most of it would go on getting a big apartment and I did. My apartment in NY is great and although it costs a lot more than it should, I feel like I can breathe there. Or I did until Julia's bombshell.

I parked in the drive, behind my father's old BMW, a car he'd had for ten years but refused to update. My father believed that things should be made to last, therefore you only buy one of them. Hence, everything in our house was pretty outdated. If something broke then reluctantly he would replace it, but if it wasn't broken then it stayed. It was a trait that my generation ill understood but one I found endearing. I picked my bag off the back seat of my hire car, wondering if it was a good time to buy something of my own. I was fed up of driving around in a hire car. I needed something a little bit more stylish. It was yet another decision that hinged on Holly. I didn't want to buy a car that she didn't like. Perhaps it would be more sensible to wait until we'd sorted things out. We could shop together. I smiled at the thought of that.

I opened the front door and announced myself. My mother called back that she was in the conservatory. I found her huddled over her sewing machine, making what looked like floral curtains. She looked up at me and I kissed her cheek. She looked older, something I hadn't noticed at Christmas. But then she was getting older. Weren't we all!

'What's that?' I enquired.

'Curtains for the spare room. I fancied a change.'

'Is this a bored retiree speaking?' My mother had been a teacher until retiring a couple of years ago to spend more time with my father. My father, who was an insurance broker retired at the same time to spend more time playing golf. To keep her busy, my mother changed the curtains in the house. I presumed that was what she did; being in New York, I didn't really get to see. I missed my parents and sometimes felt I missed big parts of their lives, maybe that was another positive aspect to living back in the UK. I'd get to see more of them. In New York, we'd talk over the phone, but I could never picture them both in retirement.

'Do you want tea?' she asked. I nodded. I knew that I had as long as it took to make the tea before she was going to give me a 'talk'. I shrugged and sat down. She would soon see that I was doing the right thing.

'Where's Dad?' I asked.

'Golf club as usual. But actually today I asked him to go. I wanted to talk to you.' So she wasn't even going to wait until the kettle boiled. 'I want to know what you think you're playing at.' She didn't sound cold exactly but she didn't sound full of love either. My mother had always doted on me. I was the boy who could do no wrong. So, I was having trouble accepting the disapproval in her voice and in her eyes.

'I am fulfilling my destiny.' I told her all about Cordelia.

'George, what on earth do you think this is going to achieve? I don't know what's behind this but whatever it is we need to sort it out. We need to sort you out. If you need a counsellor then we'll get you one, but you have to stop all this nonsense. I didn't approve when you tried to take Holly to court, and now you say you're going to make her realise what she means to you by splashing your story all over the papers. George, this isn't love.'

'But it is. It took rejection by Julia to make me realise that Holly is the one for me.'

'No, you're doing this *because* Julia rejected you. You don't want to be alone and for some insane reason you think Holly is the answer.'

'No. Holly *is* the answer. But not to my loneliness; to my happiness.' Our voices were raised and it hurt me to shout at her but I felt that her refusal to understand was deafness. I had to make her hear me.

'George, for a lawyer you can be quite poetic. Don't you see you've deluded yourself about all this. You were in love with

Julia, you raved about her, and when your father and I met her in New York we both thought you were perfect for each other. You know how much I adore Holly, but I have never thought you two would end up together; you're too different. I know Julia hurt you, I saw you straight afterwards, remember? Don't punish Holly for what Julia did to you.'

'Is that what you think I'm doing?'

'Yes. I think that you are lost and lonely having split up from the most important relationship of your life and I think that you have turned to the one person who has always been there for you. Because she's happy you're punishing her by trying to wreck her happiness, just as Julia wrecked yours.'

'I am not doing that! I *love* her!' I banged my fist on the conservatory table.

'George, when did you realise you were in love with Holly?'

'When I came home, after Julia and I split up.'

'Exactly.'

'Exactly what? You don't know everything about us you know.'

'What don't I know?'

'You don't know that when I came home to tell Holly about Julia, yes, I came to London especially to tell her that I was going to propose to Julia. Well, we slept together.'

'You . . . ?'

'Yes. For the first time ever and that put doubts in my mind about Julia. Holly and I were so good together but I wasn't expecting it; and she felt the same. So when I proposed to Julia, I was confused but when she turned me down I realised it was fate's way of telling me that Holly and I should be together.'

'I didn't know that.'

'It's a bit ungentlemanly to go around telling everyone that I've had sex with her. And certainly not the sort of thing I was going to discuss with my mother. The reason I am pursuing this is because Holly is scared of hurting Joe, so she won't admit her true feelings. I have to make her realise because otherwise, well otherwise doesn't bear thinking about.'

'It still doesn't add up. Maybe Holly sees you sleeping together as a mistake. Mistakes are easy to make.'

'No. She just doesn't know what to do.'

'George, I've been married to your father for thirty-three years. We met, we fell in love, we worked hard to stay together but there was never any doubt that we were supposed to be together. That's how you approach marriage. Not by trying to *make* someone marry you. Not even if you have slept together. There is no way you are being fair to Holly. If you are meant to be together then she'll realise for herself. If you loved her you'd step back and wait. You talk about fate, but it seems to me that fate is a convenience to you because you certainly don't trust it.'

'I am doing what I have to do. I hoped you'd understand.'

'George, you're my son and I love you, but this . . . no, I can't understand this. I can't understand how you can drag yourself, Holly, and both families through the press like this. It's not fair on anyone, least of all yourself.'

'You don't know. No one knows. I drove for hours to get your support, but you won't give it.' I felt tears prick my eyes. I was getting lonelier by the second. My parents had always been there for me, I couldn't understand why they were turning against me; that wasn't what parents did.

'No, George, we won't and I know your father feels the same way.' I glimpsed tears in my mum's eyes as I stood up, grabbed my unpacked bag and left the house. Until it was over and Holly agreed to be my wife I knew I wouldn't be back.

I tried not to be too upset as I drove away. My past was my future after all, it was all intrinsically linked. Temporarily, and I knew it was temporary, I seemed to have lost my grip on my past: my family and Holly, but I knew it would come back. It was my future, of that I was sure, so this was a mere blip.

# Chapter Twenty

———◆✕◆———

## *Gaining Weight*

I did what any self-respecting woman who was fast losing her self-respect would do. I panicked. I hadn't told Joe yet and he was concerned because he thought that after the whole court thing we could put George behind us. He thought that our relationship would be fun, and it wasn't; I wasn't. I hadn't broken the news to him yet that his life was about to suffer from a distinct lack of fun. *By the way Joe, George has hired a bitch woman PR to turn our lives into a media circus and at the same time I'm pregnant and I don't know who the father is. Oh, did I forget to tell you I had sex with George? Well I forgot to tell anyone so you're in good company.* I was really looking forward to that conversation.

Freddie persuaded me to talk to Francesca. After all, on top of everything I probably was going to be fired. George had given me warning of Cordelia's involvement in our lives, but had omitted to tell me when she would kick off, so we didn't have time to rest on our laurels. I tried to tell myself that no newspaper, magazine or television show would be interested in George's story, but then I knew if that were the case then Cordelia wouldn't have courted him in the first place. I was so angry, but not necessarily with George. He looked so dejected when he had left court and I was victorious. I watched him walk away having been rejected yet again, and I knew that he was vulnerable, hurt and probably a bit nuts, so I couldn't blame him for being persuaded by Cordelia that this was a good course of action. She was completely and utterly taking advantage of him. I would have slapped her if I had seen her, no, I would have kicked and slapped her and pulled her hair. My thoughts were stubbornly refusing to get into line.

I wanted to talk to my old friend George, believe it or not, I missed him more now than I had in the last five years. I wanted to see him and talk and get the impostor George banished. And I would say that I understood how awful he must feel and that he must still be heartbroken about Julia, which I know is a dreadful, awful affliction. When it happens you think you're going to die, or at best never recover. I would tell him that I'd support him and we'd work through it together as we used to when we were growing up. Because our friendship made us invincible; we could solve anything together.

But I would never say any of this because I didn't know where George was. A stupid drunken shag, a marriage pact, a court case and a pregnancy discovery later, I knew I would never find George again.

Francesca, Freddie and I sat in the boardroom. I was tired. As soon as I'd discovered I was pregnant I had become pregnant. I craved sleep all the time and I developed the habit of rubbing my stomach, with a natural urge to protect whoever was growing inside me. I was confounded by the desire to get used to being pregnant, but at the same time trying to avoid the mess that was my life. Because no matter which way you looked at it, it was a mess.

Retribution. I am not a totally bad person, but I am quick to judge and I can be a snob. Before, if anyone had talked about a woman who didn't know who the father of her baby was, I would have been quick to condemn. I would have immediately thought that the woman was a tart, probably a drunk, someone who was selfish and didn't think about the life she was bringing into the world. It certainly couldn't happen to a woman who was intelligent, who didn't open her legs for a half shandy and a packet of peanuts, and who was on the pill and took it religiously, i.e. it couldn't happen to me. But it had, and was this punishment? Was it because I had been judgemental? Was it because I was happy? Why was I, all of a sudden, being so irrational. I blamed it on my hormones. The other thing about being pregnant was that I had something to blame all of my emotions on.

'Can we just get this straight? You're three months' pregnant, and you don't know who the father is because you slept with George?' Francesca asked. I nodded. 'Which wouldn't be a problem if it weren't for the fact that George has hired Cordelia Dickens to be his PR and to get media coverage for his plight.' Again I nodded. 'The thing is that George knows he slept with you, but Joe doesn't know that. So no matter how we try to cover it up, unless we do the old trick of pretending you're not as pregnant as you are and saying you gave birth prematurely we're left with a number of problems.'

'I'm not doing that. I've lied enough and look where that's got me. I need to be honest. If I did pretend that I was less pregnant than I was, George wouldn't believe it. Can you imagine what will happen? He'll demand a test anyway and where will that leave us?' I was getting slightly hysterical. I didn't believe the situation could be any worse than it was, but it was sounding worse by the minute.

'Holly, calm down, we have to look at the whole picture before we can decide what to do,' Freddie said, sensibly.

'Firstly, let's look at the media side of things. There is always the possibility that the story won't be picked up.' Optimism was something I had already said goodbye to, so that didn't soothe me.

'Francesca, you know as well as I do that that is highly unlikely, Cordelia will twist it until someone picks it up, you know that.'

'But is it enduring?'

'Probably not as it is, but with the baby twist, that gives it another six months life.'

'OK, so damage limitation. You have to tell Joe about the baby and about sleeping with George. I know that that is an awful prospect but you need to tell him straight away.'

'But I'll lose him.'

'The only way you can guarantee not losing Joe is if you get rid of the baby and say that George is lying when he tells the world he slept with you.' Francesca sounded harsh, but then she normally did. I still burst into tears.

'Francesca, don't be so hard on her, this isn't easy,' Freddie pleaded, as I sobbed.

'I'm not trying to be hard, I am trying to be practical. I'm sorry if I sound sharp, but life is going to get tough.'

'I know you're right, but maybe we could be a bit gentler with her?'

'Freddie do you think the press are going to be gentle once this gets out? If we're going to implement some damage limitation then I don't think we need to do it by being fluffy.'

I sobbed louder, which was awful because I sounded like a silly girl. I felt as if they were talking about me rather than to me, which they were because I had turned into a snivelling idiot who had probably lost her marbles. I pulled myself loosely together.

'You're right. Freddie, Francesca is right. I should harden myself but I think it's hormonal. All this crying and stuff. Anyway, I would just like to say that I am not getting rid of the baby. I know that would be the easiest option, but not one I can entertain. I already love it, even though it's partly responsible for my life becoming anything but a picnic. So, can we go from there?' I was astounded by my composure, and by the surprised looks on Freddie and Francesca's faces, so were they.

'Glad we've established that. Firstly you need to talk to Joe. The sooner the better. We don't want him learning of this through the newspapers. Freddie, you need to call the tabloids and find out if any have been offered the story and if so when they're planning on running it. The only thing I can think of is to offer Holly's side to whoever isn't running the story, but if we do that we're going to have to predict what George, or Cordelia, will be saying. The other option is to ignore it and hope it goes away, which I favour. If we put our side of the story across in the media, that gives ample opportunity for us to be criticised. It will be hell but I probably would vote for maintaining a digni-fied silence at first and then offering to put your side across to a chosen publication. What do you think?'

'I know the media, if I put my side across they'll probably twist everything. Also, although I can pretty much guess what George is going to say, I would rather wait and see. With the pregnancy I don't feel that I have a strong defence and all I want to do is to keep that from him for as long as possible.'

'Which means that you are going to hibernate for a while,' Francesca said.

'What? I can't do that. What about work?'

'You'll work from home. And also, when I've found out when the story is breaking, then you will need to call our clients.'

I looked at her. 'They'll freak.'

'No they won't, not if we explain things to them properly. Holly I am not worried about our clients leaving us over this, anyway I am certain that won't happen, but only if we're honest with them in the first place.' Francesca looked serious, the situ-ation was serious but at least she hadn't fired me. I probably would have fired me.

The thought of calling all my clients filled me with dread. Actually the thought of talking to Joe did as well. There was a lot of dread about. My increasing body weight was dread. However, I knew that I had to do it. Both things.

'Can we work out an official line?'

'What for Joe, or for your clients?' Freddie quipped.

'Both,' I replied.

Francesca said I was to tell our clients the story from my point of view. It didn't sound too bad in the retelling, or should I say in our interpretation. I was going to warn them that George would be portraying me in the worst light he could, whilst protesting my innocence. It was complicated. I was going to tell them that George was in the grip of madness and believed we should enforce a marriage pact made ten years earlier. Then warn them that he would probably tell of an incident that passed between us, when we both had too much to drink. I was to assure them that the whole press invasion, if it were to come to that, was a highly exaggerated chain of events. I wouldn't tell them about the pregnancy just yet, as we were still keeping it under wraps but I would promise them that whatever happened, their interests would be looked after as well as ever. I had to persuade them to stick with us because I knew, that although Francesca was fantastically supportive, if I lost clients over this then I wouldn't have a job.

I would tell them that any press invasion would not affect my professional life and I would explain that Freddie and Francesca would personally be ensuring that. Finally I would beg them to stay, if necessary. I might have to take the same line with Joe.

'Can you take a paternity test now?' Francesca asked. I hadn't told them about what the doctor said, although I wasn't sure why.

'No, I've been told it's dangerous for the baby. I could lose it and anyway apparently there are some ethical issues as well. My gynaecologist said I would have to wait until after the birth.'

'That's bad.' Freddie looked upset.

I just shook my head, but deep down I was relieved. How can I explain? I didn't want the baby to be George's. I couldn't cope with what that would mean for the future. For a start it would mean no more Joe, although I think that was going to be the case anyway. It was too confusing and too complicated and even if I could have a test, I didn't want to find out that the baby was

George's and the way my luck was going, I believed a paternity test would confirm my worst fears.

'How will Joe feel about that?' Francesca asked.

'To be honest, I think that Joe is going to be upset about the fact I slept with another guy and that will preoccupy his thoughts first of all. Then, he'll want to know, but not at the expense of the baby's health, although I am not sure I can say the same for George. Shit, I can just imagine George turning up with some horrible, private doctor who will do anything for money and demanding we take a test and then hurting my baby.' This scene became so vivid in my thoughts that I became slightly hysterical.

'OK, I vote we keep the baby issue from the press, and from George, for as long as possible. You're barely showing any signs of pregnancy, so no one would guess.' Francesca tried to re-assure me, but I wasn't convinced.

'But I have hospital appointments and antenatal and stuff like that. Actually I have no idea what I have to do but I will have to go out.'

'Just wear baggy clothes. I think the best thing is to hope that the press interest dies down before anyone finds out about the baby.'

'Francesca, I think I should resign.' My stomach was knotted and I just couldn't see how any of this could make any sense to anyone: clients, Joe or me.

'No way. You have worked hard and successfully for my company and now you need this job more than ever. I'm going to set you up to work from home. Freddie will run the office side of things and we'll hire other people if we need them. After all it is time we expanded the business.' I loved the way Francesca was making out I was almost doing her a favour.

'I'm worried about my clients, they'll probably go elsewhere.' In my mind, the conversation with my clients had gone badly: 'I'm sorry Holly but we can't have someone as loose as you working for us, especially as you're in the media. We have reputations to uphold and your actions will reflect on us adversely. Therefore we are rescinding our account with Francesca Williams PR, effective immediately.' They would all say exactly the same.

'No they won't. None of this questions your professional judgement. What we'll do is convince them that we'll plug them whenever we can. It's all publicity after all. You've got a pretty good relationship with them, and they value you, so you know that they'll be fine. We just need to ensure that we explain the situation and they don't find out from anyone else. Call them when Freddie has found out when the story is going to break, not before. And Holly, go home. Take the laptop, I'll send someone over to install the e-mail network, another phone line and anything else necessary. Is that all right?'

'Francesca thank you so much. I don't know how I'm going to get through this but your support and Freddie's means the world to me.' Fresh tears streamed down my flushed cheeks.

'Shit, you can tell she's hormonal,' Freddie said. Francesca smiled.

'When the story breaks, we'll issue a press release giving our side. We know the media, and we know it has the attention span of a gnat. We'll ride the short storm and then one day we'll look back and laugh. Well, maybe we will.' Francesca squeezed my hand. She should have been sainted for letting me stay on.

Dixie booked me a cab and I went home feeling slightly better. At least I had a job, I wasn't going to be a 'single mother on social' cliché. Which I know sounds snobby, but at least I could afford my child, even though it hadn't been planned. If I needed to salvage something from this, it was a tiny vestige of pride. That gave it to me. But what I needed to to do next would take it away.

I got home and changed out of my office clothes into a pair of grey exercise leggings and a hooded sweatshirt. Then I set my laptop up on the small wooden dining table that sat behind my sofa in the living room. I grabbed a faux suede cushion from the sofa and wedged it behind me on the wooden chair. My new office. I inserted the lead into the laptop then plugged it into the wall. I stopped there, there was no point in switching it on because I couldn't focus on work and besides I didn't know what work I should be doing. Instead, I rooted around in a drawer until I found a pen and pad, then I sat back into the cushion and started writing a list.

Lists, I find, give clarity and focus. I also believe that they give me a semblance of control. The first part of my list consisted of everyone I needed to tell about the situation: Joe, my parents (who I was still seeing at the weekend, although not to announce my engagement any more but to tell them that their daughter was knocked up and didn't know who the father was). At this point my list broke down as I broke down. My actions would hurt so many people. I stopped thinking about myself for a moment and thought of others. When I returned to the list, I wrote my sister's name, and Lisa's. Actually Lisa wasn't someone I would worry about, but I knew Imogen would be full of disapproval. Imogen had always been an angel. An angel that liked to tell her younger sister what to do.

I thought for a second how much easier I could make this by having an abortion. It was late, I knew that, and when the doctor had mentioned it I fobbed him off. Probably because I worried that if I thought about it for more than a second it might be a good option, or at least an easy one. But I couldn't. I had never been broody, but all of a sudden I felt totally maternal. There was one overriding certainty in the whole mess, and that was that as soon as I found out I was pregnant I wanted the baby. When my thoughts were just tuned on that, I felt euphoric. When they strayed to the practical side of my life, I was desolate.

Time seemed to pass so slowly. I was at home by lunchtime, and although it seemed like hours it was only minutes. I had never felt such loneliness as I did now. There was only one thing for it. I had over five hours to get through before Joe was coming round; the only person I could talk to was my baby.

I didn't know if it was a bit too soon to be chatting to my unborn child, but I felt comfortable with the thought. It was a bit weird at first, not knowing what to say, but I soon got the hang of it.

'Hello, little bump. I saw you yesterday, and you looked a bit like a new potato but I know that you are going to be beautiful.' I felt very emotional. I was talking to someone that I didn't know, but who would soon take over my life. 'I haven't given you the best start that I could, but I promise you that I will get better. I didn't mean to hurt you, I'd never intentionally hurt you. I am afraid that your welcome to the world might be in the public eye a bit. I will do everything to avoid it, but if that's the case then we will deal with it. I want to tell you about your father, but all I can say is that it's one of two men; one I love deeply as a lover and the other I used to love deeply as a friend. I hope and pray that Joe is your father because he's so wonderful and if you can be a bit like him, then you will be very special. I will bring you up the best I can.' I wiped away the tears.

'But I have got lots of love and you'll get it all, and more, and whatever happens I will protect you. Hopefully I will give you a good life and I promise that although I might be very sad at the moment I will laugh a lot, because laughter is so important. Your maternal grandparents will love you too. I don't know if you'll ever meet your other grandparents, it scares me to think about that, so I am sorry, but I will sort it out when you come into the world properly. And in the meantime I promise to look after myself, which means that I'll take care of you.' The tears streaming down my face stopped me in my tracks, then the buzzer went.

Not expecting anyone, I answered the intercom to be told there was a delivery for me. I waited at the open door, and was presented with a basket of things. It was from Francesca. In the basket were a whole load of vitamin supplements and a book on pregnancy by Dr Miriam Stoppard. The courier looked terrified as I sobbed while signing his docket.

I think it was a relief that I had a package to focus on, because I had really run out of conversation with my belly. Then I did what I always did when I felt low; I tucked myself into bed and read. This time I was reading about pregnancy.

I could have skipped quite a lot, like the section on deciding to conceive and how to conceive, but I read it. I wanted to devour every word. I was still reading it when the buzzer went again. I looked outside, it was dark. I then realised that the buzzer was telling me Joe was here.

I knew I looked a mess, but there was nothing I could do or wanted to do about that. This wasn't the sort of conversation when you needed to look glamorous. It wasn't the sort of conversation you normally had, full stop. As I watched Joe appear from the stairs, I looked at him long and hard because I knew that I might need to memorise his beautiful face in case I didn't get to see it again.

So much can change in the space of a few days. I had gone from being engaged to the man I loved, to here. With the days' tears still etched into my face I saw him look at me questioningly, I let him into the flat, sat him down with a glass of wine and prepared to answer his questions. He was wearing a black V-necked jumper over a pair of black Prada trousers. Joe had more designer clothes than I had, and I used to tease him about that. Tease him about how scary it was for a girl to be worse dressed than her man most of the time. I wondered if I ever would again. If there would be any more of that intimate familiarity. His hair was shorter than normal, he must have just had it cut. Would I see it grow longer? I resisted the urge to touch it.

'Holly, what's wrong?' He sat on the sofa and drank his wine. At that moment I would have loved a glass, but resisted the temptation. I was drinkless. He pulled out his cigarettes and I went to get him an ashtray. Again, I had the urge to light up, more because I knew it might calm the storm that was raging in my stomach. I hoped my baby wasn't going to get sea-sick.

'Joe, you have to listen to me. I need to tell you something and I need you to promise to listen to every word I say. This might be the most important conversation of our lives.'

'Shit Hol, you sound so dramatic.' He didn't know the half of it.

Then he did. My words tumbled out, but they carried the whole truth. I left nothing out, my honesty was brutal. When I had finished I saw that his eyes were moist.

'You slept with George?'

'Yes.'

'When we argued?'

'Yes.'

'And now . . . you're pregnant?'

'Yes, Joe.'

'And you can't be sure who the father is?'

'Not without tests.' I was struggling, the tears that wouldn't go away were waiting to return and I was feeling sick and dizzy. It was all I could manage.

'And George is going to the papers with the marriage-pact story.'

'Looks that way.'

'And he doesn't know you're pregnant.'

'No. But I have a feeling I can't keep it from him for ever.'

'You know that when he finds out he'll hound you even more. He'll be convinced that it's his baby and he'll use it to try to get you to marry him.'

'I know.'

'I want a test,' he said, suddenly. I looked at him and a pang of love shot through me.

'I can't, it might harm the baby, or even bring on a miscarriage. We can't find out until it's born. Joe, what do you want to do?'

'I don't know. I have no idea. I never in a million years imagined that I would be having this conversation with you.'

'Me either.'

'I need to leave now.'

'Of course you do.' We stared at each other for as long as we could bear it, and then we both turned away. He stood up and very hesitantly he walked out of the flat. He faltered as if his feet might change their minds and turn around; but he never looked back at me, not once.

When he had gone, my sobs returned. I was frustrated with all my tears but feared that they would soon have squatters rights, they spent so much time on me. What I needed was a laugh or two, and that meant it was time to call Lisa. If she couldn't cheer me up, then no one would.

When she heard my voice begging her to come over she dropped everything. Lisa isn't big on questions which is another reason why she was so perfect. I called Freddie and told him about Joe, or as much as I could bear and he told me that he was making progress with the tabloids but didn't have anything confirmed yet. Then I called Francesca and thanked her for the parcel and she seemed to understand that I didn't want to talk further. Then I read Miriam's view on pregnancy and alcohol.

Reading it, I knew I was being punished. Although it implied that a little (very little) alcohol would not be harmful, it was just ambiguous enough for me to make the decision: booze was out. For the duration of my pregnancy anyway. You see, I felt guilty because I had been drinking during the first three months, and if I'd known I was pregnant then I wouldn't have done, so if anything is wrong with my baby I will be to blame totally. It struck me then how hard it was; forget George, forget Joe, this pregnancy was hard enough.

There was so much to know; when I had gone to my doctor I had been in shock. When I saw the gynaecologist I was definitely in shock. Then I had to tell people, so that occupied my thoughts, but now it hit me: pregnancy is terrifying. How do you protect the baby when it's inside? How do I know that I am doing the best for it? I picked up the book and started to read.

I was learning about anxiety and trying to ignore the section on the father's role. Yeah the father's role. A quick roll and then off he goes. Bastard. Whoever it was. I was bloody angry. Not sure why, but I was. It was better than crying I guess, although then I considered that anger might be bad for the baby. I tried to find 'anger' in the index but it wasn't there so I contented myself with reading about ankle exercises. Then the buzzer went. Relieved I went to answer it. Any longer on my own and I would be certifiable.

Lisa came to greet me with a big kiss. She had no idea about the scene that awaited her. Actually, as soon as she bounded into the sitting room and saw the book she realised.

'Fuck are you pregnant?'

'Yes.'

'That's the crisis meeting you called with me?'

'Yes, that and the fact that George has hired a PR and is going to the papers with the story of me refusing to marry him despite the marriage pact.'

'He's what?'

'Oh and I don't know who the father of my baby is because I omitted to tell you but I shagged George when he came home in early December.' Lisa looked at me, her mouth opening and closing like a very pretty goldfish. Then she slumped into the sofa.

'I need a drink.' I went to pour her a glass of wine. There was plenty left from the bottle I had opened for Joe's brief visit. When I walked back into the sitting room she was hanging out of the window.

'What are you doing?'

'Having a cigarette. I don't want to pollute the baby.'

'That's sweet.'

'Yeah, but I need to smoke. You can't give me all that news and not expect me to smoke.'

'I don't care if you smoke, you can come in and just pull a chair up to the window if you want. I've been round Joe for three months, and you know how much he smokes. Oh shit, I hope him smoking hasn't harmed the baby. Come to think of it, George and I smoked the night it might have been conceived. You don't think it's going to be stunted do you?'

'Holly you're pregnant not insane. You're not insane are you?'

'I feel it. I found out almost straight after going to court that I was pregnant. Freddie guessed; it hadn't even entered my mind. Then I had to admit that I'd slept with George. Oh, and before that, Joe asked me to marry him, I didn't tell you that because we were going to see my parents this weekend to tell them first. Then I went for a scan, organised quickly because the doctor thought I might be quite pregnant and I couldn't remember my last period. Then my worst fears were confirmed: over three months pregnant. Either Joe or George could be the father.' I paused and took a deep breath. 'Then before I could do anything, I got a letter from George saying he's hired Cordelia Dickens to be his PR and they're going to the papers to make me see sense. So today Francesca and Freddie spent the morning trying to decide what to do. Then I told Joe about the baby and he left abruptly without talking about whether he wanted a spring or summer wedding and now you're here.'

'It's been a shit few days then.' I couldn't help laughing at her evaluation.

'You could say that.'

I made myself a cup of tea while Lisa drank, smoked and tried to digest my news. When I took my tea in, she was the picture of serenity again.

'Here's how I see it. Francesca will look after the press. Well her and Freddie will. If you get some publicity then don't worry.

It'll all blow over. People have far worse stories coming out than the fact you won't marry him. Then this is how I would deal with the baby. Maintain to George that it's Joe's. If he doesn't believe you then refuse a test. As long as you refuse a test then he can't prove he's the father. He might take you to court again to get a test but my guess is he won't, because there will be a little doubt in his mind if he is the father, and if he has the test and it is Joe's then his story has lost its oomph. Following me?'

I nodded, amazed. Lisa was not only addressing my problem rather than changing the subject, but she was addressing it well.

'Now your parents will support you as will I. Joe will come round, leave him alone to get over the initial shock, but I would write him a letter, telling him you love him. In the meantime I will be your birthing partner or whatever they call it and we'll go to antenatal or whatever they call it.'

'Wow Lis, what's come over you?'

'What do you mean?'

'You're being so practical.'

'I am, oh fantastic. I've been trying.'

Relieved of a conversation that didn't involve me I decided to pursue this. 'What do you mean?'

'Well I thought that it was time I did something.'

'Why?'

'Well you know, my career is all but over. I get some work but the other day I was offered an assignment to pose as a married woman who needed to borrow money so her and her husband could extend the house because they have too many kids. I'm thirty-five, I don't feel like a harassed mother of three. Anyway I turned it down and decided that if I'm over the hill in the modelling world I ought to do something else. You see, Max's career is on the up and up, whereas in the early days it was the other way round, so it feels a bit weird. I guess I was feeling a bit put out by the fact that I'm not in demand and he is, but I love him to bits so I wasn't going to let it spoil things. Or not since I've thought about it anyway.'

'When did you get so sensible?' I was a little worried that Lisa had turned into someone like me.

'Oh, not really sensible. Anyway I decided that I was going to give up flogging my dead career and help Max with his. And he is really pleased, you know men like to have the little woman flocking round them. And then I thought we might have a baby, but now I don't have to worry about what it'll be like to be fat, I can see how you get on before I decide.' I was relieved to see she hadn't changed that much.

'OK, Lisa, and if I can do fat successfully, then you can try it.'

'Exactly.'

'My main problem now is how to get Joe to forgive me and how to get George out of my life while ensuring that my baby is all right.'

'You need a fucking miracle.'

'Thanks Lis, have another drink.' Although it had been one of the longest and most traumatic days of my life, I went to bed with a hint of a smile on my lips.

# Chapter Twenty-one

I borrowed Lisa's BMW for the trip to my parents' house, because Joe was supposed to be driving us and I didn't want to sit on a train. I hadn't yet told my parents that Joe wasn't coming, so I thought that if I turned up needing a lift from the train station I'd have to answer questions before I was ready. I listened to Classic FM on the journey, deciding that it would be a comfort to me and the baby. I also thought that if babies were aware of their surroundings whilst in the womb then my baby would come out cultured.

I had slept soundly the night before, but that wasn't surprising because I was exhausted. I was afraid that my broken heart might keep me awake but it didn't. I was also afraid of bad dreams about what lay ahead, but if I did dream I didn't remember. I awoke, showered and dressed and then packed a small weekend bag for my trip. I then went to a local card shop where I chose a blank card, with a picture of a boat on it, to send to Joe. I have no idea why I chose that card but I knew how the little boat, all alone on the sea, felt. I went home and wrote to him from the heart. A short, but simple note telling him I was sorry, and saying I loved him. It didn't seem enough, but then I knew that it would never seem enough. My thoughts flicked to George. I wondered if he knew the damage he'd already caused. Would he put a stop to it? I guessed the answer was no. George had become a man on a mission, and there was no way he could be stopped. Unless I hired a hitman. But then I didn't want my baby to be born in prison and knowing my luck, I would be caught. And I didn't know any hitmen anyway so it was a bit of an unrealistic idea.

As I drove, I tried to enjoy the scenery. The A303 which went past Stonehenge offered some lovely views, but all I could think was that I was going to disappoint my family at the end of that journey and there is nothing lovely about that. I just concentrated on the road, and on not driving too fast or putting myself and the baby at risk. As I don't drive very often I thought that maybe I would have been more sensible to take the train, but then I wouldn't have had the time alone to gain my composure. I really needed that.

As soon as I parked my car outside our house, just on the outskirts of Barnstaple, my mum came out to greet me. She looked so excited, but then her face fell.

'You're on your own?' My mother had never been the type of mother to hassle me about relationships but I knew she was looking forward to meeting Joe. I had raved about him so much.

'Yes. I need to talk to you and Dad, and Imogen, is she around?'

'Imogen's here. We all are. We were all waiting to meet Joe.' She sounded upset and my heart went out to her. This was only the beginning.

'Shall we go in? I've got something to tell you.' Not surprisingly my mother looked puzzled as we walked in, and knowing how she worried I decided to tell them everything straight out. I relayed the now familiar story, from George's first appearance back in my life until today. My father looked at his shoes, my sister looked at my mother, my mother looked at me. I looked at my stomach (it was a sympathy tactic. Don't shout here's your grandchild, sort of thing). Imogen was the first to regain composure.

'You don't know who the father is and it's about to be splashed over the press. Oh God, what's Jack going to say? He's famous, he has a reputation to maintain, as soon as they discover you're his sister-in-law he'll be tarnished.' Imogen was more hysterical than I had been when I found out.

'Immi, they don't know about the baby yet. Hopefully the media coverage will die down before anyone finds out. And if it doesn't then I am quite happy for you and Jack to issue a press release condemning my actions if it'll help save his career.'

'This isn't about Jack, or Immi, or us. It's about you, Holly.' My father spoke.

'But it affects us all,' Imogen repeated. My sister had been known to throw the odd tantrum, so I wasn't too surprised by her outburst.

'Are you all right Holly?' My dad asked and on cue I burst into tears.

'I am so, so sorry. I made a mistake, a big mistake, and now I am paying the price but I don't want anyone else to suffer. It's enough that Joe's left me and will never be back, and George is insisting we should get married; without the fact that my baby not only won't have a father, but won't know who his father is. And sorry seems totally inadequate. I don't know, Daddy, I don't know what to do.'

'You don't have to do anything, Holly, it was a mistake, but you can't take it back. We love you and will support you. Can't you come and live here for a while?'

'No, not with George's parents living nearby. Besides, I have to keep working, after all someone has to support the baby, and Francesca is being fantastic. I'm going to work from home for a while. We'll issue a press release telling our side of the story in response to George. Other than that we have to play it by ear. You know, this has been a complete emotional upheaval, but I'm OK, I really am. I'm a little scared, and upset and heartbroken and angry, but I'm OK.'

'Sounds like it. Holly, you're not to be alone. I'm going to organise a roster of people to take care of you.' It was the first time my mother spoke. She spoke with the efficiency of someone used to organising the church flower rota.

'I can't have someone with me, I'll be fine.'

'If the press story takes off you won't. Look how they were with Princess Diana.'

'Mum, it's completely different.'

'Even so, they might hound you.'

'I don't understand how this story can be that interesting,' I protested.

'Right, I'm going to call Lisa and have her stay with you when you go back. She can take week one. Then your father and I will come up, we need a holiday. Then Imogen, you can take a week. Then we'll review things. I am not having my daughter left on her own while she's carrying my grandchild, and is also an object of press intrusion.'

'We don't know if the press will be intrusive,' I protested.

'Well if they are then we have a plan, if they're not then at least you'll have support through your pregnancy. Any objections.'

'I'll do it because you're my sister, but I am bloody angry with you,' Imogen said.

'Imogen, I hardly think Holly needs this right now,' my father said.

'That's right, wrap her in cotton wool. If only she'd kept her legs shut—'

'Imogen!' my father exclaimed. He rarely raised his voice. I had to suppress an unexplainable desire to laugh.

'Daddy, she's right. Half this problem is the fact that George has some preposterous idea about us being made for each other, the other half is my fault. I understand Imogen's anger.'

'Even so, it's not going to help. Now I'm going to make some tea.' My mother closed the conversation.

It hadn't been as painful as I had feared. Actually, apart from Joe, none of it had been as bad as I'd imagined. My parents faces showed no signs of the disappointment I had anticipated.

Francesca hadn't been angry with me like I was sure she would be. I was guilty of underestimating people; even Lisa had reacted differently to how I'd expected.

I spent the rest of the weekend with my parents (Imogen was sulking, which surprised me because she was never usually angry with me for long). My mother plied me with fruit and vegetables, my father told tales of when my mother was preg-nant, I cried a lot, not just because I was sad, but because I was happy too.

Freddie called my mobile on Saturday evening to tell me that the story had been picked up by the *Daily News* and was being run on Monday. He had been told it would be on page thirteen, definitely unlucky for me. The reality hit hard.

Although with Cordelia behind it, we had expected press coverage; now it had happened. The *Daily News* was probably the fourth biggest tabloid, and page thirteen wasn't exactly a priority page; more of a filler. Freddie calmed me down and said that the two biggest tabloids had, it seemed both turned down the story for now, which meant that we could perhaps get one of them to print my response to his allegations. The *Daily News* was also known for being as downmarket as a tabloid could be; there was a small amount of comfort in that. The situation was containable. So Freddie said, anyway, and I needed to believe him.

I returned to London on Sunday evening, bracing myself for whatever happened next. There were a few messages on my answerphone but only one I cared about. It was from Joe.

I listened to it over and over trying to discern from his voice what he wanted because I couldn't from his words. All he said was that he wanted me to call him. I wondered why he hadn't tried my mobile, but the fact he had called was enough. I took a deep breath and dialled the number that I knew so well.

'Hello.' His voice still made me weak at the knees.

'It's Holly.' There was a silence that would break all silences. I didn't want to say anything in case I said the wrong thing. Finally, he spoke again.

'Why?'

'Why what?'

'Why did you sleep with George?' He asked me the one thing I couldn't answer.

'I don't know, I really don't, Joe. I didn't want to.' I had never felt more inadequate in my entire life.

'He didn't . . . you know . . . force himself on you?' I realised what he needed to hear, but I couldn't tell him that. No more lies.

'No.'

'Right.'

'Joe, I can't explain because I don't know myself.'

'But you did.'

'Yes,' I whispered, as I heard the phone go dead.

I don't know how long it took me exactly, but I know I held on to the receiver for a while before putting it down, almost as if that was my last link with Joe. I cried. Of course I cried, it was all I ever did these days. Then I went to my kitchen, opened the cupboard and took out the chocolate biscuits that Freddie had bought for me. I hoped that the baby wouldn't mind; at least I wasn't feeding it with spinach or something bland. I was sure it would be grateful that its mother was turning into a chocoholic. I decided not to consult Dr Miriam on the matter, just in case.

I sat on the floor leaning back against my kitchen cupboard and munched. I don't know how long I was there, but I munched and munched until I had run out of Hobnobs. Then I pulled myself up ready to get some more. I looked at my stomach which seemed to be growing by the day, but still wasn't exactly huge. Still I didn't think anyone would guess I was pregnant just by looking at me. Well, they wouldn't if I stopped eating so much. I resigned myself to a cup of herbal tea and that was all. I had to look after myself and chocolate wasn't good, it had caffeine, sugar and all sorts. I didn't want a hyperactive baby.

It was all so confusing thinking constantly of someone else. I had just lost the love of my life. Pre-pregnant me would have drowned my sorrows in style. Booze, cigarettes, anything to numb the pain of losing him. But I couldn't do that. I had to be strong. I had to cope. I had to keep my unborn child healthy. It was all far from easy. I missed Joe so much. There was so much pain. I'd never known this pain before. The worst period of my life was, as I have already explained, when George had left for America. But that pain had nothing on this.

There was this fear, a massive fear which was rooted deep inside me. I could feel it constantly. The worry I felt about the baby, the paternity issue and the press, could be identified separately. At times I felt happy about the baby, at times scared, I was worried about the paternity issue, and the press onslaught, but that was nothing to the fear I felt about losing Joe. That was all encompassing; that was the worst I'd ever felt. I could only deal with things (and I wasn't coping that well), by separating them. Each was a separate issue. The woman that was crying herself dry over Joe was different from the woman that was talking to her unborn child, different to the woman who fretted over the father of that unborn child and different to the woman who was about to appear in a national newspaper. There were four Holly Millers. That was the only way I could keep my very precarious grip on life.

I picked up the phone and called my mother. Although my father had been the stronger parent when I told them, I needed the reassurance of my mother, as a mother. When she answered the phone, I just cried. I felt as if I was five years old again and had scraped my knees. I wanted my mummy.

'Holly, listen to me darling, it is going to be all right. I know that seems impossible at the moment, but you are still the same wonderful, strong, independent woman that you were before all this. There will be an end. Just remember that. Because when you know that this nightmare will be over, you can live. Remember you're carrying our first grandchild and your father and I can't wait to be grandparents, it doesn't matter who the father is, it's still your child. I can't solve this one, but I can tell you that it will all work out for the best, as things do.'

'I don't know if I can cope.'

'You can. You will. You're not the sort of person who runs away. Don't let him force you away. Listen darling, I've arranged for Lisa and Max to come over this evening and they're staying for a week.'

'But they can't leave their flat.'

'They can and they are. You need to be in your home, and your friends are there to take care of you. Max has a job in Scotland from Tuesday, so it'll be the two of you. Don't argue with me, I won't allow you to be alone.'

'I love you mum.'

'I love you too.'

Is it awful that it takes a crisis to make you appreciate what you've got? Probably. But the way my family and friends had supported me was wonderful and I made a vow to never take them for granted again. Although I am sure I would, because it's only when people are so supportive that you do take them for granted. But I would try.

Lisa and Max arrived shortly after my phone call. Lisa was clutching wine and a big bunch of flowers, Max had enough luggage for a month.

'Sorry, Hol, Lisa insisted that these were all essentials.'

'Don't apologise, I'm sorry that you had to leave your flat.'

'Not at all, it's like going on holiday,' Max said, and I burst into tears again.

'Fuck, I always cry. I am trying to put it down to hormones because if this is the new me I really don't like it.'

'Don't worry, if you carry on crying all the time I'll tell you to stop. But I'll let you for now,' Lisa said, as she uncorked the wine and pulled a bag of celery out of her handbag.

'Lisa, why have you brought celery?' I asked.

'I decided not to smoke around you. It's not good for the baby.'

'I don't think it'll really harm it, unless of course I sit in a smoky pub for the next six months.'

'Well I think that it's better to give it a healthy environment, so celery has become my substitute cigarette.'

We all settled down with drinks and food. Max ordered pizza and garlic bread, they drank wine, but I abstained and stuck to my herbal tea. I drank herbal tea (no caffeine, no badness), which I hated, because that and water were the only things that were completely good for you, apparently. I was behaving irrationally, I know, I was probably going mad.

'When do we find out the sex?' Max asked. He was patting my stomach and asking why the baby wasn't kicking. When I told him it was too soon he seemed disappointed. I got the impression he was a bit broody.

'We don't.' I had thought about it and decided against it. I don't know why, but it felt like tempting fate. I wanted the baby to be healthy, I would do anything I could to ensure it was healthy, that was it.

'But then how do we choose names?' Max asked, disappointed.

'She'll choose names for either sex of course,' Lisa said.

'No, I'm not choosing names until it's born.' Lisa and Max exchanged looks, then they both looked at me.

'There's more to this, isn't there?' he asked.

'It's George isn't it?' she added. I nodded.

'The truth is that George is going to find out about the baby at some point. Then when the baby is born we will have to do the test and I'm scared, petrified, that when we do the test, the baby will be George's and he'll take the baby away from me.'

'Shit, Holly, you should have said,' Lisa put her arm around me.

'We won't let George take him away, even if he is the father,' Max said. He reminded me of Joe when George had been trying to get me to marry him. Joe the protector; now Max the protector.

'Thanks,' I whispered, but I didn't believe it. My mother had said it would be over at some point, but I had no idea when. It was an evolutionary process. If George wasn't the father then it would be over. If he was, then he would take me to court for custody and there'd be yet another battle to fight. So many battles all of a sudden. One shag and I had managed to get myself into this much of a mess, it barely beggared belief.

'Holly we will. I promise that Max and I will do everything to protect you from that abominable man.' Lisa was angry. I was touched and impressed; I didn't know Lisa knew words like abominable. 'So, when is the first antenatal?' she asked.

'I should have gone before now but as I didn't know I was pregnant . . . I don't think I'm going to go. They're full of happy couples and I don't think I could cope. Francesca has given me the number of her yoga teacher, she does private lessons for pregnant women, that's meant to be just as effective.'

'What does your doctor think?' Max asked.

'She doesn't know. I'm seeing her tomorrow, I'll ask her then.'

'I'll come to yoga with you,' Lisa announced. 'I quite fancy getting bendy.'

I raised my eyebrows and stifled a giggle. 'It'll be more to do with exercising my birthing muscles.'

'OK, well then I'll be there for support.'

'But Holly, if your doctor thinks you should go to antenatal you will won't you?' Max sounded worried and that made me feel so much better. These people were all in this pregnancy with me, because Joe was not.

'Only if it's essential.' I really had made my mind up. I wanted to do something privately. I wasn't interested in meeting other pregnant women and swapping stories. For obvious reasons.

Everything was fine until I decided to go to bed. I kissed my friends goodnight and thanked them again, then I realised that I was going to bed alone and I felt that fear more keenly than ever.

I dreamt about the baby. I dreamt about how it would feel about its mother having made such a mess of her life. I dreamt it looked like George; then I dreamt it looked like Joe. I woke up, feeling more anxious than ever as I realised that it was Monday and George's story was going to be in the paper.

I looked at the clock, it was half past six. I got out of bed and pulled on a pair of jogging bottoms. Then I found my biggest jumper and put it on over my T-shirt. I found my keys at the bottom of my handbag, grabbed some change and went out. There was silence from the spare room, and I tried to be quiet so as not to wake my guests.

It was bitingly cold and still dark. The sky was filled with dark clouds; I shivered as I realised how sinister it looked. Then I shivered at the cold. I walked as slowly as I could to the tube station, to the newspaper stand, that I knew would already be catering for the early-morning commuters. When I got there I realised how odd I looked against the smart suits clutching *The Times*, *Telegraph*, and *Mail*. I waited in the queue until it was my turn.

'*Daily News* please.' I thought the man behind the counter looked at me oddly, but then I was paranoid. He handed me the newspaper, I handed him the money. Then I walked home.

I resisted the urge to open the paper and read the story straight away. My hand shook as I clutched the paper to my chest. I don't know if I was torturing myself, but I let myself in the flat, went to the kitchen and made myself a cup of herbal tea. It was only when the steaming mug was in front of me as I stood at the kitchen counter, that I opened the paper.

It seemed to take me ages to get to page thirteen. I was trying to breathe slowly, not panic because I could feel the anxiety building up. I cupped my mug as tightly as I could with one hand, while I turned the pages, slowly and deliberately with the other. Then I reached page thirteen. The first thing I noticed was a photo of George, looking forlorn, groomed but forlorn. It was typical Cordelia. Then I read the headline.

## THE MARRIAGE PACT MAN

### JILTED SWEETHEART GOES TO COURT OVER BROKEN PROMISES

*George Conway, thirty, had everything a man could wish for. He was a successful lawyer living an extravagant life in New York. But although his career was steaming ahead he had more important matters to attend to. He left New York for London to seal a promise made ten years earlier. He arrived in London with the sole purpose of being reunited with childhood sweetheart, Holly Miller.*

*Since the age of twelve Holly and George had been inseparable, as friendship grew into love, and adolescence gave way to adulthood that love grew. When they were twenty, they both declared that they would be together for ever and they signed a marriage pact promising to marry each other at the age of thirty. Both were building successful careers, so much so that when George was offered a job in New York, Holly felt she wasn't ready to give up her job in public relations. They parted tearfully but knew that one day they would be together.*

*At the beginning of December last year, George returned home to claim his bride. Their passion was instantly rediscovered, but Holly then turned against the man who loved her. Despite sleeping with him, she told him that she had a new man in her life, Joe McClaren, thirty-two, and she had no intention of marrying George.*

*Distraught, he didn't know where to turn, so he turned to the law to help him. Unfortunately it did not. Now George is appealing to Holly, to the love that they share because he knows that they are meant to be together.*

*'Although Holly has behaved despicably towards me and towards Joe, I forgive her because she is the love of my life.' Conway said. 'All I can do is use the powerful medium of the press to appeal to her. Holly I love you and I know you love me. Please marry me.'*

*Wiping away a tear, George Conway manages a smile as he leaves and waits for his one true love to respond to him.*

*If you know Holly Miller, or if you have a marriage-pact story contact the Daily News.*

Oh I knew Holly Miller all right, but not the one in the paper.

# Chapter Twenty-two

When Max and Lisa emerged about two hours later, I had my head in the oven.

'Shit Hol, what are you doing?' Lisa screamed.

'Cleaning the oven,' I replied, pulling my head out and displaying my pink rubber gloves for them to see.

'You scared me,' Lisa said, going to the fridge to get her morning piece of celery.

'Sorry.' I peeled off the gloves and put the kettle on. 'I'll make you both coffee to compensate.'

'Holly, the newspaper. Do you want me to get it?' Max asked.

'No need.' I pointed to the counter where the newspaper lay open at page thirteen. Max and Lisa started to read it when the phone went. I went into the sitting room to take the call.

'Hello.'

'Hol, it's me.'

'Oh Freddie, thank goodness. Did you see it?'

'Yes, so has Francesca. We don't think it's anything to worry about. I mean I know it's a pack of lies, but it isn't that damaging. It's on a crap page, and it's not that big, well it does fill the whole page but most of that is the photo.'

'Freddie, why do you sound so stressed?'

'We called the *Daily News* to refute the story, they refused to print your side.'

'Why would they do that?'

'Not interesting enough.'

'Shit. Can't we make it interesting?'

'Well not unless we offer them the pregnancy exclusive. That might make it too interesting.'

'What are we going to do?' I needed Freddie to tell me that it would be all right.

'Well for now, nothing babes. I've blackmailed every sub-editor on every tabloid to call me if they pick it up. Luckily, we've given them enough good stuff to get into their good books. I'm preparing a press release for you which we'll send round to everyone if the story isn't dead today. Even the *Daily News* have agreed to let me know if they are going to continue running the story. They don't think it's going to get any more coverage to be honest. If that is the case then it's over.'

'Freddie, you know Cordelia won't let it be over.'

'She might not have any choice. Shame there isn't a general election or something. Unfortunately it's a quiet time for news, that's our biggest problem.'

'Yeah, well I'm not enough of a bitch to wish for a world disaster just to suit me.'

'I know. Hol, Francesca and I are on top of this. I'll e-mail the planned release for your approval, and we'll take it from there.'

'What would I do without you?'

'That's a bloody good question.'

I went back into the kitchen where my two guests had made their own coffee.

'So?' I asked.

'It's a pile of shit,' Lisa said.

'Yeah and we're going to e-mail the paper and tell them that,' Max added.

'You'd do that?'

'Of course. I have to go into the studio now, so I'll mail them from there. What does work say?'

'Freddie thinks it will all be over soon.'

'Fingers crossed.'

By the end of the morning I was exhausted. Lisa had been brilliant, fielding calls from people; but I spoke to my parents, who were very reassuring; my sister, who was hysterical should they connect me to her famous husband; and again to Freddie. No news from his end, I wanted to believe desperately that that was good.

Lisa made lunch, which was no mean feat for her, and I guess the reason we had a tuna salad.

'It's very good for you,' she explained, when she put it in front of me.

'It is,' I replied.

'You know that oven thing earlier?' she asked.

'Um.'

'Is that you nesting?'

'What?'

'You know they say pregnant women get urges to clean everywhere because they are nesting.'

'Makes me sound like a bird. I guess I did get an urge to clean though. Normally I have to bribe myself to go near that oven. How come you're an expert on pregnancy all of a sudden?'

'I told you, we're thinking about trying for a baby, but I still want to see how yours turns out first.'

'Any baby made from you and Max is bound to be gorgeous.' Not only was Lisa in possession of model looks, but so was he. I didn't think my baby would stand a chance in the beauty stakes compared to theirs, even if it was Joe's. Lisa just smiled.

She came with me to my doctor's appointment. I saw the same doctor as before, who told me much the same as I had been told at the hospital. She went through all the tests I needed to have done, gave me leaflets, said she would arrange an appointment with a gynaecologist and finally she asked me how I was. I decided to give her a potted version as I knew she had a waiting room full of people. I was growing to like her. She had sympathetic eyes, and a comforting smile. She wasn't one of those cold horrid doctors who made you want to stay away. I could imagine she was ultra busy because everyone would want to come to see her, even if just for a chat. I pulled myself out of my silent thoughts as I heard her mention antenatal. I asked her if I could go to Francesca's yoga teacher and she seemed to think that that would be all right. As long as I had a chat with my gynaecologist about it, and went to at least a couple of birthing lessons. I promised I would.

Even though I could picture the scene and I didn't like it: Lisa, clutching her celery, accompanying me, a class full of happy, smiling, smug couples, assuming that we were lesbians and probably keeping well away from us in case it was contagious. The men would be calling their pregnant women honey, and Lisa would be taking the piss out of each and every one (the only silver lining). The teacher, although I am not sure if they are called teachers, would tell us both off for giggling too much and I'd sulk like I did at school. I really, really didn't want to have to go through that, but if it was my punishment I would take it like a woman.

By the end of the day, there was no news about any more media interest in my life. I received the press release Freddie had prepared, I approved it, dealt with a couple more work-related things, then I made a chicken casserole for dinner. As I was never that keen on cooking, I guessed I was 'nesting' again, but after consulting Dr Miriam discovered it was probably a bit early for that. Actually I was trying to keep myself occupied and my mind off other matters. Max came home, we had dinner, and then, straight after, I fell into bed exhausted. It was a dreamless sleep.

As soon as I got up I logged onto the laptop. I was eager to do some work, and needed something to focus on other than the mess that was my life. I didn't have any e-mails to check, which upset me, so I fired loads off to Freddie, Francesca and Dixie.

That way I knew that they would reply to me and my inbox wouldn't feel quite so lonely. Neither would I.

Then I went to buy all the newspapers, ignoring Max's offer to go. He had to get ready for a lunchtime flight to Scotland, and I wanted the fresh air. I walked to the local newsagent, bought all the tabloids, and carted them home.

I had learned early in my job to read newspapers quickly, looking for specific references, which is what I did, whilst sipping another cup of hateful herbal tea. Lisa and Max offered to help, but I waved them away and they could see I was on a bit of a mission, so they left me alone. I was pretty sure they were talking about me, but I didn't mind. This roster that my mother had arranged for me was probably organised on the basis that it wasn't safe to leave me on my own. When I thought about the next person on her roster, I was sure it was either her and Dad, or Imogen. They were the only people who didn't have full-time jobs to go to, my parents being retired and Imogen being the wife of a rich man. I didn't have the energy to tell my mother that I would be all right on my own, but also I wasn't sure that I would be. At times I felt I was slipping into the realm of madness and I didn't want to be alone for that reason.

I read until I had covered each paper. There were no mentions, not one.

'It's clear,' I shouted, giving Lisa and Max the opportunity to join me. I wasn't sure who was more relieved, them or me.

That afternoon I was diverted from my problems, when Lisa took me to a London hotel spa. It was a lovely surprise and I filled up when she told me. I was taking the afternoon off work, but actually I hadn't got any to do. Freddie and Francesca were definitely covering for me, which annoyed me a bit because I wasn't totally incapable, but I have to admit the idea of a relaxing afternoon being pampered was more fun than work.

'I can't believe how much you've done for me.'

'Oh don't be silly. You're stressed and stress isn't good for the baby. But a massage, a manicure, a pedicure and waxing. Do you want anything waxed?'

'No need.' After all, waxing was something I did religiously for Joe. Now I could become really hairy and no one would notice.

'OK, then manicure and pedicure. No need to let yourself go.'

'I wasn't going to,' I lied.

We arrived at the spa which looked incredibly expensive.

'I can't let you pay for this,' I said, knowing she had already booked two passes.

'You don't have a choice. Birthday present.'

'My birthday has gone.'

'Christmas then.' I gave her a look but didn't pursue the argument. I knew I would have to find a way of paying everyone back but had a feeling that if their support were translated into money, I'd need to win the lottery to do so.

We parted ways once we'd changed into our fluffy white robes. I was having a massage, and I think Lisa was going for colonic irrigation, although she didn't tell me that. I actually didn't want to think about it, so as I lay on my treatment table and felt warm hands unknotting me, I really did relax.

It started slowly, as at first I could almost feel my tension. I was rigid. A couple of comments from the masseuse confirmed this. But after a while I felt the knots dissolving and fell asleep.

Still drowsy from my massage I offered my hands to the manicurist and then my feet. I couldn't decide what colour I wanted them painted because I was too relaxed, so she went for a neutral colour. When she finished I put on my swimming costume and went to the spa where I got into the warm, bubbly water, wishing every day to be like this. There were no worries in the spa, no concerns, because it was a haven, a protective haven where nothing and no one could get me. As I felt the bubbles working magically up and down my body, and my mind more settled than it had done in ages, I realised that if I really could keep stress to the minimum I would be all right. But then I knew that as soon as I stepped out and I left the spa and went home all my problems would be there still. I couldn't drown them in the jacuzzi even if I wanted to.

Lisa looked relaxed as she came to join me.

'This place is amazing,' I said, giving her a kiss on the cheek.

'I know, it makes you feel as if you're in heaven or something, and there's no outside world.'

'That's exactly what I was thinking.'

'Which is why I thought it would be so good for you.'

'Lisa, you're a wise woman.'

'No one's ever called me wise before. Holly, you have to promise me something.' I nodded. The way I was feeling I'd promise anything. 'If you ever get into a proper state and you're really stressed, and you can't afford to come here, then come and talk to me. We'll do something to get rid of it, but you were ready to explode and that's not good for anyone.'

Lisa was getting wiser by the second.

We still hadn't heard any more from the newspapers, no news was still good news. Francesca gave me some proposals to write, to keep me from driving myself mad, and Lisa went shopping for groceries. There was an element of calm in my flat, but that scared me because everyone knew what calm came before, didn't they?

# Chapter Twenty-three

The ripple in the calm came at the end of the week. One particular columnist on the second biggest tabloid had picked up on the George story, highlighted it and said that it was difficult to enforce a broken promise in this day and age, as if that was a bad thing. There wasn't much, but it was implying sympathy for George. That wasn't a disaster in itself, but it was inasmuch as columnist Lindsay Black was one of the most popular and widely read. Freddie told me, reluctantly, that the story would probably now be pursued by that paper, he then sent our press release to each paper and the said columnist.

Days were merging into each other. I was constantly on the lookout for press coverage, I was trying to keep it together, but not succeeding very well. As Lisa and Max packed up to leave my flat and resume their lives, I changed the sheets in the spare room, in preparation for my parents' arrival. My second set of babysitters were due the same day Lisa and Max left.

I was managing to keep on top of things. I wanted to kill Lindsay Black, whom I had always found intelligent reading until now, I still wanted to kill George and I still hadn't heard from Joe.

My parents arrived with enough food to keep me going for the whole remainder of my pregnancy. I was approaching my fourth month, and I was steadily (daily) gaining weight. I thought that it would only be a matter of weeks before I would show. I had a couple of weeks for all the media interest to die down, but as it hadn't really started, so I didn't know when this would happen.

I settled my parents into their room, then we had dinner, cooked by my mother. They tried to reassure me the way parents do, but I was too preoccupied. For a moment, I blanked out everything but the fact that I could do something about the mess; I could make everything all right. I was going to be a mother, it was my duty to behave like *my* mother, a woman who always made everything all right. When you're fighting for someone, other than yourself, someone you love very much you fight that much harder. I imagined all those terrified soldiers going to war, fighting for the safety of their loved ones, and although I wasn't in any way comparing myself to them, I needed some of their courage.

That was exactly what I was going to do. I was going to be brave; take control, I'd put an end to the nonsense of the press threat by facing the enemy and I would also tell my loved ones how I felt. I was sure that this was the best course of action, I knew I was doing the right thing.

My first brave act was to write a letter to Joe. I begged an early night, and tucked up in bed with my hot water bottle (my mum), I took out a pen and pad and began composing.

> *Dear Joe*
> *I agonised over writing to you, not only because I didn't know if I could find the right words, but also because I didn't know if you would want to read them. My intention is not to cause you any more pain, if you feel a fraction of what I feel then I have caused you far too much already.*
> *I still have no answers for you as to why I slept with George, but all I can tell you was that I was reeling from the shock of finding that I was in love with you, and fighting with you at the same time. That is no excuse but fear can make people act irrationally; turn for comfort in any way they can. Falling in love*

*with you was the most wonderful thing I did, but also the scariest. I was terrified, especially as I hadn't heard from you and I didn't know how you felt.*

*George is familiar. That sounds awful but he is. Or was. When I saw him again I remembered how secure my childhood was, which had a lot to do with him. He was my security blanket as I grew up.*

*There are no details to give you, because that I know is too painful, but what I want to say to you is simple. I love you with all my heart. I miss you in a way I have never missed anyone. I go to bed each night and pray that the baby is yours, that is all I want because then maybe you'll feel able to be a part of my life again.*

*That is all I hope.*

*Joe, I love you. Ignore this letter if you want to, but please don't ignore that I really do love you. Hollyxx*

I didn't have to tear up any pages, it flowed the way I wanted it to right from the start. I had a warm feeling inside me. I was taking some control back. I was going to do anything in my power to fix things, I would never stop fighting for what was important. Not in the way George was doing, but in the right way.

Do you lose the ability to sleep when you get older? Or is having kids the end of your late mornings? My parents were at the kitchen counter drinking tea when I got up at seven the next morning. They were fully dressed, and my father had taken over my job of buying all the papers.

'No mention, love,' he said.

I smiled. I needed to check my e-mails and make a phone call. 'Why don't you guys go out and explore a bit?'

'But we can't leave you.' My mum looked horrified.

'I'll be fine for a couple of hours, Mum, I just want to check in with work. I do still do some occasionally,' I pushed. Eventually I managed to get them out of the house armed with an *A–Z* and an umbrella. I had no idea where they were going, but guessed that a walk around the common would be it, before they'd start fretting and return to check I hadn't run away.

I didn't need to check e-mails, after all it was only Monday morning, but I needed to send some. I sent one to Freddie copying Francesca requesting I be given more work. It felt weird and I knew they were protecting me but I also felt as if my role in the company was diminishing. Yes, I'd been writing proposals, talking to clients, bossing people around, but I had been out of the office for so long that I felt out of touch. I also felt as if they were protecting me too much. I was pregnant, not ill, and I needed to keep busy more than ever. Although I wasn't one hundred per cent sure I was doing the right thing, it had seemed like a good idea last night. I was trying to sort my life out, so I made a phone call.

I dialled the number and took a deep breath.

A sing-song voice answered straight away. 'Cordelia Dickens PR.'

'Cordelia Dickens please,' I snapped, in my most scary, curt voice.

'Who shall I say is calling?'

'Holly Miller.' Within seconds, Cordelia's voice came on the line. It sent a shiver down my spine.

'I didn't expect to hear from you,' she said, with a sinister tone.

'I'm sure you didn't. Cordelia you did your best, it didn't work. One story in the *Daily News*, one tiny mention in a column, it's not your best ever is it?' I tried to sound threatening, but my resolve was leaving me fast.

'Oh Holly, I know that you work for Francesca Williams and her firm is only a tiny little tadpole in the pond of PR, but I thought you would know better.'

'I do know better, and if my company is a tadpole, then yours is pond scum.' I was feeling quite pumped up by the argument. It was definitely therapeutic.

'Is there any point to this conversation?' Cordelia was as cunning as a hungry fox.

'I just want to be left alone.'

'Then marry George. He's a good-looking man with a great career. If he wasn't a client then I'd be jumping him.'

'That would solve all my problems.'

'I know, which is why I'm not going to. Apart from the fact he is totally in love with you anyway, so there is no way he'd even look at another woman.'

'Bullshit.'

'I'm really busy, Holly, but I can tell you one thing. This isn't over, not by a long shot.'

'What do you mean?'

'Just what I say. You haven't heard the last of this and your silly little attempt to threaten me has just made me more determined.'

'Why? Why this?'

'I heard about George and saw an opportunity. For both of us.' She sounded so mercenary.

'You can't be making too much money from him.' It was a last attempt. My bravado had completely dissolved.

'Oh, I get a percentage of the money he gets for his story, so at the moment he's not making me rich.'

'So it wouldn't hurt you to drop it.'

'I can't do that, you haven't heard the last of this. You better get comfortable Holly, because it's going to be a long ride.' She laughed then, a Cruella de Ville laugh.

'Why do I get the feeling this is personal?'

'Because it is. Actually I didn't know anything about you before I started working for George, but now I do there's a little bonus there for me.'

'What?' I felt hot, then cold. I certainly felt confused.

'Ask Francesca,' she replied, before slamming down the phone. What did she mean by that?

I came off the phone fuming. But then I calmed down and panicked. I checked my e-mail and saw that there was one from Freddie and one from Francesca. Shit, they would kill me when they knew what I'd done.

Freddie sent me a ton of work to do with the message: '*You're bloody welcome to it.*' Francesca said that I should come into the office if I felt like it. I mailed back saying I would go in the following morning. I decided not to tell them about my phone call until then. Although they couldn't kill me over the phone, if I cried in person they might forgive me for ruining everything.

Because I thought I had. By having a bitchy conversation with Cordelia I had just managed to make her more determined than ever. There was only one possible option left to me. Perhaps I could call George and persuade him that Cordelia was only acting in her own best interest. Could I do that? Should I? I decided to wait until I was in the office and take advice. I couldn't rely on my own bright ideas.

I went to my bedroom and picked up the letter I had written to Joe. It was from the heart so there was no way *that* could be wrong. I went to the post office and mailed it to him. I kissed the back of the envelope and hoped that it would bring me some luck.

My parents arrived back shortly after me. I explained about going to work, and they looked concerned, but I managed to put their minds at rest.

'It's lovely having you to stay, but I don't need anyone here,' I said. 'After all nothing has really happened.'

'We'll be here just in case. It's a scary time for you with the pregnancy and everything. I'd rather you weren't alone.'

'OK.' There seemed little point in arguing. Actually I didn't want to be alone, I never minded being alone but since Joe and I had split, I hated it.

I spent the rest of the day, making a dent in some of the work I'd been sent. I felt like I was fifteen again and doing my homework. Especially as my parents hovered around me offering to help. As if they could help.

As I took the tube into the office I was excited – for five seconds. Until I remembered what a nightmare journey it was. As I snuggled up to a man with a very scratchy suit, and tried not to scream as someone stood on my toe, I considered telling someone I was pregnant to see if that would get me a seat, but then it was a secret and tubes had ears. Actually they didn't, but I was paranoid. If Cordelia got hold of it, then she would make my life hell. I was wearing a shift dress which was quite loose on me in the old days, but had become tighter. I wasn't exactly showing but my stomach was definitely rounder. My mother said you couldn't tell that I was pregnant just to look at me, which made me feel better, because I felt huge.

I marched into the office feeling almost normal again, until I saw the look on Freddie's face.

'Did you get the papers today?' he asked. I shook my head. It was only nine thirty and the office was still quite empty. 'Boardroom,' he said as he took my hand and led me there. Every tabloid was spread out on the table. They were all open at a certain page. The headlines screamed at me. The photos sneered at me. Cordelia had managed to carry out her threat. I was the subject of four national newspapers that day:

BETRAYAL: THE MARRIAGE THAT NEVER WAS
FROM BROKEN PROMISES TO BROKEN HEARTS
THE MARRIAGE-PACT MAN AND THE SCARLET WOMAN
THE HEARTLESS WOMAN AND THE HEARTBROKEN MAN

I was in shock. There was no way I could comprehend what I'd read. I looked at Freddie with tears in my eyes.

'I'll get you a coffee, sit down and read them.'

'I don't drink coffee any more, only fucking herbal tea,' I spat through clenched teeth.

The thing about the stories, I gleaned, once I'd been able to regain control and read them without my tears blinding me, was that they were consistently inaccurate. Actually they weren't all lies, but mostly. Because, surprise, surprise, the thing that they'd done was to spice up the story. Cordelia, spurred on by my stupid phone call, had reshaped the facts to sound more tabloid. The 'sex sells' principle had been employed. And it had worked.

I was a nymphomaniac who had had a very long sexual relationship with George in my youth. As well as having sex with everyone else. I manipulated him totally from the beginning, and told him that although I loved him, I needed to try other models out. Then, when he felt vulnerable about our relationship I signed the marriage pact, promising that it would come true because I loved him. Of course that pact was all that kept him going. Then he moved to New York and I told him that I would join him just as soon as I'd sorted my career out, and he'd believed me. I kept him going with phone-sex for years until he could bear it no more and came back to claim me. (Note: I have never had phone-sex with anyone. I find the idea a bit embarrassing to be honest.)

He did that and I jumped into bed with him immediately and told him that I would marry him, but that I had to dump the bloke I was seeing at the moment, viz. Joe. He went back to New York, believing me but when nothing happened he came back again, and started the legal proceedings.

Freddie came back with my herbal tea.

'So, what do you think?' he asked, flinching slightly as if I was going to hit him.

'I'm not about to shoot the messenger,' I replied. 'It's all lies, bloody lies. I can't believe it.'

Francesca walked in as I was sobbing into Freddie's black top, and she read all the papers before she spoke.

'Can we sue?' she asked.

'How can we prove it. They haven't said anything that's quantifiable. How can I prove that I only had sex with him once? How can I prove that I'm not the total slut that he has made me out to be?'

'You're right. She's a clever bitch.'

'Cordelia?' Freddie asked.

It was as good a time as any to tell them. 'It's all my fault.'

'Why?'

'Because I called her yesterday and told her that it hadn't worked and that she'd be best to leave me alone.'

Both Francesca and Freddie paled. 'Shit.' They voiced in unison.

'I know, she got really mad and said that I should ask you about it.' I pointed at Francesca, I was lacking the energy to even address her properly. She sat down beside me.

'I would have supported you anyway. You see, Cordelia used to be a friend. We both started in PR together and we both worked for respectable firms. But somewhere along the way she discovered the celebrity, or minor celebrity arena and decided that she wanted to concentrate on that. Mainly, I think, because the people she represented were so desperate for fame that they would do what she told them. Not a brain to call their own, most of them. She wanted me to work with her and she didn't like it when I refused and opened up my own company.'

'Sounds like a pretty ridiculous grudge to me,' I said, thinking it sounded like something from a Jackie Collins' novel. But then, Cordelia sounded like someone who wanted to be in a Jackie Collins' novel, so it almost made sense.

'*And* I slept with her husband.' Francesca coloured.

'You what?'

'Well, he was quite a dish and she was getting on my nerves, pestering me all the time to go into business with her, then threatening to ruin me if I didn't. It was only the once, but she divorced him because of me.'

I laughed, really, really loudly. Freddie and Francesca looked scared, as if I had jumped over the edge.

'It's all about sex. I slept with George. You slept with Cordelia's husband. Christ, we're in this mess because of sex. Sex with George was all right, it was functional but it hit the right spots. I mean there were no emotions involved, like with Joe but technically it was fine.'

'Graham – Cordelia's husband – was the same.'

'Fucking hell, can you two hear yourselves,' Freddie said. 'We're in the middle of a crisis and you're comparing notes on the two men who put you here. Can we have some decorum.' Freddie was visibly upset. I looked at Francesca and we both burst out laughing once more.

Cordelia found, or was led to George, and as she said she would have worked for him anyway, but with the added bonus of getting her revenge on Francesca, she was a little more determined in her quest. It all fell into place.

The office was in full flow, and I noticed that my staff were working as if everything was normal. I went to talk to them.

'Are you all right?' I heard a few times. Some were embarrassed at first but I think I managed to convince everyone that I missed them and that I was still sane.

'How's the bun?' Dixie asked.

'Making me fat,' I responded.

'You look well.'

'Thanks Dix, but I feel like shit.'

After I re-established my staff relations, I went back to the boardroom where my two allies were discussing the war.

'I'm going to get Sarah to draft a press release saying it's all lies.'

'OK.'

'Then we'll send it out. But Holly, my instinct is that we should ride the storm. I think that anything else would be a bad move. All we need to do now is to make sure that you keep a low profile and that you keep your pregnancy hidden, if you know what I mean.' Francesca was now solemn.

'I've got a hospital appointment later this week, but if I take my mum and we get a cab then that should be all right.'

'Some photographers might start following you, although I can't imagine they will,' Freddie warned.

'I should go home now, shouldn't I?' I asked.

'Yes, and Holly . . .'

'Um?'

'Don't have any more bright ideas. Check them with me first.'

'Right boss. I was going to ask if you thought I should call George.'

'Do you think that you can get through to him? Better than Cordelia?' Freddie asked.

'I might. I thought that maybe if I told him how hurt I am by the press coverage, I might be able to appeal to his better nature.'

'OK, but let's draft what you're going to say, then you can call him from the office while we're there.' I had the feeling that they already knew it would go horribly wrong, but were humouring me. At least if it did go wrong, this time they'd be there to catch me when I fell.

I paced Francesca's office as Freddie went to instruct Sarah on the press release. I could see that everyone in the office was giving me sympathetic glances. I smiled. They must think that I am on my way out, but they still seemed to care.

Francesca drafted what I would say to George; we all knew how good he was at twisting my words. However, I was taking him by surprise, which was a very sound war tactic.

Francesca dialled the number and handed the phone to me. I hoped it wasn't his answerphone. It wasn't.

'George Conway.' The voice was even more arrogant than last time.

'George, it's Holly.' Pause to let that information sink in.

'Holly, what a surprise. I'm not sure I should be talking to you.' I had anticipated that, or Francesca had.

'I know you probably think I should go through Cordelia, and I tried that, but George we share a lot of good history.'

'True.'

'Have you seen the papers today.'

'I have.'

'And are you happy about it? The fact that I have been having sex with you all our lives practically. That I used and abused you but promised to marry you. George, it's all lies.'

'That's one way of looking at it.'

'And the other is?' I raised my eyebrows at Francesca and shook my head.

'That I have to do whatever it takes to get you to realise that your rightful place is by my side.'

'George has it not occurred to you that by telling these lies about me it'll just make me hate you?'

'Yes, but you won't hate me for ever. Believe me this is totally necessary.' Again, Francesca had anticipated this response.

'I could sue you for defamation.'

'I'm a lawyer Holly, I know what you can and can't do. Sue me if you want but you won't win. In the end you'll realise that I love you and you love me. If it takes a bit of disruption in your life then I'm sorry but you could always just admit to how you feel.'

'George I feel like my best friend is stabbing me in the heart. I feel like the one person who would never hurt me has hurt me. I feel as if there is no way I will ever be able to love you, not in the way you want me to. This crusade of yours is fruitless, and it's hurting me. Surely you don't want to hurt me.'

'Of course not, but if it's necessary . . . Holly please, just agree to marry me and we can put all this behind us.'

'I can't do that.'

'Then I have to go.' He hung up.

Francesca looked at me.

'The problem is that he absolutely believes he is doing the right thing. I can't understand it, but he does.' I put my face in my hands in total despair, and Francesca, at a loss of what else to do, held me.

# Chapter Twenty-four

---◆◆◆◆---

## *Human Interest*

I put down the phone and felt wretched. Why couldn't she understand that I didn't want to hurt her? That hurting her was tearing me apart. It had been hard ever since I had agreed to work with Cordelia. Sometimes, like now, I questioned my actions. I just wanted to issue a nationwide appeal to Holly, so she could realise her life was with me. That was all.

At first I thought Cordelia had been wrong. The story hardly set the world alight, and it seemed poised to die before it even got anywhere. I began to think that my quest was fruitless. Then Cordelia suggested that we spice up the details. It had all the makings of a great human interest story, but it needed a bit more of a kick to it. That was what she said. I know about the law and she knows about the media. We worked together.

When I was with Cordelia I felt relaxed. She was reassuring, she was patient, and she listened. All I wanted was to marry Holly and I knew, knew without a shadow of a doubt that that was what should happen. My family weren't speaking to me, Holly wasn't speaking to me, but I would prove them all wrong because they *were* all wrong. I was right. If I had to use dirty tricks to get Holly, so be it, because the main purpose of the story, unknown to Cordelia, was to split up Holly and Joe. Once he was off the scene then there would be no one standing in my way.

Cordelia was impressed by my suggestions and, as I knew they were legally sound, we went ahead. I was amazed how quickly the story broke. I'd spoken to her in the afternoon and by morning we were in the papers. Cordelia was pushing me but that wasn't it. I was pushing myself just as much. I knew that this was perhaps my big chance and I wasn't going to blow it.

At first I was nervous about talking to journalists but by the fourth interview I did that day, I got used to it. And the photographs. I have never been that keen on having my photo taken but when you have a professional photographer and they are telling you how great you are, then you begin to believe it. I began to understand how Holly's old flatmate, Lisa, got so vain. She was a model and had people pandering to her all the time. Holly and I used to take the mickey out of her something rotten. I wondered if she still did. So, I had five photographs taken, four interviews with national dailies, and one interview with a weekly gossip magazine. I was beginning to feel like a bit of a celebrity. I smiled to myself that we'd come so far, so quickly, and I knew there was only one person I had to thank for that. I vowed, as I set off to meet with her in her office that I would tell her so.

'Cordelia, I am gratified by the way things are going.'

'I'm pretty pleased myself.'

'So, what next?'

'Well, I have had offers from some television shows. Now, we need to be careful not to choose the wrong ones. I am recommending *Wake Up Britain!* that's broadcast really early but has a very high viewer rating. *This Afternoon* with Nancy Witter will be good for you as she's really friendly. Then I think we'll try *Michael Martin Discusses*, it's a Jerry Springer-type show, it might be a bit boisterous, do you think Holly would agree to appear?'

'Definitely not.'

'Good, then you can get your views across without any difficulty. Then we've also had an offer for you to go on Keith

Northam's show, you know . . . the gay comic. It's a very funny and highly popular show. He might take the piss a bit but I think you can handle him. Also that show has an evening slot, so by the time we're finished everyone in the country will know who you are.

'Wow, I can't believe it!'

'This is only the tip of the iceberg, George. By the time I've finished, Holly will be crawling on her hands and knees to you begging you to take her back.'

'But we were never together in the first place.'

'You were, George, I remember, for the purposes of this campaign you were. Now we are going to cram all this in pretty quickly. You'll do two shows the day after tomorrow, then next Monday you do Michael and you're doing Keith next Thursday evening. I think you can cope.'

'So this is already arranged?' I wasn't sure that I liked her agreeing things without my say so.

'Only provisionally, we don't have time to mess around George, I've told you that enough times.'

'Sorry. This is great. I'm certainly impressed.'

'I'll send Holly a schedule of your TV interviews. I'm toying with the idea of you doing some radio but we'll see how the TV goes first.'

'You're the boss.'

'George, have a good restful day tomorrow because you're going to be busy. Busy, busy, busy.'

'I will.' I kissed Cordelia on the cheek and left to go home. Holly would soon be putty in my hands.

At home I read through the papers again, and for a fleeting moment felt bad. But then I pulled myself together. I was doing what I had to do. It had become my mantra. *Doing what I had to do.*

I made some notes for my forthcoming television appearances and I also looked up the shows on the Internet. I wanted to be prepared. Then I turned to the question of wardrobe. I didn't want to look too flashy, I wanted to look smart and serious. My court suit would be perfect. I decided to address my television appearances the way I would address my court appearances. When I went to court, I always wore the same outfit. I had five identical suits, I had countless white shirts, and I used the same tie. Consistency. If you looked the same dependable you, other people unwittingly began to trust you. Not quite subliminal, more amateur psychology. So that would be what I would do on TV. I smiled as I realised that I could be very good at this.

The journalists I'd faced so far had all been so sympathetic that I wasn't worried about the TV hosts. One female journalist had hit on me, I was sure of it. She said it was a crime for a man like me to be on my own and then she winked at me. Another said Holly must be crazy to turn me down. The male journalists sympathised as well. We guys must stick together. I was being encouraged and that reinforced my feelings that I was doing the right thing.

I ran my fingers through my hair and thought about getting it cut. But then I decided against it. I didn't want to look too well-groomed, too clean-cut. Wearing a sharp suit and having my hair slightly messy would convey that I was upset by the situation; and I was.

OK, so there was an amount of calculation and a certain manipulation of public sympathy, but at the same time I was working for the greater good.

My mobile rang as I was contemplating my opening lines.

'George Conway.'

'George it's Clive.'

'Clive, I've been meaning to call you to thank you for putting Cordelia in touch with me.'

'I see by the tabloids that it's working out.'

'Well it seems to be. Of course Holly hasn't capitulated yet but she will soon.'

'George, be careful won't you.'

'Clive you are one of the most cautious bastards I know. Too long in the British legal system.'

'I know, but Cordelia can be dangerous.'

'What in a mad axe-wielding sort of way?'

'No, but I've dated her and believe me she's got a ruthless streak.'

'I'm sure, but she has to in her line of work. Anyway, why would she be doing this for me, for not much money, if she was so ruthless.'

'I don't know, but that's what worries me.'

'Clive, you're not bitter because you broke up are you?'

'We're not all like you, George. I just want you to be careful.'

'I appreciate your concern but I can look after myself.'

''Bye.' He hung up.

Clive wasn't someone I was interested in now, he was way too cautious, but I was grateful to him for getting me and Cordelia together, even if he regretted it. It was hard to understand the feelings and motives of other people. No one but Cordelia was supporting me at the start, but now, the press were behind me. Clive could go to hell.

Straight away my mobile rang again, it was Cordelia.

'George I've confirmed all those interviews and I'm biking round details as we speak. Also I've spoken to the papers, they've had very positive feedback so far, apparently the public have been sending e-mails in support of your plight. We're winning.'

'That's all I need to hear.' Clive was a fool, Cordelia was doing her absolute best. I had to trust her because she was all I had.

# Chapter Twenty-five

My first appearance was on *Wake Up Britain!* Which meant I had to get up in the middle of the night and travel to the studio in east London. There I was met by a lovely young lady called Sally and taken to make-up. I was a little taken aback but they said it was normal 'so my nose didn't shine under the studio lights'. I felt nervous, as I sipped at a coffee and waited for my turn on the sofa with Anton Harvey and Felicity Long, but I didn't have long to wait.

'Our second guest this morning is a man with an unusual story to tell. He actually took his childhood sweetheart to court to try to get her to marry him. Ladies and Gentleman . . . George Conway.'

My legs wobbled as I walked on to the set but I faced the camera, gave them a smile, shook hands with Anton and Felicity and sat down.

'George, welcome,' Felicity said, smiling brightly.

'Thank you,' I replied.

'So, George, a bit weird to say the least, suing someone to get them to marry you,' Anton said. My first reaction was to punch him; his voice was so mocking. But I was here to win sympathy.

'It might sound strange but I felt I had no other option,' I replied, again, with a slight smile.

'Why is that?' Felicity asked. I wondered how long they had been working as a double act. They were probably screwing each other which would have explained a lot.

'I have been in love with Holly for as long as I can remember. We've been pretty inseparable since we were twelve. But of course, growing up it's not healthy to have only one relationship, we both agreed on that. However, we always said we'd be together. I was ready before Holly, that was it really. At twenty I told her I was ready to commit to her but she wasn't to me. Although we were sleeping together constantly, she was still seeing other men. So she agreed to sign a pact, actually it was her idea—'

'Can I just interrupt? You were sleeping together but she slept with other men? Didn't that give you a clue that she wasn't interested?' Anton was a jerk. If he was sleeping with Felicity then she was a jerk as well.

'She reassured me to the contrary. Have you ever been in love, Anton?'

'No, I'm married.' He laughed at his hilarious joke.

'Well, then you are luckier than me. Holly said that we would end up together, she promised that and I love her as much now as the day we met. I didn't sue her to hurt her, but to make her see what she was throwing away.'

. 'But you weren't successful were you?' Felicity said. No, of course I wasn't you single-brain-celled bimbo, otherwise I wouldn't fucking be here. I took a deep breath.

'No, which wasn't a surprise. I'm a lawyer and I knew my chances of winning were slim. I just wanted her to see how much she means to me.'

'But if she doesn't want you, don't you think you'd be better off walking away?' Anton asked, looking too smug. This wasn't as easy as I thought.

'Perhaps I would, but I know in my heart that I am meant to be with Holly and she'll realise one day that she's meant to be with me.'

'Thank you George, I'm afraid that's all we have time for . . . after the break we meet Kelly, the kitten who can tell the time.'

They beamed. I smiled. Then I said my curt thank yous and left.

I sat in the dressing room and called Cordelia.

'You were marvellous,' she said.

'It was a fucking fiasco. Those brainless morons couldn't interview a chimpanzee.'

'Actually they can't even interview a kitten, which is what they are trying to do as we speak, but they are very popular, and you came across very well. Keep it up this afternoon and we'll be home and dry.' I felt slightly reassured.

The afternoon interview was with Nancy Witter. She came to meet me before the show went on air and we ran over what she knew about me, and I filled in the blanks. She was lovely, reminded me of my mother, when my mother had been talking to me.

'So, what we will do is talk a bit about your story, then I'll ask a couple of questions then to finish I'll ask if you have a message for Holly, which you can then relate.'

'Sounds good.'

And it was. I told my story without any mocking. The sympathy on Nancy's face was so genuine I wanted to cry. Then finally she asked me if I had anything I would like to say to Holly. I looked straight at the camera on cue.

'Holly, if you're watching, I want you to know that I love you so much. Please come back to me.' Then I let a single tear roll down my cheek.

I called Cordelia from my dressing room.

'George you're a genius – the tear – my God, you almost had me crying and I never cry.'

'It was genuine, Cordelia.'

'Of course it was. No question. Now if there is anyone left in the country with any sympathy for Holly I'll eat my Manolo Blahniks.'

In the taxi on the way back to my flat I thought for the first time about Holly. Had she seen the programmes? Of course she would have done. There was no way that she could resist watching. I wondered if they had swayed her yet. I wondered if we'd got rid of Joe. I had an overwhelming desire to talk to her but knew that I mustn't. I had been told by Cordelia to let her come to me. I was so psyched by the way things were going that I knew it was just a matter of time.

The press picked up on my television appearances and I got some good coverage. It was superb. There was even a phone poll in the biggest national daily newspaper asking people to vote if they thought Holly should marry me! I was gaining ground each day. By the time I came to do the show with Michael Martin, I had gained enough confidence not to feel nervous any more. I felt like an old hand and more than that I was enjoying myself. The lights, the cameras, the action. It was an amazing buzz.

However, Martin's show was different because I sat on a stage, told my story, then members of the audience asked me questions. Cordelia had told me that this was the sort of show where you needed the audience onside from the word go. I had no idea because I never watched this sort of thing. I knew there were hundreds running in America but not being the sort of person who had time for daytime TV, I never watched. Julia and I called it trash TV. I felt a pang as I was reminded of her but pushed it away. I wasn't trash and this was TV. That was all.

I was the third guest, and the show was about unrequited love. Which annoyed me because my love wasn't unrequited, it was just unrealised, which is what I said. I looked at the audience and at the scary fat man in the ill-fitting checked shirt and the woman who had warts on her nose, and knew I didn't belong there. I was going to kill Cordelia.

However, in the meantime I needed to say something, so I told my story, with the tear which now seemed to appear on demand. I told them the same I'd told everyone, there was nothing new to say and no new way of saying it. When the audience got to speak, one woman asked me if I'd marry her, another said that Holly was blatantly a fool. A man told me he admired me for being able to admit my feelings, another said that I should move on because she didn't deserve me. Unlike the ugly people that I shared the set with, I gained the audience sympathy, and their affection. When Michael read out a statement from Holly, (who refused to attend), they booed. I was once again triumphant as they applauded and cheered for me. They liked me, they supported me, they reaffirmed my belief that I was right.

As I left, I was asked for my autograph. It was such an amazing feeling, imagine being asked for your autograph for the first time ever. I signed with a flourish and whistled as I sat in yet another taxi.

Instead of going home I went straight to Cordelia's office. She was almost orgasming she was so pleased with me.

'You are not going to believe it. I've had letters and e-mails forwarded on from newspapers and the TV shows. You're a huge hit with the public. Huge. Mammoth. Let's go to lunch, I feel like celebrating.'

'Don't I have anything else on today?'

'No, nothing until tomorrow night, the *Keith Northam Show*. Besides I've got loads of other offers for us to talk about. Come on, I'm buying.'

We went to an expensive French restaurant where Cordelia ordered champagne. Before we chose food we discussed the offers.

'I've got a request from the *Mail* for an interview, they haven't covered you yet and feel a bit left out, so I agreed to that. They've got a huge circulation. Then *GQ* want to do an interview with photos.'

'A photo in *GQ*?'

'I know, fab isn't it. Then we've got a few more shows, I suggest you do. Also, the *Herald* will have the result of your poll the day after tomorrow, they want you to comment on the outcome.'

'I don't know what to say. Some woman asked for my autograph today.'

'Darling you better get used to it, because you're a hit.' She touched my hand, lightly, I smiled at her. The champagne and the success was making me horny. Beyond horny. This wasn't like anything I'd felt before, it was spreading through my entire body. I had no idea what it was but it felt great.

We ordered lunch and ate it but I didn't take my eyes off Cordelia. Of course I would rather be taking Holly to bed, but she wasn't likely to agree to that and I needed a physical release. I ordered another bottle of champagne and made sure that Cordelia drank more than me. When she asked for the bill, I pounced.

'I want to prepare for Keith Northam's show and thought I would look at some pre-recorded videos, maybe you'd care to join me?' I gave her a direct look.

'Where are they?' Her voice was husky and I knew that she wanted to.

'My place.'

'Well, you're my biggest client, I can hardly refuse.' She paid the bill and we hailed a cab back to my flat.

When we were in the cab I put my hand on her thigh but nothing more. I could tell by the look on her face that she had no objections. It was a simple gesture. I noticed she had on stockings (not those dammed tights – passion killers) and I wasn't sure who was more turned on. I paid for the taxi, and she was looking at me with a sexy expression; I could tell she was aching for it. I led her into the flat, and as soon as we were through the door I kissed her.

The kiss was hard. Months of frustration went into that kiss. When we pulled apart she was breathless.

'I thought you wanted to watch the tapes,' she said, teasingly.

'Get your blouse off.' I knew Cordelia's type. They came across all hard and bossy but really all they wanted was to be told what to do. She undid her blouse and let it slip to the floor. I didn't touch her. 'Your skirt,' I commanded, and watched as she unzipped it and let that fall. She stepped out of it and I looked at her. I wanted her. She was wearing a pair of tiny white satin pants, her bra which cupped her smallish breasts matched, as did her suspender belt clipped to her natural stockings. Her high-heeled shoes were still on her feet.

'Keep the shoes on, but take your bra off,' I snapped.

'Kiss me,' she said, her voice all girly and seductive.

'Not yet . . . do as I tell you.' My voice was commanding and I could see her getting more and more flushed. She unhooked her bra and her breasts were free, with nipples hard as peanuts. I made her stand there but kept staring at her as I took off my suit, my shoes, my shirt, finally my socks. Then I moved towards her.

'Suck me,' I ordered and she removed my boxer shorts and sank to her knees.

I had missed sex so much. Cordelia was fucking brilliant. She sucked and licked me till I climaxed, then I brought her to orgasm using my tongue. I turned her over and took her from behind, and she squealed with pleasure. We hit the top of the scale at the same time and collapsed on the floor.

'Wow! I have never had sex like that before,' she said, breathing heavily.

'Me either. You're a fucking sexy woman Cordelia.' I looked at her, although I had removed her pants she was still wearing her stockings and shoes.

'I want more,' she demanded.

'Be my guest.'

She straddled me. We had sex countless times, and each time it got better. She was the horniest woman I'd ever met. She was mine for the taking and I would be taking more and more.

The following morning when we woke up she seemed hesitant.

'What's wrong?' I asked.

'I'm your publicist, George,' she replied.

'Exactly, which is why this is so perfect. No one can read anything into us spending time together. I'm very upset at the moment, you didn't think that it was wise to leave me alone. You're the PR you work it out.'

'So you want it to happen again?'

'Right now for starters, but only for starters.'

'You're my client, I must do as you ask.' She resumed her coquettish manner.

'Then get your head down and go to work.'

Cordelia had to go into the office which left me with time to kill before my car came to pick me up to go to the studio. I thought about what had happened. I surprised myself because I'd never been the dominant type that liked to tell women what to do, I was normally too busy taking care of their needs. Julia had made me nervous in bed because what I felt for her was a mix of the emotional and physical. There was a tenderness between us. But with Cordelia, I knew she wanted me to take her hard and instruct her what to do. It turned her on as much as it did me.

The Keith Northam interview wasn't live. So, although it was due to go out that evening, we were filming it in the afternoon. There was an audience and other guests, famous guests. An England footballer (I'm ashamed to say I didn't know any England players), and a pop star called Saffron, I didn't know her either. There was a buzz in the studio that I hadn't experienced before. The audience had come to see the celebrities and the host. Suddenly it occurred to me as I went into make-up that I was a part of it. I was on the same show as these 'stars'. I winked at Tessa, who was applying my make-up, and realised that just by being here, my celebrity status was being acknowledged as well.

This was a proper television show. The host was funny and popular and the viewers cut right across the range, not just house-wives and students. I was still on a high from the realisation of who I was. I was still pumped up from the great sex with Cordelia. It was amazing the confidence that followed a good screw.

The recording started, I was the last guest on. I waited for my cue and when it came, found that the other guests were staying on set. I kissed the singer, shook hands with the footballer and with Keith.

'Oh you're a lovely boy,' Keith said, and the audience howled. I wasn't sure of his motives. Was he trying to embarrass me or come onto me? Intimidation hung in the air, but I was deter-mined not to crumble. I had to remember who I was; a rising star.

'Thanks, shame Holly Miller doesn't think so,' I replied and got another laugh. Then Keith proceeded to relate my story, in his own words.

'This poor man has been abandoned by his one true love. It turns out that she used him for sex, not something all men would complain about admittedly, but George isn't happy. You actu-ally tried to sue her didn't you?'

'Yes,' I laughed, because that seemed to be appropriate. 'I was so grief-stricken at being rejected that I took her to court to try to enforce the pact we'd made to marry at thirty.'

'Are you thirty?'

'I am, we both are.'

'So what happened?'

'It wasn't successful. The judge dismissed it, which wasn't a surprise but it left me with a broken heart. Ever since then I've been trying to get her to realise that we're made for each other.'

'Oh well, if she doesn't want you I know a lot of other people who do.' Keith winked at me and the interview was over. Just like that.

It amazed me every time, how short these interviews were. They barely gave you a chance to say 'hello' and 'goodbye' before it was over. Blink and it's gone. But I contented myself with the fact that the TV exposure I was getting, no matter how brief, was bringing me closer to my goal. It was enough. Enough to make me a celebrity.

I had to stay around while he challenged some member of the audience to eat a bowl of uncooked vegetables, then it was over. He took hold of my hand.

'I wish you luck George, you're such a nice man.'

'Thanks,' I said, and went to call Cordelia.

'George, how did it go?'

'How are your knickers?'

'Slightly damp.'

'It went fine, do you want to watch it together.'

'Yes, but your flat is so depressing, come over to mine.'

'When?'

'As soon as. I'm leaving the office now.' She gave me her address and hung up the phone.

The feeling I got after walking off that set was unreal. It was awesome. People clapped and cheered for me! All I did was tell my story and they all applauded. I wasn't the freak that Holly and my family made me feel like; I was no longer isolated. Someone cared about me. More than one person cared about me. Suddenly I had gone from being alone to being a hero. I was in demand. It was incredible. I felt more like my old self; I was regaining control of my life. I felt as if I was seven-foot tall when I walked out of the building. The preceding weeks had bowed me but now I was walking tall once more. Not defeated, never going to be defeated; invincible. At the door a couple of young women approached me.

'Could we have your autograph please?' one asked, and

shoved a piece of paper in front of me. I flashed them my best smile.

'Do you know who I am?' I asked, using the old celebrity line but not in the way it was normally orated. I wanted to make sure they hadn't mistaken me for the footballer. I needed them to know who I was.

'Course we do, you're George Conway, we're your biggest fans. I can't believe that girl doesn't want you, she must be insane.' I laughed aloud, I couldn't believe this was happening to me. I took the pen and asked their names then I signed their pieces of paper, bestowed a cheek kiss on each one before climbing into my waiting car. I wound down the window.

'I really do appreciate your support,' I said. 'It's been very hard.'

'We think you're great.' As the car pulled away I realised I was sexually aroused.

I was a celebrity. Somehow or other I was. Offers from *GQ*, the newspapers, television shows, even some women's magazines were flooding in. Radio 1 wanted me to appear on a show, as did Virgin, Capital and others. I was in demand. Real demand. And I couldn't believe how good it felt. This would show Holly. She would see how famous I was becoming and then she'd be more than sorry about the way she'd treated me. Adulation is the biggest high you can ever get, and I was getting it daily. If I had known it would feel this good, then I would have joined this world years ago. It was so easy. Not only was it sexier than law, it was more rewarding than law.

When Cordelia opened the door she was wearing very little. A black basque covered her slim body. Black lace stockings held up with a black suspender belt clasped her legs. No knickers. High heels. I was out of my clothes in a flash. I looked at her and wondered if it was her that was turning me on, or my new-found career. I think it was a combination. After we'd had a quick fuck, I wanted to get down to business.

'Can we go through all the offers I've had before we settle down to watch the show?'

'How romantic.' Cordelia licked her lips and went to get her notebook. We went through the list twice (I couldn't believe the offers I was getting), then we had more sex. Fame is such an aphrodisiac. I wondered if, when it all died down, I'd ever be able to raise an erection again. Or maybe it was here to stay. The fame not the erection. 'George, you are becoming a star, you realise that don't you?' Cordelia said.

'I do, and I know exactly who I need to thank for that.' I was aware of how invaluable she had become, and I figured that if I wanted this level of fame for a while longer then I would need to keep her happy. Luckily, I knew just how to do that.

# Chapter Twenty-Six

---

## *Kiss And Tell*

Safety in numbers, that was my new motto. My mother was right, it wasn't a good idea to leave me on my own. Ever since the tabloid story and the ensuing television appearances I had felt more and more threatened by what George was doing. It had been only a week but I was part of the daily news. Or George was. Past the fact I was the evil nymphomaniac slut who ruined his life, no one was interested in me. The sad thing was that George was fast becoming a national hero for doing nothing but concocting a load of lies. No one would be captivated by the romance of the real story; nor would they be enamoured by his behaviour, so he changed it. It had very little to do with me and it was driving me crazy. The worst thing was that I knew his story had a limited shelf life, but then the pregnancy would extend that, and at some point they would find out about it. I had no doubt of that.

I thought about telling him myself, but then why should I feed his story? I didn't have the strength to battle with him but I wasn't going to give him the ammunition. I was driving myself round the bend with my musings on the whole thing so having people with me was keeping a degree of sanity in my life.

My parents were leaving at the weekend and my sister was arriving for a week. I wasn't looking forward to it. She was the only person who was cross with me and I didn't really like being told off. But my mother decided that we needed to spend time together and Imogen was sacrificing a week of cooking dinner for Jack (or more likely a week of going out for dinner with Jack), to take care of me. I was supposed to be grateful and I was, honestly. I was just a bit scared of her and her opinion of her little sister.

To have people round to watch Keith Northam, or more accurately George on Keith Northam, had been my mother's idea. When we watched him in *Wake Up Britain!* I shouted at the television and ranted for hours afterwards. When I saw him with Nancy I cried. The Michael Martin show reduced me to screaming at the screen, and when they read my statement and people booed me, I cried again. I couldn't believe the exposure he was being given. I certainly couldn't understand the hype.

Reading the newspapers was becoming an ordeal. In my job we used to celebrate even the tiniest mention in the tabloids, now I dreaded looking. My work was suffering because I was so wrapped up in myself and my new interactive relationship with my television, and I know that Francesca and Freddie were carrying me. So, my mother had decided that I would feel better if I had people to take the edge of my reaction, hence the party that was awaiting George's latest appearance. My mother had even bought nibbles and wine. Anyone would think we were celebrating, except that the atmosphere didn't match the refreshments. We had the television on in the background but no one was watching and the conversation was definitely stilted.

Lisa was sitting on the floor, in front of the armchair which housed Max. She was looking at the day's papers, catching up on the life of her wayward friend. Lisa said to me that she never thought my life would be more interesting than hers but it was. I believe she meant well.

'Oh my God,' she shrieked.

'What now? I read that paper and there wasn't much, Oh God this is a nightmare,' I shrieked.

'It's got nothing to do with you, Hol. No, there's this thing you can get to make your boobs bigger just for a few hours. But then they go back to normal size. Apparently it's very popular in the States.' I heard myself laughing loudly, out of relief that I hadn't actually missed anything.

'I would sue,' Freddie said.

'What are you talking about?' Francesca looked at him sharply.

'I'd sue any bird that did that to me. Imagine, you spot this woman in a bar and you think to yourself "nice tits love", then you go up to her and buy her a drink. You get talking, have a few more drinks, maybe go to dinner and then you go home with her and before you've had time to say whey hey her tits have shrunk and they're pretty much like fried eggs and you're sizzling in bed with them. I would sue for having been seduced under false pretences.'

'You are so sexist, Freddie,' Lisa said.

'No shit,' I added.

'Actually I think he has a point,' my father said, which shocked us all.

'But you wouldn't chat up a woman because of her bust size would you dear?' my mother said. I think it was more of a statement than a question.

'I wouldn't chat up anyone full stop love, but if I were a young, free, single man like Freddie I would agree with him.'

'What do *you* think, Max?' Francesca asked. 'We might as well get the whole male point of view.'

'Well I'm not really a breast man, obviously,' he said looking at Lisa's flat chest; she took a swipe at him. 'But I think that the point is why? Why would you increase your bust size for a short time anyway? And how on earth would you know what size of bra to buy?'

'That's a good point. I wouldn't do it,' I said, looking at my ever expanding chest, 'but then I wouldn't need to the rate I'm going.'

'Well I might give it a try. It's only sixty quid a tube. We could have five hours of fun, Max, and then I'd go back to normal, and that's not all, apparently it works on men's bits too.'

'In that case, I might give it a try,' Freddie said.

'You've got a nerve, I'd bloody well sue you,' Francesca said.

'Ah, but I'd use it just before and you'd be long gone by the time five hours was up.'

'Freddie you're a monster.'

'I think it's starting,' my mother said, initiating silence in the room.

'Oh for God's sake, can we talk normally for a while, at least until he comes on,' I asked, as I heard the irritating opening credits.

'What shall we talk about?' Lisa asked.

'I don't know,' I snapped, feeling myself tense up. I was sure that all this tension and stress wasn't good for the baby, but I consoled myself with the fact I had started my yoga sessions last week and the instructor assured me that not only would they benefit the baby and the fitness of its mother but also it would help to control my stress. I definitely needed that. I knew I should make more of an effort to stay calm, but it wasn't in any way easy.

'I don't like this chap very much,' my father said.

'I think he's sweet,' my mother countered.

'Bent as a two-bob note,' my father replied.

'No, really?' My mother sounded genuinely surprised. I wished the silence would return.

I chewed my hair through the guests that preceded George. I wasn't interested, I couldn't concentrate, and I don't think I heard a single word they said. Then, all of a sudden, he was on screen.

'He always wears the same fucking suit,' Freddie said.

'Shush,' Francesca chastised. We all watched.

'Well that wasn't so bad,' my mother said as cheerfully as she could muster.

'It's strange,' Francesca said. We all turned to look at her.

'What is?' I asked. I had managed to refrain from shouting at the screen but I was feeling utterly depressed by the warm response he got from Keith and the audience. I couldn't even begin to comprehend how this story, even his version of it, had captured the public and the media. The Marriage Pact story was known to so many people thanks to the newspapers and his television appearances. George was known as The Marriage Pact Man. I was the hated villain, or should I say The Marriage Pact Villain. It was incredible. All this just because I signed a marriage pact with my best male friend when I was twenty and drunk. They say things in your past come back to haunt you, but no one could have envisaged this, surely.

'He's changed an awful lot this week. Have you seen how at first, when he was on that breakfast show he was quite timid, well not timid exactly but not as confident as he came across there,' Francesca continued, pulling me out of my thoughts.

'What are you saying?' Freddie asked.

'That he is beginning to enjoy himself.'

'Shit,' Freddie said.

'But what does that mean?' Lisa asked.

'It means that George is no longer doing this to get Holly to fall in love with him, he's doing it because he likes it.'

'Which makes him a hundred times more dangerous than he was,' I finished.

'Oh dear,' my mum said. Understatement of the year.

'I'm not sure what to suggest,' Francesca said, looking worried.

'Me either. I thought that he'd give up on me at some stage, I thought it would all die down long before the baby thing came out, but now, now he's enjoying his notoriety, so he'll keep it going as long as he can.' Now I was getting a tiny bit hysterical.

'But he'll need something to hinge it on. Look at the *Big Brother* contestants, they got famous for being on TV, but when they were off TV only a couple went on to stay famous,' Max said reasonably.

'You're right, but George is so determined, and relentless. If he is enjoying the fame, he'll make it last a bit longer, maybe not for ever but long enough for this to continue until everyone knows about the baby, which will give him his lever, at least until after the baby is born and the paternity is determined.'

'I wish you'd take a test, just so you could tell the press that you do know who the father is,' my mother said.

'And if it's George?'

'Then at least we'll know.'

'Mum, you know it's dangerous. I can't do that, not yet.'

'I'd like to take a shotgun to him,' my father said, suddenly.

'Me too,' Max echoed.

'Perhaps if we all went round with baseball bats and acted threateningly,' Freddie suggested.

'I don't think that I will dignify that suggestion with an answer,' I stated.

It soon became apparent that we weren't getting very far, and the 'party' broke up soon after. I was too exhausted to think any more so I went straight to bed.

When I woke the next day, I thought of Joe. He hadn't responded to my letter and although I wasn't really surprised, it still hurt. I couldn't help thinking how humiliated he must feel. I was pretty humiliated but men felt it more keenly than women. According to the press and according to George, I was in love with him and had slept with him for most of my post-pubescent life. According to me I had only slept with him once. That must have been hurtful for Joe and I knew that he couldn't ignore it.

Or ignore the poll that voted eighty-seven per cent in favour of me marrying George, or ignore the fact that I might be carrying his baby. I had been so busy thinking of myself, feeling sorry for myself that I hadn't given Joe much thought apart from the usual broken-heart ones, and even they were about me. I knew, as soon as I woke up, that whatever happened I had to see him.

I felt a stab of jealousy as I wondered if he had someone else and I willed that not to be so. I decided to call him in the office, that way if I managed to get through to him he couldn't be too nasty to me. Not that he had ever been nasty to me. I still loved him ergo he had to still love me. I should have tried harder to make things easier for him, instead of thinking selfishly. I was angry with myself for the first time, as I realised how truly self-centred I had become.

I had my morning cereal and tea, and then, when ten o'clock struck I grabbed my mobile, shut myself in my bedroom and called him. I felt brave and scared at the same time.

'Joe McClaren.' My insides flipped over at the sound of his voice.

'Joe, it's Holly.'

'Hi . . .' he sounded uncertain.

'Please don't put the phone down, although I know I deserve it. Joe, I know it's only been a couple of weeks, but . . . all the press stuff.'

'It's horrible. I can't believe he could do that to you.' He was speaking quietly, but at least he sounded compassionate.

'I know, but I was worried about you?'

'Me, why?'

'It might be horrible for me but at least I am responsible, you didn't ask for any of this and you shouldn't have to read those lies.'

'Holly, I do know that most of it is lies.'

'It's just that I worried.'

'Worried that I'd believe George and not you?' His words

reiterated my selfishness. I hadn't called him to ease my own conscience. Had I? No, I had called for him, not for me, just for him.

'Yes.' I hung my head in shame. Even when I was thinking of him I was really thinking of me.

'I wouldn't do that.'

'Joe can we meet, please, even if just for a few minutes?' There was a pause in which I prayed for him to say yes.

'OK.'

'Thank you.' We arranged to go for lunch the following day, at a pub round the corner from his flat. That way, there was no reason for him not to turn up. Then I spent the rest of the day worrying about us meeting until I decided to read some more of Dr Miriam.

Apparently I was about to see my stomach grow very quickly. I was really looking forward to that. I would soon be obviously pregnant, visibly pregnant. Fat. I wondered about wardrobe and decided that I needed to go shopping. Although if you don't know how big you're going to get how do you know what to buy? Or do you just buy a shit load of elasticated stuff and watch it expand with you? I didn't really like the sound of that. I already had some things that I couldn't fit into. My very sexy Juice jeans for one thing, and my tight black Joseph trousers (actually I had a few of those). I had to wear my baggiest clothes and even my hipsters were no good because all of a sudden I had hips. I was pear-shaped. It was bloody depressing. I had been dumped, the victim of a media campaign, and now I was getting fat.

I went swimming with my mother that afternoon. Yoga and swimming were my chosen pregnancy activities. Designed to contain my expansion a bit. We went to the local swimming pool, where I had become a bit of a regular (well I'd been twice already with Lisa). My mother changed into her extravagant floral swimming costume and me into my black Lycra one which was about to become too small along with everything else I owned.

I hadn't told anyone, not even my mum about my forth-coming meeting with Joe. They were leaving in the morning, and Imogen wasn't arriving until the afternoon, so thankfully I was unsupervised for long enough to see Joe. I felt almost happy as I began my lengths.

I had always thought swimming a most boring activity, you go up and down and then turn around and go up and down again, but now I had begun to find it relaxing. Not only was it helping me burn calories but it was relaxing my mind. As were my yoga classes. Actually, I was rarely calm but imagine how I would have been without yoga. I would have been like a wild woman. Probably I would have taken to biting things and not washing my hair, or not washing full stop. I wouldn't talk any more I'd just wail and wail. You see, the yoga *was* really helping. So, although I would at some stage have to go to birthing classes, I was doing all right.

My mother said that in her day you just got on with it. Bearing in mind that 'her day' was only thirty-four years ago with Immi and thirty with me, she made it sound like it was the dark ages. And in a way, mum was right. She never had stretch-mark cream and all the expensive vitamin supplements I was taking. She didn't go to yoga, she went to a class run by the local hospital. She didn't have the choice of drugs I was having. And she certainly didn't believe in all the fuss pregnant women seemed to make these days. By the end of that conversation I almost felt guilty for all the modern developments and technology that would make having a baby so incredibly easy for me. But actu-ally I was more than grateful.

I swam my fourth length and noticed my mother was sitting on the side dangling a foot in the water. I swam towards her.

'Why aren't you swimming?' I asked. After all, she had insisted on coming with me.

'I don't much like it really and it's terribly cold,' she replied. I rolled my eyes and continued until I'd done the requisite twenty lengths.

The swim had relaxed me but I still felt nervous about my forthcoming meeting, especially as I couldn't tell anyone. The good thing was that Joe was so much in my head I didn't even bother to get upset about the press slaughter I'd suffered that day. Keith Northam had been quoted as saying that George was one of life's true gentlemen. I had been called 'mad' by him and just about everyone else. Actually, there was only one small mention of me in one of the tabloids and also two readers' letters, so it wasn't a bad press day. With that and with Joe agreeing to see me it was a pretty good day in all, especially compared to recent days. I tried to hold that thought as it was the most positive I'd had in a while.

# Chapter Twenty-seven

I waved my parents off, crying because I really would miss them. More than likely they would be back, but I wasn't sure because mum didn't want to give me too much advance information about her roster. I assured them that I would be able to cope for a few hours until I met Imogen at Paddington Station, and finally they seemed to believe me.

As soon as they'd gone, I ran back in my flat and started panicking about what to wear for my meeting with Joe.

I'd already had a bath, and washed my hair but I brushed it until it shone. Actually it was really shiny at the moment anyway. Being pregnant was making my skin and hair look good. Of course that could be attributed to the fact I hadn't had any alcohol, but I didn't want to think about that too much. I was beginning to miss alcohol, which is a little scary because it would imply an addiction, however slight. But, after the self-righteous, pious, Holly finally realised that punishment was not a reason to give up drinking and that the baby was, I finally admitted to myself that it was harder than I thought it would be. Just as I thought I might allow myself a little to drink after all, I then realised I couldn't. My doctor told me that a glass of wine here and there was fine. She said it as if she was suggesting a treat (look pregnant woman, a glass of wine, how exciting). I didn't tell her I was more a-bottle-a-night girl. What fucking good was a glass? Or Guinness, which is apparently good for you because it's jam packed full of iron. But I hated the stuff. So I kept to my self-imposed drinking ban. It was better for the baby and it was much easier than having just one glass. It was if you're me.

I had no idea what to wear, especially as I had trouble finding anything, but I wore a black skirt (just above the knee), which still fitted because it had always been a bit too big, and a red top. Did I look like a mum-to-be? No, I didn't, I looked sexy, especially as I pulled on my high-heeled knee-length boots. I tried to ignore the fact that my calves bulged a bit as I shoe-horned myself into them. I wanted Joe to see me looking as if I was in control. Even if I wasn't. I ordered a taxi to go to Camden. It was decadent but it meant I could avoid public transport which scared me. There had been a few photos of me in the press and although I definitely wouldn't be as familiar to people as George, I felt safer in a cab.

To say I was nervous would be like saying I was quite upset when Joe walked out on me; a huge understatement. I was excited to be seeing Joe; I was desperate to see him. But, still I was nervous. What if he couldn't cope and we had a row, or he walked off before we'd even talked? I didn't expect him to come running back to me, I wasn't here for a reconciliation no matter how much I wanted that, I was realistic enough to know it wasn't an option. I just wanted to see him. To look at his face, to know that he was real. I knew he was real but since he had left my life, there was a huge gap. I just needed to see him and to know that he was all right. I didn't expect the hole to close up; I knew it wouldn't go away, but it felt right to be seeing him.

I was early, so as I pushed open the door and walked into the pub I didn't expect to see him there. But he was. My heart felt as if it was snapping in two, like a pathetic little twig, that stood no chance when trodden on. He was hunched at a small table with a pint of lager in front of him. I felt tears stinging my eyes and I begged them to go away. He was still as gorgeous as ever, sitting in his black jeans and black shirt. I wanted, no I needed, to go over and throw my arms around him. But I certainly couldn't do that. Instead, I took another deep breath and I walked over to him. As if he could feel my presence he turned around just before I reached the table.

'Hi,' he said.

'Hi,' I replied.

'Can I get you something?' he asked.

'I'll have an orange juice, please.' I sat down. I fiddled with the beer mat until he returned. He put the orange juice down in front of me and I took a sip. I wished it had some gin in it.

'Joe, I have no idea where to start. I just needed to see you.'

'How are you?'

'I've been better.'

'What about the baby?'

'The baby is fine. I've started yoga and I go swimming, although I'm running out of clothes that fit me.'

'You look fantastic.'

'Thanks.'

'How are you coping with the press?'

'That's what I wanted to ask you.'

'Holly, I can't imagine how hard this is for you, but I know one thing, I wish I'd given him a good kicking when I had the chance.' I resisted the urge to fall about laughing at Joe's hard man act, but I was flattered, I could tell he still cared about me even if he hated me a bit.

'I know, but I'm not sure that would have helped. I wish I knew what to do.'

'The baby?'

'What?'

'You haven't done a test? You haven't told him?'

'I haven't, no.'

'Good.'

'Good, why?'

'I don't know but I was afraid you were coming here to tell me the baby was his.'

'I'm not telling you that. I hope to God it isn't. I know that doesn't make things better Joe, but I would do anything for this baby to be yours.'

'I know that, I believe you Holly. I'm just not sure how I can do, what I can do. I'm so fucking confused. And I'm angry, Holly, really angry. I have never let myself care for someone like I care about you, I've never been so vulnerable, and I certainly have never been so hurt.'

'If I could take it back.'

'You can't though, can you.'

'No.'

'I don't know where we go from here Hol, I need some time, I don't know. Part of me wants to take you in my arms and go back to when we're planning the wedding, and planning how we're going to take care of the baby, but I don't know if I can.'

'Joe, if you ever ever feel you just might be able to, then please call me. I'll be waiting.'

'So, no chance of you marrying George?'

'I don't think George even cares about that any more.'

'What?'

'He likes being famous. I'm not important.'

'You made him famous.'

'I didn't mean to.'

'I know. But sometimes we do things that we don't mean.'

'And then have to live with the consequences.'

'I guess we do.' I held the tears in check, but I could feel them. Waiting in the wings.

I stood at the end of the platform at Paddington Station waiting for Imogen. It was with a mixture of emotions. I was slightly scared of the week-long lecture I was going to get; I missed the easygoing and nurturing nature of my parents, but I also felt that I deserved the hard time Immi was no doubt going to give me. After leaving Joe and feeling the full brunt of the effect I had on his life, I deserved to be beaten with a sharp stick whilst being made to lie on coals. That was the only way I felt that I would be able to deal with the immense sense of guilt that had settled in.

The train pulled in, and I stood there as a deluge of people passed me. I felt nervous looking for Imogen, as if she wouldn't appear, but then I saw her emerge from the throng, and I felt relieved. She was wearing her city outfit. My sister was hilarious, when she was at home she lived in jeans and casual clothes but when she came to London she always wore suits. Today she was wearing a dark red trouser suit, with high-heeled black boots. She looked as if she was going to a business meeting instead of coming to babysit her pregnant sister. She kissed my cheek, and automatically I rubbed it as her lips were thick with lipstick. Even though I had made more of an effort with my looks than I had in ages, I still felt dowdy in comparison.

Imogen and I had never really been very good at sibling rivalry. I never wanted to be her and she certainly never wanted to be me. We were lucky in that we had a four-year age gap and strong personalities. We were both OK looking, I had dark hair, hers was fair. Our colouring was different but our features the same. She was about two inches taller than me, but I was tall enough not to worry. We got on as children, but there was always a line we never crossed. We became friends as we got older but, again, friends in a sister-type way, not in the same way George was my friend.

When Imogen left home I knew she would never come back, and I followed her soon after. We never gave our parents too much to worry about, well, not until now anyway. Imogen had always been immensely sensible. She was the sort of person who would make a pros and cons list before making a decision. 'Shall I buy the red dress or the black dress? Well the red dress is more dramatic, the black more practical.' That sort of person. I loved her for that, because she was as cautious as I was not. I would never ponder a decision for too long, which is probably why I was in the mess I was in. Imogen would never have got as drunk as I did with George. Then she would have pulled away from his kiss so she could weigh up the options. Then sensibly she would have left. I used to think that my sister was boring, but not any more. Imogen is happy, she might be controlled but she is happy. And I'm not.

'Have you got your car?' she asked, letting me go from her light hug. I didn't feel it was the time to point out that I didn't actually own a car as it hit me how little we really knew about each other. It was going to be a fun week.

'No, I got a cab. I've been to see Joe.' I led her towards the taxi rank.

'Holly are you sure that you should be spending your money on cabs? Babies are expensive you know.'

'Well, you can pay for this one then,' I snapped, then regretted it. Arguing with Imogen was a new thing, and not one I was entirely happy about. I liked our relationship; liked the fact it wasn't over-emotional in any way. I didn't want it to change. Too much was changing.

'Holly, I didn't mean that. Let's just get home, huh?'

'Sorry.'

I asked Imogen about her favourite subject: her husband Jack. That kept the conversation flowing for the journey home.

I let us both in, and took her straight to the spare room.

'It's not a bad flat to bring a baby home to,' she said.

'Thanks.' I hadn't thought about the baby as actually living here. I supposed there would be time for me to decorate the nursery, and buy clothes, but I had done none of that yet. Saying that, I still had five months to go, so there was no great hurry.

'It's big enough, you don't have to negotiate too many stairs, and the spare room will make a lovely nursery. Here, I've got you a present.' Imogen rummaged around in her small suitcase. It was an air-hostess suitcase, albeit a Prada one. One thing that was in direct conflict with Imogen's organisational manner was the way she had packed. Everything was thrown in.

'Do you need hangers or anything?' I asked.

'No, apart from my travelling suit, that needs to be hung. I've got jeans and tops otherwise.'

'Imogen, why do you dress up to sit on a train? It seems a bit crazy.'

'I don't know really, I just always like to look my best. Holly, I know you think I'm old before my time.'

'I don't. It's just that that's the sort of thing mum would do. She would wear her posh outfit to travel and then wear casual clothes the rest of the time.'

'Maybe I'm turning into mother.'

'I feel like I am,' I replied sitting on the bed and rubbing my stomach. Just then Imogen found what she was looking for and pulled out the sweetest set of babygrows in a range of colours. She handed them to me. They were so small, how on earth where they supposed to fit a person? They were tiny. I couldn't hold something that tiny, look after something so small, it would break. *I* would break it. I touched the soft fabric and the enormity of my predicament hit home. I burst into tears.

'If you don't like them I can change them,' Imogen said, coming to sit next to me and putting her arm round me.

'It's not that. How did I get into this mess Immi? I am going to be responsible for a baby, a baby that is going to be so small it will fit into these, and what sort of start have I given it. I'm known in the press as this bitch woman, I've lost Joe, I don't know who the father is. And that will be reported in the papers soon, now George has become the nation's darling.'

'Let's calm down. Everything is unimportant apart from the baby. You have to keep yourself together for the baby's sake if nothing else. What did Joe say when you met him today?'

'Basically that he loved me, and he hated what was happening but he still didn't know if he could forgive me.'

'But it was a start.'

'If I could tell him for sure that the baby was his then maybe we could get back together, but I can't tell him that.'

'And you don't want the test because you could lose the baby as a result.'

'Yeah and can you imagine George. He'll be unbearable if it is his. The thing is as soon as the press find out, and I reckon they'll find out soon, then he will probably demand a test. What I'm hoping is that I can stall him, and the only way he can make me have a test is to take me to court. In a perverse way I feel as if this is the only ammunition I have against him now. He'll be so frustrated by me that maybe he'll start to realise how awful this whole situation is. Do I sound petty?'

'Yes, but I understand. George has totally lost it. I can't believe that he's turned into this monster. Is there anything we can do to stop him?'

'Nothing that I can think of.'

'Holly, can I ask you something?'

'Sure.'

'How did you get pregnant?' I looked at her.

'Immi, you've been married for years, surely you know the basics.'

'Holly, don't be so facetious. You know exactly what I mean. You were on the pill I take it.'

'You really are turning into mum.'

'Holly, I am trying to be supportive but you have to be honest with me.'

'The pill isn't always one hundred per cent safe.'

'If you take it per instructions the chances of it failing are very slim.'

'Well I'm just one of those unlucky cases.'

'You're not.'

'I never forgot to take it, not once.'

'Right. So why didn't it work?'

'I don't know.'

'You do.'

'I don't.'

'Holly, we never had these pathetic arguments as kids, I'll be dammed if I'm going to start having them now.'

'Well then, perhaps you should leave it alone.'

'Or you could be honest for once.'

'I was ill.'

'Right.'

'That's the truth. I had been ill, I was on antibiotics. I slept with Joe while I was on them and I also slept with George. I also drank heavily, and didn't take the tablets that seriously. I had some sort of ear infection, but I forgot all about it. The doctor told me it might make the pill ineffective but I forgot that too.'

'I have never known anyone as good at denial as you.'

'Yeah, I could teach classes.'

'Holly, don't you see, you're to blame for this mess, not George. OK, so most men wouldn't have gone to the lengths he has to pursue you, but the pregnancy, the baby, the paternity, that's down to you.'

'I know.'

I hadn't thought about it like that. The reason I hadn't was because, as my sister so correctly pointed out, I was good at denial. Look how long I was pregnant before I noticed. I remember being ill and feeling miffed because I needed to take antibiotics. I remember having a debate with Freddie about why they tell you not to drink with them. He said it was because it decreased their effectiveness, I said it was because they got you really pissed, an idea that appealed to me. We agreed on a compromise where I would be allowed the odd glass of wine, which is what happened. Then Joe and I had the fight, then I got steaming drunk with George. And not once did I think that my pill wasn't working. I just didn't think. I did it, and afterwards when it was too late to think I put it to the back of my mind.

Until now. Now, when my sister, who is turning into my mother, decided to make me face up to the fact that actually I was responsible for the situation I found myself in. There was no one else to blame.

Self-blame can be quite liberating.

I cooked a chicken while Imogen changed, and then she called Jack and chatted for ages. What they could talk about as they'd been apart only for half a day was beyond me. I liked my sister's relationship, it made me think that love was worth it after all. She stopped me from being a cynic. Eventually when she came off the phone I dished up dinner and we sat at my table in the sitting room. Imogen drank wine, I sipped at my ice-cold water.

'You are funny. Normally you drink like a fish but now you won't go near it.'

'I don't want to do anything else to harm my baby. I've done enough don't you think.'

'More than enough, Holly. You know that you need to take some control back don't you?'

'How?'

'Start with Joe. Keep in touch with him, try to meet him regularly, I think that as long as he can forgive your indiscretion with George, then he might be able to accept things with the baby.'

'Maybe, but I don't know if he'll ever be able to accept bringing up another man's child. I will keep in touch, because I still love him and I pray nightly that this child is his, but I need to get on with life for the two of us. I also need to know what I'm going to do if it does turn out to be George's.'

'Get a damn good solicitor.'

'Exactly. You know, the more George hogs the limelight, the more I want to hurt him because he's dragging my name through the tabloids and the TV without a thought for how it's affecting me. I don't even think that he's thought about what would happen if I went running to him. He doesn't want me any more, he wants the fame now. That's why I am so confused.'

'Holly, I'm not going to let this man beat us. We're the Miller sisters, we can get the better of him.'

'What do you suggest.'

'I don't know but I'll work on it. I might be angry with you, well only because of your head-in-the-sand stance, but I still love you and if it's the last thing I'll do, I am going to get you out of this mess.'

Later as I lay in bed, cocooned in my duvet, I felt better than I had in ages. I was going to fight George, somehow, and I was also going to fight for Joe, but most of all I was going to take care of the baby, because that was my main, if not my only priority.

# Chapter Twenty-eight

Although it was Sunday, Francesca and Freddie were coming over to my place to talk about what we were going to do next. The initial burst of media frenzy had come to a halt but we expected more the following week. Not so much television, but we knew that articles would appear in the papers. We had been using all our contacts to find out who was running the story, or any story, and when, and although we could do nothing to stop it, at least we were aware.

We all sat in the living room, Imogen made coffee, then came to join us.

'Do you want the good news or the bad news?' Freddie asked. He had brought the Sunday papers with him.

'The good?'

'Wrong answer, there isn't any good. The bad news is that you've sparked a huge debate in the *Mail* about women who use men and the fact it's a growing phenomena. They use you and George as a case study, and he comments all the way through. God knows how he got any sympathy, he's an arrogant prick.'

'Freddie, can we get on with it,' Francesca snapped. Freddie looked suitably chastised.

'Sorry. The *Sunday News* have a story about you and, oh shit this is embarrassing, did you ever date anyone called Justin?' I felt the redness start in my toes and creep up my entire body. 'I'll take that as a yes. Well, the thing is that he has sold his story about how you used him.' I almost couldn't bear to look as Freddie passed the paper to me. There in full colour was a picture of Justin, a lovely man with bright orange hair. Justin was a man I dated for two months when I was twenty-six. I have to admit to using him. He worked in the City and I met him through a mutual friend at a party. I was single at the time and he had a good job. I thought it might be nice to be wined and dined for a while and I was right, it was. Sex with a man with ginger pubes was a small price to pay (although it took me months to get rid of the remnants from my bathroom, stubborn little buggers they were). Anyway, he was such a bore that I really couldn't bear it for longer than two months (and it was only that long because he arranged a trip to Paris just as I was going to break up with him). Finally when I did tell him that I didn't think we should carry on seeing each other, I must admit he did get a bit angry, especially as I told him on the way back from Paris when we were sitting in the first-class carriage of Eurostar (all paid for by him). I did feel bad, but then I was young.

Everyone watched me. I found it hard to concentrate on the story. But I did.

### I KNOW WHAT IT FEELS LIKE TO BE USED BY HOLLY MILLER

*Justin Stamp, 30, City Broker is another man used and dumped by Ms Miller. 'I can fully sympathise with George,' he said. 'The thing about Holly is that she is a complete vamp ready to reel you in, then once you've fallen for her she gets what she can and then dumps you without a second thought.' Justin's sad tale began with an introduction at dinner. Immediately he was attracted to the dark-haired beauty (pictured right) . . .*

I stopped and looked at the right-hand side of the page, then I screamed. I hadn't noticed it before, how could I? I didn't recognise this woman who was wearing a lacy black basque, and was spreadeagled across a bed, as me. But it was. Everyone, apart from Freddie, who had already seen it came to look.

'I don't fucking believe it.' I thought it was the usual tabloid 'model', part of another story. But it was me! My parents would be seeing it. I couldn't deal with this so I went back to reading what Justin said, feeling totally sick.

*. . . They went out for two months during which time Justin treated her like a princess. 'I took her to the best restaurants, bought her gifts, I even booked a weekend at a top hotel in Paris, travelled first class all the way. It was on the way back that she dumped me.' Justin is obviously not the first man to be treated callously by her, as George can concur, although he admits that they probably wouldn't have lasted the distance. 'Holly seemed to be out for what she could get. Her selfish nature was evident from the beginning.'*

*George Conway and Holly Miller were betrothed before she left him for someone else. George is still trying to win her back. Our advice is . . . listen to Justin, she is not worth it.*

'They're making me out to be totally horrible, I can't believe it.'

'Holly, is there anything in the story that is untrue?'

'Not exactly.'

'Where did they get that photo from?' Imogen looked horrified.

'I have no idea,' I replied.

'Holly?'

'OK, I let Justin take it while we were in Paris. He'd bought me all this fancy underwear, I thought the least I could do was let him take a photo.'

'With no thought of the consequences. You do realise that our parents will see this.'

'Well, maybe they won't recognise her, after all she didn't recognise herself.'

'Freddie, that's not helpful,' I said, wanting to giggle. It wasn't really funny, but Imogen looked so upset and it was my first 'kiss and tell', well sort of anyway.

'It's not the end of the world,' Francesca said. 'Our clients know that people exaggerate hugely, so I'm not worried on that score. Are there any more likely to come out of the woodwork?'

'I don't think so, well actually there could be loads. I have no idea. I never would have thought that Justin would do this.' I felt a bit horrified at just how many people could do this to me. Not millions, but enough. Then I worried about the fact that it was true. I had used him. But I hadn't used George. The whole thing was becoming quite surreal. But the worst thing was Joe. If he didn't see it then one of his mates would, and just as I was trying to convince him I wasn't a tart, Justin was doing the opposite.

'What else?' I asked, resigned to the fact there was bound to be something.

'Nothing,' Freddie said.

'So only two newspapers?'

'Which is good.'

'Well there is a government scandal,' Francesca pointed out. It did cover most of the broadsheets and tabloids.

They no longer needed to use my story to fill space. They had some real news to report. Although I wasn't thrilled about red-headed Justin spilling the beans, that would probably finish off any hope I had of Joe feeling sorry for me. And I know I used him, but I don't think he was in love with me, in fact I know he wasn't. He liked to take me out with his work colleagues, I was his trophy, and so we both used each other. I liked eating out, I liked being desired and he needed to have someone on his arm, and someone to have sex with. Fair swap I'd say. I would also like to point out that at some stage everyone has used someone in a relationship. Shit, I'm not proud of everything I've done in my life but what thirty-year-old is? If I met them I'd look them in the eye and call them a liar.

'Yeah, thank fuck for the fact the civil service is as leaky as Holly's breasts are about to become.'

'Freddie!' Imogen was on her feet. I took a deep breath, I knew this was an Imogen tantrum stance.

'It's not funny. It's not about Holly, it's about all of us. Her baby isn't even born yet and its mother is being portrayed as a whore. Every day Joe, who loved her, has to read about how callous she's been. Jack has been asked to comment on it as her brother-in-law, Jack writes children's books for God's sake. He's got an image to uphold and having a loose woman for a sister-in-law isn't going to help his sales, and let's not forget Mum and Dad. They live in a small town and they have to endure stares all the time. But they never complain because they love you, Holly. So, no, there is nothing to joke about here and two stories do not constitute good news.' Imogen was shouting and I had to resist the urge to cover my ears with my hands as I had when she'd had tantrums as a child. It wasn't easy.

Freddie and Francesca stared at Imogen as if they'd never met her before. Which, thinking about it, they hadn't. I didn't know what to do, or say. She was right, this affected many more people than just me. I was the least of my own worries. Or I should have been. The *whole* situation wasn't my fault, but it was more my fault than it was theirs. I burst into tears.

'I know, Immi, you're right, but I don't know how to stop it. I so want it to go away but I have no idea how to stop him from doing this. I don't know if I should just fall apart or laugh. Immi don't be mad at Freddie, it's him who keeps my spirits up. We've tried to put our side of the story across to tell people I'm not the bad person that I'm being made out to be. But it's hard because no one wants to know my side. They all like George's version, and the television shows, well, now everyone loves George, so they need to hate me. I'm Lex bloody Luther to his Superman. And it is damn unfair because I know I'm not the only one who's hurting. And it's going to get worse. That's what I can't bear, it's going to get worse when news of the pregnancy gets out. Joe will be dragged into it fully and I can't bear it when I think of Mum and Dad being stared at, because they are the most loving people ever, and they don't deserve this, nor does Joe. He doesn't deserve it and neither do you and Jack, or Francesca or Freddie. I almost can't bear it.' I could feel the tears rolling down my cheeks, the snot dribbling from my nose but I was unable to do anything about it.

There had been jokes, yes, but there were no more jokes to be had. This wasn't flippant. This wasn't funny. It was utterly desperate and that was how I felt at that moment. I felt as if I had nowhere left to turn. Nowhere to go except down. But things were going to get worse and that thought was panic-inducing; I had no idea how I would cope. I was aware of arms around me, but I don't know who they belonged to. I was aware of tissue mopping me as if I were a helpless child. I *was* that child. Thoughts came and went with a speed I couldn't contain. I was in a box with them flying around me, trying to grab them, but being unable to clutch a single one. Then there was blackness, but I don't know when that came either.

I woke up and didn't recognise my surroundings. Actually I did, I was on the set of *Casualty*. Then I shook myself as I realised I was still in a half-dream like state, or that's how it felt. My mouth was dry and furry, but I wasn't drunk. I panicked as it occurred to me that I was in hospital, and I looked around me for someone to tell me what had happened. As I tried to move my arm, I found a head lying on it; Freddie's head. I jerked my arm and watched his head stir, he shook himself awake.

'Hol, are you OK?'

'You tell me?' My mouth felt dry.

'You passed out. The doctors think you just fainted, but they did some tests. We were so worried.'

'The baby?'

'The baby is fine, that's the first thing they checked. I kind of lied to them and said that I was the father, so I got to see the scan, my God, Hol, it's incredible.' I smiled at Freddie.

'You're the only man I know that definitely isn't the father,' I joked, weakly.

'Well, I would like to be. Actually I wouldn't because that would mean I would have had sex with you.'

'I could have got you so drunk that you wouldn't remember it.'

'I guess that would be all right. Seriously honey, I was so worried, so is Francesca, she had to go into the office, but she said to call her as soon as you woke up. Also, a very guilty Imogen is pacing the corridor outside.'

'Why is she guilty?'

'Because she said all that stuff to you, then you cried, I've never seen you cry like that, you totally lost it and then you blacked out.'

'It's not Immi's fault.'

'That's what I told her. I told her it was probably the shock of seeing yourself in the newspaper.'

'Actually I'm used to that by now.'

'But not in your underwear.'

'Freddie, can you get me some water please, and then find Immi for me and a doctor.' I couldn't talk about the newspaper or yesterday any more.

'Sure.' He passed me a glass of water, then he left.

I patted my stomach, it seemed to have grown. The door opened and Imogen appeared. I tried not to notice how awful she looked but it was hard. Her hair was greasy, and her make-up smudged. I had never seen my immaculate sister looking so ghastly in public. I felt guilty again.

'How long have I been here?' I asked.

'It's only Monday. You've been asleep since yesterday. I haven't called Mum and Dad yet, I thought I'd let you decide on that.'

'They don't need to worry any more. Imogen, I'm sorry.'

'No, I'm sorry. I shouldn't have said what I said. This isn't your fault.' She sat on the side of the small bed and took my hand. 'I was out of order, Holly. You're the one who has to deal with this, and you've got a baby to think of. I shouldn't have got angry. You know how hard I find it to be frivolous about things at the best of times.' Imogen was right. She was too serious-minded, a bit like George actually.

'I don't need you to apologise. The baby is really OK?'

'Yes, it's fine.'

'Then there is only one thing left to do.'

'What?'

'Immi, I think it's time I told the world.'

'You mean, announce it?'

'Yeah, the sooner I do it, the sooner they'll lose interest in publishing stories about me. And I don't want the media, or George to find out by any other means. I want to tell the truth. It seems that lies are the only things that hurt anyway.'

'Don't decide yet, get your strength back. You need to do that.' I nodded and closed my eyes. I was so tired.

I awoke to find Imogen, looking slightly smarter, sitting next to my bed.

'How long was I asleep?'

'All day, it's eight now, and Lisa is here. She's just gone to get some coffee, apparently the lack of nicotine is getting to her so she's trying caffeine.'

'Why doesn't she go and have a cigarette?'

'She's given up. Just not very successfully at the moment.'

I smiled, at the familiar. 'What about the doctor?'

'You missed him, but you're suffering from exhaustion, hence the need to sleep. Actually he recognised you, and said it's not surprising that you feel the way you do. But the baby is fine although you have to try to stay healthy for it. I know that's easier said than done.' Just then the door opened again and Lisa breezed in. I was so pleased to see her.

'You silly cow, what were you thinking of?' She walked over and gave me a big hug.

'What are you wearing?' she was in fact, wearing a pair of high-heeled red shoes, and a polka dot dress. She looked a bit like Mini Mouse.

'I was working on the set right, and when Freddie called me I ran out in their outfit. Hideous isn't it?'

'I thought you'd given up.'

'I had, but this job was well paid and I thought why the hell not? What should I care if I look a total tit as long as I'm being paid. But it's the last time. And I think they're probably going to have me arrested for stealing this.'

'You should be arrested for just wearing it.'

'Imogen is coming to stay at mine tonight. I thought it would be better.'

'Thanks Lis.'

'I'll be fine on my own,' Imogen said, looking anything but.

'No, it's settled, you're coming home with me.' They stayed for another hour, until I told them to leave. I needed more sleep.

I was allowed to leave hospital the following afternoon and I managed to stay awake. He prescribed more sleep and told me that although he realised I couldn't avoid stress, I had to try to minimise it.

'Tell that to my ex-boyfriends,' I said.

'Maybe if you said you were pregnant, they'd leave you alone.'

'Or maybe they'd have a feeding frenzy like crocodiles in a zoo.'

'Point taken.' I smiled. After all, he was a doctor, I wondered how much of the real world he had time to live in.

Imogen called a cab and took me home, insisting on making up a bed for me on the sofa. It reminded me of when I was younger, my mother did the same. If we were ill (and we had to prove it), she would make up a bed of the sofa, give us a hot water bottle, switch on the television, and spoil us all day. I loved being ill. I smiled at Imogen.

'You know I think I was just really tired. I feel so much better for the hours and hours of sleep.'

'Francesca is coming over after work to talk to you about what you said yesterday.'

'Shit, you guys are worse than the WI. You all talk about me more than you talk to me.'

'Holly, that's not fair. I told Freddie what you said when he called to see how you were. Lisa agreed with me that they should advise us.'

'I work in PR, I know about the press, I could write my own press release, why do I feel as if you all think that since this happened I've suddenly turned into a moron.'

'It's not that and you know it. We're trying to do the best for you.'

'Sorry, I know you are. I'm just a bit frustrated. If only George would bog off.'

'Yeah, well I'm sorry to say that he was on another breakfast show this morning, he's done an interview in the *National Herald*, and the *GQ* issue with his feature article is out in a week's time.'

'Freddie told you all this?'

'Yes, he's on top of it. Listen, Hol, George has also done some local press in Devon.'

'Shit.'

'I know, but it's just regional. What's important now is to make sure that you are all right, health-wise.'

'I know. I want to wave my magic wand and make him go away.'

'Jack suggested having him kneecapped.'

'You are joking.' Why did all the men think that violence was the answer?

'Actually I think he sounded quite serious. He's really upset for you, not for himself, but for you.'

'Jack's a love. But knowing our luck if we did that *I'd* end up in prison.'

'I know. But it's quite a nice vision.'

I giggled. 'Yes it is. I never thought of myself before as violent but I would like to chop his balls off.'

'With a blunt knife.'

'Immi, you're shocking.' We both hugged and laughed, because, I decided that if I didn't laugh, I would bawl my head off.

That afternoon, Imogen and I read a bit of Dr Stoppard's book, a section on what was going to happen next. Apparently I would start to feel more energetic. I cried with laughter at that given the mammoth sleep I'd just had. The good doctor also said I would be hungrier now so I would probably expand at a fast rate.

'Oh God, I'm going to be like a person with a bicycle pump up my bum. I'll keep growing and growing until the baby bursts forth.'

'No, because you aren't going to be stupid about it. But we ought to think about buying you some maternity clothes. It says that you are probably going to need them now.'

'I'm *not* wearing smocks.'

'Holly, they've come a long way with maternity wear since mum was pregnant.'

'Thank God.'

'Holly, can I ask you how you feel about the baby?'

'I'm excited, terrified, but even though I would never have chosen to get pregnant and have a baby in these circumstances, I know that I love it more than I've ever loved anyone. Well, a different kind of love, I feel so protective. The first thought when I woke up and realised I was in hospital was for the baby. I was terrified in case it was hurt.'

'You really want to be a mother, don't you?'

'Um, yes, I really do.'

'I wish I felt like you.'

'Immi, I only feel like this because I'm pregnant, I didn't want a child before.'

'But I've been married for ever and people keep asking us when we're going to reproduce, but I don't know if I want to.'

'How does Jack feel?'

'He's a children's writer, he loves his audience, and he'd love children of his own.'

'You've talked about it with him?'

'Yes, but I stall him, I'm not too old am I? I still have plenty of time. It's just seeing you pregnant makes me want to feel broody, but I don't.'

'How about we wait until the baby is born and you'll be an aunt, see how you feel then. But don't have a baby if you don't want one. Immi, I don't know what you're scared of but it's not scary, it's wonderful.'

'I'm scared of not loving it.'

'Why would you not love it?'

'Because . . . I don't know. I think I should talk to someone about it because it's not fair on Jack.'

'Have you talked to Mum?'

'No, she wanted kids from the word go.'

'Well then maybe you should see a therapist. There is obviously some reason you feel this way, but I don't think for one minute that you wouldn't love your baby.'

'You don't think I'm crazy?'

'No, I think you're very normal and I think you're very brave for admitting that this is how you feel rather than just getting pregnant. I'm sure that's what most people would do.'

'Thanks, Holly.'

'You're welcome, sis.'

I was learning things about everyone. About Lisa, about my sister, about my parents, even about Freddie and Francesca. It was amazing what a crisis could do, and I suppose that at least the way it was bringing us all together was positive. If there was a positive to be had.

# Chapter Twenty-nine

'Holly, I've brought you loads of work,' Francesca said as she walked through the door.

'Really?' I was pleased, work was just what I needed. Among other things.

'I know we've been making you take it easy, but now I need you, I've got a few proposals that you need to write, and also I need you up to speed on all accounts so you can check that the clients are being serviced properly.'

'I'm sure Freddie's doing that.'

'Yes, I know, but he's new to this responsibility, he needs to know that *you* know he's doing a good job. I need to know as well.'

'I'm thrilled, I was beginning to think that I wasn't really necessary any more.'

'Of course you are.'

We spent an hour going through all the things that needed doing and I felt the old me return. I was a career woman, not just a pregnant messed-up blimp. I also knew that the work would help to take my mind off other things and give me a focus other than myself.

'I don't think you should overdo it,' Imogen said, as she brought in tea. She had made the tea in a teapot I didn't even know I owned, and she carried it on a tray with a plate of biscuits. She was so like my mother.

'Immi, I'm not even going into the office, I'm just working

from home. It'll be good for me. Most pregnant women have to work up to a month before the birth.' I wasn't sure of the exact accuracy of that statement but I sounded authoritative.

'Most pregnant women don't have the media attention you have.'

'Nothing compared to Victoria Beckham.'

'Yeah but she chose her media attention, you didn't.'

I sighed. If Francesca wasn't intending on sacking me, she would once Immi had finished. She'd feel far too guilty to keep me on.

'Imogen, if at any time Holly can't cope she can stop. We're fully behind her, and she can slow down at any time.' I smiled at Francesca with gratitude. Sometimes it was nice to have someone else to do battle with my formidable sister.

'Fine then.' Imogen raised her eyebrows then left the room

'Are things all right between you two?' Francesca asked.

'She's just concerned, and she is sweet but you know, fussing a bit much.'

'Who's on the rota next?'

'Imogen just announced that she's taking a double shift. She won't leave until she knows I'm fully recovered from the fainting episode. Then it's Lisa again, thank goodness. Francesca, I'm worried about the effect all this is having on our clients.'

'You know what I've discovered? Our clients love any press coverage, even if it isn't centred around them. Since all the pieces in the paper about you mention where you work, I've had more new business enquiries than ever.'

'You're kidding?' The world was twisted.

'No, seriously. I think what you have to remember is that everyone is obsessed with celebrity, and although you're not really one, the fact that you're in the tabloids is good enough. No one aspires to the broadsheets any more, or our clients don't. I reckon that I'm going to have to give you a raise for all the potential business you're bringing in.' I looked at her to check if

she was going to break out into a hearty laugh and declare: Joke!'
But she didn't; she looked in earnest.

'You're not just saying that to make me feel better?'

'Holly, I know that you don't see it at the moment, but I'm a
businesswoman first and foremost and as much as I love you I
love my business more. If you were harming it in anyway I'd pay
you off. As it is, you're actually doing me no end of good, albeit
unintentionally. So, can we agree to stop the paranoia. Anyway,
you've got to write the new business proposals. And you've got
to present them. That's the stipulation I have for you. You can't
stay in the background when people have come to us as a direct
result of you.'

'You mean that they want to see me, which is why they've
come to us?'

'Probably, but that's OK. Because we will get some business
from this, well we will when you present the amazing proposals.'

'Am I a freak show?'

'Not exactly freak, you are an object of interest, people are
intrigued. But as I said, these people are serious potential clients,
I'd know if they came to us out of curiosity.'

'I suppose if some good can come out of this, then I'm not
going to complain. But it's bloody perverse. I almost don't know
if I can condone it.'

'Lose the morals Holly.'

'I don't even know where they came from.' We laughed. 'I
think that in the case of the flourishing business it might be a
good time to talk about the pregnancy.'

'Remind me, how pregnant are you?'

'Four and a half months. Halfway there, can you believe it?'

'No, you're not that fat.'

I pulled up my top to show her my rounded stomach.

'My God, that's amazing.' Francesca came over and put her
hand on my stomach. I wasn't entirely comfortable but thought
that it was something I had to get used to. 'Does it kick?'

'I can feel it moving a bit, it feels like a butterfly fluttering its wings. It's truly amazing.'

'Oh, Holly I can't believe you're going to be a mother.'

'Nor can I.'

'It's so exciting. And as you are about to start showing, and as you are going to be going out a bit more, I would advise that we pre-empt the media interest this is going to cause and issue a release.' Francesca was right, she was all business first.

'That's what I was thinking. We might as well get it over and done with.'

'There is always the danger that the interest in you will last until you give birth and paternity is established.'

'There's nothing I can do about that.'

'I know, but you might be in for a good few months of media coverage. Can you handle it?'

'Yes.'

'You know how we think George is in love with the publicity and the fame? He is going to exploit this, with the help of Cordelia. God I wish I'd never slept with her husband.'

'I don't think she is doing this because of you sleeping with her husband. She didn't even know I worked for you when she first came across George. Anyway that's not important. It's obvious that they are going to exploit this, but I bet you they won't try to make me take a DNA. They won't want to risk that the results ruin their little plan. Shit, if I wasn't so terrified that the baby might be hurt I'd have the damn test.'

'I'm going to write a press release. Actually I'm not, Freddie is. It'll say that you're four and a half months pregnant, and that the father is almost certainly Joe, but there is a chance it's George because of a one-night stand. However we put it it's not going to sound very good.'

'No, it isn't. Francesca, I'm going to tell George myself.'

'Are you sure, I don't like the sound of you talking to him.'

'I don't want him to read it in the paper, or have some hack calling him up and asking him his reaction. He was reasonable once upon a time, I need to remember that. This is temporary insanity, I'm sure of it.'

'It's hard to lose friends isn't it?'

'You know it really is. I can't equate the George that's doing this to me with the George that was my best friend. It hurts every time I read the paper or see him on television, because he was the most important person in my life for so long. I grew up with him, I knew him so well, and there is no way that he would have ever hurt me, I know that, which makes this so hard to understand.'

'I know, Holly. I'm going to get Freddie to write the release tomorrow; can you call George tomorrow?'

'I need to call him just after we fire the release out. Otherwise he might go to the papers before us, we need to time it just right.' The world, or the country would know tomorrow that I, Holly Miller, was pregnant, unsure of paternity and then they would hate me more than ever. Imogen was right, unlike Cordelia's type of scraping-the-barrel-celebs, I wasn't courting publicity, nor was I in control of my own image. They had branded me the baddy and ignored my defence. Things, without a doubt were going to take a turn for the worse.

'OK, we'll write it in the morning, you approve it, then we'll have it ready to be faxed out as you call George.'

'I want to come into the office to do it, is that all right? Then at least I'll be able to help.'

'Then you can get started on the work I've given you at the same time. Will Imogen let you come to work?' Francesca's mouth twitched.

'She'll probably insist on coming with me, just like a mother on her child's first day at school.'

'You're lucky to have her.'

'I'm lucky to have all of you.'

'Holly, there's just one more thing.'

'What?'

'You need to call Joe and tell him about this. He is going to get dragged into all this you know, he deserves to know first.'

'I'll call him tonight.' What Francesca didn't know, what no one knew was that I wanted so much to hear the sound of Joe's voice, that even giving him bad news appealed to me. I missed him so much, I missed his voice, his smile, his smell, everything. It was so horrible to feel that life could be empty with just the absence of one person, but it could. It was even worse than when George went to live in New York. That was how I knew that I had found my soulmate, I'd just been a bit careless with him and I was paying the price.

I was just sad that he was too.

# Chapter Thirty

———◆✕◆———

'I have to tell George about the baby, and I wanted to warn you that we're also sending a press release out.'

'Right.'

'I hate to have to tell you this but it'll probably be all over the papers, and George will have a field day with it. He'll probably insist that the baby is his and therefore I have to marry him.' I bit one of my best fingernails as I waited for his response.

'Right.'

'And you're going to get dragged into this, I'm so sorry, but Joe, I don't know what else to do.' Another nail. This one tore a bit close to the quick. I bit my lip to stop myself from squealing.

'Right.'

'Can't you say anything else? Shout at me, or something.' I had been so nervous about making the call, so excited about hearing his voice, now I needed him to tell me something, anything. 'Right' wasn't going to do it.

'Holly, there's a lot to take in. My parents ask after you all the time despite the fact that you're in the paper. They still think that I should give you another chance. I told them that you're pregnant and they already think you're carrying their grand-child. They're over the moon. My mates all think that I should go and have a showdown with George, although they admit that I will probably be portrayed as the bad guy in the papers, they think I should fight for you. My sister thinks that I should kick your arse into space, as do most of my female friends . . .'

'I didn't know you had any female friends.' Oops, think before you speak Holly.

'Well maybe you don't know as much about me as you think. Anyway, the point is that every bloody one of them has an opinion about what I should do because our lives are being played out in public. And when they find out about the baby, there'll be more of it. Shit, Holly I was the victim in this, I didn't do anything to deserve this except fall in love with you, and now I am paying the price. I'm paying way above the price. I don't know what to say to you, Holly, because there is no script. I never in my wildest dreams believed that any of this would happen. I've been cheated on before, but I've never been the potential father of a child and I've never had my girlfriend splashed across the newspapers because of the alternative potential father.'

'I know, and I am sorry. I've probably worn that word out I use it so damn much. I don't know what to say.' I really didn't. I baulked at his accusation that I didn't know him. I did know Joe. I knew him because I loved him and that was my one remaining certainty.

'Nor do I, Holly. I would love to tell you that it'll be all right but I can't because I don't know if it will.'

'I love you.'

'I love you too, despite everything. I just don't know if I know you any more.' There was a silence, I needed to say something, to do something to keep him on the phone, to explain to get him to come back to me, anything, there had to be something. 'Bye Holly.'

'Joe . . .'

'Bye Holly.' He put down the phone and I looked at my bleeding finger and cried.

It was impossible to explain exactly how I felt after the call. He didn't say anything that was unfair, he wasn't as angry as he could have been. He sounded upset, fed up, tired and confused. Joe was this great, great guy who had a successful job and a nice flat and good friends and a loving family but then this woman came into his life and turned it upside down. That woman was me. She pulled his life apart and not only that, she did it publicly. He wasn't a heat-on-his-sleeve type of guy. He liked chatting, he liked banter, occasionally he would want to talk about his feelings but not always. If it weren't for the papers I'm not sure how many people he would have told about our situation. I would put money on it being a lot less than a million.

His normal life, which was only normal in the way it was normal to him, like mine had been to me, had suddenly been replaced by chaos. There was nothing average, regular, typical, sane or right about our lives now. Normality by our own definition or by anyone else's was long gone.

All I could think of was him, and the people he knew giving him advice on what he should do. It was as any friends would do, only for Joe, everyone knew the situation whether he wanted them to or not. He didn't have to talk to them, he didn't have to moan, they all knew what was going on. I'd not only robbed him of me, but I'd also robbed him of his privacy. Just as George had done to me. How on earth could I ever expect him to forgive me? I couldn't forgive myself.

All I could think was that when finally I was able to take the paternity test, we'd find the baby was Joe's and he'd forgive me because he admitted he still loved me and I would be the mother of his child. On the other hand, the reason I couldn't find the courage was because if the child wasn't Joe's, then I would lose him for ever. 'Please be Joe's,' I said to my bump, wishing it could be that easy.

Imogen found me lying on the sofa, trying to make sense of the situation.

'Joe will come back,' she said matter-of-factly.

'How do you know, you've never met Joe.' I didn't mean to snap but my temper was frayed.

'I know, I just do. I can see in you the way I felt when I met

Jack and I know that he feels the same. He's angry now, but he won't always be. Anger can't last for ever you know.'

'You think?' I looked at her, my sister. She reached out and stroked my hair, an action I found so comforting and unreal. Imogen had never reached out to me like that, emotionally or physically.

'I do. Anger wears you out, that's why it's good, and when you're tired you feel it ebb away, until the anger is gone, and what's left is a feeling of serenity.'

'Well I'll look forward to it.' I wasn't convinced but I was too tired to argue.

'Trust me, Hol, I know.' I looked at my sister and not for the first time wondered how much there was that I didn't know about her. It began to occur to me that there would have been so much she didn't know about me until now. Joe was right, the press had made our lives public; George had made our lives public.

'You mean . . . did you have an affair?' I asked, realising that the conversation was no longer about me.

'No, Jack did.'

'He what?' I was incredulous. Jack, the passive, successful, loving, devoted husband had cheated on her. 'Why didn't you say?'

'Because we wanted to keep it out of the public arena. I know Jack isn't exactly a celebrity, but he does attract his share of publicity. Anyway, it was hardly an affair, it was a one-night stand.'

'I'd have killed him.'

'Like Joe should have killed you.'

'Touché.'

'Anyway, I was angry, so angry, but eventually the anger subsided and I realised I still loved him and so I forgave him.'

'Was it that easy?'

'No, it wasn't easy at all, and it took a long time. I made a decision, but it still affects us. Remember I said about not being sure about a baby, that's one of the reasons. I don't think he'll do it again, I really don't, but it made everything feel unstable, and I still haven't fully recovered.'

'Immi, I wish you felt you could talk to me.'

'I didn't. I do now though, somehow, now I feel I can tell you anything.'

After that revelation, Imogen went to phone Jack and I went to bed. It was strange how I felt angry at Jack, yet he'd done what I did. But he was married, but then again I loved Joe, so did the fact he was married make it worse? No, of course it didn't. I suppose I realised that it was easier to make a mistake than you would think, and I also knew that although love was wonderful, it made people miserable. The way we were able to hurt the people we loved was sad. It shouldn't be that way. We should only make them happy. I wondered as I drifted into sleep if I would ever make Joe happy again.

I woke the following morning, feeling slightly sick. The way you feel when you wake up not entirely ready to welcome the day, but you're too sleepy to know why. It soon became clear. Today I would tell George that I was pregnant and I would also tell him that there was a chance he was the father. Oh, joyous day.

Because I was going to the office I went straight to the bathroom and showered, then once I'd dressed, I went to get some breakfast. The familiarity of the morning routine made me feel better. So many days with nowhere to go had taken their toll. Imogen was sitting in the kitchen nursing a cup of tea.

'Are you all right?' I asked, putting on the kettle.

'Yes, I didn't sleep so well. It's not always good to stir things up you know.'

'I know.' I squeezed her arm. 'So, what are you going to do today?'

'Jack's coming up.'

'Really?'

'I told him that I missed him and he's coming up for the day. He can't stay over because he's working flat out on his new book, but it's nice of him to come up for lunch isn't it.'

'It is. Immi, you can go home, I don't want you to feel that you have to stay.'

'I don't feel that, I want to stay. Absence makes the heart grow fonder.'

'I hope so.' I trailed off thinking about Joe again. That would be the sort of thing he would have done for me. He would have come to wherever I was just for lunch, just to see me. My eyes filled with tears.

'Hey, Hol, what's wrong?'

'Apart from the usual?'

'Point taken. Come on, I'll make you some toast and then pack you off to the office. And if you say again I'm like mum I'll slap you.'

I got to the office to be greeted like a long lost relative.

'Thank fuck you're here, Freddie is driving me mad,' Dixie said as she threw her arms around me. 'I can't believe how round you look,' she finished.

'Thanks lovely, I've missed you too.' I hugged everyone else, except one guy I didn't recognise.

'I'm Zig,' he said.

'Hi, I'm Holly.' He nodded at me as if he knew me.

'He's freelance, helping out,' Freddie explained, as he whisked me into Francesca's office. Even though my job was safe and I was being given work to do, I felt like an outsider. I more or less ran the office but now it had one additional person I'd never even met, interviewed or hired. The fact that he was temporary didn't matter. It wasn't how it used to be, I didn't like the fact that my role had changed and it had changed not because any of us wanted it to, but it simply had to. George had a lot to answer for. At times I would have loved to wring his bloody neck.

Freddie presented me with the press release that he'd drafted. It was short and to the point. I didn't feel that I could add anything that would make me look better but I took it to my desk. I telephoned all my clients, first to explain the situation to them. Most were sympathetic, however *Zoom* sounded positively thrilled. 'Do you think that next time you're being asked something you might mention us by name?'

'I'll do my best.' I shook my head. I could just imagine it. I'm pregnant, unsure of the father, but I smell nice because *Zoom Deodorant* are one of my clients. Francesca was right, my clients seemed to think that bad publicity was better than no publicity. Which was lucky because otherwise they probably would have demanded I resign their accounts. I determined then that I would mention my clients in the press release. George wasn't the only one who could exploit the media. Even if it was reluctant exploitation on my part, I owed them for sticking by me.

'Freddie,' I called over to where he was in conversation with Sarah.

'Yes,' he shouted back.

'I want to make a few adjustments.' I took the press release over to Sarah's computer and started typing.

'Holly.' Freddie was laughing at me. 'They're not going to print that.'

'They might,' I replied, as I hit the save key.

All I had done was inserted a paragraph, in the middle, listing all my clients. They were standing by me and they could have deserted me. They could have taken away my job. They could have left me up shit creek.

'Well at least we might salvage something. I was going to suggest you front the new *Zoom* campaign: "In times of extreme stress, *Zoom* keeps you dry".' Freddie fell about laughing.

'Don't even joke about it. If you suggested it to them they'd probably go for it.'

I looked at the open-plan office. All the team were working intently as they always did but snatching surreptitious glances at me. I presumed they were unable to resist looking at their tabloid, pregnant, absentee boss. I looked at the computer monitors, the walls covered with press cuttings, the cluttered bookshelves. I looked around and I knew that I wanted to be back there; it was my second home.

'Let's go to lunch before you call George,' Freddie suggested.

'OK.' Anything to put it off. I remember when I was at school, just before my A levels I was supposed to be revising but I would rather do anything but. I would polish my shoes, sort out my underwear drawer, I think I even washed my dad's car; rather than work. It felt like that now, but I didn't have my underwear drawer handy.

'It's better to wait until the fax has arrived before you ring him, anyway. That way you'll be telling him about it at the same time as the journalists get it.'

'What if they get it first and call him?'

'No chance.'

'I must be costing the company a fortune.'

'Don't be silly. How did it go with Joe last night?'

'He got angry.'

'Oh.'

'But that's good. Imogen says anger makes you tired, so you forgive more easily.'

'Really?'

'Freddie, it makes sense, Imogen's right. I feel like I'm going through this weird sister bonding thing at the moment. We never did it, when we were young or anything. Now I feel as if we're building a relationship.'

'So, how about you. How are *you*?'

'Better now I've got all this work to do. Weird, thinking that people want to use our company to get a look at me. But it keeps my mind off things. I made a start on the pitches last night.'

'Holly, it's going to get a lot worse.' Freddie's voice had dropped to almost a whisper.

'I know.'

'People will want photos of you now.'

'As long as I'm not in my underwear.'

'They'll want photos of you looking pregnant.'

'Pregnant I can do.'

'Holly, I know you're really good at denial, but can you stop. There is every chance you're going to be hounded.'

'Oh, don't be silly, I'm certainly not that interesting.' Freddie was prone to being melodramatic.

'I was thinking about moving you into my flat.'

'What on earth for?'

'Because I think that you might have journalists and photographers outside yours.'

'Don't be silly. Now, can we order because I'm eating for two and that means I need lots and lots of food.' Freddie shook his head but he indulged me. After lunch we made our way back to the office.

'I don't want to call him,' I said.

'I know, but you have to.' We went to Francesca's office. Francesca sat me down at her desk and handed me the phone. I looked at it as if I'd never seen one before.

'Number,' Francesca demanded. I pulled out my mobile, and scrolled down the phone book until I got to George. I gave the phone to Francesca and she dialled. I squeezed the handset to my ear, willing him not to pick up.

'Hello.'

'It's Holly.'

'Holly, what a lovely surprise.' The thought of the George on the end of the phone made me feel like throwing up. He was so far removed from the man who used to wipe up my tears and make me laugh and bring me Lucozade when I was sick, and persuade me to cook for him, and do his laundry most of the time. He wasn't my best friend. He was an impostor. That is what I believed. I think that post-Julia, he had gone nuts. He was a lunatic, someone who had lost all reason; deranged. The court case alone provided evidence of this. Unfortunately instead of the lunacy subsiding he was actually getting worse. I wondered why, I alone, could see this. The man was clearly unhinged and the media and the public hadn't noticed. This enraged me almost as much as his behaviour did. But in the absence of having him certified there was nothing I could do, so instead of having sympathy, I used anger. Mad or not he was still ruining my life.

'Where are you?' I asked.

'In my apartment, why?'

'I wanted to check that you weren't in a television studio.'

'I'm at home. It's a day off, actually.' He let out a sort of chuckle. I tried to keep myself calm but I could feel the anger rising. I could feel it rolling in my stomach; swishing through my blood, filling my head.

'Don't rest on your laurels too much George, you don't want the media to lose interest.' Francesca shot me a sharp look; Freddie stifled a laugh.

'Holly, you know why I'm doing this. I'm doing it for us.' At that moment I honestly believed that he believed what he was saying. He was obviously a victim of psychosis.

'Whatever. That's not why I'm phoning you.' My voice was sharp, cold even. I was trying to antagonise him. If it gave me pleasure, and my life was a little short of that right now, then I was entitled.

'Why are you phoning me?'

I took a deep breath. 'George, you're my oldest friend, you know that. Whatever this is all about, I have never valued a friendship the way I valued ours.' Good start: when dealing with insanity sound patronising.

'Me too.' He sounded pleased, so obviously, it was working.

'And whatever happens, I hope you remember that.' I spoke slowly and clearly, as if he was an imbecile, a mad imbecile.

'Holly what are you talking about?' Now he sounded confused.

Freddie mouthed, 'get to the point.' I scowled at him.

'George I'm having a baby.'

'You're pregnant?'

'That's what I said.'

'But, how?' I wondered what was going through his mind at that precise moment. He was probably upset because he thought I meant I was pregnant by Joe which would foil his little plan. Unfortunately that wasn't the case, but it didn't hurt to let him think that, to tease him with that thought, for a few seconds anyway.

'The normal way, George, a little sperm swam up my you-know-what and fertilised an egg. Like most women, ovaries were involved.'

'I didn't mean that. How does Joe feel?' He sounded nervous. He was no doubt imagining his new-found fame crumbling around his arrogant ankles. As much as I would have liked to prolong the agony, the time had come. Not only were Freddie and Francesca gesturing frantically at me to hurry up, but I was also in desperate need to pee.

'Well he probably feels the same way you do, as I have no idea which one of you is the father.' Probably could have been a bit gentler with the news, but then, he didn't deserve it.

'You mean it might be mine?' I could almost hear his mind ticking over.

'Yes, I'm sorry to say the most accurate prognosis of conception date is the end of November or the very beginning of December.'

'Oh Holly, this is wonderful news.'

'Really? Well it might not be yours. After all I shagged Joe loads of times and I only had sex with you once.' Francesca was giving me her stern look again but I was past caring. Whatever I did, I couldn't make George behave any worse.

'But it might be. I have to call Cordelia.'

'George, you're priceless. I tell you you might be the father of my unborn baby and the first person you want to call is your publicist.'

'It's not that.'

'What is it? You need her to get you some more interviews based on the new developments. What now, *This Morning, Coffee Break, London Tonight*? All to say how right you were to insist on marrying me, because now I might be carrying your baby. Well, don't worry, I've issued a press release so everyone will know. What you do to exploit the situation is up to you.'

'I'm sorry you feel like that. If we're going to be parents then we have to start planning the future.'

'For God's sake listen to me – it might not be yours. It might be Joe's.'

'Then we'll have a test.'

'I'm surprised you want a test, after all if it turns out to be Joe's then that will be the end of your media career.'

'But . . .'

'Ask Cordelia, I'm sure she'll recommend not pushing for the test. Besides they're too risky. I've got to go now, 'bye George.'

'But Holly, I need to know more. Do we know the sex? Should I come to antenatal with you? Are you eating healthily?'

'Actually George, we don't know the sex, I don't bother with antenatal and I drink shit-loads of brandy and smoke forty ciga-rettes a day so I don't have much time to eat.' I put down the phone.

Francesca was staring at me with her mouth wide open.

'What?'

'Imagine for a minute that someone had just told you that you might be about to become a parent, then they followed the news with that tirade. How would you feel?'

'I don't give a shit how he feels because he hasn't considered me in any of this, not at all.'

'Well, the press has the information; George knows, Joe knows. I guess what happens next is out of our hands now,' Freddie said reasonably. 'But Hol, maybe you want to be a bit careful about what you say in future.'

'I'm sure he wasn't even listening, he was already imagining the television career he's going to build on the back of me.'

Despite my bravado and my bitchiness I looked at Freddie and Francesca, put my head in my hands and wept.

'Bloody hormones,' I croaked between sobs. 'They won't stop making me cry.'

# Chapter Thirty-one

———◆◆◆———

## *Fatherhood*

I was going to be a father. I was having a baby. I knew, deep down that the baby was mine. No matter how much Holly tried to protest, or how much she kept on about it being Joe's, I knew it was mine. It all made sense. Fate had led me to the conclusion that I was supposed to be with Holly, and to make sure that we knew, it had given us a sign – a baby. We were definitely intended to be a family. I couldn't give up on making her see that. If anything, the baby made me more determined than ever to carry on my crusade. It was only through the media that I would be able to persuade her. The only way.

I could forgive her for being so horrible on the phone. I have to forgive her because she is in a different place to me right now. I know that she will regret her actions, and I know that she will tell me she's sorry. But that will be the time she tells me that we are meant to be together and that the baby is mine. It will all happen because it's written in our stars.

I called Cordelia with the good news.

'Guess what? Holly's pregnant and it might be mine.'

'But that would make her over four months.' Cordelia didn't miss a trick, which was why she was so good at her job.

'Exactly.'

'So, how come we didn't know about this sooner.'

'She kept it quiet, but she's sent a press release out to all the papers.'

'Well then we better act quickly. Can you get yourself here straight away?'

'I'll see you in half an hour.'

We were sitting round the meeting-room table, drinking coffee. Our sexual relationship, or any evidence of it was absent when we were in the office.

'So, how do you feel?' she asked me.

'Elated.' I was over the moon. Before I asked Julia to marry me I knew that I wanted kids pretty much straight away. I was definitely into being a father. I'd be a good father.

'But we don't know for sure it's yours.'

'I know.'

'George, we can't go to the press saying you're convinced the baby is yours, they'll think you're mad. On the other hand if she has a test, and it turns out to be Joe's then our story is dead in the water.' She looked pensive.

'She said she didn't want a test.'

'Really? Well that's handy. We will tell the press that it must be Holly's decision to have a test and we're not going to push her. That way it makes you look as if you're being ultra-reasonable and it keeps the story alive.'

'So it's good news all round.'

'It is, very good. Couldn't be better.'

'So, what now?'

'I'm going to call round and offer you for interviews. Papers will want your reaction to the news. Television shows can have you on when they talk about paternity issues, and they all love to flog that topic to death. I'll get some magazine interviews. Your line is that you are happy, although you don't know for sure if you are the father. Your main concern now is to take care of Holly, and also to let her make her own decisions about paternity tests and so on. Make it clear that you would love nothing more than to be a father.'

'Actually I would love to be a father. When she told me and there was this possibility that it might be mine, I was filled with this warmth. It was truly amazing. I might have created a life.'

'George, save the sentimental crap for the interviews. Right, let's start setting them up. Do you want to hang around? We could go for dinner after we've finished.'

I looked at her and thought about sex. Great sex. 'Sure thing.'

I smiled as I watched her stand up and go into her office. While I waited in the meeting room with my coffee and the newspapers I imagined Cordelia in action. She is amazing when she works, really something else. She picks up the phone, always manages to get through to the person she wants to speak to straight away, and then she goes in for the kill. She is pretty sexy when she works. After what seemed like hours she returned.

'What we have here is a situation. The media love it. They all want your response so I'm organising a press conference. We might even get some television coverage, actually I'm sure of it. Sophie is booking us a room for the conference; I've arranged it for early evening.'

'Isn't that a bit quick?'

'Not at all, we need it to be in the papers tomorrow, and maybe on the news this evening. We don't have time to procrastinate.'

'If you're sure.'

'Trust me George.'

'I do. What about dinner?'

'It'll wait until after the press conference. I think you'll be hungry by then.' Then she kissed me. 'That's something to keep you going until I get you home, bad boy.' I couldn't wait.

I just had time to go home and change into a suit before getting a cab to the hotel for the press conference. It wasn't exactly the

Hilton but then it was all arranged at short notice. I was worried that no one would show up. Surely journalists were too busy to drop everything. It would be embarrassing if no one showed. I have to admit to being nervous. I'd seen a number of press conferences on television but had never been the subject of one. Sports stars, TV stars, they were the people who got press conferences, along with parents of missing kids and various other crime victims. So where did my press conference fit in? It must be on the celebrity side. If the press turned up and if there was a good number of them then I would know that I was a star. If they didn't, then I would sit down with Cordelia and figure out how to make me one.

Cordelia met me in the entrance of the hotel and informed me that we had a full room.

'They've all come, even a television news crew. What I am going to do is to introduce you and tell them that we're here because of Holly's pregnancy and then you say a few words – what I told you earlier – then they can ask questions. Try to answer all the questions because you need these guys to be on your side. Ready?' I nodded.

She led me into the room, and it was just like the press conferences you see on TV. There was a table and two chairs for Cordelia and myself, and then a room full of photographers and journalists. As I sat down the flashbulbs went off as one blinding me. I blinked as the flashing continued. Finally one after another they began to stop until I could see again. I blinked and smiled. These people were all here to see me! Cordelia stood up.

'Ladies and Gentlemen, I do not need to introduce George Conway, as you've all been very supportive of his plight. The reason for this gathering is that we all know that Holly Miller, his marriage-pact girl, is pregnant and unsure if George is the father or not. George wanted to share his reaction to the news with all of you. He will say a few words and then he'll take questions.' I smiled at Cordelia and stood up. They were all here for me.

'I have mixed feelings about the news. On the one hand I am delighted at the thought I could be a father, but because I don't know for sure I feel reticent. I want everyone to know how happy I am, but there is something preventing me from being completely happy and that is the thought that Joe McClaren might be the father. As you know I love Holly with all my heart and only want to support her through her pregnancy. I have no intention in pushing her to take a paternity test and respect her feelings that this is a decision that she has to make. Thank you.' I smiled broadly as I sat down. Cordelia nudged me.

'Don't look too smug,' she hissed. I rearranged my facial expression accordingly.

'Any questions?' Cordelia asked as people started shouting things out. It was impossible to know who I should listen to. Finally an order emerged, I wondered how these things happened, but had no idea. It was as if I was addressing a rabble, which then subsided and everyone became quite civilised. I'm sure Cordelia must have given them a secret code or something.

'Do you still love her despite the fact that she has no idea who the father of her baby is?'

'Yes, I absolutely love her and stand by her.'

'Why aren't you pushing for a DNA test?'

'Because I think that the most important thing now is the health of the baby, and tests are risky on unborn babies. I do not want to put the baby or Holly under undue stress.'

'What about Joe? Does he want a test.'

'I don't know, I haven't spoken to him.'

'Do you know the sex of the baby?'

'No, there is no indication that Holly knows either.'

'Would you prefer a girl or a boy?'

'If the baby turns out to be mine, as long as it's healthy I don't care about the sex.'

'Do you still want to marry Holly?'

'More than ever. She really is the one true love of my life.'

'Don't you think she's a tart?'

'No, I think she has made some mistakes, but I can forgive her.'

After a few more questions, all along the same lines, we called a halt and stood up, said thank you to everyone for coming and left.

I waited in the lobby for Cordelia who wanted to speak to a few of the journalists and to find out when it might appear on the news. I sat in a faded velvet chair and thought about what had happened. It was amazing, the buzz I continued to get from talking to people about myself. I felt heady, as if I was slightly drunk, even though I hadn't had a drink.

The cameras had been uncomfortable at first but after a while it was OK. I was thankful that I was photogenic, I looked good in the photos that had been published so far. Life was strange, so much had happened, and now I was able to command the time of important journalists. It amazed me how much we'd achieved.

'George.' I looked up and recognised Freddie, Holly's work colleague.

'What are you doing here?'

'I found out about the press conference and thought I'd come and see it for myself. Holly doesn't know yet, I'm going to go to her place and break the news to her. I hope you're proud of yourself.'

'What do you mean?' I was angry that he had interrupted my high, and was trying to take the shine off my success.

'I mean that you haven't considered Holly in any of this. None of it. She has been dragged continually through the mud by you. All the papers think that you two had this long love affair that didn't exist. You had a one-night stand with her, engineered by you. That's all, and now you won't leave her alone. You're ruining her life and you're putting the baby at risk.'

'What crap. You know nothing about me and Holly. We grew up together, we shared more than you can ever know. As for love, well you're wrong, we're meant to be together.'

'No, no you're not. I know that for a fact because I know that Holly loves Joe.'

'Freddie, I don't really have time for this, nor am I interested in your opinion. If that baby is mine I intend to play a big part in its life and Holly will eventually realise that we are supposed to be together. Nothing is more certain.'

'But the baby is probably Joe's.'

I knew he said that to taunt me. 'No, I know it's mine. So if that's all you've come to say then you can leave now.'

'I should knock your fucking infuriating head off.'

'Go ahead, the newshounds will be out any minute, I'm sure they would love to see that.' I smiled as I watched Freddie walk away.

'Who was that?' Cordelia asked as she came up to me.

'Holly's colleague. He was trying to do a macho "leave her alone" thing.'

'Well the good news is that the papers are all carrying the story and you'll be on the Ten O'clock News tonight. It will probably only be a brief mention but we're lucky because it's a quiet news day.' She smiled. 'You were brilliant, and your reward will be given to you back at my place.' She licked her lips in that way that drove me crazy. I just couldn't wait until they were round my cock.

'Fantastic. Let's go.'

There is nothing like a good fuck while watching yourself on television.

# Chapter Thirty-two

We got the papers in the middle of the night from King's Cross Station. I loved that, it was something that Cordelia and I had been doing more often, almost a routine. We would be part of the seedy side of London for a few minutes as surrounded by prostitutes, drunks and the night people, Cordelia would park up her Mercedes while I would get out and buy the tabloids. I always bought the later editions, but the early editions in the middle of the night, that was something else. I would clutch them to my chest while we drove back to Cordelia's flat. When we got back we would lay the papers out, and go through them, one at a time. Both with the same sense of anticipation. When we found something about me, I would get so excited that I would barely be able to read the copy. In just a few weeks, this had become addictive.

The newspapers were my friends; they didn't disappoint. Our story was in all of the 'populars'. The four main tabloids had a small picture of me on the front page. It was one taken at the press conference and thankfully I looked quite startled as if I had had a shock, not as if I had been taken by surprise by the cameras, which was the reality. Although most of it was taken up with the latest government scandal, there was still a small bit dedicated to my story. And more inside. I looked at Cordelia, unable to stop smiling as I read each one twice.

*Daily News*

## WHO'S THE FATHER?

*Poor spurned George Conway was given another shock yesterday when fickle Holly Miller told him she was four-and-a-half months pregnant and had no idea if he was the father or if it was Joe McClaren (31). George bravely told us that he was delighted with the news, and believed in his heart that the baby was his. He also said he would give Holly his full support during her pregnancy. Does he care too much? Opinion on page 13 looks at the whole picture.*

*Herald*

## A TALE OF TWO DADS

*George Conway (30) yesterday discovered his marriage-pact girl and the love of his life was up the duff with no idea who the father was. Joe McClaren (31), is the other contender for paternity. If it wasn't enough to break his heart, Holly Miller (30), has gone too far. We think George should insist on a paternity test, and clear up any misunderstanding. Full story, page 7.*

*Daily Informer*

## MARRIAGE PACT GIRL PREGNANT!

*Holly Miller, the girl involved in the marriage-pact scandal has announced she is over four months pregnant. The problem is that she has also admitted she has no idea if the father is George Conway, her childhood sweetheart, or Joe McClaren with whom she was having an affair. George called a press conference last night, keen to give Holly his love and support and to say that he would be overjoyed to be the father. Full story, page 3.*

*Post*

## UP THE DUFF WITHOUT A FATHER

*George Conway, the man rejected by the girl he was set to marry has been shocked to discover that he may be the father of her baby. Holly Miller is heavily pregnant and has announced she doesn't know who the father is. She says it could be George, or someone else, but sources say that it could be any of a number of people. For full story see page 6.*

'George, this is amazing. We've really hit a nerve. Do you know how difficult it is to get this sort of coverage?'

'I know, it's unbelievable,' I concurred.

'I hope that you know how lucky you are.' Cordelia licked her lips. I knew what was coming next. She got incredibly horny when we got good coverage.

It was intoxicating. I could almost smell it. Powerful. An aphrodisiac greater than the freshest of oysters and the finest of champagnes. Julia flitted across my mind. If only she could see me now. I was irresistible; I felt irresistible. Life looked, smelt and tasted so sweet. The sweet smell of success.

It was so different now. Just a month ago, the greyness encompassed my very soul. The look, the taste and the smell of life was rank, weak, empty. Now life was aromatic.

I explained this to Cordelia. She was an incredible woman. Not only sexually alluring, but also synchronised to my every thought, my innermost feelings. When the transformation was complete, I felt as if I could look at Cordelia and see something of myself. The lost and found. That was how I felt when I looked at her and I think she knew that.

Holly's refusal to see me that way was irritating. There was nothing I could do to change that, but allow her to slowly realise what she was missing. I knew that she needed me, she had always needed me, and now I was so strong, she needed me more than ever. I could afford to be patient now, generous with my time. Because I had a new chance, a new life and I had to make decisions about my future. Holly was my future, but I could wait.

I had to decide what I was going to do about my career. Law was fine, but I had never felt quite as satisfied by winning a case as I did by appearing on television. I knew about my personal future, but not my professional one. Did I stay with law, or did I go into the world of media, or could I combine the two? I know I wanted to keep the buzz, and therefore didn't feel my future lay in the courtroom. If I were going to stay in London, I needed to build on my current fame. The idea of a future in London coupled with a glittering TV career was appealing.

'Cordelia, how easy would it be for me to make a career out of this?' I pulled up her skirt.

'You can't make a career out of the pact story, it'll be old news fairly soon, you know that.' I started stroking her crotch through her knickers.

'But television, radio, I like the feeling, I love the whole business.'

'Well, you come across well, you certainly look good . . . faster George . . . so I don't see why you can't pursue a successful career. I've watched people build long careers with far less going for them than you . . . harder mmm . . . I'll put out some feelers.' I started stroking the inside of her thighs, then I moved her hand down to my throbbing bulge.

'When?'

'I'll get on to it straight away . . . ah . . . yes squeeze it there . . . Trust me George.'

'I want to . . . long strokes, mmm . . . get this sorted as soon as . . . ahhhhh . . . possible.' I nipped her and rubbed her.

'OK. Oh God, George, oh fucking hell.'

'Straight away Cordelia. Faster, you're losing it, keep going.'

'Sorry, yes of course.' She moved her hand faster along my throbbing penis. I started using my fingers at the same speed.

'You're the best ever, George, oh hell, yes. Yesss, you're the best!'

'I know Cordelia, I know,' I whispered breathlessly, moving faster and more urgently. She did the same. We orgasmed.

Cordelia pulled down her skirt and went to the phone. She returned about fifteen minutes later with the news that she had arranged a meeting with one of the producers of *This Afternoon*.

'I think I should reward your efficiency,' I said, and led her to the bedroom.

I knew our relationship had a shelf life. Much like the Marriage Pact story. More than ever we had to exercise discretion, it was paramount that we were never discovered. I knew that as my fame increased, so would the scrutiny. There would be no more risks. There would be no more Cordelia. Or not in the biblical sense anyway.

The following day we set off to see Charles Wright, the producer of *This Afternoon*. We took a cab to the now familiar TV studios and I decided that as an office, it would be OK by me. I smiled at Cordelia; she delivered in more ways than one.

We waited in the reception area which was decorated with framed portraits of people I barely recognised (I hadn't been in the country long enough to familiarise myself with its celebrities). Cordelia filled me in. Ten minutes later, Charles came out. He was tall, about as tall as me, with thick, greying dark hair. He was wearing chinos and a shirt, I guessed that celebrity was less formal than law. He introduced himself. He led us into his office, which wasn't massive, nor was it ostentatious. It was functional. He was a man after my own heart.

We sat down and made small talk while he got his assistant to organise coffee, then he cut to the chase.

'What exactly is it you want? I know the story, I know that at the moment you have the sympathy of most of the nation, but that's for your current situation. But that can't go on for ever.'

As I said on the phone, we're looking for a regular TV slot,' Cordelia explained. 'And as George started on your programme it seemed natural to approach you first.' I smiled but kept quiet.

'What exactly do you suggest? We're not looking for a main presenter.'

'What about a legal expert? Imagine how the housewives

would be jamming the phone lines just for the opportunity to ask George for legal advice. Divorce, wills, you name it, he can do it.' I wasn't exactly enamoured by being a TV lawyer but Cordelia had assured me that it was the easiest way to get a foot in the door. They may not be looking for a main presenter, but they'd found one.

We chatted some more, and finally Charles said he'd talk to his production team. He didn't seem to be giving anything away as to whether I'd be hired or not. He stood up; the meeting was over. I was slightly perplexed as to how short it had been, but Cordelia seemed happy.

'It went well,' she said.

'You're sure?'

'Fame. It makes you feel as if you'll live for ever right?' She laughed, but I didn't see the joke.

'It does, yes.'

As we left, we talked further about what sort of appearances I'd be willing to do. I said I would do anything as long as Cordelia felt it was the right thing. She urged caution and promised she'd take care of weaning out the good opportunities from the bad. But there would be opportunities, she promised that much.

I was going to be a father. I was going to be a television star. Once fame is established, if you are canny you can use it for all sorts of things. That was exactly what I intended to do. Adoration would become the norm, and Holly would be my wife. We'd be a family, and my child would be proud of his dad. And my parents would be proud of me, once more. Everything made sense, clear as crystal. It had all clicked. Thirty years old and my life was heading the way I wanted it. That was a comforting thought.

'Cordelia, are you going back to the office?' I asked, looking at her in a way I knew she couldn't resist.

'I've got a pile of work, honey, but I suppose we could make a quick detour.' I stuck out my hand to hail a cab, then I put my hand on her bottom as I instructed it to take us to her flat.

As soon as we opened the door, I undid her trousers and pulled them down.

'You should wear a skirt when you see me,' I told her.

'Sorry,' she said, sounding contrite, just as I liked.

'I'm going to punish you now,' I said, slipping my hand into her knickers.

'How, how are you going to punish me?' she asked. I looked into her eyes, they were looking into mine, waiting for me to get her to do exactly what I wanted. I squeezed her between the legs.

'I'm going to make you wait for what you want, and give me what *I* want.' I took my hand out, and I pushed her head to my crotch.

Half an hour later, as I lit a cigarette, Cordelia left to go back to the office.

# Chapter Thirty-three

———◆✕◆———

## *The Media Circus*

Imogen and I decided to go shopping, because I couldn't fit into anything hanging in my wardrobe. I felt fat and miserable.

'I still want to look sexy,' I lamented, as I looked at my stomach poking proudly out of the loosest trousers I owned. I wondered if I would ever look sexy again.

'Pregnant women *are* sexy,' Imogen said.

'Yeah, but not in tent dresses.' It might have been hormones, it might have been George, but my moods were swinging more unpredictably than my grandfather's old pendulum. It was a good job that my grandparents were no longer around, although I loved them very much, I am not sure they were the sort of people who would cope well with the news that their grand-daughter was a slut.

'Why are you crying?' Imogen asked.

'Fucking hormones,' I replied, and grabbed my coat. My moods were rather like my footwear. I went from being Manolo Blahnik (feeling gorgeous and special), to a pair of smelly trainers (disgusting and unloved), in the space of a few seconds. I had no control and even in my worst PMT ridden moments I had never felt so unhinged. I reapplied my mascara in the mirror by the front door and blew my nose.

'Do I look a mess?' I asked.

'Honestly? A bit, but we're only shopping,' Imogen replied, not entirely helpfully. I shrugged. Tomorrow, I'd have clothes that fitted and I'd look lovely. Or lovelier at least. I charged on and half opened the door. I stood, rooted behind my front door as I heard the noise and saw the cameras.

'Holy shit Hol, get back in.' Imogen grabbed me and pulled me back in. Then she shut the door and shut out the noise. I started breathing quickly, panic rose up through me like bile. I blinked, finally able to see again and then I began to wonder if it had been an apparition. I looked questioningly at Imogen, everything was in slow motion.

Imogen didn't speak, but grabbed my hand and pulled me upstairs and into my flat. Then she ran to the window at the front and looked out. Cameras went off and people shouted, it sounded monumentally loud.

'Keep back,' she shouted, a little too forcefully, as if I was being attacked. I was superglued to the floor by the door of the sitting room. Imogen was behaving like a madwoman. She wrapped herself in the blind and peeked out of the window again. I caught the tail end of another flash. She turned around with her knees slightly bent, she looked as if she was about to launch herself. She gazed around the room, then suddenly sprang into action. She pulled the blinds fully closed (actually we hadn't opened any of them that day otherwise we might have noticed the activity outside), then she ran to the telephone.

'What's Freddie's number?' she asked, breathing heavily as if she had just been out jogging. I reeled off the number and kept still as if I was playing a game of musical statues and really, really wanted the prize.

'Freddie, thank God. Oh thank God, you have to help us.' I wondered what Freddie's reaction was, he probably thought I had been attacked or something.

'I can't be calm. There's fourteen photographers and journalists outside the flat.' I couldn't believe she'd counted them.

'Exactly fourteen. We opened the front door and it was like this big shower of light. All the cameras went off and they used flash even though it's daytime, why would you use flash in the daytime?' Now I knew she was getting a bit too hysterical but still I couldn't move.

'What are we going to do? We can't go out?' There was a longer pause this time.

'I can't pass the phone over to Holly, she's immobilised. I think it's the shock.' I could hear the words but I couldn't do anything about them.

'Thank God, see you soon.' Imogen put down the phone, she looked marginally calmer.

'Freddie's coming round. Come on we have to go into the spare room, either that or the bathroom.' She steered me to the room and then sat me down on the bed.

'Holly, please don't cry?' she begged.

I didn't know I was crying. I couldn't feel the tears. She hugged me then she started crying as well. Did I ever mention that Imogen is not the best person in a crisis?

There are a number of good things about my mother. An infinite number. One being that when all this first started she made me get spare sets of keys cut and distributed to Freddie and Lisa. For emergencies, she said, although I hardly think she had ever imagined this kind of emergency. I didn't hear anything until I heard the flat door open and then I saw Freddie, standing in the doorway.

'Thank God,' Imogen screamed, launching herself at him.

'Calm down,' Freddie commanded, and pulled out his phone. He dialled a number, I had no idea whose.

'Francesca, it's me.'

Silence.

'I know, well I'm here now, and I know Imogen was hysterical but she's not exaggerating. When I tried to get in they went mad. They wanted to know who I was, and if I knew Holly and if I could get her to come out. They want photos and comments. They said they got a glimpse of her when she opened the door but they couldn't see her bump. That's what they're after. I have no idea how the story got this big but there is one thing, there's no way I can let her near the door. They're like animals. Shall I release a statement?'

Silence.

'I'll write it here, but there is no way that I'm going to get any sense out of these two. I think Holly's in shock.'

Silence.

'OK, I'll call Lisa, she's normally quite good in a crisis and at least she's used to photographers.'

Freddie put his mobile in his pocket then he crouched down in front of me. He took my hands, but I couldn't feel them.

'Holly,' he said in a voice designed to soothe a child. I looked at him. I heard him. 'Holly, are you all right?' he asked. I continued to look at him. 'Of course you're not, you've got a shit load of journalists outside. Holly, I am going to give them a statement and try to get them to leave, OK?' I just stared. I wasn't sure if I knew how to nod. He stood up and looked at Imogen who had calmed down now there was someone else here. 'Imogen, can you call Lisa and get her to come over?' Imogen bolted for the phone. He then left the room.

I have no idea how long I was alone but it felt like ages until they both returned. Imogen had a glass of brandy in her hands. She shoved the glass towards me. I stared at the amber liquid as if I had never seen it before, then Imogen changed her mind and drank it herself.

'Lisa is on her way,' Imogen said. 'Do you think she needs a doctor?'

'Wait for Lisa to come, maybe she'll be able to do something.' Freddie looked at me. 'In the meantime, maybe you can make us all some tea.'

'Oh, good idea, lots of sugar.' Obviously she had seen too

many TV programmes that responded to crises with sweet tea, or maybe the brandy had gone to her head.

'I don't have sugar, it's bad for the baby,' I said, and then I fell into Freddie's arms.

We moved to the sitting room, because it felt strange being in the spare room, but the blinds were firmly down. Imogen couldn't help but peek out of them, and give us a commentary, but nothing had changed. There was a plethora of journalists and photographers on the street outside my flat. How on earth were you supposed to deal with that? Imogen told us that one journalist had gone and got four coffees to distribute while the others looked on enviously. One photographer steamed into action when someone left my building, it was someone from the downstairs flat. Apparently they looked stunned and Imogen heard them ask the woman a question, to which she replied by running away. From Imogen's description I deduced it was the cleaner who worked for the couple whom I had nodded to a million times, who shared a mailbox with me (names were Jacquie and Dave Hooper), but whom I had never had more than a one-line conversation with.

'We ought to put a note of apology through their door,' I said. Imogen (who was getting a tad annoying), was dispatched to do this. She returned triumphantly and resumed her position by the window.

'Why don't you all just piss off,' a voice streamed up to the window.

'Oh Lisa's here,' Imogen said, although we had guessed that.

'She's pointed at some guy, and she's swearing at him. Oh, now she's shoved some woman out of the way – ouch – she just kicked a photographer's shin. She's nudging people out of the way. Now she's reached the front door.' We heard her open it; Freddie had obviously told her to bring keys. We heard some more swearing and then the door slammed shut, I felt the flat shake. I went to the door to meet her.

'Oh, Holly,' she said, before engulfing me in her elfin arms. I started crying. She pulled me into the sitting room.

'At least she's out of shock,' Freddie said.

'But none of this is good for the baby,' Lisa protested.

I nodded. I was scared. My trance, my panic, the fact I couldn't leave the flat, and I was supposed to be at yoga. None of this was helping the baby, or the baby's mother.

'Darling, breathe slowly.' I was glad that Lisa had joined me for my yoga sessions because she took me through the breathing technique and it worked. I felt slightly less panicky and a smidgen more in control. Despite the fact I could hear the low murmuring of the people camped on the pavement, I could think more clearly.

'Shit. That's it,' I said, jumping up. Everyone looked at me as if finally I had lost it. 'No, if George thinks the baby is his, then we can tell him that this behaviour is putting the baby at risk.'

'I guess it's worth a try,' Imogen looked unsure.

'Oh God, we ought to tell Joe. I promised him I would keep him informed. He would have seen the papers this morning, all that "who's the father stuff." Do you think they're stalking *him*? Oh shit.'

'Holly, don't get into that state again. Firstly I am going to go outside, and read this statement. Are you happy with it?' I took it from him. Freddie was amazing. He had managed to get me calm, sort Imogen out, and type and print out a statement. I kissed his cheek and started to read: *Holly Miller released a statement telling the press that she was pregnant and unsure of the paternity of the father. Her honesty has been total and we would like the press to respect that. We would also like the press to respect her privacy and leave her doorstep. If there are any developments we promise to keep you fully informed. Thank you.*

'I guess that sums it up,' I said. 'Can't we call the police?'

'Yeah because the gutter press will really go away and not

come back. They'll be back as soon as the police leave. I'll go and read this, then I'll come back. Holly, go and call George and Joe. Lisa, monitor her and make sure she doesn't lose it. Imogen, get away from the window.' Everyone jumped at Freddie's command. Even Imogen stopped blind-twitching for a minute.

I went to the phone and dialled Joe's mobile number. I felt awful about what was happening to him, really awful. He answered it immediately.

'Joe, it's me,' I said.

'I wondered if you'd call, are you all right?' I had thought he would sound angry, but he didn't, his voice was full of concern.

'I've got fourteen reporters outside my flat . . . yes fourteen, Imogen counted them.' I tried to sound flippant about it.

'I couldn't believe the newspapers, I know you said that you'd tell them but it's plastered everywhere.'

'I am so sorry.'

'They found me. I had two photographers and a reporter waiting outside my office. They took some photos of me and asked for a comment, I told them to bugger off. I don't think that was wise.'

'Joe, don't say anything unless you want to and if you do, call me and I'll get Freddie or Francesca to say it. The press will twist things anyway so that might be a better move. I feel really dreadful but I don't know what to do to stop it.'

'Are you all right?' he asked again.

'I'm sort of coping. To be honest I'm going to call George and make a last ditch attempt to appeal to his better nature.'

'Hol, even though it might not be mine, I am worried about the baby.'

'So am I. That's why I'm going to call him.'

'*I* wish we could get the fucking test done.'

'Joe, it's too risky and even then my doctor won't do it anyway.' I had mixed feelings about this. I didn't want the test,

I didn't want to lose the hope that Joe was the father, but then if it was Joe's then life would be better. But with the risk to the baby I knew it wasn't an option.

'I know.'

'Sorry.' That word had been hollowed out and stuffed with cotton wool.

'Me too.'

It was getting worse. Suddenly I felt cold.

'How did it go?' Lisa asked, although I knew she had heard my side of the conversation.

'He got photographed outside his office and he told a reporter to bugger off.'

'Freddie's finished,' Imogen announced. 'He's coming back in.' I heard the door.

'Lisa can you get me a jumper, I'm really cold.' I shivered.

'How did it go?' Imogen asked, the minute Freddie walked through the door. It was then I realised she had been listening to my conversation rather than watching Freddie deliver his speech.

'Not great I'm afraid, they want photos of your bump, Hol.'

'Tough shit,' Lisa said, as she returned with a cardigan.

'I'm going to have to go out at some point. I've got an appointment with my gynaecologist.'

'Maybe they'll be gone by then,' Imogen said hopefully, but not convincingly.

'I'm calling George,' I announced, and went back to the phone.

'George, it's Holly,' I said, as he answered his mobile after the first ring.

'Holly, how are you?' His voice was dripping with insincere concern, he was probably with someone, or worse still being interviewed. I looked at my watch, it was four in the afternoon.

'Are you alone?' I asked.

'I am,' he said, which surprised me.

'George, I've got a bunch of reporters and photographers camped outside my house.'

'Really?' he sounded genuinely surprised.

'Yes and I've missed my prenatal yoga class and I can't get to the doctor because I can't go out.'

'Why not?'

'Because they are hounding me. They keep shouting for me through the letter box. Freddie went out to read a statement and they said they wanted a photo of me looking pregnant. They won't go until they've got it.' My voice had become hysterical yet again.

'So let them take a photo.' He sounded as if the paparazzi had politely asked me to let them take a photograph and I was the one being unreasonable.

'George I can't, there's masses of them, they're scaring me and the baby.' I burst into unplanned tears.

'Holly, I don't control the press. The only way you can get them to leave is by coming to your senses.' He had hung up by the time I thought of a suitable reply.

I thought I knew it, but I realised something then, something I should have realised a lot sooner. George didn't care about me one hoot and much worse he didn't care about the baby. He cared about the press, his exposure and his new status as a celebrity. I know we'd discussed it, but it was only now I fully comprehended it.

I had never worked for any famous people, I worked with brands, big companies, but I had never worked for an individual. But George had taken advantage of the new celebrity. No longer did you need to sing and dance, all you needed was to get some exposure and there you go. You can book a table in the Ivy and you're a celeb. Go to parties, go to premières, go anywhere that will have you and will give you some publicity, any publicity.

George was dangerous when he took me to court, dangerous when he first went to the press but now he was more than dangerous, he was famous and would do anything to stay that way.

Freddie came over and hugged me as he saw the panic-stricken look appear on my face. I think he had already worked out what I had just realised. Imogen had moved away from the window and she was fidgeting, clearly as baffled as I was about what to do. Lisa had gone to the kitchen and come back with some biscuits and she had also made a pot of coffee. Lisa being practical was almost as scary as the people on my doorstep.

There are situations where the people around you, the people that care about you, have a really tough time. This was one of them. I knew that no one really knew what to do, that Freddie had tried his best and been unsuccessful, that Imogen and Lisa felt helpless, and I was falling apart. I could feel myself coming apart and I knew that I couldn't let it happen. Rationalising, I realised that they wouldn't doorstep me for ever. They'd lose interest before I needed to go out. Surely. I grabbed my Palm Pilot and checked my diary. I had a yoga lesson, which I could skip, a birthing lesson that wasn't until the beginning of the following week, and an appointment with the hospital. I realised how much my life had changed, I was used to having a diary with stuff in it, now it was empty. I walked over to the table and fired up my laptop.

'What are you doing?' Imogen asked.

'I'm going to do some work. Freddie, shall we?' Freddie came to join me and we checked my e-mails, sent one to Francesca, then we started working.

'What should *I* do?' Imogen asked, still looking anxious. I glanced at Freddie and smiled.

'What would be really great is if you and Lisa could go and get me some clothes. I mean I can't go out and my waistline has expanded at an alarming rate since last week. I'm getting really fat.'

'You do look a bit porky,' Freddie chipped in, supportively but not sweetly.

'But you need to choose,' Imogen protested, ignoring Freddie as I kicked him in the shin. Actually that action made me feel better than anything else had.

'I trust you and Lisa.' Actually I trusted Lisa. 'I don't have any cash but I'll give you a cheque if you pay.' I knew that Imogen had about a million credit cards.

'What a good idea,' Lisa said catching my eye.

'How do we get through the press?' Imogen asked, still not convinced.

'Just walk past them, as long as you make sure they don't get in the front door, you should be all right,' Freddie responded while typing an e-mail to our team in the office.

'Yeah, come on Immi, if anyone gives us any shit I'll sort them out.' For a minute Lisa sounded like an extra from a Guy Ritchie film, but I smiled, gratefully.

'What size? I mean what size do we get?' Ah, I had no idea about that.

'Just buy expanding things, I'm sure that's all you need to do if you go to a maternity shop.' Finally Imogen seemed convinced.

'Good idea, we'll be really helping won't we?'

'Absolutely, even my tracksuit is straining on me.' I smiled and waved them off.

I heard the door shut behind them, then I heard them walking down the stairs. Both Freddie and I peaked round the blind to see them emerge on to the doorstep. The second the door opened the cameras went off.

'Shit, I'm blind,' Lisa said, pulling Imogen out of the doorway and slamming it.

'Are you friends of Holly's?' someone asked.

'Actually I'm her sister and I'd appreciate it if you left us in peace.'

'Yeah, just fuck off,' Lisa added for good measure. I just couldn't wait to see the quotes in the papers.

'Have we done the right thing sending those two out together?' Freddie asked, smiling.

'Who cares, at least they can do something useful and also stop pacing my flat. I'll need to put down a new floor by the time Imogen leaves.'

'Which is when?'

'Well, according to mum's roster in three days' time, but she is insisting on staying until the press leave.'

'Oh dear.'

'Well it's another incentive to get rid of them. Do you think I should give them a photo?'

'No they've written and will continue to write horrible things about you. You don't owe them anything.'

'I know, but at least we might be able to get them to leave.'

'No, Holly, trust me on this. They'll start to trail away when they realise you're not coming out.'

'But I might have to go out at some stage.'

'Disguise?'

'Let's get this finished.' I turned back to my laptop screen and lost myself in work.

It made me feel like a person again. Not just a person but a useful person. Here I was worrying about George; being pregnant; missing Joe; having the press on my doorstep – that was Holly. I lost the person I used to be; career girl; smart; slim; in control. That person had disappeared and I was now trying to figure out how life was, or what it would be like. Baby; job; no partner; that was my future, and I was so busy thinking about that that I'd stopped thinking about anything else. Now, as we wrote a proposal, I felt as if I was normal again. And feeling normal was the best feeling in the world.

'Do you know how long it is since we had a good old heart to heart?' I felt as if I had lost my grip on not only my life, but the lives of those around me.

'You're totally self-absorbed,' Freddie quipped.

'I am, it's true.'

'Hol, there's a lot going on.'

'Yes but that's no excuse to lose sight of what is happening around me. Tell me something.'

'What?'

'Are you seeing anyone? Have you come any closer to falling in love or are you still tarting around?'

'Pot and kettle.'

'Freddie, don't start.'

'Well, I'm a bit busy at work to be falling in love.'

'You see, I'm not only ruining my life but I'm ruining everyone else's.'

'No, you're not. Actually I'm enjoying being given more responsibility at work and I'm also handling it quite well. It's good for me to have time to put my career first.'

'Well there's no doubt that you are more than capable of doing my job.'

'I'm not trying to take your job.'

'I'm not saying that. I wouldn't let you if you were. No, I'm talking about promotion. I'm going to be trapped in here for God knows how long, and then I'm going to be on maternity leave, and I've spoken to Francesca and we think we should re-organise the company, especially as it's expanding. It's a case of us all expanding our roles, that's all.'

'If you're sure.'

'Well, you're basically doing my job, so you should get paid more and get a title to go with it. I'm going to work full time when I've had junior here, but I'll probably take on a more administrative role, that's what I've discussed with Francesca.'

'So you've both been scheming behind my back.'

'Course we have, we're women.'

'I should go and work in a male-dominated environment, I think I'm losing my testosterone.'

'That'll be the day. So, no lucky ladies on the scene?'

'None. I am going to leave women for the minute and concentrate on my career.'

'How grown up of you. Or is it because you've run out of people in the office to sleep with.'

'Ouch. I've never slept with you or Francesca.'

'But you want to.'

'Not with you. Seriously, I wouldn't mind if she wasn't my boss but I think there's something a bit sordid about sleeping with the boss. I'll stick to her PAs.'

'You are awful.'

'I know, but Pippa is really quite cute.'

'And very willing.'

'Well, there is that.'

'I've missed this.'

'What my sex life?'

'Just banter, normal banter, I only talk about myself nowadays. I've become self-obsessed and a complete bore.'

'Well I'm not going to argue with you and if that was why you said it, it's backfired.'

'You're a good friend, Freddie, I really mean that.'

'You're not bad either.'

'Better than George?'

'Not difficult.'

'Freddie, if there is ever anything that I can do for you, anything, you have to promise to ask me.'

'Oh, I intend to. First there's the pay rise and the promotion, and then there's putting me in charge of hiring the female staff, oh the list will be endless.'

'And if there's anything that isn't incredibly shallow, you can ask me for that too.' We looked at each other and laughed. Friendship can never be overrated.

# Chapter Thirty-four

We worked solidly until I noticed the time, it was six thirty, and I realised that there was no sign of Imogen and Lisa.

'They've been gone ages.'

'Women and shopping.' Freddie shrugged.

'What if they had a fight? Lisa could have killed her.'

'Hol, this isn't an action film. They'll probably come back the best of friends.'

'It feels like an action film. *Under Siege*, that's what it is.' I stood up and looked out of the window, through the tiny gap in the blind. Imogen had developed a technique for doing it without being seen, which I copied. The phone rang. I looked at Freddie, but I answered it anyway.

'Holly, are you all right?' It was my father.

'Oh Daddy, there are a load of journalists outside.'

'I know, Imogen called. How are you bearing up?'

'I'm lucky, I've got Freddie, Imogen and Lisa here, although the girls have gone shopping.'

'Do you want us to come up?'

'No, we'll be OK. What about you guys?' If I hated being hounded by the press the thing I hated more was the idea that they were doing the same to my parents.

'We're fine, darling. Some of the hacks have made a trip here but your mother and I always say "no comment", like on TV. George's parents are having a hard time of it too. They didn't ask for any of this. We went to see them, they're devastated.'

'Daddy, do you think George is mad? I mean really mad. He is hurting so many people and the George we knew wouldn't do that.'

'Who knows love. How's my grandson?'

'Grandson? How do you know it's going to be a boy?'

'Too many women in the family. We need a male.'

'I'll see what I can do. Give my love to Mum.'

'Will do. Call tomorrow.' I promised I would and I hung up.

'Shall I make some coffee, or tea in my case? Then you should think about going, I'm sure you have things to do.'

'Not really. Anyway, I am not going until Imogen and Lisa get back.'

'Freddie, you're all heart.' I went to the kitchen, pausing on the way to have a bit of a curtain twitch.

'I think some of them have gone.' Freddie came to join me.

'Yes, but there's still a fair few. I wonder if they're going to camp overnight.' Just then the buzzer went. I looked at Freddie, we had told Lisa to use her key.

'Hello,' I said.

'Pizza.'

'I didn't order pizza. Freddie, it's pizza.'

'Whatever you do don't let them in, it's just a ploy.'

'Piss off,' I said and put down the intercom. For the next hour the buzzer went every few seconds. Taxis, pizza, flowers, the journalists angry at me for ignoring them all day were now doing their best to extract their revenge. As if camping on my doorstep wasn't enough. Freddie took the helm and showed a very broad vocabulary of expletives while he dealt with each one. Then the phone rang.

'It's Lisa.'

'Where are you?'

'We're outside, but there is some bloke at the buzzer.'

'Just push him out of the way, because if he sets foot inside I'm calling the police.'

'OK, there's just one other thing.'

'What?'

'We've got Jacquie and Dave with us.'

'Who the hell are Jacquie and Dave?'

'Your downstairs neighbours.' London is a very unfriendly place.

'Of course. Apologise to them will you?' I had seen Jacquie and Dave, only a few times. They were probably a few years older than me and had lived downstairs for a year. I hadn't had time to get to know them yet.

'Oh they're fine, they think it's exciting living downstairs from a celebrity. Actually they wondered if they could come up and say hello.'

Oh God. 'Fine, but Lisa if I find out they're journalists in disguise I'm killing you.'

'I promise they're genuine neighbours.'

Freddie went to the window and gave me a running commentary.

'Lisa's leading them up towards the door, she's elbowing everyone out the way . . . go girl. Oh, Imogen is next and she's got a million shopping bags, and it looks as if your neighbours are carrying some of them. They *are* the downstairs couple, I recognise them. Lisa has just slapped the man standing near the buzzer and he's swearing at her, and the cameras caught it all. That'll make a nice picture in tomorrow's paper. She's just unlocked the door and is ushering everyone in. The press have moved forward. Oh, brilliant, the man from downstairs has just slammed the door and someone's fingers got caught.' Freddie laughed.

'Knowing my luck they'll probably sue.'

'Don't be so bloody dramatic.' We stopped then and watched the door open. In trooped Lisa, Imogen and the neighbours.

'I really am very, very, sorry about this,' I said.

'Oh that's fine. It's probably the most exciting thing to happen since we've lived here.' Dave shook my hand, then gestured for Jacquie to do the same.

'We think you're great, no matter what they say,' she said.

I thanked them and then we all stood around unsure of what to do next. 'Can I offer you a drink?' I said, but I didn't want to, I wanted them to go.

'No, no, thank you. Imagine, Holly Miller offered us a drink. No, we must go we've got to make dinner. Cheerio.' After I showed them out I looked at Lisa.

'This is quite a funky, trendy district, so why did they choose to live here?'

'Ah, well they must have thought it was a nice, quiet neigh-bourhood. Poor things.

'What do they do?'

'Loss adjusters. Both of them.' Well that was a profession to avoid.

'So then, what did you buy for me?' I asked, excited at the prospect of what lay in the carrier bags.

'You are going to be so pleased with us, isn't she Immi?'

'You certainly are, look.'

Imogen began emptying the carrier bags and passing items to me. Firstly there were some pyjama-type black trousers which were nice; plain and not too frumpy. Then some tunics, actu-ally quite a lot of tunics and some shirts. Then a black shift dress, and a red shift dress. Some evening tops, some maternity trousers that were almost jean-like, and some bras.

'You bought me bras?'

'Well the sales lady said your tits are probably about to take over. They get really big apparently and as they're not very big now so we got these.' Both Lisa and Imogen looked really proud.

'It's all fantastic, in fact I'm going to try it all on now.' I stood up.

'OK, how about I make dinner while you all get really giggly and girly,' Freddie said, grimacing at the sight of the bras. 'Christ real passion-killers they are,' he added, before heading out into the kitchen.

Everything they bought made me feel human again. I slipped on the red dress.

'I can't thank you enough,' I said, as I went to show the dress to Freddie.

'Wow, it looks fantastic,' he said.

'You sound shocked?'

'Well I'd never thought of pregnancy as sexy before, but you do look sexy.'

'Freddie, I think you'll find you've never thought of me as sexy.'

'Oh yeah, I forgot. Anyway, come and taste this, it's a sort of curry.'

'How can it be a sort of curry?'

'Well I found some chicken, and loads of veggies, so I put them all in this pot and added stock and curry powder.' I leaned in close to the spoon and sipped.

'Umm, that's nice. Don't make it too spicy, I don't want to give birth yet.'

'Isn't that an old wives' tale?'

'I have no idea.' I wondered if Dr Miriam would know.

After we ate Freddie's curry, I decided it was time for everyone to go home.

'Come on, Lisa, Max will be expecting you; and Freddie you've been here long enough.'

'Oh before I leave, we did get something else,' Lisa said.

'We weren't entirely sure how you would feel,' Imogen finished. Lisa went over and pulled a number of bags from behind the sofa. I looked at her as she presented me with some tiny leather booties, a baby denim jacket and a cashmere blanket.

'Oh my God, I don't know what to say.' I felt the blanket, it was so soft, I held it up against my face. This would have my baby in it. It would keep it warm and make it feel safe. My baby.

'I told you it would make her cry,' Lisa said.

'Everything makes her cry,' Freddie added.

'I'm going to have a baby,' I said through my tears. They all looked at me.

'Don't you see, I'm really going to have a baby.' And at that moment, despite the fact that the press were still camped outside my flat; and that George was mad; and that Joe had left me, I was the happiest person in the world.

# Chapter Thirty-five

The press proved more resilient than any of us imagined. When, on the following Wednesday I had to go for a check-up they were still there. Admittedly the numbers had diminished, but not by many. There was a lot of money at stake for the first shot of me looking pregnant. And pregnant I sure looked, especially in my new maternity wear.

The day after the press first arrived on my doorstep the papers all carried the picture of Lisa slapping the journalist. Of course, the story ran that I was a complete cow and had sent my bitch friend down to hurt the poor innocent journalist who had done nothing to deserve it. And the press agreed with me when it came to my relationship with George. They didn't think we should get back together. Only because I was no way near good enough for him. My favourite line read: '*Holly might have the looks and she might be carrying George's child but we advise George, save yourself from a life of misery with her, save yourself for someone who deserves you.*' Then they quoted George as saying (with a sigh no doubt), '*You don't choose who you fall in love with.*' Cheers. Another newspaper, ran an opinion poll: '*Holly's Baby – who should be the father, Joe or George?*' Well, although in this paper I wasn't being made out to be a complete harlot, I didn't like the way they involved Joe. Oh, and by the way, Joe got three per cent of the votes thanks to Lisa who phoned up quite a few times), and George got the rest.

At least something positive came out of it: Joe and I talked briefly on the phone. He was no longer being followed by the press, they already had a few shots of him, but when asked about me and the baby, he regretted saying 'George is a nutter and should be locked up and made to stay away from small children of any origin.' This did not make him popular. But I was just happy to hear his voice again.

I resented this invasion into my private life, any person would. George commanded his army – the press – to march on my life, to take no prisoners, to show no mercy and like the devoted army they were, they obeyed.

The mental torture I endured was gruesome. I lost a part of myself in those days and I didn't know if I would ever recover. I would sit in bed and wonder how many people had talked about me that day; how many passed judgement.

*'Oh, it's dreadful, that marriage-pact girl is a complete slut.' 'How she can live with herself after what she's done to that poor man is beyond me and now she thinks she is capable of being a mum.' 'Imagine, sleeping with two men, getting pregnant and not having an idea who the father is.' 'She says it is one of only two people . . . makes you wonder doesn't it?'*

Then the tears would roll down my cheeks because I knew that I would probably have judged my story in much the same way, were I reading it, and what thought did I ever give to strangers who were condemned for doing something wrong. Affairs, betrayal, it is easy, so easy to criticise. Now, I was being judged and although I didn't doubt that some people were guiltier than others, I believed that there were definitely some people who were probably victims in much the same way I was. Of course I had to take my fair share of blame. We all make mistakes and we all have to live with the consequences, but they are normally things we have to deal with in private, like losing Joe. But on top of that, everything was public and the people reading the paper would be judging me the way that I had judged others in the past and that pained me to the core.

The story had some sort of mention every day. Mainly they focused around me being in hiding and George being distraught at my continued rejection of him. The good news was that my clients were getting coverage on the back of me, but Imogen accused me of being no better than George for that. She was right. This is where confusion seeps in. Working in PR I rejoiced whenever I got any press editorial for my clients. Well, now *I* was getting it by the bucketful. They had managed to track down some of my clients.

'*She made a mistake but she's a great account director*,' Phil from *Zoom*.

'*We have a good working relationship and her private life has nothing to do with it*,' Sarah from *Jet*. (The most effective household cleaner in the land).

'*I admire Holly professionally and none of this has any bearing on that*,' Helen from *Final Mile Shoes*.

'*The team is a team and Francesca Williams PR is not just Holly Miller. They are an effective company and Holly is an effective leader. We have no plans to review our representation*,' Michael from *Software Store*.

'*I should be so lucky as to be in her shoes*,' Brenda from *Stop!* (spot cream). I think she was a bit confused as to the situation.

Flattered as I was by their words (apart from Brenda's), they were excited only about the free coverage they were getting, not about the fact they'd supported me.

I was using my predicament to promote my clients, albeit indirectly, my company were reaping the benefits. Not only had we received a record number of new business enquiries but we'd won two new clients in as many weeks. Far from being a liability I was an asset thanks to this crazy situation. So, although I hated it (I really did hate it), I also felt guilty for benefiting from it. On top of everything else I was prone to moments of guilt about that, as well as everything else, but also happy that I was speaking with Joe, even though our conversations revolved around the bloody press. He didn't say how he felt about me and I didn't ask. The time wasn't right, I was just grateful that he was still talking to me. It was more than I deserved.

I had developed the habit of talking to myself, in an attempt to maintain my sanity. I was working really hard. Imogen was fully ensconced and refusing to go home. The good news was that she had become friendly with the loss adjusters from downstairs so she spent a bit of time with them. Actually, I loved having her, especially as she had got used to the press and was really quite impressively blasé about them. We were becoming close friends as well as sisters. It felt quite special. Jack had been up a couple of times to see her but because of the press siege and the fact he was a 'bit famous', I didn't get to see him. Imogen came back smiling though and I tried to persuade her to go home, but she said that Jack appreciated her so much more now. Absence *did* make the heart grow fonder. She missed him like crazy and he missed her like crazy and that was fantastic. There was even a positive side for her. She was also keeping my parents updated as to the developments, which meant that I didn't have to talk about it too much. I thought about it all the time but thoughts are thoughts and talking about it was different, and it upset me too much.

I gave myself pep talks, something I'd practised since child-hood but now they were so much more important. I was keeping the misery away from my door more successfully than I was keeping the press away.

My pep talks: You have a lovely flat (spending so much time in it was making me appreciate it more). You have great friends and a great family. You have a baby on the way. You've got your health. *It could be a lot worse . . .* You won't be fat for ever (please God). You have known love. Your skin is looking fantastic. *It could be a lot worse . . .* You still have a career.

The photos in the paper have shown your good side.

It will all blow over shortly and then everyone will forget.

You will be able to go where you want, when you want.

*It could be a lot worse* . . . My final pep talk was verging on the desperate: Your hair hasn't fallen out.

You can afford nappies and Baby Gap. Just.

There are so many nice names you can choose from for the baby.

Sleep is overrated.

*It could be a lot worse.*

Well, it worked for me anyway. I used them when I woke up in the morning with a sinking feeling or a mild panic. I used them when I looked at the daily papers and saw my story still there. I used them when George made his ever-increasing television appearances, (*Ready Steady Cook, BBC Breakfast, Blankety Blank, London Today* to name a few). I used them before I called Joe, or before I spoke to anyone. I used them all the damn time.

I was using them today for two reasons. One, I was going out and the press would at last get that elusive shot of me. I was wearing my black trousers (the pyjama-type ones) and a cream tunic top. I even put on high heels. I was only going to the hospital but as I had to face the press I decided to make sure I looked my best. I took ages over my hair and make-up. The other reason was that George had managed to get an *Aloha!* magazine feature, that was due out that day. A mixture of *OK!* and *Hello!* magazines, *Aloha!* was a British publication, that was growing in popularity. Mainly because it always seemed to have chocolate attached to its cover.

'Imogen, it's time to go.' She was standing at her sentry post by the window. I had tried to get her to move a few times at the beginning, but I gave up. You would almost think she was enjoying herself, but I knew better. Apparently the loss adjusters liked staring at the press as well, they had got to know each one of them by sight and they got very excited when a new one appeared. Together, with Imogen, they had become the paparazzi equivalent of train-spotters minus the anoraks.

'Are you going to be all right?' she asked, moving away. 'There're ten there today, which isn't bad really, well not as bad as some days, but most of them have cameras and well they're going to get overexcited when they see you aren't they?' The touch of hysteria in her voice worried me.

'Keep calm Immi. I spoke to Freddie and Francesca about this and all I have to do is go out, let them snap their cameras, say a few words . . . I'll be fine.' Actually the bravado was completely false. Francesca had told me that biting the bullet and going out was the best thing. There had been so much speculation. Some papers claimed I had gone into hiding, others claimed sightings of me staring out of the window (it was Immi in the blurred photos), some said I was too humiliated to leave the flat, others said I should be too ashamed of myself to leave it. They were having a field day with my life. Only it wasn't my life any more. I was a bystander; they were in charge. Freddie had wanted to come and get me and do the male thing by escorting me, but I wouldn't hear of it. We had an important presentation the following day and he needed to work on that. So I pretended to everyone that I was fine about going out, even to Lisa, who also wanted to come over, but I knew that that particular situation would probably end in violence and that wasn't something we needed.

Also there had been two more 'kiss and tell' stories, but unlike ginger Justin, they were both made up. One guy called Bruce claimed that I had promised to marry him too but in the end just used him for sex. I promise I have never met a Bruce. And Clint said that he was also a contender for being the father of my child. I knew no one called Clint. Francesca gave those particular papers *hell* for printing the lies, and in all fairness they both printed retractions. But no one reads retractions do they? Especially when they are positioned at the bottom corner on an inside page. I didn't even try to discover if I could sue, there seemed no point in antagonising them any further. George did leap to my defence over Clint, saying there was no way that the baby could be his. But that was because he didn't want to share the limelight. For once his selfishness worked in my favour.

The thing that worried me most of all was Joe. We spoke about the kiss and tells and he laughed and said he knew they were all crap because the guys didn't even know me. That made me feel happy *and* sad. Happy because Joe knew me and he knew me enough to recognise that they didn't know me. Sad because he still wasn't with me and there weren't any signs of him coming back.

'Holly, you haven't moved,' Imogen said, questioningly. She had gone to touch up her make-up while I had been day-dreaming.

'Sorry.' I smiled, gave her a hug. 'Let's go feed the lions,' I joked as bravely as I could. We turned towards the door. 'Ouch!' I bent over with unexpected pain. I think it was more shock than pain that led to such a reaction.

'Oh my God, what's happened?' Imogen grabbed hold of me. I straightened myself up and she saw the tears in my eyes. 'Shall I call an ambulance?' I shook my head and smiled, this time genuinely.

'It moved,' I said. 'It kicked.'

'Really, let me feel.' Imogen put her hand on my stomach. 'Oh my God, my nephew or niece kicked! Wow, this is amazing, I can feel it.' We laughed then, and hugged before I went to repair my mascara. The baby was OK, therefore its mother would be OK too.

'Four deep breaths. Breathe in. Hold. Breathe out.' We repeated this four times before opening the door. Imogen went first, holding on to my hand, I followed her. I can't describe how it felt to have all eyes on me. I would say that it was a bit like the first time I ever appeared in a school play. I was about seven but I can remember walking out on stage and looking out on to what seemed to a small child like a million faces all looking at me. At first there was silence, almost surprise I think. Then they all synchronised their actions.

'Holly, smile for the camera,' a voice shouted. I did smile but only because I was trying to work out what to do next. The cameras clicked away in unison. Someone asked me to turn towards them. I did. Obediently taking stage directions because I had lost my own. I looked at Imogen, still clutching my hand but also smiling moronically for the camera. You could tell at that moment that we were definitely sisters.

'Where are you going?' a woman shouted, frantically waving a microphone in my face.

I cleared my throat. 'I've got a hospital appointment,' I replied. I had no idea how confident or not I sounded, I could barely hear my own voice.

'Are you going to have a DNA?' another voice asked.

'No. I don't wish to discuss that right now.'

'The *Daily News* will pay for you to have the test if you give us the exclusive on the result,' a male voice shouted. I blinked wondering if I had heard right.

'My paper will do that too.'

'No, we'll do it, our circulation is bigger.' The clamour of voices was overwhelming, offering money for the result of a bloody test. The test I hadn't even agreed to have.

'I don't wish to discuss this further. If you'll excuse me I really am going to be late.' I walked down the short path, and on to the pavement. The cameras kept clicking, the reporters firing questions at me, but they let me pass.

'Can I ask *you* a question?' I said. 'When are you going to leave me alone?'

'When the story has an ending,' one of them replied. I wished that I could give them an ending. But I couldn't.

I had been a hostage in my flat for what felt like years. I wasn't feeling stir crazy exactly but I was very aware of the freedom we all take for granted. Want to go to the shops, easy. Want to get a pint of milk, go for a walk, got to a pub, a restaurant, easy. Go to work. Everything taken for granted. There were so many things I needed to re-evaluate, the list was growing longer by the minute, and freedom of movement was up there near the top along with friends, family, my health, being slim, and my work. That was an upside, there were upsides.

'Aren't you the marriage-pact girl?' the taxi driver asked. Oh, and there were downsides too.

On the way to the hospital we got the taxi to stop at a newsagent's and Imogen ran out to get a copy of *Aloha!* She came back, slightly breathless, and jumped into the cab.

'Shall we?' she asked, ready to open the magazine. I shook my head, gestured to the taxi driver. I don't know why I didn't want to do this in front of him but I suspected it was something to do with his lively conversation with the next passenger: 'Yeah I had the marriage-pact girl in my cab today and she read this magazine article, some interview by her intended and you should have heard her language, it turned the air blue.' I certainly didn't want to be a part of that. I took the magazine from Imogen and looked at the cover. Spreadeagled on a zebra-print rug was a well-known soap star actress. *My joy at baby news,* ran the headline. There was an item on Kylie, something about a few minor TV stars and then were was a mention of George. *My marriage pact hell,* the header screamed, and although it wasn't a huge headline it had made the cover, which was bad news. I rolled up the magazine and determined I would deal with it when I was back home.

We pulled up outside the hospital entrance and I paid the taxi driver who I am sure looked at me disapprovingly. I gave him a curt goodbye and then led Imogen to the gynaecology department. We pushed open the big glass doors and walked into reception. The waiting room was quite full of pregnant women, some who looked about to burst. Most had men with them

– husbands or boyfriends. I felt a pang. This was the sort of thing that I know Joe would have wanted to be a part of, were things different. And maybe even though he couldn't forgive me, or didn't want to be with me, he could still be a part of it. If it were his baby I was depriving him of this whole experience which was unfair. If the baby were George's then I didn't give a shit.

'I've got an appointment with Dr Langton,' I said to the receptionist.

'Your name,' she smiled, kindly.

'Holly Miller,' I whispered.

'Pardon?'

'Holly Miller,' I said slightly louder.

'I really can't hear you,' she said again.

'Holly Miller,' Imogen boomed. I scowled at her, as the woman behind the desk went a bit pink and the waiting room became very quiet. Everyone was staring at me and all I wanted to do was to cry. The silence gave way to whispers and I knew they were talking about me. The receptionist, who still looked embarrassed, told me to go right through. The perks of celebrity status perhaps?

I could feel the eyes following me as I made my way along the hospital corridors; boring into my back. Why did people have to recognise me? Or my name. I hadn't asked for any of the exposure but people knew who I was. Even hiding from the press on my doorstep hadn't made too much difference. I was a household face and a household name, although I don't think anyone liked me and I certainly hadn't received any fan mail.

I knocked on the door and waited to be admitted. Imogen was still with me and I felt it would be better to let her come in with me rather than leave her with the starers in the waiting room. She looked mortified, she really did, poor thing. It was hard for her having a sister who was the object of such derision. We walked into the room and sat down.

'How are we?' Dr Langton asked. I assumed he meant me and the baby.

'Fine, it kicked today.' I smiled and patted my stomach. 'This is Imogen, my sister, she's been taking care of me.'

'Right, well I need to examine you and make sure that you're on track. Then the nurse will weigh you. I notice from your records that you haven't been to any birthing lessons yet.' He spoke quickly as if he didn't really have much time. He probably didn't because this was the NHS after all.

'I'm going later this week. I want to give birth in a hospital with drugs. Lots of drugs. Maybe an epidural, can I order one right now?'

'I'm not sure that's necessary, but a hospital birth is sensible. Don't worry. You should talk through the options with the teacher in the birthing lessons if you have any doubts.'

I didn't. 'Fine. There is something else though,' I said as he carried on with his examination.

'Yes?'

'When can I have a paternity test?'

'As soon as you want, after the birth. We can only do it if we get a sample from one of the prospective fathers. Will that be possible?'

'I hope so.' I knew that it was time to talk to Joe. Although we had no way of knowing until the baby was born, I wanted him to be part of this. I knew then that I had to do what it took to get him back into my life.

After the doctor we saw the nurse who weighed me, said I was in good shape, and was really lovely. Then I went to sign up for a birthing lesson the following week. Being pregnant was really quite time-consuming. Imogen maintained a dignified silence all the time this was going on, only because there were other people around. As soon as we stepped outside the hospital door she started.

'Are you sure that a test is such a good idea?'

'I have to know at some stage. Look at the facts. The newspapers have no story when they know the identity of the father. It's the guessing that is keeping the story alive. Once we know, it'll be dead, uninteresting. It'll run for a bit longer but not much. Now if I am truly cursed and George is the father of the child then I might keep quiet a bit longer, but if I am lucky and Joe is the father, then that is the end of George. How can he expect me to marry him when I have someone else's baby? Besides, George has started doing stuff which is totally unrelated to the story anyway. Although I'm not sure appearing on *Ready Steady Cook* is going to make his career, it's still nothing to do with me. I don't care if he becomes a TV star as long as it has nothing to do with me. And if the baby isn't his maybe he'll piss off back to New York. The other thing is Joe. If it is his baby he has a right to know. He could have been involved in the pregnancy already.'

'I suppose you're right, I'm just scared for you Hol.'

'I'm scared for me too.'

We took a cab home (the driver didn't recognise me thank God), and the press numbers had seriously depleted by the time we drew up. I smiled at them while they took some more photos and asked some more questions then Imogen opened the door and pulled me inside.

'Bye,' I said as I walked in the door and waved to them.

'Have you gone mad?' Imogen asked.

'If I'd known how easy it would be I'd have gone out a week ago.' It was a lie, because it hadn't been easy, and all I wanted to do was scream.

'Holly, that isn't the point, the point is that they are going to print stuff, and it might not be nice.'

'Oh yeah, I'd forgotten. They'll probably choose the photos that make me look the fattest as well.'

'They probably will. I'll make tea.' I called Freddie and told him about the press. Then he asked me if I had read the *Aloha!*

interview and I remember the rolled-up magazine I'd been carrying around. I came off the phone and opened it to the correct page.

My heart fell into my shoes. There was a huge photo of George looking dashing, I have to admit, sitting on a sofa, with his arm draped over the back. It looked like it should have been a picture of George with someone next to him. It implied it should have been a picture of George and me. I read the interview feeling my earlier euphoria disappear.

*Life for gorgeous lawyer George Conway gets stranger and stranger – a statement the effervescent man would agree with of his own free will. A successful lawyer in New York, his life lacked only one thing: Holly Miller his childhood sweetheart. Betrothed by a marriage pact, George returned home to claim his bride. Passion was reignited immediately but then the shock came. She already had a boyfriend and had no intention of marrying him. Grief stricken, George tried to take her to court but was halted at the first hurdle. So he turned to the media to appeal to Holly to see sense and admit her love for him. If that wasn't enough for him to cope with, Holly then announced that she was pregnant and George may or may not be the father. We met George at the Hanman Hotel and Country Club to ask him how he was coping.*

Tell us why you came home?
*For love. Pure and simple. I realised that I was still in love with Holly even though we'd been apart for five years. We always said that we'd get together when we were thirty, and as I'd just turned thirty I knew that it was the right time.*
What was it like when you saw each other again?
*Wonderful, brilliant, perfect! All the old feelings came flooding back immediately, which led me to uproot from New York to be with Holly for good.*
You didn't want to leave New York?

*It was nothing to do with wanting to leave or not wanting to leave. I came back to London for Holly, nothing else.*

You're known in the press as the 'Marriage-Pact Couple'. Tell us about that.

*We were very young when we got together, well we grew up together really, so we knew that we would have to spend some time apart, to each explore our own careers. But we knew we would end up together so we signed a pact to that effect. We said that we would get married when we were thirty.*

But you have never published a copy of the pact. Why is that?

*Because it's too personal. The world may know the whole story but that pact was signed in love and I wouldn't want to tarnish that love by letting anyone see it.*

Were you shocked when Holly turned you down?

*Totally. She had slept with me before I knew she had a boyfriend. I was devastated as you can imagine.*

So you tried to take her to court . . . ?

*Yes, it wasn't a sensible move, I realise that now, but I wasn't thinking straight. I love her and I was heartbroken.*

Were you shocked by the news of the pregnancy and the fact you might be the father?

*I was overjoyed when I found out. I know there is a possibility that it's not mine but in my heart I feel it is. It reinforces my belief that we're meant to be together.*

So how do you cope with the situation?

*Well, I don't ever lose sight of the love I feel for her. And I never give up hope. It's all I have left. But I have to put myself second and Holly and the baby first. I have made it clear that I am here for her . . . always.*

How do you feel about being in the public eye?

*It is strange, but the support I've received from the public has been overwhelming. I really want to thank everyone for that.*

So what does the future hold?

*I can only take one day at a time. I hope Holly will remember our love and accept our future is together. I hope that we will have a healthy baby and become a family. There is nothing else I can ask for, is there?*

I finished reading and laughed.

'What's funny?' Imogen asked, she had finished reading at the same time.

'He is so fucking earnest, isn't he? All that shit about love and putting me first it's all such crap. I can't believe it. And the photos, they are amazing.' Photos of George in this wonderful hotel, looking upset, serious and appealing. It was so staged it made me feel sick.

'We better start praying that this baby is Joe's. And talking of Joe, I think I should phone and get him back into my life.'

'Holly, do you think you'll be all right if I go home? It's not that I don't love being here, I do, but I think that Jack and I need to spend some time together.' She looked so worried as she asked, I felt a huge surge of gratitude for what she had done.

'Of course you must go home, I'll get Lisa and Max to stay.' I tried to sound more confident than I felt. I was a child in an adult body, with another child on the way. If I was going to be a good mother I'd have to be much stronger than I was. I had to cope.

'You can't be on your own near the birth.'

'Immi that's months away and anyway you think Mum would miss that?'

'No, I guess not. Not the birth of her first grandchild.'

'I bet no one would have ever imagined that I'd be the provider,' I laughed.

'I know. They probably think that Jack and I have problems. But I think I might prove them wrong, I think maybe we will give them their second grandchild.'

'Are you sure? You seemed so unsure.' I was struck by the

idea that I was turning everyone around me, broody. Imogen and Lisa were already voicing thoughts about motherhood. I wondered how Francesca felt about it. If she declared that she was going to try for a baby then I would know I was the instigator.

'Well I've been thinking, and if Jack and I are rock solid then I think we'd make wonderful parents, but I won't rush into anything.'

'There is no doubt of that.'

Imogen went to check the train times while I phoned Joe.

'It's Holly,' I said as he picked up the phone.

'How are you?' his voice was always so gentle when he said that.

'The baby kicked today.'

'It did? That's brilliant, what did it feel like?' His rush of emotion was touching.

'It took me by surprise, it didn't really hurt but it felt strange. I thought about it then, because it's real now Joe, and if you are the father, if it turns out to be yours then you will have missed out on all this, all the pregnancy. And I don't want that. Do you?'

'I'm scared Holly.'

'I'm terrified.'

'I don't know what I'll do if it's not mine.'

'Will you at least come with me to my next scan?'

'Yes. Give me the address of the hospital and I'll meet you there.'

I cried when I put down the phone because he sounded so lost, but I wasn't as lost as him because it was happening to me. If that sounds stupid or doesn't make sense that's because life doesn't make sense a lot of the time.

# Chapter Thirty-six

———◆◆◆◆———

## *Climax*

We'd been tipped off that there were going to be photos of Holly in the papers so we took our usual trip to get the early editions. Sure enough, there she was in all her pregnant glory. Pregnancy suited her, her eyes were shining but she was definitely fat. The journalists all attacked her; she'd been rude to them. As she had been rude to me on a number of occasions, that wasn't hard to believe. Still, the sympathy lay with me, which was all that mattered:

> *'She leaves for the hospital without a thought for the father of her child.'*
> *'Holly shows no remorse for what she is doing.'*
> *'She sticks two fingers up to the press as she flounces out.'*

There was no evidence of her sticking up two fingers to anyone, it was a good story, and good coverage for us. The story was outlasting our expectations.

'I can't believe how well we're doing,' Cordelia said, as we read the papers from cover to cover.

'I'm very pleased,' I agreed. 'I'm pleased with you.' I had appeared on several television shows, in a major glossy magazine and had become a celebrity in my own right. *This Afternoon* were close to giving me a regular slot, there had been discussions and outlines, although nothing was set in stone. Cordelia was confident that we'd be signing a contract soon.

'But George it isn't going to last for ever. You might and your career might but this story will soon lose its appeal. When paternity is determined there's not much left. Although if the baby is yours we can get some more coverage. *Aloha!* have said they will pay handsomely for the first pictures of the marriage-pact baby.'

'Holly won't let that happen.' I could imagine her reaction to that suggestion. I felt bad at times about Holly and the baby. I hoped that the stress she accused me of putting her under was just her way of trying to warn me off. That was what Cordelia said. But I couldn't stop pursuing my goal. Holly was trying to make me feel guilty and that wasn't fair. After all I wasn't the one who had no idea who the father of her baby was. This wasn't my fault.

'Let's worry about that nearer the time. People love you, that's what you need to remember and we can use that.' Her usual exuberance was notably absent.

'I am not going to let things slip away, we have to keep going.' Fear of losing what I had was foremost in my thoughts.

'George, relax, we will. I'm doing my best and so far have I let you down?'

I looked at her, sitting crossed-legged on the floor with all the papers laid out in front of her. She was sexy even when she was doing something as mundane as reading the paper. She hadn't let me down; she had been responsible for where I was now. But I had to ensure I stayed there. I had kick-started my TV career but it needed developing. I needed more.

The public loved me. I received a huge number of letters of support via the shows and the newspapers. They liked me, not just the story, but *me*. I was recognised in the street. I'd signed bucket loads of autographs. That made me a celebrity. The thought of losing it all didn't warrant thinking about. It would be fine. I would be able to build on my fame, but it would help if I was the father of Holly's baby. That would give me so much more leverage. However, that was something that Cordelia couldn't fix.

'She will have to take a test at some point,' Cordelia said.

'Which could be good for us or bad.'

'We'll deal with it when the time comes.' I leaned over and kissed her, hard.

'George, this whole story is about you being in love with her, but *are* you really?' She didn't look at me.

'What do you mean? Of course I am.'

'It's just that you say you love her but you're sleeping with me.' She still didn't look at me.

'I thought this was a mutually agreeable situation for us.'

'It is, it's just I wondered if you were still in love with her.'

'I'm going to marry her and have a child with her, of course I love her.' I hadn't expected this conversation. I could have sworn that Cordelia looked upset, which surprised me.

'I've got an early start, the person who came second in that reality TV show wants to talk to me about representation. I'm going to bed.'

'Bed sounds like a good idea.' I put my arms out to her.

'George I'm tired, I need sleep,' she snapped.

'What is this?' I snapped back. I hadn't faced rejection from her before and I didn't expect to.

'I have feelings George, I'm human. I just wish you appreciated that a bit more.'

'But I do. This works for us, you know that. You never believed it would be for ever. I never gave you any reason to think it would.'

'No, I didn't but that doesn't mean that I like it.'

'You've never complained before.'

'George, I'm falling in love with you. That's it.'

Cordelia was necessary to my life for a number of reasons. Sex was but one, love wasn't an option. I was stunned. Was she crazy?

'I don't know what to say.'

'Then don't say anything. I work for you and I sleep with you and I do my best for you. OK, so the situation is a little unorthodox. I made you famous on the back of your love for someone else and in the process I fell in love with you. Not something I expected or planned. So tonight, instead of bending me over and giving me one, perhaps you could come to bed with me and hold me.' I looked at her, aghast. Why did all the women in my life turn out to be a pain in the ass.

'I need to go, I have some things to do. I'll call you tomorrow at the office.' I stood up to leave, and could have sworn that I saw tears in her eyes.

''Bye,' she whispered.

''Bye,' I said, and left.

It was late and it took me ages to find a cab. I was annoyed because, as always, just as things were going my way, someone, some woman tried to ruin it. Julia, Holly, now Cordelia. What is it with women? Why do they appear to be put on the earth to cause confusion and disruption among men? I'd had enough and vowed that the following day I would sort out Cordelia. I was her star client, she needed me and she would have me, but on *my* terms.

The following morning I woke in my rented flat, alone, feeling wretched. Loneliness had just been banished, and I didn't want it back in my life. Ever since I met Cordelia I had woken (even before we slept together) feeling positive and amorous towards the future, but not that morning. I felt flat and empty. I was a star and stars got what they wanted. That was the whole point. The only bloody point. Cordelia had no right to make me feel the way I felt.

I put on a tracksuit and went to my local café for a coffee. They knew me in there, although I hadn't been much recently due to the amount of time I spent at Cordelia's. There was a girl behind the counter, who had asked me if I was 'George the marriage-pact man', the last time I went in.

'Can I have a large cappuccino and a poppy seed bagel to eat in,' I asked, smiling through the tiredness I felt.

'Of course, George,' she replied. 'I'll bring it over, go and sit down.' I liked that. Everyone else queued up and waited for their food and drink, but I got to sit down and be waited on. A few people looked at me as she said this and I smiled, my most enigmatic smile. Within a few minutes, the girl was at my table.

'I'm at a slight disadvantage here,' I said. 'You know my name but I don't know yours.'

'Debbie,' she replied, almost shyly.

'Thank you very much Debbie. How much do I owe you?'

'On the house,' she replied.

'Thank you.' I got freebies, no one else did. It made me feel special. She smiled at me again, and I noticed her pretty eyes. The rest of her wasn't bad either.

As I ate and drank I read the *Financial Times*, then I got up to leave. I had to deal with Cordelia before I could deal with anything else.

''Bye Debbie,' I said as I walked out past the counter.

'Oh 'bye George,' she replied. Very pretty eyes.

Back in my flat I considered how I would handle Cordelia. I didn't want to end the relationship I was having with her but then if she was going to be difficult about it I had no real option. Without warning I thought of Debbie. How she looked as if I'd made her day by talking to her, just a simple thing of asking her name. That was what was wonderful, that was what intoxicated me. The fact that I was famous meant that I was so important to ordinary people. That was a commodity that no one would want to give up.

'Cordelia Dickens,' she answered her private line immediately.

'It's George.'

'Hi.' I heard her sigh.

'We need to talk.'

'The phone hasn't stopped ringing. Two papers want your comments on Holly and the hospital thing. Another magazine has requested an interview. *This Afternoon* want you to host a phone-in for men on paternity issues, from a legal point of view, as a prelude to your regular slot. What do you want to do?'

'Say yes to all of them if my schedule permits. No such thing as overkill is there?'

'No, there certainly isn't.' I heard a bit of the old Cordelia.

'When should we talk about us?' I asked.

'Is that necessary?' I presumed she was embarrassed about her outburst the previous night. I hoped she was. Things could go back to normal then.

'After what you said last night I think it is.'

'Dinner, my flat, tonight?'

'I'll be there.' I had no idea how I was going to win her round but I knew I had to. I had to ensure that she still worked effectively for me, and that was the only thing hanging in the balance. Sure I could get another publicist, but I wanted her, I liked her, I just didn't love her.

# Chapter Thirty-seven

She looked amazing when she opened the door. She was wearing a tight red top, a black pencil skirt and her trademark high heels. I was immediately aroused.

'Hi.' I kissed her cheek. Then I leaned in and kissed her lips.

'Come in.' She seemed a bit nervous, like someone on a first date, although perhaps I was imagining that. I followed her into the sitting room and plonked myself down on the sofa.

'So what's for dinner?' I asked, winking at her.

'Takeaway. I didn't have time to shop for anything.' She left the room and came back with two glasses of red wine and a bunch of takeaway menus.

'I think Chinese,' I said, taking the wine.

'Whatever you want, George.' I thought I could detect a hint of tiredness in her voice. We ordered food, drank some wine and talked about work while we waited. Then the food turned up and she set the dining table. While we ate we talked about my appearances. It was strictly business. But, I was so turned on by the amount of offers that I'd had, I needed Cordelia.

'Come here,' I said, leaning across the table to kiss her gently. She looked a bit taken aback but she didn't protest. I did my officer and a gentleman impression; I picked her up and carried her to the bedroom. There I slowly peeled off her clothes and she did the same to me. I made love to her for the first time ever.

There was no roughness, no talking dirty, no commands. I moved slowly and she moved slowly with me. As I kissed her

I knew I was giving her what she wanted. Which in turn, would give me what I wanted. Afterwards we lay side by side.

'That was amazing,' she said, her voice softer than normal.

'It always is.'

'But that was different. I love you George.'

As if someone had stuck a pin in my bottom, I sat upright.

'Pardon?' I shook my head, I must have been hearing things.

'Surely that was what that was all about. I told you yesterday how I felt and tonight you show me that you feel the same.'

Fuck. Women.

'Cordelia, I don't love you.' How could she not have known that?

'What?' She sounded shocked.

'I love Holly, I thought you understood.'

'Fine, then I can't do us. I can work for you although I think we'll have to stop seeing so much of each other. But that's it.' She was the consummate professional.

'No sex?' She looked angry as I asked this. I was the one with the right to anger. Where did she get off?

'No sex. George, when we first met I fancied you, I never, ever, before in my life have slept with a client. Even though my job turns me on, I have never bedded someone I represent. Until now. And now I know that it's been all about sex. Sure, great, great sex, but I'm not used to having feelings like this. I don't know what to do with them.' She sounded like a stranger, not the woman I knew.

'You do realise that if we got together properly my career would be over.'

'Yes, I know. But maybe when your career is established it would be different.'

'It's not in either of our interests for this to happen.'

'Depends if you're talking professional interests or personal ones.'

'Cordelia, you know how hard I've worked for this. I can't give it up now.'

'I knew you'd say that. I can't sleep with you again.'

'Which is a shame.'

'Yes it is, isn't it.' She looked pissed off, but had no right to be. I didn't ask her to fall in love with me. I certainly didn't encourage it.

'You're sure you can still work with me?'

'Of course, this won't affect our working relationship at all. George, would you go now?' I got out of bed and dressed hurriedly.

'Sophie will be e-mailing you next week's schedule. I've also got some money to pay you from last month. I'll call you as soon as I have anything else.' Her voice had hardened, it was cold and unfamiliar.

'Thank you.' I left, knowing that my mind wouldn't change. I couldn't risk everything for her, especially as I didn't love her. She must have been mad to think that I did.

I was seething as I hailed a cab and climbed in. I had to force myself to be nice to the driver. He had recognised me and wanted to talk about the problems he had in his marriage. I was relieved when he pulled up outside my flat. I was about to go inside, then decided that I needed a drink. I was frustrated. Cordelia and I had a perfect relationship. We worked well together and I liked waking up next to her. How dare she end it like that? Why did she have to do something stupid like fall in love with me. She didn't strike me as the soppy type, which was why I liked her. Were they really all the same? Even the ruthless ones?

I went to a nearby off-licence and bought a bottle of whisky. As I handed over my credit card I felt a tap on my shoulder. I turned around to see Debbie standing behind me.

'Hello,' I said, surprised, but pleasantly so.

'Settling in for the night?' she asked shyly.

'It's been a hellish day.' I smiled.

'Tell me about it, my feet are killing me. I was just buying some fags on my way home.' She sounded more confident since our meeting that morning. She looked lovely.

'Do you like whisky?' I asked.

'I do.'

'Want to share a glass with me?' I asked, with an eyebrow raised.

'That would be lovely.'

I let her into the flat and sat her down while I went to get glasses.

'I know it's a bit boring, I'm just renting it.' I gestured around me.

'I think it's great,' she replied. I handed her a drink and got an ashtray.

'So, Debbie, tell me about yourself.'

She was twenty-four and worked in the café full time. She didn't seem to be too well-educated, but then I wasn't after her intellect. She lived round the corner, with a friend, that was pretty much all there was to it.

I then told her my story. My sad, sad story.

'I can't believe a woman would turn you down,' she said.

'Would you?' I asked, teasing her. She blushed.

'I don't know.'

'Well, would you turn me down now or would you let me kiss you?' She answered by moving closer to me.

We had sex on the sofa and although it was far gentler than was the norm with Cordelia (Debbie wasn't the type who liked to be spanked), it was still satisfying. Afterwards we had another drink and another cigarette.

'I should walk you home,' I offered. She looked hurt.

'The press, you know. We have to be careful,' I explained. Which wasn't altogether true. I wasn't the one being followed by the press, and they only snapped me if they saw me out and about. But I had no further need for her tonight; I wanted to be on my own.

'Of course, it's just . . . will I see you again?'

'How about your café, breakfast, tomorrow morning?' I kissed her and she grinned.

I checked there was no one around then I walked her home. Her flat was only a five-minute stroll away. Dropping her at her door I pecked her on the cheek and made a hasty retreat.

# Chapter Thirty-eight

## *Combat*

It was the day of the scan. And Joe was accompanying me. I felt
so nervous, like I used to the morning before I had to take an
exam. I had to persuade Joe to be a part of this baby's life, even
now, because when we took the test eventually and it turned out
to be his (in my hopeful moments this is what I believed), then
I didn't want him to be resentful because he had missed out on
the prenatal experience. Also, if it turned out to be George's then
I would need him more than ever and slowly getting him back
in my life was the only thing I could think of to ensure this. I had
no control over the outcome, I couldn't revise for this particular
test. I couldn't be sure if I would pass or fail. Because that's what
it came down to. If Joe was the father, then I'd passed. If George
was, I'd failed miserably.

The newspapers were now boring me. I had managed to laugh
at the coverage up till now (well some of the time). But I had
become more and more detached; it was as if they were talking
about someone else. Actually they were. Imogen still got so
angry, not upset and hysterical, but angry. She wanted to go
down to where they still camped and 'give them a piece of my
mind'. I managed to talk her out of it, by telling her to think of
Jack. But now the media circus was being held in a three-man
tent. A couple of resilient photographers stayed, according to the
loss adjusters, in case anything unforeseen happened. Like me

being rushed to hospital, in which case the photos would be worth a lot of money. The loss adjusters were quite friendly with the press now, I think they were going to miss them when they were gone. I was amazed that they stayed as long as they did. I never imagined that they would have maintained such an interest in me.

Before they trailed off, they had made a last-ditch attempt to get me to take a paternity test, and they didn't seem to care that it might harm the baby. That, and the birth were the only events that held any interest for them. The story was almost dead, or if not dead, sleeping.

Unfortunately, the same couldn't be said for George. Now, instead of being a headline, he was featured and photographed in his everyday life. George on *This Afternoon*; George arriving at the BBC studios; George in Waitrose; George in San Lorenzo. The television appearances were increasing, he had constant exposure. Amazingly, most of the time he forgot to even mention me. What was laughable was the image he'd cultivated. Cordelia had torpedoed George into daytime TV. The housewives' favourite. How long would it be until he was hosting his own TV show? Eamonn Holmes watch out; your sofa is under threat.

Imogen had gone and Lisa had replaced her. Max was away, so she said that I was doing her a favour rather than the other way round. I missed Imogen, funnily enough, although Lisa was far more cheerful.

'Do you want me to come with you?' she asked as she came into my bedroom and handed me a cup of tea.

'No, I want to see Joe on my own.'

'On your own with a doctor?'

'Yeah all right but at least I might get to talk to him.'

'How long is it going to take?'

'Usually about twenty minutes.'

'When he sees the tiny little thing on the screen I know he'll fall in love.'

'Thanks Lis. How do I look?'

'Beautiful, you'll melt his heart.'

As I left the flat I said hello to the bored looking photographers.

'Where are you going?' one asked casually.

'Gynaecologist. Want to come along for the ride?' I had become cocky in my old age. He shook his head.

'We've heard that Kylie is in South Kensington, shopping, we're going to get photos of her.'

'Good.' I smiled. They had lost interest in me, for now.

I got the bus to the hospital, enjoying every moment. Freedom of movement had resumed. A few people stared at me but no one said anything, and I know how people stare normally, so they might not even have recognised me. I still felt nervous as I got off the bus and began the short walk to the front of the hospital where I was meeting Joe. I prayed that he would be all right.

He looked a bit dishevelled and was smoking a cigarette. God, he was sexy.

'Hi.' He stubbed out the cigarette, as I approached.

'How are you?' he asked.

'Nervous.' I managed a weak smile.

'Me too. I couldn't sleep last night.'

'I'm so sorry.'

'Holly, this is still really hard for me.'

'I know. How's work?' I asked him as we walked in.

'Pretty crazy at the moment. I'm working on a huge corporate identity for a computer firm. These guys spend loads of money on stuff like that.' I missed hearing details about his job, it made me realise how distant we had become.

We made small talk while we waited to be called to the doctor. The butterflies in my stomach weren't just because of the baby.

'How's Freddie?' he asked, keeping on the safe ground of small talk.

'Fantastic. Freddie and Francesca have been brilliant. I'm

sorry that you didn't have anyone to fall back on. Well, I mean anyone who works in PR. We should have helped you more.'

'Oh I think you got the worst of it. Anyway, it'll soon be over. The mad media will lose interest.' He laughed, uneasily.

'That's what I keep telling myself. Actually they've pretty much lost interest now.'

'It was weird though wasn't it, seeing our lives in the papers.'

'Beyond weird.'

'He's always in things and on television. It drives me mad whenever I see him.'

'I know. He's done his best to screw up everything, although I'm not entirely blameless.'

'But it was a mistake wasn't it? One with huge repercussions but a mistake all the same.'

'That's all it was, a mistake.'

Joe nodded and fell silent. I bit the bullet and took his hand. I squeezed it, he smiled and gave a little squeeze back. There might not have been much but there was still hope. Just a tiny glimmer, but that was enough for now.

We went in to Dr Langton's surgery and I sat on the trolley and pulled my top up to reveal my ever-growing bump. Joe looked scared as he watched the screen, as if he was watching a spooky film. But soon I saw the amazement in his eyes and I knew that I'd done the right thing.

'Oh boy, that's amazing,' Joe said. He looked at the screen mesmerised and then, without prompting took my hand.

'It's growing so quickly,' I said, thinking aloud.

'It's amazing.' He smiled at me and I wanted more than anything to fall into his arms. We left the hospital together and for the first time in the whole mess, I felt normal. I was a normal mum leaving hospital with her boyfriend, the father of her baby. Even if it was based on fantasy.

'It is amazing.' Joe was a stuck record. I adored that about him.

'I know.' I stood outside and shivered. The weather was warmer now but I still felt cold.

'Can I drive you home? I've got the car.' Oh how I missed his car.

'That would be lovely.' We walked to the parking bay and I heaved myself into his low Porsche.

'Not the most practical transport for someone my size,' I quipped.

'No, you're a bit of a fat bird aren't you.'

I laughed. 'Not fat, pregnant. I'll be lovely and slim again in no time.'

'Yeah or you'll be one of those cuddly mothers.'

'I will not. I'll be one of those slim, glamorous mothers that all young boys fall in love with. A yummy mummy.'

'You will. Everyone will fall in love with you.'

I smiled, sadly. Because he did, he did fall in love with me, and look where that got him. 'Do you want to come in?' I asked before we reached the flat. 'Lisa's there, she's babysitting me.'

'What about the press?'

'Two at the last count and they were leaving to go and find Kylie.' I looked at him beseechingly, I didn't want him to leave.

'I better not,' he said in the end. 'I've got loads to do at work.' I nodded and bit my lip to stop the tears. I had no right to cry in front of him.

'What next?' he asked as he pulled up.

'I want you to be involved as much as you can. We need to go to antenatal and birthing lessons. I know this is hard but if this baby is yours then you have a right to know it now.'

'Give me some time.'

I nodded, and bolted from the car, tears streaming down my face, as I made my way to the front door. I bet a photo of me heaving myself out of Joe's car, fleeing to the flat in tears would have been a great one. I was so relieved that they were no longer interested enough and so that latest humiliation, would be kept from the front page.

I let myself in with shaking hands, barely able to see, and was relieved to find both Lisa and Freddie there. I fell into his arms. My surrogate boyfriend.

'What happened?' Lisa asked.

I told them how he looked so gorgeous but so nervous. I told them how we had a normal conversation just like in the old days. I told them how he'd teased me when he drove me home, how he didn't want to come in, how he knew that he needed time to think about what next.

For the first time I would have given anything to know who the father of my baby was. I really would have. 'I can't bear it, I just can't bear it,' I sobbed, as Freddie held me in his vice-like grip and didn't let go.

Finally when I regained some semblance of composure, I realised that Freddie shouldn't be here.

'Is something wrong at work?' I asked.

'No darling, look I came here today because we knew you were seeing Joe. Francesca is joining us after work. We're your support. But there is something.'

'Really, what?'

'Wait until you hear this,' Lisa chipped in, animatedly.

'Well, Francesca received an anonymous phone call from some woman, who said that George wasn't all he seemed and that there was more going on. She said that he was only interested in himself and that it wouldn't be hard to prove that his claim to be in love with you was false.'

'I don't get it. How?'

'Apparently he hasn't been living like a monk. We don't know any more because when Francesca asked, the woman hung up. But this is the weird thing, Francesca could have sworn it was

Cordelia, she had tried to disguise her voice but as you know Francesca knows her pretty well.'

'What do you think it means?' Lisa asked, rubbing her hands together.

'Well, our guess is that he slept with her.'

'But why would she tell us?' I was trying to process the information, which still made little sense.

'Because he dumped her?' Freddie smiled.

'No, Freddie, none of this makes sense. Cordelia is making money out of him, he's making money out of me. He wouldn't risk that.'

'You'd think, wouldn't you.'

'Anyway, if he dumped her then we've no proof.'

'But he could be doing it with someone else.'

'Doing it?' I laughed. 'You mean being unfaithful to me.' I couldn't quite take it in after the day that I'd had, and anyway I didn't believe it. It was too ridiculous.

'It's worth a try. Until we know the results of the paternity test, then there will be some interest in the story. Especially when the test is finally taken and if it turns out to be George's then, well.' I flinched. 'Sorry, Hol, sorry, to be so blunt but we know that's a possibility. Therefore if we can make George look like he's not whiter than white, then you get the sympathy vote. Game over.'

'What a tosser,' Lisa stated. We couldn't argue with that.

'OK. But say he did shag Cordelia – yuck, that's a coupling not to imagine – and then dumped her, he might not be with anyone else.'

'Or he might be. Worth having him followed.'

'I'll follow him,' Lisa offered.

'Don't be silly, he knows you. Freddie, are you suggesting a detective?'

'Why not. What have we got to lose?' It was a good question.

'I just don't see it.'

'Well, maybe that's because you're secretly flattered that he loves you and you're jealous.' I hit him. 'I know; that was a joke. But it's worth a try. Lisa?'

'Absolutely. Do you think we should go one better and hire one of those honey-trap women.'

'A what?'

'I'm sure I read about it in *Cosmo* or something. Women you pay to test your boyfriend's fidelity.'

'No way. Hiring a detective is bad enough but paying someone to set him up. No, no way.' I rolled my eyes. Ever since George had come back on the scene, not only had my life been turned upside down but he had also cost me a small fortune. Solicitors' fees, taxis to avoid the press, maternity stuff (although I hoped I wouldn't be blaming him for that), the costs that Francesca endured, and now a detective. If George ever came to his senses and scuttled back to New York then I would definitely be sending him a bill.

'OK, but let Francesca persuade you to have him followed. It was her idea.'

'Fine, if you think it'll work . . . after all there really isn't anything to lose.' I shrugged because I wasn't convinced.

Suddenly things were looking very different, but I didn't quite understand. Freddie's joke wasn't near the mark, I wasn't jealous. But, and this is the age old but, for me, this was George we were talking about. Despite the fact he'd been an absolute sod to me he was still George, somewhere he was, and I couldn't believe he would do that. I couldn't believe he could have been so stupid. Why would he risk everything? How could he have changed so much, way beyond all recognition? We knew he was broken-hearted, but that didn't seem to be enough of an explanation any more. I had talked it over with Imogen and Lisa and we'd reached the conclusion that George was still in love with Julia. It's just that I'd become an easier target to hit. It might not have made perfect sense but it made more sense than the fact he was in love with me and it certainly made more sense than him and Cordelia. But then what did I know? I had been wrong every step of the way so far.

By the time that Francesca arrived, I was still unconvinced. Or I had unconvinced myself again. Freddie was definite about the course of action and wasn't relenting. But I wasn't sure. George had played dirty but that didn't mean I should. Should I? And there was the fact that the anonymous tip-off had been anonymous, and it was only a guess that it was Cordelia and that wasn't even a sensible guess. He was her client, why would she try to ruin him? And then the speculation that he was sleeping with her was ridiculous. It would be like a fly arranging to go and have tea with the horrible, big, fat, hungry spider. George wouldn't stoop that low.

But supposing, in the tight grip of madness, he did sleep with her, that didn't mean he would sleep with anyone else. If it was her on the phone, then that meant she was being vengeful, which meant that they were no longer sleeping together and there would be nothing for the private detective (which was probably going to cost my childcare savings), to discover. Not that I believed that he had slept with her. No, not George, not even mad George would do that. Surely.

'Make her see sense, she's driving us nuts with her head-in-the-sand attitude,' Freddie said. I gave him my best sardonic smile.

'Holly, I think this could turn things around for us. If we have him followed, and he is doing something we can nail him for, the press will turn against him just as quickly as they turned against you. It will be a perfect solution. A final solution.'

'But it doesn't make sense,' I reiterated, sounding like a repetitive song. It was becoming my theme tune. '*It doesn't make sense, it just doesn't make sense.*' Put a monotonous dance beat on that and you've got a number one.

'Holly, are you OK?' Lisa asked. Actually I was fine, I was daydreaming, or hallucinating. I wondered if that was hormonal. Had my pregnancy finally driven me insane? I patted my stomach and apologised, silently, to my baby. I tried to refocus on the situation at hand but I was so, so tired.

'I'm fine, a bit tired that's all,' I replied.

'At least if we try this and it works you could sleep again. I can't believe what a sleaze he is. I know he's a shit for what he did to you alone, but he's even more of a shit for sleeping around while destroying your life in the press. I'd like to break his balls myself.' Lisa was stomping around my living room in her tirade. Freddie was nodding vigorously. She was a soldier rallying her troops, he was her troop. Not much, but more than nothing. I shook my head at my ever-wandering thoughts. Was the drifting mind I was experiencing part of pregnancy? It never ceased to amaze me that there were so many symptoms and side-effects. Getting fat was only a tiny bit, it was the easy bit. Nausea, exhaustion, trapped wind, constipation, backache, oh I could go on and on with my list of ailments but I didn't want to sound like the medical encyclopedia I was fast becoming.

'Holly, listen to me.' Francesca stood in front of me and held on to my arms. I must have been wandering around. Or waddling, because I waddled now. I wasn't entirely comfortable with my extra bulk and instead of walking in a straight line I seemed to move from side to side. Only slightly, but Lisa had noticed it. She said I looked like a duck. Francesca gave me a tiny shake and continued. 'Maybe it doesn't make sense, maybe it does, this whole situation from start to finish hasn't made sense. We are trying to get you out of the mess you're in and this is a lead. My instinct is that we can turn things around. The press are losing interest but the media still loves him. At the moment George isn't showing signs of disappearing into obscurity and that is the only thing that you should want. That and a George-free future. Look, I am prepared to stake my reputation on this.'

'I don't know.' I didn't. Because he might be the father and if he was and we discredited him would that make me a bad mother? My child might never forgive me for ruining its father's career as a celebrity because that was what we were trying to do. No matter how we dressed it up we wanted to ensure that George had no more friends in the media, no more fans among the public, and no future in broadcasting. Then he would pack his bags and head back to New York. He could be a lawyer again and I could have my baby and George wouldn't be in a position to exploit that. No, he wouldn't be able to do a thing about it. But then how would my baby feel that I had denied him or her a father? What was the right thing to do? I thought about the problem page in the tabloids that I was, by now, so familiar with. They could do a great photo casebook.

### HOLLY'S BABY DILEMMA!

Picture one: *Holly with a big bump (or blonde model pretending to be Holly), wearing a dressing gown (because they always do). Speech bubble from model's mouth; 'What should I do? Should I ruin the potential evil father's chances of stardom while I can, and then I will be free from his clutches?'*

Picture two: *Blonde model Holly wearing same dressing gown and discussing things with her beautiful brunette friend. Holly: 'Should I follow him? If he really is a sleaze bag sleeping with loads of women then I worry about the baby and how it will feel when it is grown up.'*

*Beautiful brunette friend: 'I know it's a worry but it is your public duty to expose this man.'*

Picture three: *Model Holly (still in dressing gown), beautiful brunette friend and private detective who looks like Inspector Gadget.*

*Holly: 'OK, but I still don't want to hurt him.'*

*Beautiful brunette friend: 'You are doing the right thing.'*

*Inspector Gadget: 'Leave it to me, I'll sort it out.'*

*End commentary (from agony aunt): Holly, you have been through a tough time and you have made a difficult decision but your baby will thank you in the end because while you let George get away with it, it is the baby's mother that is suffering the most.*

'Holly will you take your fucking head out of the fucking clouds and just let us fucking do it!' Freddie shocked me out of my reverie. I stood and looked. They were standing in a row: Freddie, Francesca and Lisa – my three musketeers. They were giving me stern looks. I felt ganged up on. I wished I could stop my daydreaming and make a decision, I was so tired.

'They're right. Remember we have to take control,' Lisa pointed out. The baby kicked. I looked at Freddie; I looked at Francesca; and I looked at Lisa. The baby kicked again, reminding me of its presence and the fact that I had a duty to protect it.

'I can't afford a private detective,' I said, quietly. I was losing my grip on reason, but then there had been no reason for a long time.

'It's paid for, Hol,' Freddie told me.

'What?'

'Look Holly, don't take this the wrong way but we already decided to have George followed. We need to get your life back to normal, or at least a bit more normal and we have taken the decision, along with your family, who had paid for the detective.' Francesca looked tired and I again felt responsible.

'I'm sorry, you're right. I'll do whatever you think is best.'

'Thank God for that,' Freddie said.

'The detective starts tomorrow. Fingers crossed that George is misbehaving.'

'I still think we should send him a honey-trap,' Lisa said.

'Don't, Lisa, she's agreed to this, don't scare her off now.'

Later, in bed, I thought about what was happening. Despite everything I felt sad as I realised how destructive our friendship had become. When George and I were around twelve and we walked home together from school, and he teased me and I punched him in a very girly, not very hard, way and we never knew that as we sealed our friendship and it endured beyond all others, that we would be here where we were now and that we would be hurting each other. He had hurt me, and now I was going to put a stop to it, which would hurt him. Some friendship. Time to let go. I wasn't finding it easy despite the fact that George had done a great job in making me detest him, perhaps that was because I was a sentimental, nostalgic, sad person trying to hold on to the good memories of my childhood, like a child clutching at her mother's legs, clinging on tightly, asking for protection.

Or maybe it was because I might be carrying his baby.

# Chapter Thirty-nine

'Darling, you are doing the right thing,' my mother said, when I phoned her in the morning.

'But it must be costing a fortune.' Even I was getting bored of my repetitiveness.

'If it works, it's worth it.'

'I guess.'

'So how are you?'

'Confused. Horribly, horribly confused. About everything.'

'I know. But things are looking up.'

'They are?'

'Yes, they are. Trust me darling everything is going to be just fine.' I tried, desperately, to believe her.

I knew that I shouldn't have used my initiative, not with my history, but I did. I phoned the person I hated most in all of this. I called Cordelia. I knew that the last time I did this, it actually backfired and made her more determined than ever to ruin my life, but there was something I needed to know and only she could tell me.

'Cordelia,' she announced, when I was promptly put through to her.

'It's Holly.'

'What a surprise.' I imagined her sharpening her claws.

'Look, I'll cut to the chase. Someone called Francesca about George.' Logically, it was a bit of a gamble. If it wasn't Cordelia who had phoned Francesca, then I was tipping off the enemy. I could imagine the scene now. Freddie would kill me; Francesca would help him. Lisa would provide the weapon.

'And . . . ?' she sounded bored, rather than surprised.

'Yes, and they said that he'd been doing things he shouldn't be doing.'

'Well, you know full well that George has done a lot of things he shouldn't have done lately.'

'So it's true.'

'No comment.' I knew then that it was true. Indirectly she was confirming the story. George had made a big, big mistake; he had crossed the most vengeful woman in the world. Even I wouldn't have been that stupid. Perhaps.

'Cordelia, I never thought I'd say this, but thank you.'

'Don't thank me Holly. I'm not doing this for you.'

'I didn't for one minute think you were.' I came off the phone smiling.

Francesca and Freddie were right and this was all going to come crashing down around him. But that's what I wanted now. I managed, finally, to get as angry as I should have been. How dare he do this to me. How dare he come back into my life, disrupt it, lie, cheat, and make himself famous on the back of me and all the time be sleeping with the woman he was paying. I hated him. I realised that, I really did hate him. Him and his fame and his quest for more fame and the fact that he didn't give two hoots about me. Or the baby. Because if he did he would have left us alone a long time ago. And if the baby turned out to be George's then I would fight tooth and nail to keep him out of its life. Because he wasn't a good enough person to be a father. Not by a long way.

Actually I found my new anger quite refreshing.

'Freddie, it's me.'

'And today's objection is?'

'None, I'm really happy.'

'You are?'

'Yes, I just know that it's going to work out.'

'How?'

'I called Cordelia.'

'You did what?' he exploded.

'Don't worry I didn't say anything that I shouldn't . . . actually I did. I told her about the tip-off. I had to know that it was true, and it was. She said "no comment" and her tone, well I know that that is one woman scorned.'

'Holly, you could have ruined everything.' Freddie let out a sigh.

'Sure I could but I didn't. So has the detective started work?'

'He has. How are the paps today?'

'Not here, not even one.'

'Well, that's good.'

'It's great but it's not enough. George still has the public's sympathy. I want him stopped. I want him back in New York. I want to get on with my life.' I was ready to let it all go. I sounded more assertive than I had in months.

'Don't worry Hol, we're on to it.'

'Holly Miller has resumed normal service,' I announced to Lisa who was on my laptop surfing the net.

'Really?'

'Yeah. And I've got work to do today. What are you up to?'

'I'm going to work, too.'

'What?'

'Well, I'm doing Max's accounts.'

'Do you even know how to do accounts?'

'You're not the only one with a laptop you know.' I laughed as Lisa went to the spare room and came back with a very sexy looking laptop. The girl was amazing, even her computer was good-looking. She set herself up opposite me and we worked, mainly in silence, all day. I felt as if I was in the office, the day was so constructive. My mother was right; things were looking up. But then I remembered the paternity question and things began to nosedive.

The following day I received two phone calls which led me to believe that maybe my mum was right. The first was from Francesca, saying that the detective had unearthed some information for us and we were to have a meeting. The second was from Joe.

Lisa answered the phone, and passed it to me. As soon as she said his name I felt sick. What if he was phoning to tell me that he had thought about it and couldn't be in our lives? There was only one way to find out.

'Holly, I've been thinking.'

'Right.'

'And, well, this isn't easy, please don't think it's easy.' My heart skipped a beat.

'Right.'

'But you are right. If this baby is mine then I want to be involved and as we can't know that for sure, then I am going to have to swallow my pride and be braver than I have been.' My eyes filled with tears.

'Joe, are you saying that you want to be part of our lives?' Oh, please God, let that be what he was saying.

'Yes.'

'That's fantastic.' I laughed. Then Joe laughed and in laughing I felt the release of all my fears. 'You're the most amazing person ever,' I said, full of emotion.

'I need this Hol.'

'Me too.'

'Can I see you, later, to talk?' he sounded nervous.

'I'll cook dinner, tonight, my place at seven thirty?'

'I'll be there.'

After I'd hung up, the smile wouldn't go away, neither would Lisa's.

'I'll prepare something this afternoon and then I'll spend the evening at my flat,' Lisa offered.

'Are you sure?' I was dubious as to Lisa's cooking talents and I really wanted to impress Joe.

'Don't worry I won't cook but I'll buy stuff and plan the menu. What about oysters?'

'Yuck. I'm pregnant remember, I need to eat good wholesome food.'

'But that's not very sexy.'

'What I want is toad-in-the-hole, with onion gravy and apple crumble and custard.'

'Not all on the same plate?'

'No, of course not.' Disappointingly I hadn't had any weird cravings. Just normal cravings; sweets, especially cola bottles, chocolate (any kind) and frozen yogurt. I was addicted to frozen yogurt.

'OK, I can shop for that. Trust me.'

'I do.' At that time I trusted everyone. I even trusted myself. I was right about Joe. One hundred per cent right.

# Chapter Forty

I was so happy. Joe was back in my life, he was going to be there for me. I knew that it must have been the hardest decision he'd ever had to make, I knew it was a huge sacrifice on the part of his pride and I was so grateful.

I could see the light; it had been there all along. It might seem harsh but my reservation being that George might be the father of my child, therefore I shouldn't ruin him, no longer bothered me. George might be the father but there was no way I was going to let him continue to ruin my life. Even if I had to ruin him. I was dealing with things, the way Freddie always told me that I should. I was going to have Joe in my life and get George out of it. Something I should have done a long time ago.

I felt amazingly empowered as I arrived for the meeting with the private detective. Actually I was quite excited, because I'd never met one before. I was kind of hoping he'd be a bit like Inspector Gadget. Complete with gadgets.

I swept into the office and kissed every member of staff. Happiness was just the warmest feeling, like being wrapped in the softest blanket; it was the best day ever. I was the happiest person ever. Joe might not be my boyfriend per se, but he was back in my life. It seemed more likely that he would turn out to be the father of the baby, and maybe he would forgive me. The way things were going, all going my way, I actually believed he would forgive me.

I was still beaming as I went into the boardroom with

Francesca and Freddie behind me. The private detective was already there.

'Hi, I'm Holly,' I said, flashing him my new super special smile. It was a smile to end all smiles. He was wearing a rather smart suit, with a pink shirt and tie. His hair was neatly combed. But even the fact that he wasn't a cliché couldn't disappoint me.

'I'm Tom Broadbent.' He shook my hand.

'Shall we get down to business,' Francesca said, as Freddie poured coffee. Tom pulled his briefcase on to the table and opened it and reached inside. He pulled out a brown envelope. It was the tiniest bit James Bond.

'It seems that Mr Conway isn't as devoted to you as he makes out,' he said.

'Really?' Part of me didn't care, he could have been in love with a donkey as far as I was concerned. But then part of me did care because I wanted rid.

'No. He's seeing a young girl called Debbie, who works at a nearby café. He goes there every morning for breakfast if he doesn't have an early appointment. She serves him at the table, which she doesn't do for anyone else—'

'Sorry Tom, but can we cut to the chase,' Francesca interrupted.

'Of course. Well for the past few evenings she has gone to his flat and left about four hours later.'

'Shit, he's improved since he shagged me, if he can last four hours,' I said, then covered my mouth in shock horror. Everyone looked a bit disgusted, but I giggled. Joe's phone call made me happier than ever, I could only have been happier if I knew for sure he was the father and he told me that he wanted me back. But for now, this was good enough.

'I've got photos of them together, although they are not very compromising. I know that something is going on. She goes to his flat late at night, I think it's just sex. I spoke to her in the café, pretended to chat her up and although she brushed me off and said she had a boyfriend, she didn't give away anything else. Here are the photos and her name and address, also the name and address of the café. Do you want anything else from me?'

'No, that's brilliant,' Freddie said, taking the photos and looking at them. 'She's pretty,' he added. I took a look.

'Oh, poor girl, she could do so much better.'

'Yeah, well he's famous and fame is a powerful aphrodisiac,' Francesca pointed out, wisely.

We said goodbye to Tom, and Freddie showed him out. Then he came back to the boardroom and poured more coffee. I was halfway down my second cup before I realised I'd given up coffee.

'Oh dear, I don't think I should drink this,' I said, putting it down and frowning.

'I'm sure one cup won't hurt. What are we going to do next?' Francesca asked.

'Well I can come back to work now,' I answered. I didn't need to hide away now that George would be out of favour with the media.

'Yes, you can, which is great but I meant about George.'

'I reckon we should tip off a newspaper,' Freddie suggested, rejoining us at the table. 'I heard that the *This Afternoon* show is about to offer him a daily slot, but I don't think they will if he is embroiled in scandal. At the moment he's a bit of a housewives' favourite but only because they all think he is so completely devoted to you. So I say we tip off the *Daily News* and let them uncover the scandal. We can sit back and enjoy the ride.'

The old Holly would let things rest, but the new Holly would secure the future for her child, and maybe for her relationship, but definitely for herself. If George was stopped, if all he had built his celebrity status on was taken away from him, he would be left with nothing, but then that was no longer my problem.

'Do it. Finish it for good.' The war was nearly over and I was the victor elect.

Freddie called a journalist from the *Daily News*, and arranged for Dixie to bike over the photographs and details that Tom had given us.

'He was really pleased, says he owes us one for the tip-off,' Freddie said. The irony is that it was the *Daily News* that first ran George's story, so he owed his success to them, but now he would blame them for his downfall. Them, and us, but most of all his own stupidity.

The marriage-pact story was about to be dead and buried. Although another story was just beginning.

I arrived home to find Lisa and a stranger in my kitchen.

'Hello,' I said, looking at the unknown woman who was wearing an apron. Not my apron, because I didn't own such a thing.

'Holly, this is Sarah, she has come to prepare your dinner.'

'Really?'

'Hi,' Sarah said.

'Where did you come from?' I asked, wondering if Lisa had hired a caterer, which seemed a bit extreme even by Lisa's standards.

'We're friends,' Lisa explained. 'And when I told her it was you, and why you were celebrating, she offered to cook dinner.'

'Toad-in-the-hole, with rosemary and onion gravy, fresh baby vegetables and for dessert, home-made apple crumble and custard.'

'Fantastic.' My stomach rumbled in anticipation. 'I tell you the thing about pregnancy is that I'm hungry all the time. Now all I have to do is find something to wear that makes me look sexy and not like a sack of potatoes.' That wasn't easy. Even maternity clothes couldn't perform miracles.

Lisa and Sarah left just before Joe arrived. All I had to do was to take the food out of the oven and serve it. I was wearing my red maternity dress which was a bit shorter than it had been, because I was a bit bigger. A lot bigger. I thought back to the early days, before it all went wrong, but after I'd slept with George, when I asked Freddie how to get a man to fall in love with me. He suggested a red dress and no knickers. As I looked at my red dress I guessed this wasn't exactly what he had in mind. And as for no knickers, well I couldn't do that. I didn't want my baby to catch a cold.

I was applying perfume liberally when the buzzer went. I felt a bit nervous but I was still euphoric. I'm not sure how those emotions mixed, but I felt heady, relieved, and also shy. I felt like I was on a first date.

'Hi,' I smiled, and this time I did kiss him – on the cheek – but it was a start.

'Hi,' he hugged me.

'My God, you are enormous. I'm sure you weren't this big last week.' He laughed and I looked at him. The eyes, the lips, the trademark grey jumper and black trousers.

'Thanks, Joe.' I put his hand on my stomach and willed the baby to move. It did.

'It's amazing, I can feel it.' Joe looked delighted. I led him in and sat him at the table. I wanted to get the food out of the way, I don't know why but it was something less to think about. While we ate the most delicious toad-in-the-hole ever, I told him about George and the private detective.

'So the media circus will be over now?' Joe asked. I hadn't seen him smile for a long time and it felt so amazing. I wanted to keep pinching myself because I almost couldn't believe that Joe was here. What if I was dreaming. Imagine how pissed-off I would be if I woke up and found out all this was a dream. But it wasn't. I was definitely awake. The baby kicking, my exhaustion, and a little tiny pinch on the leg confirmed my status.

'It's his fault, he did this. He started it and now I'm going to finish it.' It was fighting talk but I hoped the fight was over.

'He's a sleazebag.'

'We know that. I think he's actually made the worst mistake a minor celebrity can make.'

'What's that?'

'Believing his own publicity. But I don't care about him, not even a bit. How do you feel about this?' We'd finished our main course and I was watching him sipping his wine, while I drank water.

'I just know I need to be here. When you told me you were pregnant all I could think about was the fact you cheated on me, and then I was so angry that it might not be mine. I'm not angry any more just hurting a little. But Holly, I can't ignore all this and I want to be a part of it. I figure that when we do the test then I might have more difficult decisions but for now I want to be around, I want to be involved as if it were my baby.'

'I really hope it is.'

'So do I. I want it to be mine more than anything.' His eyes filled with tears and I realised how hard this was for him. 'But I want to be there from now on. I need to be there from now on. Is that all right?'

'Of course. You can do the whole caboodle if you want. Birthing classes, hospital appointments, shopping for the nursery. I have to warn you that it's not all fun. You have to watch videos, read books, there is a lot to learn.' I felt as if I was addressing a child, but then Joe was childlike that evening.

'God there's so much I don't know. What about names? Have you thought about names? And the birth. Can I be there?' As his words gushed, I cringed at the thought that the man I wanted to win back was going to see me with my legs spread open and looking horrific like the woman in Dr Miriam's book. But then I thought, if he was there and if he saw the birth maybe he'd fall in love with the baby, regardless. That was what I wanted, and that was what I needed. My baby deserved the best in life and Joe was the best. There was no doubt of that.

'If you think you can handle it,' I joked. 'I haven't chosen any names yet and I don't know the sex. I'd like it if we chose names together.'

'I'd like that.' He looked at me, deep into my eyes and I wondered if he was still looking for the woman with whom he fell in love. 'Holly, I love you, but I am still dealing with other feelings; jealousy, betrayal, I'm trying so hard to forgive you.' I smiled through the tears that were threatening to fall. I hadn't forgiven myself either.

'I'll go and get pudding shall I?'

I showed him my shopping list and the conversation turned to the practical. I didn't want to broach the subject of money (I had already discovered that this was going to cost a small fortune), but Joe wanted to. He said we'd shop together, and he became quite bossy.

'If I am going to be involved, then I need to be involved in everything,' and – quite male – 'Are you sure you should be working?'

I loved it. I know it wasn't normal, but it was more normal than it had been for a while. I was planning my impending parenthood with the man I loved so very, very, much and that was normal. Even *if* we still didn't know if he was the father. I was so touched by his concern, by his behaviour and I was full of hope for our future.

'I've given up smoking, Holly.'

I had noticed this. 'How long has it been?'

'A week, but it's a start.' He smiled, tentatively.

'Do you want coffee?' He shook his head. We had so much to talk about, but I felt the conversation slipping away. It had been intense, and we were both tired.

'I better go, you need your sleep,' he said. I nodded. I called a taxi for him, and of course it turned up straight away, just when I didn't want it to. I walked him to the door.

'Goodnight, Hol. Goodnight, baby.' He kissed my cheek, then he kissed my tummy. I tingled.

'Goodnight, Joe.' I watched his back as he walked down the stairs and out of the door, then I went to the freezer and ate an entire tub of frozen yogurt.

# Chapter Forty-one

---

## *Screwed*

'Cordelia have you seen it?' I was shouting down the phone. Never had I felt this much rage; I was seeing red.

'I have,' she said, calmly.

Why did she sound disinterested? This was *our* livelihood being flushed down the pan, not just mine. Ever since our affair had stopped she had been annoying me. Sure, she still got me work, and plenty of it, but her manner was abrupt; almost dismissive. Most of the time she had Sophie call me. Things had deteriorated so much, that I had actually started looking for a new agent. With my regular television slot on *This Afternoon* about to be finalised, I needed proper representation. My career was taking off, I was happy with the direction, but I wasn't happy dealing with Cordelia any more. I did complain to her on one of the few occasions I was able to talk to her, but she said that as long as she did her job then I had no cause for complaint. But complain I did. She was infuriating and insolent and I wasn't going to stand for it. I was her client and the client is always right. I hadn't actually gone as far as to meet any agents yet but I had put out feelers. It was probably time to upgrade.

Until the papers threatened to take everything away. I was screwed.

'Well, what the fuck is going on?' I was breathing fire.

'You slept with a café girl, George.' She was colder than ice.

'But how did it get into the papers?' I was fuming. I don't remember ever being this angry. Everything had been so secure, now it was rocking on the edge of my personal career cliff. And the woman who was supposed to be in charge was doing a great impression of someone who didn't give a shit.

'It's only in the *Daily News*, although I'm sure other papers will feature the story tomorrow. Your waitress kissed and told by the looks of things.'

*Devoted George Betrays Holly With Waitress*. Fucking great!

Debbie had spoken to a journalist, either knowingly or not. At a guess, not, she wasn't the brightest spark in the book. But she had told him of our meetings. I had no idea how the journalist had got wind of it in the first place, or why Debbie hadn't kept her mouth shut. Fucking women. They all screw you in the end. I panicked. Everything that I had built was beginning to crumble. I couldn't let it all slip away.

'It's ridiculous. Tell them it's all lies and we'll sue if they don't retract it.'

'Is it lies then George?'

'No. But we have to do something.'

'This changes things slightly, George. You see I've had phone calls all morning asking for your blood. These people, it seems, are angry that you cheated them. They thought you were in love, they supported you, and they're not happy that you betrayed them. They believed that you loved Holly so much you'd go to any lengths to win her, but not, apparently, by sleeping with waitresses. The TV companies are a bit unhappy as well. In fact all your appointments have been cancelled. Dear, dear, it looks like the fun is over.'

I could have sworn I heard her cackle. 'What do you mean?' There was a stampede going on in my stomach; a riot in my head.

'Your fame. It was given to you and now it's being taken away.

You pretty much became a star overnight, and now you're going to be a nobody overnight.'

'But we can't let this happen.' The windows in my mind were being smashed; someone was throwing rocks. Smash, smash, smash. No future.

'There's really nothing I can do. Apart from resign as your publicist.'

'But we have to do something. Cordelia do not give up on me.' Desperation hung in the air.

'I'm sorry George, but with this, apart from hate mail, I don't think you can expect any other interest.'

'So that's it. Your saying it's over?' How could she do this to me?

'It sure is.' Cordelia laughed, then hung up.

At first I wanted to scream, but instead I punched the wall. I pulled back my fist and launched it as hard as I could. At first I didn't feel the pain; but soon it set in. I looked at my knuckles, shocked by the redness and the immediate swelling. Then I looked at the dent in the wall. I couldn't believe how the fates had suddenly conspired against me. One minute I was the media's favourite son. Now I was their black sheep. I thought I was going to be a star. But now I had had that snatched away. I called Cordelia back, I couldn't let things end like this.

'Cordelia Dickens.' She sounded so smug.

'Why did you laugh at me? This is going to affect you as well. You weren't doing badly out of me.' At least I had another outlet for my frustration, other than the wall. I rubbed my knuckles and saw how they were changing colour, the purple beginning to blink at me angrily. I knew how it felt.

'George. shouting at me isn't going to help. Now, the thing is that you're right when you say that I make money out of you, but well, there are more important things in life than money.'

'What?'

'George, you screwed up. Simple. This is your fault. The press is fickle, one minute they love you the next they're your enemy. The public is the same. It's over, face it, and I for one won't shed any tears.'

'You can't be serious.'

'Oh, I am. And when I said that *you* screwed up, well you did, but your downfall had a little help.'

'What are you talking about?'

'You've learned a valuable lesson, I hope. You shouldn't have fucked with me.' She hung up for a second time.

I had come full circle. I was alone. I was unloved. I was upset. More than that I was angry. I grabbed my coat and left the flat.

As I opened the door on to the street I saw them. They were huddled together like a pack of wild dogs. The photographers and journalists who had supported me, had come for my blood.

The noise was deafening as the cameras popped, and the hounds bayed. It was the scariest thing I had ever faced, and fear replaced my blood in pumping itself around my body. I couldn't focus on what they were saying and I felt myself lose control.

I pushed through them, they were grabbing me, pushing tape recorders and cameras into my face, shouting some more. Animals.

Eventually, I broke free of them, but they pursued me all the way down the street.

People stared as I pushed open the door with as much force as I could muster. I saw her, standing behind the counter, looking as pretty as ever. But really she was ordinary. What was I thinking? All I wanted was a bit of comfort when Cordelia had rejected me and look where it got me. The scheming cow probably planned the whole thing. Planned to seduce me and then to make money from me.

I was aware of the press behind me, squeezing themselves into the small café, leaving the door open, fighting to get a bit of space to get close to me. The customers were stunned; the press were drooling. I didn't care a shit.

'You bitch!' I screamed. The café fell silent. The cameras started up again.

'George, I'm sorry, I didn't know that they would print it,' she said. She sounded emotional; looked upset. I nearly believed her. The cameras were in overdrive.

'Debbie, you spoke to a fucking reporter, he's quoted you. Did you say this or not?' My voice was tight with rage.

'Yes,' she whispered. Some big guy came out from the back room and glared at me, but I stood my ground.

'How could you tell everyone that we were in love? That I loved you, not Holly? It's total crap. I had sex with you but I didn't love you and now you've ruined everything.' The counter separated us but I moved my face as close as I could. I wanted to hurt her. I wanted to destroy her, the way she had destroyed me.

'Hang on mate, you can't talk to her like that.' The big guy came round and looked at me threateningly. He glowered at the journalists, then looked at Debbie.

'She's ruined everything. Everything!' I screamed.

'Out!' he shouted and pushed me. I wasn't in the mood to be bullied so I turned round and punched him in the stomach using my good fist. It wasn't my finest punch. He grabbed hold of me and wouldn't let go. Again, I heard the orchestra of cameras in cruel harmony. Somewhere in the back of my mind I knew that I would regret what I was doing, but I had no idea how to stop myself.

'Let go of me, you fucker,' I yelled with all the frustration I felt. I was giving the press such a show. I could, in the back of my mind (the only remaining sane bit), already see the headlines: *The Rise And Fall Of George Conway*!

In real time, it had been a fast rise to fame. I had gone from being a nobody to a somebody overnight. And it had disintegrated just as quickly. Here today . . . gone today.

'If you don't leave I'm calling the police.' He didn't exactly give me a choice as he frogmarched me on to the street, depositing me on the pavement.

I went back to the flat, not knowing what else to do. It had all gone. Evaporated. No more television, no photo calls, no interviews, no nothing. When the last shot of me was taken – sitting humiliated on the pavement – the press walked away. They had what they wanted; they didn't need me any more. Apparently no one did. My answerphone was silent, my publicist no longer working for me. I had nowhere left to turn and no one to turn to.

'Fame is fickle,' Cordelia had said. And she should know. Because what I had was all gone, and now I had nothing. Less than nothing, because as I nursed my bruised knuckles, took off my soiled clothes and looked at my red, angry face in the mirror I realised that I had also lost my self-respect.

# Chapter Forty-two

I woke the next day feeling ill. I was cold and hot all at the same time. I had a fever. I had never felt more dreadful in my life; a life that had changed beyond all recognition. No longer was I the smart lawyer, the New Yorker, the man in a stable, grown-up relationship. No longer was I the famous person, the house-wives' favourite, and the tabloid king. No longer was I the Marriage Pact Man, the father of her baby, no longer was I . . . anything. It hurt, I ached. Everything was dull. I had no idea what my next move would be. I was alone. Totally alone and devastated.

I stayed in bed for days: I'm not sure how many. I couldn't move. I got up to go the toilet, but I didn't wash, clean my teeth, change my clothes, or eat. I didn't leave the house, I didn't see a newspaper and my phone was loudly silent. I hadn't watched it ebb away, I had watched it sprint away. Ready, steady, go! GONE. I had a bottle of water which I managed to sip when I really needed to, but that was it.

What made me get up? I don't know but I did and I showered and I changed and I went out of the house and I bought the papers. There was no mention of me. I had been phased out as if I had never been there in the first place. I watched the tele-vision; all the shows I did, and the ones I should have done, and again it was as if I had been obliterated from everyone's memory. I no longer existed.

I was no one and nothing.

What possessed me to call her I don't know but I did. I called her and I told her everything. I was painfully honest with her and with myself, for the first time. I admitted that I had slept with Holly, that I didn't love her but felt so drenched in rejection that I convinced myself I did. I told her that Holly had been the only person in my life that had never hurt me, that was why I chose her. I told her that when I found the marriage pact it all seemed to make sense but actually it made none.

I told her that after the court case I was more alone than ever which is why I saw Cordelia as my saviour. I told her that the media attention really got to me, made me feel special and loved, and sexy. How I started the sordid affair, and how it was more sordid and sexual than anything. How Holly was pregnant and I used that to get myself more sympathy. How I turned her life upside down as well as splitting up her and Joe. How I rejected Cordelia, discounted her feelings when she said she was in love, how I then took up with the first girl that I met afterwards, and used her for sexual gratification.

How I believed I was special, a star, how I believed I actually had a television career ahead of me. A long and successful career because I was a celebrity. How people asked me for my auto-graph, and how they all recognised me, and how I enjoyed that adulation. How special I believed I was. I told her how it had all gone wrong. Cordelia was involved, but young, sweet Debbie had talked to the press, told them we were in love. That I loved her and not Holly, because that's what she believed. I told her how I'd behaved so badly towards Debbie, shouting at her at work, how I'd hit the big guy, how he'd thrown me out on to the street. How the press had captured it all; my last and finest moment. How I hadn't seen the papers, how I hadn't spoken to anyone. I told her that I called her because something told me to, and that something was my reason returning. I told her how I stayed in bed for days and days and how I felt empty and alone. I told her that I hated myself, detested myself. And as I told her,

I felt as if I was hearing it for the first time; hearing what really happened. But it hadn't happened to me, it had happened to a stranger. A stranger that was me. Finally I asked her for help.

She came as soon as she could. The moment I saw her I knew that she was the one for me; had been all along and always would be. I knew that whatever I had been doing, I was wrong and now it was time to stop. Stop and start all over again.

'I've missed you so much,' she said. I held out my arms and felt so relieved when she walked into them.

'I've missed you too, Julia,' I replied.

# Chapter Forty-three

She looked exactly as I remembered her. She was wearing her favourite perfume, Obsession, that was it. I realised the moment my senses registered the fragrance just how much I missed her. She looked jet-lagged and I loved the way her eyes smouldered when she was tired. Sexy eyes. I always told her that. Her hair was slightly messy, but I wanted to stroke it. I wanted to touch her, to make sure she was real. I needed her so badly.

We held each other and talked for hours and hours.

'I'm not sure how I feel, George,' she said when I had told her my story again. 'I feel responsible, as soon as I found out you had left I felt awful but it took longer to realise how much I loved you. I did the wrong thing but I didn't get a chance to tell you that, until now.'

'And now you have to listen to my crazy story.'

'It is mad, George. Those women, the press, Holly. It's too much to take in.'

I knew then that I had to make her understand. I asked her to tell me what she had been doing since we parted. Her story was simpler than mine.

It had taken her a couple of months to fully realise how she felt about me. The proposal had come as a shock and she had panicked. She believed that she valued her independence above all but once she had it, she didn't want it, she wanted me. She believed that my leaving was a sign that I would never forgive her, and so she didn't try to track me down. She found out from one of my colleagues that I was expected back at some point and decided the best thing she could do was wait. I shuddered as I realised how close I'd come to losing her for ever, and what a fool I'd been. If only I had waited in New York, not acted so hastily. If only . . . if only.

'I love you so much, Julia I behaved so badly. I am sorry. Really, really sorry.'

'George we need time with this. I can't just forget that you slept with Holly before you proposed to me, and I can't just forget the other women, not the fact that you slept with them more the way you treated them. And of course let's not forget you might be the father of Holly's baby. I knew as soon as you called me that I had to come. I do love you George, but there's so much to consider.'

I put her to bed soon afterwards, she needed sleep desperately. A few hours later she got up, showered and we started talking again. The initial relief at seeing her, holding her, hearing her voice had been wonderful, I couldn't risk losing her again. If I did, I would only blame myself.

'Julia, I have no idea how or why I went so mad. You know me, I am normally a stable, sensible, person. Always serious, always doing the right thing. Never acting hastily. I don't know what came over me. I'm not trying to make excuses but I am trying to make you understand. Even though I can't fully understand it myself yet.'

'George, I think you may have had a nervous breakdown.'

'Maybe. But breakdowns don't happen to people like me usually. That's what I always thought.'

'They can happen to anyone. You were always so certain about your life that you couldn't cope with something happening that wasn't in your plan. I mean George, only a complete control freak would fly to London to sleep with someone before proposing to their girlfriend, just in case they might be the right woman.'

'I know.' I hung my head.

'We need to do a lot of talking, and a lot of soul-searching. Can you give me time?' I nodded.

Over the next few days we did just that. We didn't go out of the flat; ordering in food when we needed it. We talked, ate, slept, and talked some more. There was so much to figure out and I think we succeeded. I think we figured it all out.

After three days of this, she asked me a question.

'George, you asked me on Christmas morning if I'd marry you. I said no, I said we should break up but I've spent so long regretting it. So I want to ask you, will *you* marry me?' I cried and hugged her and I accepted because this was the girl I wanted, I was sure of that now. I was more than one hundred per cent sure, and I always should have been.

She persuaded me to call my boss and tell him I was ready to come back. It was amazing how quickly I pulled myself together. It wasn't just the media that had obliterated George-the-Marriage-Pact-Man, I had too. My boss told me he would be more than delighted to have me back. Thankfully, the story hadn't made it to New York. I could really start all over again and erase that part of my life from my memory. In New York there would be no one to remind me. I would be George the lawyer once more.

We made plans for the future; I *had* a future. But I also had a past which needed dealing with.

I took Julia to visit my parents. They were so relieved that I was all right that they forgave me without recrimination.

'I am so sorry for the distress I must have caused you,' I said.

'George, we knew you'd come to your senses,' my mother said. 'That's why we let you be, because we knew you'd be back one day.'

'Is that it? Don't I get a telling-off?' I don't know what I was expecting.

'I haven't seen my son in months. The last time you came

home I didn't recognise you. George, I am just so relieved to have you back that I would forgive you anything.' They didn't dwell on it, and Julia and Mum talked weddings while Dad and I went to the golf club.

'You know son, mistakes are all right, as long as you know they're mistakes.'

'There's a lot of things I'd like to take back.'

'I know, and that's what life is about. Of course you went too far, you went to extremes but now you've regained your senses.'

'I hurt a lot of people.'

'George, if they can forgive you then you can forgive yourself.' My father was a wise man.

Arriving home I asked Julia to go for a walk with me. I led her round my childhood haunts.

'My father said that if other people can forgive me then I can forgive myself.'

'Well, I've forgiven you, although I blame myself so that's no surprise.' She laughed nervously. 'They've forgiven you, your parents, I mean, so that's good.'

'Why did you forgive me?'

'Because I love you and I want to spend the rest of my life with you. I'm just such a bonehead.'

'We both are.'

'I think the three days we spent talking were the most honest of our relationship.'

'We should talk more, then.'

'Things have to change. I have forgiven you, I've just about forgiven myself but we need to make our relationship stronger as a result of this.'

'I agree.'

'I was so relieved you called. I began to think you'd never come back.'

'George the celebrity, nearly didn't,' I smiled.

'This tour you're giving me, it's not really the childhood tour, it's the George and Holly tour isn't it?'

'It's hard to separate my childhood from Holly.' I felt like a different person as I held on to the hand of my future wife. I felt sane and sensible and heady and happy. A weird mix of emotions, but none which I remember from my time in London. That man was horrible. I cringed when I thought of some of the things I'd done and said, and the way I had treated Holly. I was pretty embarrassed about the way I had spoken to her, the way I had spoken to everyone. I believed I would be cringing over that part of my life for a long, long time.

'She'll always be a part of you, because she is a part of your past.'

'Yeah, but I screwed things up for her.'

'It wasn't all you, but you're right. You need to speak to her.'

'No way.' There was no way I could ever speak to her again, no way she'd want to speak to me.

'George, you need to explain, you need her to forgive you.'

'I doubt she ever will.'

'But you at least should try to speak to her before we leave.'

'A parting shot?'

'Let's leave all our ghosts here shall we?'

'Meaning Cordelia and Debbie?'

'Write to them at least. Write apologising and then after you speak to Holly, there will be nothing left to haunt us.'

'The baby?'

'George, I wish to God that the baby is Joe's. I don't know if I can cope with a reminder of that, I don't. But there is no way to prove that yet and what I want to do is get us working before we have to deal with that, *if* we have to deal with it. I love you enough, I know that and I can't lose you, but let's just deal with the things we can for now.'

'Yeah we will.' I turned and kissed her and remembered that

I had Julia back, which is more than I could ever have asked for. My story had a happy ending even if it didn't have a public one. Although, I didn't deserve it.

As I dressed to meet Holly I wondered if I'd miss Celebrity George. Even though I knew that I shouldn't have done it, the way it made me feel was undeniable. I thought my ego would always miss it a bit.

I wore a pair of jeans, and a blue shirt. All clothes that Julia had made me buy when she went through the wardrobe and saw what I had been wearing.

'You wore all this to be in the public eye?' she asked, looking at the suits, the shirts, the ties.

'I did.'

'Then you will give them to a charity shop, you need a new image. The man in those suits is gone for ever.' I needed her assertiveness. I didn't care about the clothes, they weren't important, Julia was all that mattered now.

No, I didn't miss the fame, that man was a different man, Julia was right. That man wouldn't have asked for forgiveness, he didn't think he needed it. He was in the right, he was hard done by, he was a moron.

When I called Holly she sounded surprised to hear from me, reluctant to listen to me and definitely not keen to meet me. I begged her, I apologised over and over, and begged some more. At first she said that she would have to think about it, but then I kept pushing because I couldn't leave with baggage. I wouldn't be able to sleep, or get on with my life until I explained something to her. I know, even after everything, I was still a selfish bastard. Finally, she capitulated and we agreed to meet in a café on the Kings Road. She chose it, I think because it was neutral territory, although I didn't question her.

'Wish me luck, honey,' I said, as I left.

'Good luck and remember, whatever happens I love you.'
That was all I needed.

I walked down the street and people looked at me. I groaned as
I realised that this was the kind of thing I'd invited not long ago.
Someone shouted something but I didn't hear it. People stopped
and stared at me.

'There's that wanker who was in the papers,' a guy said to his
girlfriend. I felt myself turning red, my ears were hot as I felt
embarrassment. It was a five minute walk to the café, it seemed
everyone was staring at me, people stopping, saying things. I
wanted to hide, to run away, but this was all my fault and the
recognition that I had craved was now haunting me. I had to get
out of this country. New York was the answer.

She was there when I walked in, sitting at a table with a cup of
herbal tea in front of her. I smiled at her and she looked up.

'George,' she said hesitantly.

'Holly,' I said, noticing how big she was. 'Not long now,' I
continued, not knowing why exactly. I thought about the baby,
her baby and for the first time I hoped that it wasn't mine. How
selfish I was to want her and the baby just so I didn't feel
unloved. Because that was all it was.

'No, not long.'

I went to the counter to order a coffee, flinching slightly,
because it reminded me of Debbie. I had been such a bastard.
It was depressing and confusing. I tried to pull myself together.
Sorry wasn't adequate. Nothing was adequate. I sat down with
my coffee.

'There's something you should know,' Holly said. She was still
the same amazing girl that she'd always been. She was still my
best friend. Julia might have that place now, but Holly was that
girl, the first girl that I loved, even if the love then was platonic.

'What?'

'When you called me, you told me you wanted to apologise, but I want to tell you that that thing, the thing with the waitress. Well, we had a detective follow you and that's how the press discovered it. Actually, before that, Cordelia told us you were behaving like a gigolo, so we hired the detective and when we got photos of you and her, Freddie called the *Daily News*. They went to see her and managed to persuade her to talk about your relationship. That put an end to it.' Her words rushed out, as if she was embarrassed. But she had nothing to apologise for.

'I wish that *I* had put an end to it, I wish I'd stopped it. I shouldn't have let it get as far as it did. I don't blame you for the private detective, not after all I did to you, and I certainly don't blame Cordelia. She's a bitch but I hurt her feelings. Shit, I hurt everyone.'

'Why George? Why did you do it? I have tried to work it out time and time again but I couldn't. Not at all.'

'I was heartbroken, rejected, I guess. Maybe I was mad. I remember thinking that when I left New York after Julia rejected me that I would never be the same again. That the pain I had inside me would never leave. I felt more alone than I ever have; even more than when I first moved to New York without knowing anyone. I saw you, soon after, and you were so understanding and you said you'd always be there for me. I don't know why, I still don't understand myself but I suddenly thought that there was a reason that Julia turned me down and that reason was you. It seemed to make sense. That I wasn't alone because I loved you. Holly I know I didn't, I know that now, but I believed that I did. I was terrified, and I am sorry that you suffered because I scared you. The rest of it is a mad blur.

The court case was stupid, I know, but when my family turned against me and Cordelia found me I believed in her. She was the only person who was nice to me and in that state I needed someone. That's where it really went bad. I became a madman, I was already a madman but I wasn't horrible before. I basked in the adoration I received, and yes, I started sleeping with Cordelia. It was dirty, sordid, kinky, nothing like with anyone else. I feel awful to belittle it because in the end she did care about me, she said she loved me. And I paid the price for hurting her, but I'm pleased. I needed to be brought down and I needed to wake up to myself.' No matter how I said it, the explanation felt inadequate.

'And now?'

'Now I go back to New York and you stay here with Joe and have your baby.'

'Joe and I aren't back together.'

'Oh.'

'Yeah, we're friends and we're spending a lot of time together but he hasn't forgiven me for sleeping with you. Also, until the paternity is sorted . . .'

'What do you want to do about that?'

'Well, Joe needs to know, I don't know what you think but as soon as the baby is born we're going to have the test, as soon as we can.' She chewed her lip, like she used to when she was younger and upset.

'It's your decision.'

'It is.'

'Have you forgiven me?'

'I haven't even forgiven myself.'

'My dad reminded me that we all make mistakes, but if we realise they were mistakes then we're OK.' We were twelve years old again, briefly.

'I always liked your dad.' She stared at her tea.

'We have such a history, Hol.'

'Which is why I couldn't comprehend what you did to me. I couldn't believe you would behave like that. I couldn't equate my best friend with the person you had become, and well that's why I had such a hard time with it. Well not just that, every-thing.'

'Julia has forgiven me.'

'You're lucky then.'

'It was always her, Holly, always.'

'I thought it was.'

'I had a huge lapse of reason.'

'What can I do?'

'I don't know. Tell him you love him. Tell him it was only a mistake.'

'I can do that, but that doesn't mean he'll take me back.'

'If it's his baby?'

'Yeah. Maybe, one day. I still hope.'

'Always hope Hol, that's all we have.' I looked at her and she looked at me and I knew that there was so much more to say but actually nothing more. I saw forgiveness in her eyes and that was enough. I still felt guilty, but I kissed her cheek and I left.

Now I was ready. We packed up the flat, not that I had much stuff and Julia and I went home.

'I can't believe you have left your apartment empty all this time.'

'I guess the plants will have died.'

'So, where should we live?'

'What, when we're married?'

'Maybe we don't have to wait, we could move in now.'

'OK, so your place or mine?'

'Or a totally new one?'

'Hey I like that, new start.' We held hands as we walked through the departure gate and I knew that I wouldn't look back.

# Chapter Forty-four

*Forgiveness*

I don't know how long I sat there after he left but it felt like hours. It was ironic that his life had turned out so perfectly. How his life was the way he wanted it. He had his love. I wasn't her, no sirree, but she was and she forgave him. I felt a stab of anger, as I thought about how messed up I'd been and now he was going back to his former life and getting married and everything good seemed to be happening to him but it wasn't happening to me. Bastard. He was a total shit. But I did forgive him for a minute because I saw, in that café, my friend George. He was back for a short visit and I remembered how much he had meant to me in my life and I let him know that. But I was still furious, the shit. How dare his life work out so nicely when he was the one that ruined mine. When I thought of the tears, the loneliness, the fear, the press invasion, everything I'd gone through. I could hold myself responsible for losing Joe, and I did, but everything else?

He had turned my life upside down and now his life was the right way up but mine still had a way to go. But I let him see the forgiveness before he left and I wondered if he would ever think about that time, and feel guilty. I knew that the old George would, and that made me feel better. Actually it didn't make me feel better. I was bitter now. Unbelievably, he had come home bitter and twisted and here was I now feeling the same. Maybe I'd go to New York and take him to court, then go to the press.

See how he'd like that. I stared at the wooden table. I stared at
my empty teacup. I stared at the empty coffee cup. That was
where he'd sat, for the last time ever before he walked out of my
life.

I picked up my mobile and called Joe.

'Joe McClaren.'

'Joe, it's me.'

'Is everything all right, the baby . . .'

Every time I called him he said that. It almost made me smile.

'Everything's fine. I just saw George.'

'You what?' He sounded pissed-off.

'Remember, I promised you I would never lie to you again. I
saw him, he wanted to explain, to apologise. Julia and him are
together again and they're going back to New York to get
married.'

'Really?'

'Yeah, he said he was a total shit, and he was sorry.'

'And?'

'Well it's not going to change anything is it? It's happened now
and an apology doesn't make everything go away. But he made
me realise one thing.'

'What?'

'That it's time for us to put the past behind us.'

'If we can.'

'We could try.'

'We could.'

'You could try to forgive me.'

'I could try.'

'Are you still on for birthing classes tonight – apparently
they're showing the un-edited video version of labour.' I
laughed.

'It might make you not want to go through with it.'

'Yeah but I'm not entirely convinced I have a choice.'

'No, right, actually you don't, unless you keep your legs closed.'

'Not my strongest skill.'

'No, I remember you used to be quite a minx.'

'I might still be.'

'Really?'

'So, I might not be my most desirable right now but I will be again.'

'That's the easy bit, it's the stretchmarks and the floppy boobs that stay with you for ever.'

'So tonight then, meet at the hospital at seven.'

'Yup, same time, same place.'

'It's a date?'

'Well, it's sort of a date.' I hung up smiling, this was definitely progress.

# Chapter Forty-five

## *Full Term*

My baby shower was a little unorthodox. Simply because it was thrown on the day I was due to give birth. I had no idea about baby showers, what they were, or why they were called showers. Lisa proved to be an expert, which was strange. They were a present-giving party for expectant mothers and anything that involved present-giving was OK by me. But for reasons unknown to everyone else, I had evaded having one. Here were my reasons: Ever since George had disappeared off the scene I had been trying to get life back to normal. Just as soon as my life became public, it became private again. Overnight I was in the midst of disruption, overnight I wasn't. I knew how fickle the press were, but there was something from that time that stayed with me. After the press left my doorstep to my great relief, but the disappointment of my neighbours, the aftermath stayed. Once more I was a normal person, a pregnant, normal person. I once again had freedom of movement, I could come and go as I pleased. I was just another person in a city full of people.

Although I had a few offers, mainly from people wanting my side of the story after George had been shown up to be a total prat, I had refused them all. I didn't want the story to continue and it had never been my story anyway. All I wanted was to go back to work *and to work*. I wanted to be anonymous, and in a few months I had achieved that. Now, I rarely got a second glance. I had been forgotten and that suited me. There would always be the marriage-pact story, it had been chronicled and therefore records of the mad phase in my life were always going to be there, but for my sake, for the baby, for Joe, I didn't want them to be anything more than records. Dusty, old records in a cardboard box. Or was I a floppy disk in a plastic box? Because that was where I wanted to keep that part of my life – in a box.

There was still something I wanted to do: win back Joe. And I was only able to do that by giving him space. I'm not sure who it was who said that if you love someone set them free and wait because if they love you they will come back, but whoever said it, I was doing it. I had asked him for forgiveness once, but now it was up to him. George had taught me something. Actually his actions had taught me something. If you want to push someone away, far, far away you pursue them relentlessly. Perhaps I was being a little paranoid because I would never take Joe to court, nor would I go to the papers with our story, been there. It had been done.

I didn't want a baby shower. It was because I was too busy trying to put my life back together, and actually I was finding it harder than I thought. Work was fine but I was tired. So tired. And big. Enormous. Huge. I got to the seventh month and thought there was no way I could get any bigger, but I did. Daily. The clothes that Lisa and Imogen had chosen for me were beginning to strain in protest and I'd taken to wearing huge men's shirts that were the only thing that fitted. Nothing else was that big, just my stomach. I did wake up one morning in a panic and called Dr Langton to ask him if he was absolutely sure I was having just one baby. He found that amusing, to my annoyance.

I discovered exhaustion, real exhaustion. I had never known anything like it. After work I would go home and fall asleep pretty much straight away. When Joe came to see me I would fall asleep on his shoulder, which wasn't a good seduction tech-nique, so luckily I wasn't trying to seduce him. Lisa insisted on taking me out to dinner one night, saying that because I was pregnant didn't mean I had to be boring, and I found it so hard to reach the fork to my mouth that she gave up straight after the main course and bundled me home in a taxi. The driver had to wake me when he got to my flat.

Then there were the emotions. I felt I had been coping with so much before: the press, the heartbreak and the pregnancy. Now I had just the pregnancy, the heartbreak and the paternity issue, but it was still so hard. Birthing lessons, yoga, check-ups, shopping for the nursery, all the normal activities were taking their toll as they all made me realise one thing. I was having a real baby. Not a toy. It filled me with dread. I was going to be responsible for another person. I would have to feed it, to wind it, to comfort it when it cried, to clothe it, and although Joe was going to be a huge part of its life, I was going to be his or her mother. And before I could worry about that, I was also going to have to give birth to it. Have you ever seen a video of a woman giving birth? It's not pretty. And the babes are so big in comparison to the small hole they come out of. I called Dr Langton and asked him for a Caesarean. Again he laughed. I was glad that my pregnancy psychosis was providing my doctor with enough entertainment. He told me that I was behaving normally for a woman in my condition but how could that be? If this is normal then people would only ever have one baby; and that was only because they didn't know what it was really like. Unless, and this terrifies me as well, what happens if, when you do give birth, you see this tiny little cute baby and you get instant amnesia. I told Joe to remind me how I felt as soon as I gave birth. Although I probably wouldn't ever get to have sex again anyway.

It was becoming a nightmare. It had been a nightmare from start to finish but then at least in the early days I could blame George. Not that I wasn't glad that he had gone. But it was so confusing. This thing was happening to me and I ill understood it. It was causing all sorts of emotions all crashing together at the

same time, refusing to make any sense. If Joe could have forgiven
me then maybe I would have been better, or maybe I wouldn't.
I had his support and his ever-increasing presence as the birth
drew near, he couldn't have been more supportive. He bought
me food, he cooked for me, he made me endless cups of herbal
tea he even massaged my feet. We'd shopped together, we had
a flat full of baby stuff. So that was another reason for not having
a baby shower. I had most things I needed and stuff I hoped I'd
never need. I also bought a car. A very sensible Golf. It was silver
and had a really cool stereo. The only thing missing, baby-wise
was a car seat, which my parents were going to buy me.

The problem was, that I still didn't know and neither did he
and the strain of that question was constantly in the air.

But then on the day I was due to give birth I thought I probably wouldn't, because babies are never on time the first time
round apparently (Lisa said). I finally agreed to a last-minute
baby party.

My parents were staying at my flat, unable to bear the thought
of me being alone at any time when the baby might make its
appearance, because despite Joe being around all the time and
assuring me that he had his phone on at all times he hadn't stayed
the night with me, for obvious reasons. My parents also said they
didn't want to be in Devon when their first grandchild was born,
and I didn't protest because I didn't want to protest. Imogen and
Jack were also in London. She said it was because Jack had all
sorts of commitments but I felt it was because they wanted to be
near as well. They were staying in a flat owned by Jack's
publisher in South Kensington, so at least I wasn't totally over-
loaded. Then Lisa and Max also found lots of reasons to drop
in. My flat was shrinking. They came round most evenings, and
Lisa most days since I'd stopped working. Freddie was also a
constant presence, he said he needed to get my opinion on work
issues nearly every evening, and he always came with Francesca.
Everyone wanted to be with me for the birth, and if they'd been

allowed to, I am sure they would have been more than happy to witness it.

I had borrowed chairs from the loss adjusters to accommodate my visitors, and the flat did feel awfully small, but it was lovely having a houseful and I think it also took the pressure off Joe. He was there but we weren't alone which meant that he couldn't think I was trying to back him into a corner; I had no spare corners in any case.

When the due date arrived, Joe arrived at nine in the morning having taken the day off work. Although I told him it wouldn't be necessary he didn't believe me. My parents had made breakfast and were sitting in the sitting room talking about baby names.

'Are you sure you don't have a favourite name?' they asked after Joe made drinks for everyone.

'It's a secret,' I said. It was a secret. One more thing that was just mine and Joe's. We had shared a fair bit of the pregnancy with the general public. We had shared it with friends and family. We let them all be here when I was about to burst because they had been supporting me all the way and somehow, in some way this felt like a part of them all.

Joe was behaving as if this was his baby and I wasn't doing anything to discourage that. We'd even had dinner with Joe's parents, they'd come up to London especially. They were so nice and they behaved as if they were going to be grandparents which made me happy and guilty all at the same time. I asked Joe, once, in my braver moment what he would do when we knew the results of the test and guessing my meaning he just squeezed my hand and told me that it would be all right. I was terrified that he had convinced himself he was the father; I was terrified he was wrong. There was still so much I couldn't forgive myself for, but I was living my life. Getting on with it. As best as I could.

George would be planning his wedding. That I knew, because

it was related to me by my parents via his. They had told them that they were flying to New York for the wedding. The news made me feel resentful at first. Angry even. Because he had gone away and nothing had followed him. Whereas we were still dealing with the aftermath. And even if the baby was his, he would still marry Julia. Nothing would change his life.

Joe was still dealing with the fact that I had slept with George, the baby might not be his, and the fact that our lives had been so so public. I think he would be dealing with that for a very long time.

Francesca and Freddie were still being affected at work, people still wanted to know about the marriage-pact baby, because that's what it was. Although the story had died, there was still the last piece in the jigsaw to finish it off properly and they were constantly phoning to ask for the first picture, or the exclusive on the name.

My parents were still being overprotective, worried that I might not have recovered fully from events. I would never recover fully, but that wasn't the point. They didn't need any additional worry.

Imogen and Jack were the same. Imogen was being haunted by the way the press acted, and although she and Jack were stronger than ever (good things out of bad things), the time she spent with me will always stay with her.

Lisa and Max. Again, they won't forget in a hurry. The amount of tears they mopped up, the fainting episodes, the neuroses. Like true friends they will always be there for me, but they can't forget what happened.

No one can. Apart, it seems, from George.

As I stroked my baby and tried silently to coax it into the world (nine months is a hell of a long time, especially when you're the size of a bus), I knew that even my baby would never forget.

The events surrounding his or her conception and incubation had been documented. Even if it were forgotten there might be some people who will always remember. Maybe one day he or she will read the story or hear about it some way. Perhaps I, as the mother, will have to be brave enough to explain, or perhaps I won't. Although the head-in-the-sand Holly was supposed to have been buried, old habits die hard.

As he said 'I do', I wondered if George would think of us, I wondered if he would consider for a minute the repercussions of the aftermath. I don't expect he would.

I know he thought I forgave him in the end but I didn't really. Not deep down. I forgave him to preserve our memories, our childhood, because I could never let go of that, but that was it. He would never be forgiven for the events surrounding the marriage pact, the court case, the media circus and me.

'Here you go.' Joe handed me a cup of tea and sat next to me. He put his hand on the bump and I wondered if – when it turned into a real person – I would ever have any physical contact with him again.

'We're going shopping,' my mum announced.

'What for Mrs Miller?' Joe asked. My mother turned pink. It transpired that she and my father adored Joe, and I liked to think it wasn't just because he might be the father of their first grand-child.

'Call me Margaret,' she said. 'We're shopping for the baby shower.'

'Honestly mum, we don't need anything.' I had protested and protested to no avail.

'I don't think you realise how much you do need. Now we're all bringing a present and having a party, it'll do you the world of good.'

'It's hopeless to argue,' Joe said. I put my head on his shoulder.

'Do you think it might happen today?' Joe asked, when we were alone.

'No, I really don't.'

'Are you sure?'

'I don't feel different today and I thought I would. After the scare last week.'

'Braxton Hicks, that was scary.' I had had my fake contractions, which believe me don't feel fake and are enough to put you off the real thing. Joe had proved to be a real asset because instead of panicking he started timing and proclaimed them to be Braxton Hicks. Then he called the hospital for reassurance but they told him he was doing the right thing. You only go to hospital when the contractions are five minutes apart, Dr Miriam taught us that. But although the fake contractions were painful, I was glad we were given a dress rehearsal in a way. Joe was marvellous and that took some of the worry off me about the opening night.

'Joe, do you think it's going to be a girl or a boy.'

'Definitely a boy.'

'I think its going to be a girl.'

'You're just argumentative.'

'How do you really feel about it?' I had forced myself to ask this question a hundred times, which was silly because even Joe didn't know how he felt.

'Hol, more than anything in the world I want this baby to be mine.'

'Me, too.'

'But I'm a part of it now, whatever happens I'm not sure I can walk away.' That was just what I wanted to hear.

'What happens if I'm a crap mother?'

'Then the poor little bugger's doomed. No, we'll both be great.'

'We will, won't we?'

'Yeah.' I fell asleep on his shoulder and I dreamt about fish.

\*

I awoke to hear hushed voices. My parents, Imogen, Jack and Joe were all around the dining table.

'How long was I asleep?'

'Four hours,' Joe told me.

'God, I never slept so much in my life.'

'Enjoy it while you can,' my father said. I stood up and walked over to where they were standing. On the table was a baby car seat, a McClaren pushchair (hopefully appropriately), and loads of toys.'

'This is all for us?' I asked, touched once again.

'Imogen went a bit mad,' Jack explained.

'I want my nephew or niece to have the best.'

'It will have the best aunt and uncle,' I said hugging her.

'We were going to present all the gifts later, at the party.' My mother sounded disappointed.

'Well you can, we'll forget we've seen them, Margaret,' Joe said. I'm sure my mother blushed.

'Can we go for a walk?' I asked Joe.

'Sure, that way we'll have space to set up the party,' Imogen said. Everyone looked so excited and I tried not to laugh. Joe went to get my jacket and we left.

It was the beginning of autumn but summer hadn't quite packed up and left. It was slightly cold but sunny, a lovely day. Joe took my hand as we walked to the common, and I wondered how we looked to everyone. We looked like a normal, happy couple about to have a baby. But we weren't.

'Will you ever forgive me?' I asked suddenly. I didn't mean to ask it, but once I had, I had to know the answer.

'I will, you know. I'm not even sure if it is about forgiveness any more. Hol, I love you and I know that it's weird that we're still not together because in so many ways we are. Trust me, and give me a little more time.' It was good enough for now.

We returned home after drinking hot chocolate out of paper cups and talking about how we would walk the baby round the common to get him or her to sleep. It so felt like we were a family, I had to believe that we were. That we would be.

'Surprise,' Freddie shouted letting off a party popper as soon as we walked through the door.

'It's not a surprise Freddie, we knew all about it.'

'Oh well, I thought that maybe you would appreciate the sentiment, I thought the shock might get the baby moving.'

'What are you talking about?' I asked as I kissed him.

'Apparently, according to Mother Nature.'

'Who's Mother Nature?' I interrupted.

'Lisa,' he said. Joe started laughing. 'She told us that in order to coax the baby out you should have a hot bath, which believe it or not she is running for you now, eat curry and go on roller coasters. In the absence of a roller coaster I thought I'd use a party popper.' I shook my head.

My flat was a hive of activity. The presents I had already seen had been wrapped, although not the pushchair or the car seat, which had each been given a solitary bow. More presents had been added to the pile. My mum and Imogen were rushing around with plates of things, Jack and my father were watching the news. Francesca was standing watching the food activity with a look on her face which suggested that she might like to help but wasn't sure how: Lisa I could hear singing in the bathroom.

I kissed everyone then went for my hot bath.

'Oh Hol, it would be so great if the baby could appear tonight,' she said, as she locked the door and I got into the bubble-filled bath. It smelt so good, like candy which made me hungry.

'Why?'

'Because it's the date we believe it to be due and we're all here.'

'I hate to point it out but you're always all here.' I gave her hand a squeeze in case she took it the wrong way, although Lisa was thick-skinned.

'But don't you see, we can't wait to meet junior. It's been so long, or it felt so long and I just want to meet it.'

'You know, you're going to be godmother, and Max is going to be godfather.'

'Really?' her eyes filled with tears.

'Of course, although I hadn't actually talked to Joe even about a christening but there are so many reasons why you'd both be perfect.'

'There are?'

'You're both my best friends, and you're quite well off which bodes well for good presents, you're a lot of fun, which again is good and then you'll feel obliged to babysit all the time.'

'I feel really touched, apart from the money thing. Hol, we'd be delighted and you won't keep me away from babysitting, not even a bit, after all this is my trial run.'

'As long as you get it right.'

'Of course I will. Are you going to have other godparents.'

'Well, of course Joe knows nothing of this yet, but I want Freddie and Francesca.'

'Holly, traditionally a girl would have two godmothers and a godfather and a boy would have two godfathers and a god-mother.'

'When did you get to be such an expert?'

'I thought everyone knew that.'

'Well, my baby is special and no matter the sex it gets two of each.' I kissed her cheek as I heaved myself out of the bath. The baby was moving which stopped me for a minute, but then I towelled myself off and went to get dressed.

People were wearing party hats when I returned to the living room, it was more like a kids' party than a baby shower.

'Look at you.' I did look at them, the people I loved, the people who never questioned me, never condemned me, always supported me, and my eyes filled with tears.

'Shit, she's off again,' Freddie said.

'Stop it, it's . . .'

'HORMONES!' everyone shouted in unison.


'Oh, my, God!' I dropped my sausage roll on the floor and clutched my stomach.

'What?' Joe jumped up from his place by my mother and was at my side.

'I think I had one, a real one.' I looked at him, and the others in the room and my eyes were blurred and I had no idea if I'd imagined it. Joe took out his watch.

'I'll time it from the next one.' Everyone fell silent. Another one came. It really bloody hurt.

'That was just under ten minutes, I think it's starting.' The room cheered which seemed a little surreal at the time.

I endured a few more contractions which suddenly moved closer and closer.

'Six and a half minutes,' Joe announced. 'It's time to go I think.' He helped me up, but it wasn't easy. And we walked to the door. Joe picked up my little case which had been waiting there for two weeks. Everyone lined up and kissed me. I felt like I was going on holiday, not to give birth.

'We'll be right behind you,' my mother shouted as I waddled down the stairs and waited for Joe to get the car, my car, and bring it to the door.

I screamed in pain as he drove to the hospital, a little too fast I think. All I could think of was my epidural and the end of the pain. It really, really bloody hurt. I always knew it would but believe me the reality is worse. It was more like torture than giving birth. Maybe that's what happened. Someone had to give birth and so they set a test of goodness, and men were better than women (hard to believe I know), so God said that women would suffer by being the ones to give birth.

Oh dear, madness had revisited.

We were in a hospital room, and it was happening. All the emotions of the past nine months had gone as the nurses spoke to me, Joe clutched my hand for dear life, I heard that 'my party' were all waiting outside. I knew they would be there for the birth as they had been throughout my pregnancy, although not actually present. The anaesthetist arrived at some point and talked me through the epidural before leaving me again, and later returning to administer it. I had no idea of the time I had been there already but I think it was hours. It felt like hours. I was aware but I was unaware as the labour took hold, then the pain relief set in, then the birth began.

The pain I had felt when the contractions started were indescribable. Terrified, I screamed and I clutched at Joe's hand and I swore and willed them to leave. I had never known such pain, never. But as soon as the epidural took hold the pain subsided and I felt as if I could cope after all. I didn't have time to think, there were people telling me to push one minute, then not the next and it was all so bloody confusing, and all the time Joe was looking in wonderment at the whole event. Well he would, he never had to bear such agony. I managed to keep my thoughts to myself.

I could feel the sweat, I was exhausted, I didn't know how long it had been, minutes, hours, days? It felt like days. I looked at Joe and asked him through gritted teeth.

'Six hours,' he replied and he kissed my head. And although I wanted to stop, to go to sleep, to have some peace and quiet, that kiss, that little kiss made me one hundred per cent better. I could have run a marathon after that kiss.

'Push,' someone commanded and I pushed with all my new found might.

And then I saw it. A head. Gory, but it was a head. Then I pushed some more and time was suspended as was reality because something incredible, amazing, and unbelievable was happening. There was a baby.

'It's a boy.' The first words I heard properly as the baby was handed to me. I looked at him, all covered in blood and I looked at him and I loved him, more than I'd ever loved anyone. Then they took him away and I panicked but people were talking to me all the time, and I heard his first cry. He had a good set of lungs on him.

'Is he all right?' I asked.

'He's perfect, Hol,' Joe answered, and I saw the tears in his eyes through the tears in mine. We had done it. The perfect miracle, the best thing ever. And I was feeling so bloody corny.

Eventually, it seemed like hours but it probably wasn't, I was told that everyone else could come in. Joe held the baby for the first time, then went to call his parents. I didn't ask him how he felt, because I knew that the moment he saw him, he'd fallen in love too. It was written in his eyes. It had been over six hours but it was worth every bloody minute just to see and cuddle the tiny bundle wrapped in the tiny blanket. I had already forgotten the pain; I had mother's amnesia.

Everyone rushed in, which made the small room a bit crowded, even more so than my flat had been. Everyone was emotional.

'I can't believe you've done it,' Lisa exclaimed, as if I was the only person in the world to do it. But that was how it felt. It didn't feel like a normal thing that women did everyday, it felt magical and unique.

'He's beautiful,' my mother said as she held her grandson.

'Looks just like you,' my father said, although he looked nothing like me, because he was a baby.

'Are you OK?' Freddie asked, standing back and peering at the baby over my mother's shoulders.'

'I'm fine, perfect in fact.' Then Imogen held him and so did Jack, and Francesca sort of touched him but declined holding him, just yet. Max had a cuddle as did Lisa and my baby son slept through it, which I hoped was a good sign for the future.

'My parents will be here first thing in the morning,' Joe said, on his return. 'Well done, you were fantastic,' he added planting a kiss on my forehead. 'It was gruesome wasn't it?'

'I can't remember,' I said, and laughed.

After a few minutes of the baby being admired, the nurse told everyone that they should leave.

'I'd be in trouble for letting so many people in here,' she chastised, but I didn't care.

'They're family,' I said. She smiled and left.

'Have you got a name?' Freddie asked, as everyone prepared to go. I looked at Joe.

'Jamie,' he said, proudly.

'Jamie?' my mother asked, a little surprised.

'We thought about James, but decided that we preferred Jamie,' I explained.

'Welcome to the world Jamie,' I said, as I held him, exhausted. The nurse returned and ushering everyone out, took him from me and placed him in a hospital cot by the bed. He slept on.

'I need some sleep,' I said, when the room was empty apart from Joe and myself.

'I'll stay, if that's all right,' Joe said, uncertainly.

'Of course it is. You can stay for ever.' I wasn't sure if the effect of the drugs was still with me, or if it was the euphoria of giving birth.

Joe sat in a chair by the side of the cot, I could see him stroking the baby's arm as I closed my eyes.

'Hello, little fellow,' I heard him say. 'Although I'm a proud and silly man, I do love your mummy.'

I felt the smile stretching across my face. We would be fine, I knew that now. I also knew that the people who mattered, my grown up friends would always take care of us, and that Joe would always take care of us and I would take care of Jamie.

# Chapter Forty-six

*Paternity*

My fingers trembled as I dialled the number. It didn't help that I had had to wait hours so that I didn't call New York in the middle of the night, the wait only heightened my nerves. I wasn't sure why I was so worked up about the call but I believed it had something to do with the fact that now everything would be finished. Resolved. Finally. No more unanswered questions. The past was really and truly that.

I misdialled because my hands wouldn't do what my brain was telling them, and I swore. I tried to calm down, using my yoga breaths of pre-pregnancy, but that brought back memories of so much stress it was almost enough to make me hyperventilate. 'Concentrate,' I said aloud, as I made my fourth attempt to dial his number.

I hadn't spoken to him since that last day in the café. Imogen had told him about Jamie, the day he was born. She had then told him when we were taking the test. He offered to pay for it, but I refused. I didn't need his money. Imogen said that he had been so reasonable, so calm and so concerned, but I didn't want to hear that for myself. After giving birth I wasn't strong enough for George.

But now I was. I knew that no one else could deliver the news for me. I was the mother of the child, George had spent months as the potential father, so it was only right that I spoke to him myself. But it was hard.

The thought of talking to him brought back all the memories I had tried so hard to expunge. Not only the ones of the past year but also before that. Memories of our childhood, the one that I had to learn to put behind me, memories of friendship that was no longer there.

Finally, I heard the ring tone.

'Hello.' It was her.

'Julia, it's Holly.'

'Hi, hang on.' She sounded friendly, and I almost liked her for not trying to make small talk with me.

'Holly.' His voice still haunted me. Still made me feel sad and happy and confused. I knew at that moment that I would always miss our friendship, our unbelievable, magical friendship.

'I got the results.' I twisted the telephone chord around my finger as I tried to stop the nerves. Why was I feeling like this?

'Holly, tell me.' He sounded kind, not arrogant, he was commanding me but gently. I wondered how he was feeling, but I couldn't imagine it.

The pause seemed to last for ever, I willed her to get on with it, but I also knew that whatever the outcome, the telephone call wasn't easy for her. I needed to cut her some slack. I owed her that much. And more. But as I glanced over my shoulder and saw Julia, standing in the doorway, shoulders hunched, lightly chewing her lip, I knew that this wasn't yet resolved and we all needed it to be. Yeah, Julia had forgiven me and yeah, we were together for ever, but if I was going to be the father of Holly's baby, that was going to affect the rest of our lives. How could I be a father living in New York? Would I back out and let Holly and Joe bring up my son? These are questions that I have asked myself ever since I left London. They are also questions that Julia is asking me constantly.

Everything serves as a reminder of how I messed up. Holly, sitting at the end of the phone, sick with nerves, Joe. How must he be feeling? Julia, biting the skin off her lip and me, well, I felt pretty churned up. But then I deserved it. I had done all this, it was all me. It takes two, they say, that's what Julia says when I have my worst moments of guilt. And I still do. They're pretty black. I almost want to deny myself the happiness I feel just to give into the guilt, but I don't, I don't because Julia won't let me. As I feel the tension in my shoulders I glance at her again and I know exactly what I want Holly to say.

Up until now I have had mixed feelings. At first, when I found out she was pregnant I wanted to be the father, but then I also wanted to marry Holly. When I got back to New York I began to feel confused. Part of me felt that I would love to be a father, but I knew that I wanted to be a father with Julia. Part of me felt even more guilt for acknowledging that but I had no idea what I would do. Until now. Now I know, for the first time exactly what I want.

'Holly,' I prompt again, gently.

'Sorry,' she says, but still I have to wait.

'It's OK.' It is OK, although I can't figure out if the delay is a good or a bad thing.

'Joe's the father,' she blurts, finally.

I feel myself go hot, then I feel cold. Then an immense feeling of relief washes through me. However much I sound like a bastard, I am pleased. More than pleased, I am overjoyed and I am sure Holly is too. I put my hand over the receiver because there is a wonderful woman who needs to be put out of her misery.

'It's Joe's,' I call across to her and I see her break into a smile. Then I smile.

'Holly, are you still there?'

'Yes, George.'

'You must be over the moon.' I say this with genuine feelings of warmth.

'I am.' She giggles. 'I'm so happy George, I really am. So is Joe.'

'I'm happy too. Holly you deserve to be a family at last, after everything . . .'

'Past George, let's leave it there.'

'I really wish you all the best for the future.' I know I sound distant but the news means I can at last gain some distance from my guilt, from the past, from everything.

'I do too. For you and Julia I mean.' She sounds equally formal. Like a stranger almost.

But that is what had to happen. I had to sever all ties. Not just because of the guilt, but also because you can't always carry the past into the future. Sometimes you have to let go.

''Bye George, take care.'

'You take care too.'

I know, as I put down the phone, that I will never speak to her again. I will grieve for our friendship at some point, but for now I will go to the woman I love and think about our future, and our future baby and our happiness. It might sound selfish but it's not. It's right.

I feel so relieved as I put down the phone. I didn't know how he would react but he reacted the way I wanted him too. I didn't want him to be the father of course, but I didn't want him to be disappointed, although I don't know why. Probably I will never make anyone fully understand the extent of our friendship, I cannot even voice it to myself, but suffice to say I wanted him to be as pleased with the result as I was. Or not quite as pleased as I was, because I was really, utterly, amazingly pleased, but I wanted him to think that it was the right result.

Because, undoubtedly it was.

I turn away from the last conversation I will ever have with my best friend and I stop.

He is standing in the doorway. His hair is a little long because he hasn't had time for a cut, he is wearing a black polo-neck shirt with flecks of baby sick, his gorgeous legs are clad in a tight, scruffy pair of jeans, and his feet are bare. And in his arms is my son, our son, Jamie. And I see him bend down and plant a kiss on his tiny little head and I feel an overwhelming surge of love, unlike anything I've ever felt before. I smile through my tears, because I can't help them.

It was time to say goodbye to my childhood once and for all, because that was gone, past. Another childhood was beginning and that was the only thing that mattered.